Earth has been almost silent for forty years. The apocalypse left behind only fragments of civilisation, surrounded by a sea of barbarism.

But now the true End is in sight: the horizon is alight with burning villages, two cities lie in the shadow of an army gathering in the north, intent on ending the old world forever. And somewhere, a supernatural force is on the move, pushing its servants into place: a young girl with special powers, and a man whose destiny might decide the fate of all.

While ominous swarms of pigeons plague the sky, the world grows quieter, and dark forgotten secrets are revealed — secrets of betrayal, love, and obsession — the army in the north prepares to leave.

The epic *Ruin Saga* continues…

Join My List to keep up with new releases:
http://eepurl.com/V4niL

THE RUIN SAGA

VOLUME II: BRINK

Harry Manners

Brink
by Harry Manners

First published 2015 by Radden Press.

All characters in this novel are entirely fictitious, as are the events portrayed. Any resemblance to persons living, dead or imaginary is coincidental.

All right reserved. This paperback edition was published by Radden Press in May 2015. No part of this publication may be reproduced, transmitted or stored in any form (including electronic) without written permission from the copyright owner.

Copyright © Harry Manners 2015.

Cover design by Levente Szabo.
Edited by Amy Eye & Alex Roddie.
Formatting by Polgarus Studio.

PROLOGUE

Radley leapt a fallen log, holding in a scream. The way ahead was blurred by a slick of snot and tears, the young black forest swimming in the predawn light. All he recognised was the clearing of rusted metal ahead—the gates of Twingo.

The town was close, but so were his pursuers. In seconds he would be within shouting distance, but until then he had to keep quiet. If he squawked now, they would be on him before he could take another step.

The trees were close all around, winding seamlessly up and around old tarmac roads and suburban terrace rows. A town had been here once, full of people, thousands of people. But that had been long ago, before they had all vanished from the Earth. Though only forty years had passed, the trunks of these trees towered over the ruins of the Old World. They seemed to loom up at his flanks to bite at his ankles.

He knew this path through the forest better than the streets of Twingo itself, but still his mind's eye filled with terrible images of a wall of foliage having sprung up ahead, barring his path. His back muscles clenched spasmodically, expecting a bullet, spear or arrow to come tearing from behind at any moment. But none came.

He shouldn't have snuck out. His mother had warned him about it every day since the cradle, wagging her finger and tapping her foot over breakfast in the same faded apron. *"World's a dangerous place, Rad. Don't you go snooping. It'll be the end of a little wisp like you."* And he had been a good boy, most days. He scarcely went against her will.

But so much wonder lay beyond Twingo's walls. So much to touch, see, and smell. The handiwork of countless long-dead men, mysterious and powerful. They had machines that could beam your face clear across the world, his grandma used to say. All those rusted hunks of metal on the road had once been magic carts, ones that went along without the aid of a horse. And there had been food as well. All the food a person could eat, and so much more.

Not like today, where you had to scrounge in the dirt for a morsel. Last year's famine had levelled what mankind had rebuilt since the End, sucked the land dry of life and hope.

How could he stay cooped up in that godforsaken dump when the secrets of fallen gods lay just beyond the trees? If he could find something worth trading, maybe he could make something of himself and move with his mother to the great trading post at Canary Wharf, maybe even New Canterbury, home of *the* Alexander Cain. He'd heard things weren't quite so bad there.

He'd been sneaking out before sunup whenever the

guard grew lax for a few months now. It had never hurt anyone; he had always been back before daybreak. But now things had gone very wrong. This morning, things had been different; he'd known that as soon as he'd slipped under the fence. There had been something in the air, a prickle, like somebody had been watching.

And no more than half a mile into the forest, shadows had appeared in the trees, moving slow and steady toward him, converging from all directions. He ran for all his worth, but all the while they had stayed a short distance behind, as though it were nothing, as though they were teasing him.

And now, finally reaching the edge of Twingo and safety, he sensed how close they had gotten. He could almost feel their breath on the back of his neck.

He was young, only a nipper, but he was no fool. They could have killed him ten times over already. Why hadn't they?

He decided it didn't matter. He just kept running.

*

Max felt his guts twist, pulled from sleep by distant screams. He took a moment to make sure he wasn't dreaming, then sat up and sighed. He wasn't surprised, nor did he hurry. He'd been waiting for this.

Twingo had seen better days. There had been a time when dozens from all the settlements in the southern counties passed along their single thoroughfare daily to trade and share news. Nestled on the edge of the City of London, beside what had once been the green expanse of Greenwich Park, they were second only to Canary Wharf itself, the hub of commerce for all of England. But here, things had been a little looser, the rules laxer, and the trade more risky. Men of ambition and vision had traded here, where the meddling influence of the southern cities was largely absent. They had enjoyed a healthy, symbiotic relationship with the powerhouse across the way.

But then they had gone and started trouble. It was all that fool's fault. That Alexander Cain and his flock. They hadn't been able to let the Old World go. They had gone into people's lives and disrupted any peace they might have found with how things were. And now it was coming back to bite them, and everyone else who had dealings with them.

As he swung his legs out of bed and pulled on his clothes with unhurried, steady hands, the knot in Max's gut faded, turning off the fear, something he'd learned to do long ago. Once dressed, he took up his rifle from beside the bed, checked the load and safety, and pulled open the door. Across the hall, Bill emerged from his own room a moment later, his eyes set and face grim.

"Do you think it's them?" he said.

Max nodded and headed for the balcony. The Royal Observatory, empty save for the heavy barricades upon all the doors, groaned and echoed around their heads, the vast stores stacked up in each room, and the few senior Twingites who bedded here. Atop the hill of Greenwich Park, they could see all of Twingo and the surrounding landscape from here, and in the distance, London's ruined, cragged skyline. They both stepped under the murky sky, struggling toward dawn, and looked out over all they'd built.

"Today," Bill said. "I can feel it."

"Today," Max said.

Below, lights popped on. The screaming came from the trees, a single source moving straight for them. He recognised Radley Tibble's voice even from this distance, though he couldn't yet hear what he was saying. Not that it mattered. Everyone knew what it meant. Their time was up.

Smoke had been appearing on the horizon for weeks now. News had reached them of burning, raping, and pillaging. And not just here, but everywhere, all over the country. A scourge swept over the land: a new army bent on enslavement and destruction, driven by the smouldering hatred stoked by Cain and his lot during the famine. They had lost contact with the last of their neighbours three days ago.

"Looks like they saved us for last."

Max looked past the trees, across the swollen banks of the Thames, toward the single twinkling spire in Canary Wharf. "Not quite last," he said.

The others slowly joined them on the balcony, rubbing their eyes. Some uttered forlorn cries, a few scowled, while others only stared. But there was no panic. Twingites were made of stronger stuff. They had all known this was coming. Other places might have seen disorientation and fear take over, but there had never been room for that here.

Instead, the elderly founders of the rickety trading post turned on their heels and disappeared back inside, some to strengthen the barricades, others to sound the alarm. Only Max and Bill remained, still scanning the land below.

"I don't see them," said Max.

"They're using the tree cover. They'll come from the west."

At that, they too headed back inside and sealed the balcony behind them. Bill turned over his rifle to young mop-haired Jordan, their best sniper, and bade him head up to the service hatch at the top of the observatory, and cover them. "I was never any good with a gun, anyway," he said, flashing his long programmer's hands, still delicate and free of callouses after these long years of strife. Some things never changed.

"Pieter," Max called. One floor above them, a hunch-backed scarecrow stooped over the railing, eyebrows raised. "We'll be needing that alarm, now."

Pieter nodded, his brow low and untroubled over his face. The granite will and resilience was something they all had, even if a sea of broiling terror lay underneath—and Max had no doubt they were all scared shitless. But in this world, you had to look strong, even around your closest friends. Twingo Glare, some called it.

Pieter disappeared into a side room, and a moment later the whine of an old air-raid siren started up, thrumming through the corridors of the observatory, rattling Max's bones. He and Bill headed for the stairs, descending together, side by side, and stepped through the open main doors. Friends and companions they had known for these long decades sent their affections with a single flick of their eyelids. Then they were moving out across the grass, descending the hill, and the doors were barricaded shut behind them.

There was no room for soppy goodbyes. It was the only chance they had of surviving this.

They raced towards the town ahead as the siren spooled up to its full wail. The screaming in the forest continued to rise above the racket. It would be on them within the minute. Without a word to one another, sensing each other's thoughts, they broke into a run towards their lives' work.

Max Vandeborn had founded Twingo off his own back, along with Bill Bateman, just weeks after the End. The entire city of London, all of England—maybe the world— had been stripped of all its people in a single moment, leaving merely a few scattered random survivors. All there had been then was the whistling wind and millions of pieces of empty, deflated apparel littering the streets, left by their departed owners where they fell during the morning commute. They hadn't even known if there had been any other survivors. But what else had there been to do?

Max had been a city banker, Bill an e-commerce entrepreneur. Buying and selling was what they knew, all they knew. And so with an empty, naked and deathly silent world staring them in the face, they had collected supplies from the infinitude of unattended supermarkets, picked a spot, nailed up a sign, and opened the business. And they had waited.

For weeks they had waited like that. But neither of them had been fazed. After the shock of the End, little fazed a survivor. Bill had lost a family of five, young wife, kids, a big five-bedroom townhouse in plush Muswell Hill. He'd been barely thirty then, but his face was on magazine covers. A real gold-star deal. After the End, he shut down, went cold, and the businessman within took over. That was how he coped.

The End was fine with Max. All he'd had was a pet chinchilla, and the damn thing had bitten him every time he went near it. He had no attachments but his money. He might have lost it all when the world's microprocessors fizzed and turned to ash during the End, and all those ones and zero that passed for currency in the bank computers vanished right along with all those people, but you could always make money where there was demand. And he was betting on a lot of demand now the bottom had fallen out of everything.

It had been the *Maxwell and William Trading Post* then. It came to be called *Twingo* much later. The place began as a fenced-off chunk of homes and shops on the edge of the park, and spilled onto Her Majesty's—as Max insisted they still were, and always would be—lawns, leading up the dome of the Royal Observatory upon the hill. Capping the central thoroughfare, conveniently blocking off the entire width of the street, was a transport lorry with a full complement of brand-new Nissan Twingos.

Some places were named after great men, battles, or

ideas. Some were named for glory or in remembrance. Some, it seemed, were named for the sheer hell of it.

They reached the first of the huts, having slowed to a walk to stir confidence. They nodded in turn to each of the armed men and women standing atop the roofs of homes they had built with their own hands. They each nodded back, then went back to scanning the treeline. Max felt a spark of pride.

Soon, they had left Her Maj's lawns behind and strode over the tarmacked thoroughfare, past stalls and stores, warehouses, and stock pens. The children, sick, and elderly were holed up inside the deadbolted concrete store sheds, each the nexus of a cluster of armed Twingites. Everything had been battened down in thirty seconds flat, and all of Twingo was ready to face whatever emerged from those trees, despite the sleep dust fresh in their eyes.

Young Radley Tibble came tearing out of the forest a moment later, sprinting on his gangly legs across to the chain-link fence and scrambling under it. His voice had become ragged and broken, but now everyone could make out what he was saying. *"THEY'RE HERE! THEY'RE COMING! THEY'RE COMING!"*

He was on his feet and running again, all the way down the thoroughfare until Max caught him in his arms, where he sagged like a sack of wet grain. "They're coming!" he screeched, straining against Max's grip, his eyes wide.

"Hush, now," Max said. His voice was among the quietest in town, but people always listened. And even in the grip of stupefied terror, Radley heard him, and a last scream died in his throat. "How many? What direction?"

Radley only stared up at him.

"Speak!"

The eyes of a wounded fawn met his iron-hard gaze. He looked at Bill, who shrugged. "Fine," he said. "Go to your mother. Lock up tight."

Radley scrambled away towards one of the store sheds, leaving a cloud of dust in his wake.

"What are you smiling about?" Max said.

Bill turned to him. He was grinning with a nostalgic glaze to his eyes. "The dust. Like Roadrunner. Remember, in *Looney Tunes? Meep, meep!*"

"I remember a lot of things, Bill."

A moment passed, then Max let a smile blossom on his own lips. "We had a good run."

"The best."

They didn't need any more. Long, hard years of tribulation had forged a link deeper than words. All it took was a flick of the eyes, and Max knew Bill would be there next to him to the end. He flicked the safety of his rifle. "Alright, let's go see what these bastards want."

They advanced along the thoroughfare until they stood a short distance from the spot where Radley had crawled beneath the fence. There they waited in silence, and waited. Long minutes passed as they all scanned the treeline, trigger fingers at the ready. The air-raid siren cut out and wound down in a long, unspooling drone. Then there was only the wind, kicking up the usual dust devils in the dirt around the edge of town, obscuring what lay beyond.

Max squinted into the haze. Dawn broke, and fingers of sunlight clawed over the tops of the trees, further impeding his vision. But he didn't move, didn't give any sign of weakness. He just waited for whatever might come. Eventually, something did.

Two figures materialised from the dust and walked down the thoroughfare toward them. The air was filled with the sound of cocking rifles and footsteps as the entire town's guard readjusted their stance to aim down at the emissaries. One was young, thin and gangly, almost like Radley except for a heavy limp and a face that looked like it had seen things nobody that young should see. The other was older, squat, and immediately set Max's heart aflutter. There was something dangerous about him, something primal, unhinged. An enormous, curved hunter's knife hung from a sheath at his belt.

The two of them stopped twenty feet away from Max and Bill and looked around at the town for a good while, their faces untroubled, as though the place were empty and they had stumbled across a curious relic. They didn't acknowledge anyone besides each other.

Max knew he had to keep quiet to avoid appearing weak. He also knew Bill's patience wouldn't hold out that long. But he didn't try to stop him; doing that would have looked even weaker.

"This is private land!" Bill said. "We're not trading today."

The younger, gangly man looked at them for the first time. "We're not looking to trade, friend."

"Then you'll kindly get off our property before we shoot you both for trespassing."

It was the squat man's turn to lock their gaze. "Well, now, that would be a big mistake." His voice was level and calm, but Bill caught something veiled behind his eyes, something that couldn't be hidden. It frightened him. He tightened his grip on his rifle.

"State your business," Bill said.

Max wished he'd shut up. He was acting as though he could talk their way out of this.

"No business, just an offer," the young man said. "Allow me to introduce myself. I'm Charlie. And this"—he gestured to his lupine companion—"is—"

"Not an offer, a choice," his elder companion interrupted. "A real simple choice."

Charlie looked annoyed at the interruption, but pressed on. "Yes, I suppose, a choice."

"Cut to it," Max said. Three words that brought all possibility of further pleasantries to an end. He was through waiting.

Charlie paused, then shrugged. His face settled into something altogether more apathetic. "You know who we are. You know what we can do. You must have seen enough fire on the horizon by now. Your allies are gone, and now it's your turn. So choose: you can join us, or you can burn."

"Join you in what?" Bill said.

The squat lupine man grinned, a terrible, wicked expression that made Max sick to look at. "Killing scum, that's what."

Charlie held up a hand, though visibly withered when his companion bared his teeth like an excited dog. Max had the impression that the true balance of power between them was far from equal. "Our quest," he said. "We have a mission—to rid the land of the greed and injustice it's been shown by the dominant powers. These *civilised* people with their morals and books and history, waltzing into everyone's lives and taking what they see as theirs, leaving a trail of destruction behind."

Bill scowled. "It's been a bad year for everyone. The famine would have kicked everyone's arses whether Cain and his people were around or not."

"Yet those who could have helped the starving and helpless instead chose to help themselves, to further their own plans, their little schemes to bring back the Old World." Charlie laughed cruelly. "Leaving behind a trail of destruction and death wherever they went." A bitterness had infected his face. He changed tactic. "There's no need to make this hard. People talk highly of this place for miles around. Lay down your weapons, fall in line, and none of you will be harmed."

"We're not laying down anything," Max said before Bill could utter a word.

"Think about it. Things might not be so tough anymore, but the damage is done. People are starved, the Old World supplies are spent, and it'll take months for the next harvest to come in. The lands are empty." A note of genuine anger flashed on Charlie's brows. "Trading posts aren't much use if there's nobody left to trade. You rely on your clientele for your own supplies. What do you think will happen to you now?"

They didn't say anything.

"There would be no shame in it," Charlie said. He even offered a hand, as though he were a brave sailor plucking floundering fools from stormy seas.

"No shame in bowing down to bully-boys and intimidation?" Bill muttered.

Charlie ignored him. The fingers of his proffered hand waggled. "We were all different, once. We were all just like you."

Max found himself leaning back away from that hand despite the twenty feet between them. "Somehow I don't believe that."

The hand dropped. The kind expression flickered, revealing the ugliness lurking beneath. "Don't be fools."

"The fools here are those who wandered into this town with nothing but an itty bitty knife to threaten us and expected to just walk out of here." With that, Bill raised an arm and swirled a hand above his head, signalling Jordan to blow them away. Max didn't bother trying to stop him. There had been too many pyres of smoke afar of late. The time for mercy had passed.

In unison, the armed guards atop the stalls and homes all along the thoroughfare braced their stances against the lips of the many roofs and took aim. Snaps, clicks and twangs filled the air as they cocked their weapons. Max readied himself to pick one of them off if Jordan's high-calibre rounds failed to kill on impact. "I'm sorry, but we can't take any chances."

Neither man moved, nor did they show an ounce of surprise. Instead, they stared directly up the hill towards the observatory, straight at where Jordan would have been perched in the service hatch. They knew they were being watched.

Max made to turn to Bill and the others, alarm bells jangling behind his eyes, but before he could do more than start with shock, the squat man moved. Max had never seen anyone move so fast, so blurred as to be almost imperceptible. It would have looked as though he had only twitched, if it weren't for the hunting knife vanishing from his belt. All that remained was the bare leather holster. A short whistle accompanied a wisp of air that blew against Max's face as something passed by very close. For an instant he might have perceived an amorphous spinning glitter of a wicked sharp blade. Then there was a solid, meaty thump, and Max turned to look at Bill.

The hunting knife had reappeared, embedded to the hilt in Bill's chest. He was staring down at it, his mouth open in a faintly surprised O, a brilliant scarlet rose already unfurling across his shirt, radiating from the polished wooden handle. Max dropped his rifle and caught him before he hit the ground, easing him to the dirt as a single blood bubble popped from his lips. He looked up at the two men, considered diving for his rifle, but found all the strength had gone out of his legs. Instead, he turned back to his dying friend, his hands now slick with rivulets of blood oozing out in rhythmic dribbles. The blade must have pierced the aorta.

"Oh, Bill," Max muttered.

A book could have been written on the important things they had never said to one another. Too many things. Max mouthed wordlessly, and in the end, he said nothing at all.

It was over in seconds. The friend he'd lived, slept and fought beside for forty years faded to a meaty vessel in mere seconds. There wasn't time for fear or pain to settle in. The surprise simply drained from his face as the light left his eyes, and his grip spasmed and then grew slack upon Max's sleeves. Then he was gone.

Max stared into his sightless eyes. The blood had stopped oozing from his chest. His hands lay curled and limp on the thoroughfare dirt. No shots came whizzing down from the observatory, nor from the armed sentries of the thoroughfare itself. He turned back to face the two men, leaving Bill's body to slump beneath him, and struggled to his feet. He didn't bother going for his rifle. If he was going to die, he'd rather do it standing.

"You're coming with us," Charlie said.

"No," Max said. "We're not."

The young man's face flattened. His cheeks were oddly shaped, like putty. Plenty of ugly brawls had broken out in Twingo over the years, and he knew a face that had been recently stomped on when he saw one. Somebody had really gone to work on this kid. He had the stench of ruined goods about him, a good apple made bad by cruelty. "Then you'll burn."

Max turned in a wide circle, along with those standing

upon the rooftops, to look at the observatory. Even at a glance he could tell there would be no help coming from the hill. Stoic silhouettes lined the entire ridge, black against the rising sun. They outnumbered all the men, women, and children of Twingo twice over—at least two hundred. The roof of the observatory, where Jordan would have taken his perch, was spattered with at least a dozen more silent watchers. They had all come silently, without notice, and they each watched without moving an inch, yet in each hand was the outline of a weapon: all kinds, from automatic rifles to pistols, machetes to hunting bows, hatchets to pitchforks.

The wolfish squat man leered. It looked as though he was almost salivating, and a redness had crept into the whites of his eyes. "I wonder how your stuck-pig friend tastes, roasted on a spit," he said. "I guess I'll find out."

"Fuck you, and your rotten mother."

The lupine man ignored him, grinning, his tongue stuck hungrily between his teeth. "Morning's best time for a feeding."

"You all know what do to," Max called to the others on the rooftops. He didn't have to raise his voice, didn't have to rally, didn't even have to glance up. They would all fight to the end, no matter how short an end it might be. He sensed them in his peripheral vision, closing around the store sheds in concentric circles, some shaking and some weeping silently, but all ready, all Twingites. He felt a great momentary swell of love for them all, and then he turned it all off like a switch; emotion muddied the reflexes, and any chance of surviving this required an unfeeling soul.

He had hoped to have Bill with him when the end came. In a way, he was. Bill would have found that funny.

He'd always expected things to end like this. That was the way of this new world. He'd gunned down enough bent traders with the townsmen in hails of bullets to feel no real animosity towards these men. Everyone served a higher purpose, gears of a great machine. The world moved on, the tides changed, and crowns were ripped from cold, bloody hands. The Old World's ruins littered the Earth, but it and all its civility was only a distant memory. For some, it had only ever been a dream.

Max eyed his rifle, lying a few feet away, and tensed his legs, ready to dive. "I hope you brought plenty of rounds," he said, and then he lunged, and the air was alive with gunfire.

*

When it was over, Max was blinded by his own blood. A gash on his forehead was trickling a steady stream into his eyes, and with his arms tied fast behind his back, it dribbled without check over the contours of his face. Strong arms shoved and corralled him forward, kicking him when he fell, cursing him when he stumbled too fast. He'd taken a ball to the thigh, but it had only skimmed off a chunk of muscle close to the surface, missing the femoral artery.

Waves of heat buffeted his skin and something crackled and popped nearby. They had started setting fires. Gunfire crackled and the occasional scream still rang out, but the battle was almost done. He tried to judge how long they had lasted. It couldn't have been more than a few minutes, which seemed impossible. The raiders had been so fast, so silky smooth in every movement, so accurate with every shot. It was eerie.

They had looked like barbarians perched like crows on the hilltop, but they were nothing of the sort. He had taken down maybe a dozen, and they had all been farmer types, emaciated and ropey from the famine, but they had each gone down snarling, often picking off another Twingite before they bled out. Something had turned them all into trained killers.

They were heading uphill. He could hear others' ragged breathing around him and tried to get their attention, but every time he called out, somebody pressed a thumb into his leg wound, and he ended up biting clean through his lip trying to hold in the screams.

Why were they keeping any of them alive? To barter or torture, maybe for slave labour? He promised to kill the others before himself. No Twingite would be a slave, nor suffer a lingering death.

Someone kicked the back of his knees and he fell forward with a grunt, white-hot agony flashing in his pelvis and up his spine as his full weight landed on the shredded meat of his leg. Others landed in the grass on either side of him and then his hands were free. He wiped the blood from his eyes.

They were sacking the observatory nearby, hauling out

the last of those barricaded inside like hounds rooting foxes from a run. Those who blabbered and begged were shot or hacked to the ground. Those who fought back were knocked out cold and thrown on the grass beside Max and the other captives.

Charlie stood over them, unscathed. He and the wolfish man had vanished before he had ever reached his gun, even with his limp. "You people and your pride," he said and spat at Max's feet.

"Just finish it," Max growled.

"Finish?" Charlie grinned, and Max saw a shadow of the wolfish man's leer buried somewhere behind it, an infectious inner madness that seemed to radiate from every one of these creatures. "Nah. You people have a reputation for being real tough bastards, and you put up a hell of a fight. You've got the spark He wants. You're all with us now."

Max looked at the others beside him in the grass. He expected them to be veterans, nail-hard folk from before the End. But instead, most of them were young, some only kids. Among them he spotted Radley Tibble, snot nosed and whimpering in the grass, clutching a ragged strip of his mother's dress, one end charred, the other dripping red.

They didn't deserve this. He knew what it was like to lose everyone you loved in the blink of an eye. Better if they had all died down there with their families. His mental switch flickered on and off, and a wrenching twist was working into his guts. "Who's He?" he said.

Charlie stepped aside, and another figure took his

position—a tall man with a balaclava tied around his face. A pair of wood pigeons bobbed on one shoulder, cooing and cocking their heads to watch the smouldering wreckage below. The man's striking green eyes lanced into him. He felt like a pincushion, speared by that gaze.

I know those eyes, Max thought. *But no, it can't be.* "You can burn our homes, but you can't take away what we are. We're free. We'll never fight beside you pigs, so get it over with."

The tall man stepped forward and loosened the balaclava, letting it fall to one side. A few of the kids cried out at the maw revealed in the virgin light. Even Max repressed a grimace. It was hard to believe he was alive; there was so much scar tissue, so much shrunken, retracted flesh, exposed membrane and muscle. Patches of bare skull showed in a few spots around where the cheeks and chin should have been.

"It's been a long time, Vandeborn," he said.

"James …" Then Max could only shake his head, speechless for the first time in memory.

The fires of Twingo were dying low, and the last survivors were being thrown down on the grass. The flock of victors—filthy, stick-thin and stinking—gathered around the gutted observatory, surrounding their prey on all sides.

But Max scarcely noticed anyone but the tall man before him. Eventually, he found his voice again. "What happened to you?"

He didn't answer, just turned and pointed east. The

pigeons cooed, cocking their heads, as though following the line of sight drawn out by his arm. Max's eyes followed it too, and his gaze fell upon the horizon. Glistening in the early morning haze, amidst the sagging ruin of London, was the single lit spire in Canary Wharf.

PART 3

THE PIGEON KEEPER

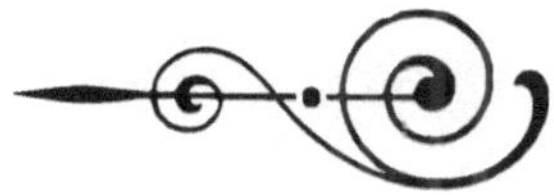

Only the dead have seen the end of war.
> —**Plato**

Every man gotta right to decide his own destiny.
> —**Bob Marley**

CHAPTER 1

"Geoffrey, get down!" Alexander Cain bellowed.

A hundred other warnings joined his own, but they came too late. The line of dark figures holed up on the mezzanine of the old skyscraper had already snaked their rifle barrels into view. Before the members of the ambassadorial convoy from Bristol could raise their heads, three dozen muzzle flashes winked in the gleaming midday heat.

The first volley killed Geoffrey Oppenheimer's son and his two nieces, along with three of his other companions. Red mist fizzed into the air as they dropped to the cracked pavement, and the procession of carts, horses, and trailers scattered like insects. Then the air filled with cracks, whines, and screams, and Alexander ducked back under cover.

So close, they were so close to home. Only fifty feet separated them from the safety of the fortified walls of the compound around Canary Wharf Tower. But it was all open ground without a speck of rubble to shield them. The bastards had known right where to spring their trap.

The guards up on the compound's walls returned fire,

still yelling for Oppenheimer's group to flee, but Alexander doubted they were hitting their marks. The majority of the enemy had likely fled already, ducked back into the endless tracts of chrome and steel that made up the city's bulk. They would never find them if they searched for a week.

Although he was stranded behind the pillar of the underground parking lot, which exploded and fragmented as rounds ricocheted all around him, he had a sense that there was little of Oppenheimer's group left to save. It had been the same since the ambassadorial convoys had started arriving from the outer settlements. They had been under siege for days.

Forty years ago, before the Old World had come crashing down, commuters had squeezed along these streets in their millions. The skyscrapers had gleamed then—steel and glass spires that stood testament to man's dominion over all the world. The concrete, too, had been fresh and smooth, and the air had been alive with radio and microwaves, transmitting billions of messages and voices.

Things had changed since the End. The City of London, the small nexus that lay in the centre of London's sprawling bulk, was a city no longer. It was a mausoleum. No computer had whirred nor phone trilled for decades. All the electronics had turned to dust that day, at the same time as almost every man, woman, and child had vanished suddenly, leaving empty clothing crumpling to the ground and a cascade of falling jewellery.

Only a few had survived. The Early Years had almost finished them, but humanity had pulled through. Since then, they had all faced countless trials and tribulations, but none as bad as now. A famine had levelled any crop worth harvesting, and a blood feud had erupted across the land. An army was gathering, bearing down on the last remnants of civilisation. All that stood between them and a new Dark Age were a few thousand precious souls.

Five of whom had just been blown away on the street outside.

Alex gritted his teeth as plaster exploded from the pillar around his head, shredded by shrapnel. Blinking the sting from his eyes, he looked around at the others crouched in the parking lot, breathless and filthy after their long cross-country ride. They'd had only seconds of warning, having flung their horses and themselves under the first cover in sight. Oppenheimer's party had been moments behind, but they had arrived from the other direction and hadn't been so lucky. The narrow city street had funnelled the convoy into a neat line stretching directly before the enemy skyscraper, right into the firing squad's line of sight.

It was a turkey shoot.

"Sons of bitches!" Marek Johnson roared over the racket, inches to Alexander's right. "Cowards, rotten cowards." The tendons in his thick neck tensed, and his face screwed into an ugly mask of burgeoning fury. Thickset and powerful, he looked absurd crammed between a ticket turnstile and the rusted carcass of an old Audi. His grip on his rifle tightened, as if he were preparing to leap from cover.

"Stay down!"

"I'm not leaving them out there."

"There's nothing you can do."

"Bullshit!"

He was scrambling to his feet when Alexander risked losing a hand, reaching out across the two feet of open ground between them. Marek easily had twice Alexander's mass and was twenty years his junior, but nevertheless, Alexander felt the usually stoic protector yield under his hand. Such were the way of things when you were heralded as the Messiah who would save civilisation.

Marek's eyes were ablaze, but he stayed put.

Alexander was reminded of Lucian, and a pang of anguish ran through him. In the firefight he had almost forgotten about his own brother. He was out there in the wilds somewhere. They had raced in aid of New Canterbury only a day ago and had spent a mere hour with boots on the ground at the suspected site of the enemy stronghold. It had been a false alarm; no shots had been fired. Yet still the silver-haired Lucian McKay had disappeared. They had searched for hours amidst the massacred corpses of countless slaves and innocents, but he hadn't been among them.

Alex wished he were here now.

Gunfire still smacked with jarring jolts against the other side of the pillar, but its rate was ebbing. He tore his rifle from around his shoulder and swung around onto his toes, signalling for the others to do the same. Ignoring the aches and pains in his tired old body, he listened with practised patience until the lull reached its zenith, and then cried,

"Now!"

They leapt from cover and fired a return volley as one, peppering the weathered glass of the enemy position until it was fine spray, leaving a gaping hole all along one floor of the skyscraper. Perhaps once, such destruction would have seemed a scar upon the face of perfection, when the world's economy had been managed from these very buildings, but not now—not among the mosses, the creepers, the fallen ceilings and walls, and all other the signs of Father Time's work.

They kept shooting until Alexander was certain the streets were empty, that whoever had survived from Oppenheimer's party had taken shelter, and then waved to cease fire. They waited in ringing silence as plaster dust rained down on their shoulders and the tinkling of broken windows settled in the distance. Alexander's legs were screaming from the effort of holding his crouched position—

Christ, I'm old, he thought.

But so long as the others were behind him, he would never show weakness, not if it killed him.

"What's the situation down there?" came the voice of a guard up on the compound walls. "How many injured?"

Alex glanced around at the taut, determined faces beside him, and all the smoking barrels of as many rifles. "None!"

"Mobile?"

"All."

"Can you make it to the gate?"

Alex darted his head to peer at the stretch of shattered

glass on the distant skyscraper. Only blackness met his gaze, the enemy nowhere in sight, for now. They might start firing again the moment they stepped into the light. But so many counted on his strength, and they were so close to safety. They couldn't afford to be beaten into submission. He trusted every man and woman in his party with his life, but even now he felt pressure on the back of his neck. All the long years he had trained his inner circle to lead others, to be his emissaries—his very flesh incarnate—and still now they were looking to him for strength.

Some things never changed.

"We'll make it!"

"Good. We'll cover you."

Alex leaned back and swept his gaze over the others. Determined, twinkling pairs of eyes bobbed in the gloom, all trained upon him, all ready to give their lives for the mission; the mission to preserve the world's knowledge, art, and science for future generations, and prevent the backward slide to barbarism that had already consumed so much of the world.

They would follow him to the end. That was the story of his life. How many had followed him to their own ends while he had lived on? How many lives had been saved by his hand, against all those cut short by the storm that had raged around him all these years?

"Are you ready?" he breathed.

They all nodded without hesitation, and as always, his heart skipped a beat at the recollection of all that had nodded just as solemnly before all the skirmishes that their mission had brought down on their heads. If only they knew of the carpet of blood upon which he walked, or how many of their predecessors' bodies he had walked over to get to where he was now.

"The horses?" Marek said.

Alex looked over to his white mare, milling in the recesses of the lot where they had reined up, watching him patiently in spite of the echoing racket. She had served him well for many years, her white coat as much a symbol of their mission as himself. She watched him even now.

"Leave them," Alexander said.

Tension stole amongst their ranks, for their mounts were among the few horses that hadn't succumbed to hungry mouths during the long famine. In the vastness of the empty British Isles, where human settlement was as common as in the Arctic Circle before the End, these animals had sometimes been the only friends they had. There would be no replacing them. But still the others stayed at his side, ready.

"Once we break cover, nobody stops until we're inside." Alexander hesitated, then added, "Leave the fallen, even if I'm one of them."

The compound gate's klaxon buzzed, and in the corner of his eye, Alexander saw the gate swing inwards. The parking lot was filled with the rumbling echo of their breath sounds, sharp and shallow. Their window was moments away.

Then from somewhere out in the street came Oppenheimer's voice: "Alexander!"

"Geoffrey! Where are you?"

"The subway station. We thought we could get under the wall this way. I led them all in here …" A lonely sob rang out across England's former capital.

Alexander cursed. They had sealed the old tunnels with concrete just before the siege had begun. There was no way out of the station but the glass-roofed bank of escalators that served as the entrance. "How many are you?"

His old friend's harried voice was broken, panicked. "Ah … seven. We have wounded."

Alex suppressed the urge to swallow. The others were listening close. Sweat tickled the small of his back as it ran in a stream down from his neck. There had been over thirty people in Oppenheimer's convoy. That had been the way of all the ambushes thus far. Only the ambassadors themselves and a few lucky stragglers had been left unharmed—the rest, slaughtered.

The gate clunked open. The guards began calling out from the upper catwalks, balking in protest. But Alexander hesitated. He looked to the others, saw them looking to him now with an air of desperation, and screamed internally. He turned back to the street.

The enemy skyscraper was still derelict, but there were at least two hundred metres between the station and the gate. It would be only too easy to pick Oppenheimer's group off once they emerged. Yet the only chance for any of them was now. "Geoffrey, the gate's open. On five, we're all going to run. Don't stop, not for anything."

"We'll be killed!"

"They'll cover us from the wall." Alexander ignored the slick of self-hatred that slithered in his gut, and readied himself. There would be time to make amends later. If any of Oppenheimer's group made it.

"One ... two ..."

Over a dozen sharp inhalations filled the parking lot, and rifles were slung over shoulders.

"Three ... four ..."

Alexander took one last glance at the enemy position, a black abyss twenty storeys above the ground. Any number of things could be trained upon them right now. But what choice did they have?

"Five!"

The world smeared into a medley of colours. Alexander launched himself out into the light, and the air was filled with automatic gunfire almost before he had even cleared the parking lot's shadow. Panting and cries of alarm flashed by as his younger companions surged past in a blind bid for personal safety, under the protective barrage of fire being laid down by the Kevlar-clad men up on the compound's walls.

Amidst the flurry and madness, he caught a few defined snapshots: a guard above his head, teeth bared over the flashing muzzle of his assault carbine; the enemy skyscraper, sporting a fresh gouge in its smooth glass walls on a lower storey from which dozens of gun barrels protruded, heedless of the returning fire; Marek, roaring in pain as he staggered along, clutching a leg that was spurting streams of scarlet; and straight ahead, Geoffrey Oppenheimer and six other figures, sprinting along the street towards them.

Oppenheimer was an old man, perhaps seventy. He had always been a dignified soul, just like the other ambassadors; a natural leader who believed in peace and justice. And just like the others, he was now covered in the blood of his family and friends, running for his life with wide eyes, his mouth ajar in a scream of naked fear.

Amidst the panic and frenzy, a single coherent thought flashed through Alexander's mind.

How far we have fallen.

His lungs seared and his legs begged for mercy, but eventually he reached the gate. The others had already dived inside, and those in the courtyard beyond were braying out for him to follow. But he tripped to a halt on the threshold and turned back.

Three of Oppenheimer's seven companions lay on the ground unmoving. The remaining four were close, but still thirty metres from the gate. Thirty metres of open ground, a straight shot from the enemy skyscraper. The cover fire being laid down by the guards had lessened the incoming volleys some, but this last stretch was the perfect bottleneck. They would never make it.

Alexander was running toward them before he knew what was happening. The anguished howls of those in the compound chased him, but to no avail. His feet carried him inexorably into a raining hail of ballistic metal. There was no room for fear, not in the scant moments it took for him to cross the distance to the bottleneck.

A curious certainty had fallen over him. For while the

enemy was barbarous, it still had a master. And while most had no clue who could be at the helm of this scourge, Alexander did.

Then he was crossing the last few feet to Oppenheimer's remaining four, passed by them—enduring the briefest and most intense expressions of bafflement he had ever seen from them—and then skidded to a halt, throwing his arms wide. Eyes squeezed shut, teeth gritted until his jawbone crunched upon his skull, he came to a standstill in the dust of the Old World, and waited to die.

And then there was silence. Sudden, absolute silence. The gunfire had stopped dead.

He gasped, blinked in the midday glare, frozen with his arms thrown high, a static five-pointed star upon the crumbled tarmac of Canada Square. Even those crying out for him on the wall were silenced. For a time that seemed like forever he stood there staring ahead at the line of gun barrels, all trained upon him, but none firing a shot.

Then a single voice broke the silence. "Alexander!" Norman Creek bawled. "What are you *doing*?"

Alex peered over his shoulder and saw men and women he would have called friends lining the walls of the Canary Wharf compound in their dozens—no, hundreds—all staring without a mote of movement among them. Mouths hung ajar and eyes were wide, and Alexander couldn't blame them. He should have been dead.

Even from so far away, despite the sun, he picked Norman out from their ranks. A crooked, slender silhouette propped up by a cane and capped by a crop of unruly dark hair, he stood upon the catwalk directly over the gate. Their eyes met, and Alexander suddenly felt very exposed, naked, and foolish.

Then he remembered all he risked by being out in the open. There was precious little between him and death. He had risked all his long years of strife, the lives of countless thousands who relied on him, and the mission itself.

The curious certainty that had overtaken him evaporated without ceremony, leaving him a lonely old relic stranded in No Man's Land.

"Get back here!" Norman again, desperate and confused.

"Alexander," Marek called from the open gate, the slimmest sliver of his face peeping from the lee of the steel door. "Step back this way. Slow and steady." He paused, then continued in a voice laced with thinly-veiled disbelief and confusion. "Mr Oppenheimer and the others are safe. You can come back now."

Alexander returned his gaze to the enemy skyscraper, and saw that the gun barrels had disappeared. They were watching; he could still feel the pressure of their gaze. But the ambush was over.

He stared hard into the blackness of the steel and glass spire. "So it really is you leading them," he muttered. The acidic burn of liquid fear bubbled low in his bowel. All the notes, the signs, the slow and creeping advance of these barbarous hordes upon their homes. All the time he had kept the truth of who was really behind it all a secret, even to those he loved, even to Norman.

Yet the reality of it all hadn't seeped in until now, not really. It had taken this, facing the firing squad, literally.

Ignoring the prickling of the hairs along his spine, he turned his back on the street and walked back to the gate. He forced himself to take his time, not hurrying, passing over tarmac studded with gouges and ragged old vehicles torn to scrap by bullet holes. And the bodies, too. Not only those of Oppenheimer's party lay scattered around the wall, but also the bloated remains of those slaughtered in ambushes earlier in the week, when the other ambassadors had arrived.

The stench this close to the compound was nauseating, a black ugly smell that clawed at the back of his throat.

He made a point to study each of their faces in turn, and they joined the endless parade that had over time followed him in the name of the mission, only to meet their deaths. He didn't dare try claiming the bodies, not even the children. He alone was being spared a bullet to the head, but how far did their mercy extend?

His nerve almost broke at the gate's threshold. It took all his mettle to stand fast and walk unhurried into the courtyard. Hands ran over him, pulling, tugging, buffeting over his clothes and face. A few secured his safety beyond the threshold, Marek's chief among them. Alexander struggled to pick out any one face from the teeming mass; there were so many. Voices gabbled their joy at his safety. Reverential and fetishistic hands caressed him.

The klaxon buzzed overhead and the gate swung shut. Those up on the catwalk held firm until it squealed to a booming close, then they too relaxed and turned to look down at him. From the tower itself, Alexander could make out the ghostly images of refugees filling every window of the lobby and several floors above, pressed against the glass, all watching.

"What the hell did you think you were doing?" Marek growled in his ear.

"Helping a friend," Alex said. He looked at Oppenheimer who crouched weeping over his one remaining young daughter.

"We could have lost you."

Alexander almost retorted that he was nothing special, but caught his tongue just in time. The masses had treated him as a demigod for so many years it had become part of the fabric of who they were. People used to pilgrimage to his home before the famine. Sometimes, he forgot how they all saw him.

That's why they all wanted to touch me. I'm something other, privy to secret truths.

He had just walked towards an enemy that had slain everything it had come into contact with, and walked away.

You might as well have walked on water, oh great Messiah.

Norman appeared in the crowd, and those around him bowed back to make room for him, affording him a juvenile form of the reverence being beamed at Alexander himself. Norman had been his disciple long before anyone had called him Messiah. It was hard to see him as anything but the embodiment of all Alexander had worked for. To see him so broken and weak was unsettling.

He hadn't turned out to be the man Alexander had hoped.

A harried, scornful voice rose above the racket, coming from the lobby. "Of all the shameful, reckless, godforsaken imbecilic things I've seen in my time, you take the candle and the dish, Mr Cain!" Evelyn Fisher screeched. A wrinkled, regal creature from a bygone era of war and eternal fear in the north during the Early Years, she let her Yorkshire accent cut a swathe through the crowd's ranks and left a tunnel of bare tarmac between them. Her eyes glowered over the relief swelling on her face. "What were you thinking?"

Alexander didn't reply, just walked over to Oppenheimer and crouched down beside him. "Are you alright?"

Oppenheimer gripped him with a bloodied hand, patting him sporadically on the shoulder while still leaning over his fainted daughter. Her white dress was torn open across the waist, the delicate trailing hem spotted with scarlet. "It's good to see you, old friend," he managed to last.

"Can you stand?"

"My girl …"

"Here, let me." Alexander helped Oppenheimer to his feet.

I'll never forgive myself for this. But they need to know we're still strong. He lifted the young girl like a trophy and held her limp body close against his, her head resting on his shoulder. "We are now all arrived," he called. "The ambassadors"—he swept a hand around, picking them out from the crowd, drawn from across the country—"have assembled, despite the attacks. The council may now convene."

Whispers exploded across the courtyard. The council summit of Canary Wharf had been the only true symbol of organised government since the End. Its word represented all the might western civilisation could still bring to bear. Even those in the cragged ruins of the North knew their names. For a long time, they had been the sole power in this land—for all they knew, the world.

How close it had all come to nothing, and how fast they had been reduced to a rabble of rats hiding behind concrete walls.

But Alexander wasn't going to give up without a fight. They might have fallen, but there was life in them yet.

"Many are still injured," Evelyn said. "The rest are weary from travel."

"Our walls can stand strong for a few hours more, I'm sure." Alexander looked skywards at the hunks of muscle manning the catwalks around the tower. As one, they stiffened, giving a single unified nod that seemed to bear down on the crowd and soothe the brewing panic.

Evelyn stepped forward and caressed Oppenheimer's cheek. "Geoffrey, you old fool," she crooned.

"Evie." Behind the haunted sorrow on Oppenheimer's mud-splattered face, the ghost of a smile flickered. "We made it."

"We did. But we still have a job to do."

His eyes hardened. Alexander had seen that look too many times to mistake it—the hardening determination, like a carapace swallowing doubt and fear. "We have a job to do," he repeated, nodding.

She took him under the shoulder, and together, they stood and faced the crowd beside Alexander.

He looked down at the pale young girl in his arms. She still breathed, but with all that she had lost, she would never be whole again. Her face joined those of the dead outside, and the endless shadow parade behind them. "Two hours," he called. "Two hours, and the council convenes."

The crowd dispersed with vigour, milling and whorling as people piled into the lobby and disappeared into the tower. In moments the courtyard had almost emptied, and the only ones left were the guards, the council members, Marek, and Norman. While the guards stared away across the city with their ears sealed decidedly shut, the others all stared at Alexander.

"You should be full of holes, chief," Marek said quietly. His leg had been haphazardly bandaged, already soaked through with blood, but he was standing on it nonetheless, staggering yet determined. "They gunned down some good fighters today, no easy targets. And you run right towards them across open ground and ..." He looked Alexander up and down, speechless.

"What were you *thinking*?" Evelyn breathed.

Alexander swallowed. There was no answer to give.

"What if we had lost you? How would we go on?"

Alexander smiled automatically. He swept an arm at

Norman Creek, and all eyes turned upon him. "For that, we have our champion. I was never going to lead the world back to glory, remember? That job belongs to Norman."

Silence. Nobody would ever question Norman's destiny; Alexander had made sure of that. The story of his succession had become sacred religion. They believed in him as much as they believed in Alexander. The council members were old, wise, and powerful, but everyone needed their comforts, even if they had to blind themselves to the truth.

Because the truth was Norman had never wanted any destiny. Even now, he cringed at the mention of his own name.

Marek took the girl from Alexander's arms, and they departed to make preparations, leaving Norman alone with Alexander.

"Where's Lucian?" Norman said. There were tears in his eyes.

Alexander touched him on the arm, but he recoiled. "Alive. I'm sure of it."

"Where?"

"I don't know. He disappeared."

"How could he just disappear?"

"We found their hideout, in the woods—at least, what was left of it. Their slaves had fought back … It was a massacre. We searched inside, and …" Alexander thought of the note he had found in a dusty old office, the one that had so distracted him, which rested even now in his pocket. "We got separated. And then he was just gone."

Norman glowered. "We have to find him."

"We will, but not now. We have much to do. And in any case"—he eyed the wall—"we couldn't leave if we tried. Not now."

"Maybe if you hadn't abandoned me here, I could have saved him."

"Norman—"

"Maybe I could have done *something*!"

Alexander whirled to face him, his patience bowing. "Norman, you're injured! The attack on New Canterbury was just a few weeks ago. Broken ribs take time to heal. I'm sorry we left you, I am, but there was little time, and in your condition …"

Norman's eyes swam with hurt. "All those years you raised me to believe in that stupid destiny, and told all those people they could look to me. When the time finally came for me to step up, you just left me, right in front of everyone." He blinked. "I'll never forget that."

Alexander didn't answer. "Like I've said before, our past isn't all roses. It never has been."

Norman smouldered awhile as they circled the courtyard. Inside the tower, a great hubbub had kicked up. People were making ready for the summit, the one thing that might still save them. And beyond the wall—no, through it—Alexander could feel the enemy, feel them all around, pressing in closer.

"Marek's right. You should be dead," Norman said finally, and stopped abruptly, turning Alexander forcefully to face him.

Alexander nodded.

"They didn't shoot. They know you."

He nodded again. "Yes."

"You know more than you're telling us. You always do."

Alexander didn't reply.

Norman waited a moment longer, then shook his head in disgust and ambled upon his cane toward the tower. "One day, you'll learn to trust your family," he spat over his shoulder.

Alexander was left alone.

The truth was he knew everything. And that was why he was still alive. In reality, the great hordes and burning and mass-killings weren't about food or land or hunger at all. It was all revenge for the wrongs Alexander had done, all stemming from the man at its head—a man who wanted to watch all he'd created burn to the ground.

He took the note he had found in the dusty office from his pocket and unfurled it:

Know this, brother: if there had ever been a time in which you could have saved them, could have ever truly saved anyone, it was the last time you looked into my eyes—when you chose your dream over your family.

Destiny calls, Alex. I'll be seeing you, soon.

— J

CHAPTER 2

Light. A metallic squeal amidst total blackness.

Lucian lifted his head, breathing stale, stinking air, and blinked fiercely. His eyes streamed, the optic nerve throbbing at the intensity of the square of orange radiance pouring into the room. How long had he been in this damp, dark cell, his hands and feet bound to this unyielding metal chair?

He thought it might have been hours, but days would have better suited the ache in his back and the numbness in his legs. He had heard others beyond his four walls, begging and babbling, some screaming. But they had seemed far away, removed from his own private darkness, as though their beatings and torture had been going on in some distant land.

A figure broke the perfect orange glow and stepped into the room with a heavy limp, accompanied by a fug of sweat, ash, and the gamey tang of coagulated blood. He would have recognised that limp anywhere. "Untie me, Charlie," he growled.

Charlie stood over him, his young face made old by pain

and hatred. It had been weeks since the people of New Canterbury—in no small part led by Lucian himself—had dragged him through their streets and trampled over him like an animal, yet still his body bore the marks, the gashes still seeping pus, the great bruises on his face and arms only now fading from green to yellow. His lip twitched. He dropped a box he had brought with him onto the ground and sat with difficulty, angling his fractured leg out to the side. "My father taught me that violence was the refuge of the uncivilised mind," he said, his eyes trained upon a spot past Lucian's shoulder. "He was a good man, gentle and kind. He believed in things, he had principles and morals, and he stood by them, even when nobody else would. Even when we had to steal so that we could eat, or cheat a tradesman out of his wares, he would make amends somehow. He'd leave a cloth full of bread crusts under a nearby tree, or send help back for them when we came to the next village. He was a seer from before the End. He thought we could be something again, live in the big skyscrapers and drive motorcars again someday. He hadn't given up." Charlie's eyes flickered to Lucian, and his gaze bore through to Lucian's memory of the night he had gunned Charlie's father down. "And then they came and took us and made my father go out on those little jaunts into your city every night. During the day, he would rest real quiet and tell me everything was going to be fine. Meanwhile, every now and then they took one of the other families outside and shot them while they grovelled in the dirt. But he was my dad. He'd never lied to me. And he said we would be fine." A twisted mutant of a smile flashed upon Charlie's lips, threaded with pain. "I believed him."

The expression vanished suddenly. "Then he ran into you. I know he wouldn't have done anything to hurt anyone. He was just doing what he had to." He inched closer to Lucian, stinking of grease and other people's spilled blood. "I know you must have sensed that he wasn't one of them. But you still shot him in cold blood."

Lucian eyed Charlie's hand, hovering close to his belt, where a rusted old pistol hung in its holster. He waited until Charlie's fingers had stopped spasming over the handle before he said, "I did what I had to do to protect my family. They attacked us, put Norman on crutches, killed Ray, scared hundreds of people half to death."

"And for that you murdered an innocent man."

"I made a mistake, Charlie. A lot of people got hurt that night. And your father was among the enemy."

"He had no choice!"

"Neither did I!" Lucian surged forward against his restraints, ignoring the pain of the wire cutting into the flesh of his wrists. "People were desperate. You know how things were then. Anyone would have slit a stranger's throat for a bag of grain."

Light erupted from his peripheral vision, and Lucian gasped, blown sideways. Nausea sent his guts heaving and he vomited bile across his shoes. Through the stars flashing before his eyes, he saw Charlie with his fist raised to strike again, teeth bared. "That was your fault! If you and your kind hadn't scoured every nook and cranny across the whole country and stolen every scrap of food for your towns and cities, maybe so many wouldn't have died." He scowled. "Maybe now you wouldn't have an army of orphaned kids, grieving widows, and childless parents burning and killing everything and everyone you hold dear."

"Like I said, what had to be done was done."

"You starved people to death. Your brothers and sisters, those to whom you're so fond of preaching, about how you'll save us all, bring back the power of the Old World. But because we're not part of your little clique, because we don't live in the wreck of some creaking city and spend all day reading dusty books searching for answers, we're not worthy. We're just dogs, cavemen."

Lucian said nothing.

Charlie sneered. "You can't even deny it to my face."

"What do you want me to say?" Lucian muttered. It took all he had to meet Charlie's gaze, because those hurting eyes hanging over him were the spitting image of his father's, the same ones that had silently pleaded for peace around the campfire, before the shooting had started— before Lucian had put a round in his chest. "I can't change what I did."

"All I want is justice." Charlie's fingers waggled close to his belt once more.

Lucian felt sweat break out on his neck. He knew the drawn, haggard look stealing into Charlie's face all too well. It was the look men got when they were fixing to kill. "That could put you on a dangerous path, Charlie. Your father wouldn't want this. You're right. He did try to stop what happened. And I bet he wouldn't have wanted this for you, signing up with the enemy on some revenge kick."

Another blinding blow caught him across the temple, and yet more stars flew in from nowhere, twinkling and fading. Then, Charlie's voice, cold and seething, "What would you know about what he would have wanted?"

"An old bastard like me gets to know a lot of people in his time. Some are bad, most are just trying to get by however they can, and a few are good—the kind of selfless good guys who don't seem real, like they're out of some book. Your dad was one of those." Lucian swallowed hard. His throat was parched dry, and his tongue rasped the back of his throat, but that wasn't why it was hard to talk. A hard orb had formed in his gullet, trembling and whispering evil things. "I killed him," he said. "I did. And I'm sorry. I took your father away from you, and there's nothing I can ever do to put it right—"

"No, there isn't," Charlie said. His fingers had grown still again. There was noise outside, a lot of noise. His eyes darted away towards the concrete walls, as though he were seeing through them, and his brow furrowed. "Save your breath. We're going to have to cut this short. We're moving."

"I take it I'm not alone?"

A smile flickered on Charlie's face. "The End might have kicked us to the dirt, but you'd be surprised just how many pockets of the Old World are still out there. Like cockroaches. And I have to hand it to your kind: we burned plenty places to the ground and they still won't bow, won't sign up, and won't even look at us like we're men and women. They see us just like you do, like cavemen."

"Think there's a clue somewhere in there?"

"Don't get smart. You get another day of living, but I can still make that day ugly." Charlie pushed the door closed as someone shuffled past outside. He suddenly looked alert, perhaps even afraid.

Lucian frowned, but waited until the shuffling dissipated before he said, "I'm not supposed to be here, am I?"

Charlie didn't answer, his ear pressed to the door.

"Do the others know who I am?"

Charlie was very still, facing the door. Lucian thought he caught a single muscle spasm in his neck.

I'm onto something, he thought. *But don't push it, not yet.*

He let it pass and waited in silence. Eventually, Charlie seemed satisfied and turned back to face him, the half-healed slashes in his cheek thrown into sharp relief by the scant light shining in through the crack in the doorway. "We've been real busy, burning up all those little quaint villages and towns. A fair few sign right up with us to keep breathing, but you wouldn't believe how many swear fealty to your ilk, to *New Canterbury* and your blessed little council in London." He leaned in close, so close that Lucian could smell the dry, musky excitement on his breath. "It's like you're gods or something. They think you'll swoop in and save them." He smiled. "But we have faith in them. They just take a little convincing."

"And this humble abode is where you do your

convincing? With a hammer and chisel, no doubt?"

"Pliers, too, if the occasion calls for it."

Lucian shook his head. He thought of Alexander and Norman, and all the others counting on him back home. He had to get back to them somehow. And if he couldn't get back, he'd have to find a way to put an end to it all fast. He would have liked to say he would never hurt any of them, would never turn, but he knew better than that.

He had seen some bad things. People could do horrific things to one another in the name of beliefs, ideals, even love. Especially love. And men were fickle creatures. Even the strongest broke eventually. In his experience, you could make anyone do pretty much anything, if you took enough away from them, and made them hurt enough.

Charlie was the perfect example of that.

What have I done to him?

Charlie was watching him carefully, hovering only a few inches away, waiting for Lucian to make a move. But Lucian kept still and kept his gaze level. He wouldn't give him his trigger. After almost a full minute Charlie licked his chapped lips and muttered, "Like I said, we're moving you."

"Where?"

"Far away. We're done with this place. Nowhere left but your little bastions."

Lucian swallowed. "So why not finish it? Just get things over with?"

"Because He has plans for your friends. And He hasn't led us astray yet."

Lucian's breath wheezed out of him. "He?" he

whispered.

"That's right, He."

So it really was true. He really was behind all this, leading the scourge. Alexander had shown him all the signs, but he had never quite believed James was really still out there. It had been easier to half-believe it and keep it at the back of his mind. Because if his brother really had returned, it meant all this was their fault. They had bred a monster.

Just like Lucian had done yet again with the young man before him.

Charlie smiled. "You don't need to worry about Him. You won't live long enough."

Lucian scowled. The wire cutting into his wrists was starting to work its way deeper into his flesh. The pain was pulsing, raw. With the damp and the dirt, he was liable to get some nasty infection soon enough. He had to get out of dodge, or else he'd be suffering long before Charlie got to him. He'd rather eat a bullet now than live through that. Dying from septicaemia was a messy affair. "I'm all for walking and talking a while longer, but why bother moving me if you're just going to kill me? Why don't you end this, Charlie? You're only here to get revenge for your father. What's to stop you pulling the trigger right now and walking away from all this?"

Charlie didn't answer, but Lucian heard the crack deep in his throat.

"You can't do it, can you?"

"I can do it!" Charlie snarled.

"Then go ahead."

A moment of silence stretched out between them, then snapped; and in the next, Charlie was holding his knife in his hand. The blade twinkled in the hallway light, reflecting Charlie's wounded, terrified face.

Lucian forced himself to keep his gaze level despite the snakes slithering in his gut and the ball of fear swelling behind his eyes. Not long ago their roles had been reversed; Lucian had held a gun right to Charlie's head while he kneeled on the cobbles of New Canterbury, right before he had set him free. It hadn't been loaded, but Charlie didn't know that. He had threatened, bullied, and beaten the kid. It hadn't been enough that he had killed his father. He had treated him as though he had been the one who had been wronged, rather than the other way around. And why? Because he had been scared and ashamed.

He could have made amends, maybe, if he had tried hard enough. Maybe he could have at least stopped him signing up with the wolves at their door. He had failed him, just like he had failed his friends and his family. He had sworn to protect them. Yet here he was. And after everything he deserved no better.

He closed his eyes and waited for the end.

I'm sorry. Jesus, I'm sorry.

Ringing silence stretched out for so long that the snakes in his gut quieted, and the sound of his own breathing returned to his attention. He peeked one eye open and saw Charlie standing with his arms by his sides. His knife was back in its sheath. In his hands was a black linen hood. "Like I said, we're moving you," he said.

"You can't do it."

A muscle leapt in Charlie's jaw. "Enjoy the trip."

Then the hood was over his head and he was back in darkness.

CHAPTER 3

Norman retched, clutching the toilet bowl between his hands. Precious, irreplaceable morsels he'd eaten for breakfast slicked the U-bend. He wiped his mouth, head swimming, his fractured ribs throbbing, and then he stumbled from the stall to lean against the door. Two weeks since he had been attacked, and still the pain was no better.

But it wasn't the pain that was making him sick, not really. It was something else. Something was at odds with the world, and the weight of two cities rested on his shoulders. They had all stared at him in the lobby. Hundreds upon hundreds of expectant, dull, cow eyes trained upon him, as though all they had to do was fall in behind him and he would saddle up a warhorse and vanquish the enemy.

He took a deep breath and headed out into the lobby of Canary Wharf Tower, cane clacking on the faded marble floors. Yesterday, the tower and its fenced-off compound had been near empty; the shining pinnacle of England's last coalition of societies, relics of the Old World. Today, it was a refugee camp. Torn knapsacks, crushed luggage, bloodied bandages, and filthy exhausted refugees littered the floor. As many wept as those who had gone deathly still, dull-eyed and lobotomised by trauma.

Canary Wharf's fortified compound was fast becoming the last remaining safe haven. The summit between the land's dwindling societies had been called weeks ago, but the ambassadorial parties had been attacked en route. Now that Oppenheimer had arrived from Bristol, they were at least all accounted for, but they had taken heavy losses. Unnervingly, the council members themselves didn't have a scratch on them. It was their families, friends, aides, and subordinates who had been slaughtered.

It was almost as though the enemy knew about the summit and was keen to let it go ahead. The thought that they wanted to let them scurry around, squabbling in politics made the hairs on Norman's neck stand on end.

The tower's concrete walls and regiment of armed guards had kept back the tide thus far, but how long would that last? Who knew how many the enemy were? This place was no fortress, and its guards were few. They were calling it a siege, but if that became the reality, Norman didn't like their chances.

And what of home? New Canterbury had guns and men, but no high walls. And they had no fewer defenceless folk than here. Now that he had heard just how many towns had been hit, it was a wonder that New Canterbury remained almost unscathed. They'd had break-ins and raids—Norman's broken ribs could attest to that, not to mention Ray Hubble's corpse—but no more. One death, one injury;

it was nothing compared to the hundreds of bodies that lay in the enemy's wake.

Again, it was almost as though they were being spared. New Canterbury had been revered as the home of the great Alexander Cain for so long that its name was synonymous with their cause. Now it looked as though its name was the only thing saving it. But that was all the more chilling, because if it were true then it could only mean one thing: they were being saved *for last*.

All that was left to them was the summit. There was still power among them. The enemy might be playing cat and mouse, but that couldn't be justified. They were rabble, after all; a mass of farmers and traders brought together by a tenuous common goal. And they didn't have Alexander.

Norman walked across the lobby and tried to keep his head held high. The looks aimed at him were the same, demanding and fawning, but he ignored them. Let them have their hopes. That was the least he could try to do for them. He would do anything to avoid the future Alexander had in mind for him, but that didn't matter now; *they* all believed in him, even if his great destiny was all smoke, and that was all that mattered.

Not far from the stairwell, he spotted Allie. She was crouched down over a frail young girl in what had once been a pretty summer dress. It was Oppenheimer's daughter. She was awake now, but lay very still as Allie whispered a constant stream of sweet babble. The little girl had just lost her siblings and her mother, but still the faintest of smiles was on her lips. Allie had a gift with words.

Norman tried to ignore the flutter in his chest, but it now came whenever he looked her way, and he could no longer ignore it. Allison Rutherford had been a spurious gossip not long ago, a newcomer in New Canterbury who could be relied on to incite rumour wherever she went.

War had changed her. Her eyes had hardened, her hearsay had shifted to fierce mummery, and even her soft rounded face seemed to have become older, more angular. In a few short months, she had blossomed into a true woman. And during that transition, Norman's eyes had begun to linger.

It had been she who had stayed by his bedside after he had been attacked.

She caught his eye, and before he knew it, he was walking toward her and the little girl.

"Someone wants to meet you," Allie said.

He knelt with difficulty beside them both, facing away from the prying eyes of the crowd, and tried to smile for the little girl. She returned the favour, though timidly, and her eyes flicked to Allie for comfort.

"It's okay." Allie gripped her forearm. "He's not a grump, really. Most of the time."

"Unless I skip breakfast. Then I grow gruffalo horns."

The girl's face remained pale and taut, but her brow relaxed a tad. Allie gave him an encouraging look, and together they leaned over her and did their best to entertain her while the worst of the wounded were stabilised in the lobby and hauled upstairs, where their old infirmary had overspilled across two whole storeys. Complimenting her on her dress, asking her about home and her favourite books; it all brought back memories of the martial arts class Norman led back home.

He had always considered teaching one of the more taxing chores on New Canterbury's duty rota, but he missed the kids. He had never appreciated how easy their lives had been until now—just what Alexander's vision had meant for their quality of life. How many years had he moped and brooded over the destiny foisted upon him, meanwhile enjoying all the comforts of electricity and baked bread and fried eggs, curated libraries, and a comfy bed? And all that time, thousands had eked out desperate livings on the edge of rotting towns, fighting off thieves and succumbing to simple illnesses, slowly forgetting who they were and all they knew.

And then the famine had come. With their mission to thrust them into swift action, Alexander had insisted that the council impose a policy of aggressive scavenging, to stock up on food to buffer the impact of starvation. They couldn't afford to starve, not if they were to continue protecting the legacy of the Old World. They had scoured all the land and taken all they could find, leaving little, if anything, for anyone else. At first they had been unaware of just what effect they were having, but by the end of the famine's height, it had been obvious that they had robbed thousands of their already slim chances of survival.

In truth it was no surprise this army had banded together. They had brought this on themselves.

"I want my mummy," the little girl was saying.

Allie hushed her and brushed a stray lock of hair away from her cheek. "Rest, now, darling."

"I want her!"

Allie's lips tightened and grew pale. She glanced to him for help.

Norman was gripped by the same paralysis, and for a moment he thought they would both remain that way; but then a bright flash winked to life in the abyss behind his eyes, and he leaned toward her, taking her hand in his. "Back home, do you go to school?" he said.

She nodded, sunken eyes glazed.

"Do they tell the story of the End?" He waited, but she had grown still. He smiled. "I bet they do. They've been telling it all over since I was a boy. Before the End, the great cities were full of people, millions, and all the old machines rang and trilled and flashed around them, doing their bidding and talking to other people and other machines across the sea. Because, of course, there were many places across the sea, and each one was home to millions more people. We were wise, and we had power. The world had big problems, terrible problems, but we strived to put them right just as we do today—and that's what's important: we're no different today than our ancestors before us. They might have lived in tall buildings and talked to others on the other side of the world just like I talk to you now, but they were just people, no different from us." He paused, and squeezed her hand. "Why do we tell that story?"

"Because they're all gone," the girl whispered.

"Yes, they are. They left us behind to carry on, and

though we don't know why they left, we have to do our best to carry on their way of life. One day we'll be ready for that power again. If places like this and people like us fail, everything they worked for will vanish just like them. And we can't let that happen, because that's how we keep them alive." He placed both their hands over her chest. "So long as we carry all they knew, felt, and dreamed, they're still here with us."

The little girl looked down at her own chest. She said nothing, but her lip quivered. She wasn't young enough for fairy tales, but a child's imagination was the most powerful thing Norman knew of; it made them tougher than diamond. He could almost see the cogs turning inside her head. After a long time, she looked back up at them and gave the smallest of nods.

He gave her his best smile, despite the swell of embarrassment swelling in his throat, and stood on shaking legs, suppressing a grunt as his ribs cried out.

"I'll be right back," Allie said, caressing the girl's cheek. "I'm going to make sure he's alright. He's special, you know."

"I know," the girl answered. She looked at Norman. "He's the Chosen One from the stories."

Norman blinked in surprise. "How did you know?"

"Daddy and the others always talk about you. Everyone does." She fingered her bloodied dress. "You're going to bring us all together someday, that's what they say." She glanced to the wall and the looming city beyond. "Are you going to save us from the monsters, Mr Creek?"

Norman felt his lips part, but his mind had gone blank. He stood lamely before her for some moments while she stared out through the lobby windows, and then he turned on his heel and hurried away. His cane clacked upon the granite floor, his throbbing ribs begged him to stop, and he sensed myriad eyes moving over him from all around, but he refused to let up, his eyes fixed on the staircase. Suddenly his attention was on escape, and nothing else.

"Norman, wait!" Allie called. He tried to ignore her, but she caught up in a few strides and caught his elbow.

He wheeled around, fury surging forth as though a cork had been yanked. "*What?*" he hissed. "*What do you want from me?*" He had managed to keep himself from yelling, but only just. His voice had emerged as a sibilant whisper, all the more scathing for its bottled intensity.

She recoiled, her face falling. Others nearby fell quiet, averting their eyes and busying themselves with the remaining wounded. "I just wanted to say thank you." She seemed unable to meet his eye. "You handled her really well. Almost like—" She hesitated and bit her lip, but then with an almost audible *clunk* her eyes rolled to stare right at him. "Almost like Alexander."

He swallowed convulsively. The others were peeking at him once more. He took a deep breath and ran a hand through his hair. "I'm not surprised," he said. "That was one of his old speeches, verbatim. He used to say the same thing to me every night when I was a kid, word for word." He leaned closer and lowered his voice. "I'm sorry. It's the pain." He scowled. "This radio message they received better be worth it. Bringing us all together like this, it could have ended us."

Her eyebrows twitched, and she touched his arm. "I know. It's okay."

"No, no it's not. I can't take it out on you. You were doing a hell of a job with her."

She shrugged. "What was I going to do? She just lost her mother."

"Not everyone would have. It's ugly, but it's the truth." They started for the stairs, slowly this time.

"Well, I don't know how much good I did. It was nothing on your performance."

"Like I said, it was Alexander's story."

He felt her eyes stabbing at him again, drowning out the others'. "That may be so, but there's a reason people look to you."

"They look to me because they've been told to. They've had fairy tales of some great prodigal son shoved down their throats since before most of them could walk, and the rest are too old to remember anything different. It's all fluff, something they can lose themselves in, something to believe that keeps them going." He suppressed a scowl. "Nobody ever really expects me to lead."

"That's not true. Maybe it was once, but not now. You've changed. There's something of him in you, in the way you move, talk—the way you are."

"I'm nothing like him."

"Norman, your destiny—"

He grunted, cutting her off. "There's no such thing as

destiny," he said slowly, enunciating every syllable. "They're just stories."

They walked in silence until they neared the stairs, leaving the body of refugees behind, and could talk freely again. "Stories can come true, you know," she said.

He shook his head. She was supposed to be the one he could rely on to be on his side, yet even she seemed be slipping under the legend's spell. He couldn't blame her, surrounded by blood and severed families. But she had been a lifeline he had been relying on. He had few allies left. With Robert back in New Canterbury, and Lucian missing …

He stopped mid-stride and gripped her sleeve, gentle instead of hard.

Clutching, he thought. *I'm clutching at her. How desperate is that?*

"Please, don't turn into one of them," he said. His voice was almost cracking. "I need you to see me, not the Chosen One. I need you on my side."

She looked taken aback, and glanced toward the others back in the lobby. Norman knew they were all watching, and knew that they must be making something of a spectacle. The grand marble staircase wasn't exactly inconspicuous. But he refused to look away from Allie and waited until she had turned back to him. "Allie, are you with me?"

She was chewing her lip again, but her gaze was resolute. "What are friends for?" she said.

Feeling more than a little embarrassed, he realised she wasn't moving with him anymore, but hovering. She was waiting to go back to Oppenheimer's daughter. Despite all the staring and his own little drama, she hadn't forgotten. In fact, she looked more determined than ever.

What a little time can do to a person, he thought. *She was just a kid not long ago. A damn annoying one. And now … what would I do without her?*

"Will you be alright with her?" he said.

"I have to be." No fear, no uncertainty, where only minutes before there had been. Had his story had something to do with that?

Maybe she's right. Maybe's something of Alexander rubbed off on me, after all.

Left with that uncomfortable thought, Norman made to ascend the staircase to find the council chambers. His focus was so distant that, at first, he didn't notice the white figures moving past him at all. It wasn't until the third of them had brushed past him—almost seeming to pass *through* him— that he froze in place.

Half a dozen pale shapes were moving on ahead of him, ascending the stairs. Three were gesticulating in conversation with one another, two were running with armfuls of folders and sheaves of paper, and the last was ambling at a leisurely pace with something held to his ear that sent the air wheezing out of Norman's lungs: a smartphone. All of them were dressed in the kind of formal office attire that had littered the cities in the Early Years, before they were picked clean by traders. Yet they were all white, like figures from a children's picture book that hadn't been filled in. As they passed through the sunbeams thrusting in through the lobby windows, each one seemed to shimmer. He heard them, too, but their speech was warbling and muffled, as though he had water in his ears.

It all lasted only a moment, but it was most definitely there, right in front of him. He could have reached out and touched any one of them. His eyelids flickered, and they were gone. No shimmer, no noise, nothing. Gone.

"Norman?" Allie sounded a thousand miles away. "What's wrong? Do you need a hand?"

"Did you see that?" he cried, whirling to face her.

"See what?"

"Walking there, people. People in suits, right there on the stairs!" He reached over and gripped her shoulder. "You didn't see that?"

Her lips had parted, and her eyes were wide, afraid. "Norman, are you alright?"

There was no lie in her eyes; she hadn't seen anything.

"I'm fine," he breathed. "I'm fine, I just … I need a rest."

"Good idea. Just make sure you show for the summit. One hour."

"An hour." He nodded. He tried to give her an encouraging smile, but his cheeks had turned to cement. The pain in his chest pulsed, sending blinding flashes up his spine to the base of his skull. Suddenly, it was hard to breathe. He turned back to the stairs and hurried away from her—her and everyone else.

It wasn't real. It was the pain. It was making him seeing things.

They were people from before the End. The voice

whispering those words was familiar, but not his own. He had heard it once before, though, perhaps in a half-forgotten dream.

Echoes. That's what they're called. Echoes.

No, it was just a hallucination. Pain did funny things, played tricks on you. The people who had once lived and worked here were long gone.

That same familiar voice spoke once more, setting free a torrent of liquid fear into his bowels: *That's right: they're all dead and gone. Aren't they?*

CHAPTER 4

Billy Peyton was dying. Tree-studded darkness lay all around her, and no matter which way she turned, the forest always looked the same. The great maze had swallowed her up, and she had been stupid enough to wander right into it. How long had she been in here?

There was no way of telling. Only thin slivers of light made it down through the dense canopy, and she was lucky if she could tell whether it was night or day. All she had to go on was her thirst, which by now had become a smouldering fire in her belly, slowly creeping out towards her arms and legs. She had tried to eat some dried berries a while ago, but they had caught in her throat and she had choked, as though her mouth were full of sand.

It was fetid and still amidst the forest's vastness, the air close and old, so humid that moisture seemed ready to bleed onto every surface. She had been licking leaves for a while now, but the scant drops were nothing compared to the torrential slicks of sweat pouring from her skin every minute. Her head was buzzing and an odd ringing had taken hold in her ears, while her muscles ached and her feet grew clumsy.

She was afraid, but what scared her more than her weakness was the fact that she wasn't as afraid as she should have been. Some part of her was already beyond the point of computing the severity of her situation.

Stupid, stupid, stupid! she thought. *Daddy always told me New Land was dangerous. I should have stayed with him. He needs me.*

She had left Daddy all alone back in the cabin where they had been hiding the last few weeks. He had been sick since they had left home and come across the ocean to New Land, but now he was stuck in bed all day. Most of the time he slept, and it was all she could do to get him to wake him long enough to get some food and water into him. They had been hiding from the monsters who had attacked them and taken Grandpa.

Billy had thought they had gotten away, too. The old cabin they had found was perched on a cliff by the sea, and she hadn't seen a single sign of another person in all the miles she had covered searching for scraps of food. But then she had come across an encampment of travellers, and found a secret copse to watch them as the days dripped by, and Daddy grew weaker. Though Daddy had warned her to stay close to the cabin, and to run if she saw anyone, she had been drawn to them. They hadn't seemed so bad, and they had had food, lots of it.

She had been on the verge of walking into their camp the morning she had come to her copse, and saw the place had been burned to the ground. The travellers had disappeared, along with all their food. Her last chance had vanished along with them.

And then Panda Man had appeared. Before, she had been alone, and the next moment, there he had been, standing in the grass beside her. The man from Daddy's nightmares, and one of the faces Billy had been seeing in her dreams since coming to New Land. Daddy had told her he hadn't been real, he was just imaginary, a boogie man they made up.

But there he had been. He promised that unless she did what he said, Daddy would die.

She had been scared, but she had listened, and though she hadn't believed he was really there—Daddy had warned her that as they got hungrier and thirstier, their eyes might start playing tricks—he had hauled her up out of the grass and set her on her feet. There had been no mistaking that he was there after that. He had been strong, too strong. He had thrown her around as though she had been a leaf.

Standing over her in his long dark coat, his beautiful yet pale young face blemished by two dark streaks under each eye, he had spoken strangely. She could hear his words echo even now. *"Something is brewing on the horizon, something you're a part of, something that will decide the fate of not only this world, but many. Maybe all. There will be time for answers later. Right now I need you to find some people."*

He hadn't needed to say any more, not really. Because she had already known who she had to find: the other faces from her dreams. Two men, one old and one young: dark haired and blond.

When she had asked where to go, she had received a final reply from the Panda Man. *"It'll come to you. Find them, Billy. Find them."*

Then he had been gone.

She had stood there in the copse for a long time after that, confused, wondering whether her mind really had been playing tricks. Daddy would have said so, but he was sick. Somebody had burned the travellers' camp to the ground, and there was danger in the air—she had felt it.

Going away in the wilds of New Land was against everything Daddy had told her. With no food or water, what hope had she of finding anything or anyone before she became too weak to go on? But the Panda Man had said Daddy would die if she didn't do it. And Daddy was barely strong enough to feed himself; there was no way she could burden him with what she had seen.

Grandpa would have known what to do. But he was gone now.

Grandpa. It burned in her chest to think of him. At night she could still hear him humming the Old World rhymes. He had given himself up so she and Daddy could escape. Losing him so soon after Ma, it was too much for her little heart to take. She had died for her as well, starved herself so that Billy could eat a real meal once a day, wilting in secret in front of Daddy and Grandpa. She had made Billy promise not to tell.

And now Daddy was sick, so sick. He wouldn't let her go for help or look for a doctor; not while the monsters were out there. "They'll never get my angel," he had been saying in his sweaty half-sleep, beet-red with fever and coughing up bloody phlegm.

She couldn't lose him too. She wouldn't let it happen.

And so she had set off without returning to the cabin, afraid she wouldn't be able to leave Daddy if she laid eyes on him. Setting out from the copse without a clue which direction to take, she had let her feet guide her. They had taken her first into the travellers' camp, and she had rooted in the smoking ruins for a few scant treasures that had survived the conflagration. Amongst the detritus she had found mostly ash, but her luckiest discovery had been a small, yet razor-sharp paring knife. It had been well cared for, without a hint of rust despite the Old World markings on the tang, and she had tested it by throwing it against a tree trunk. It had rolled end over end and snicked into the bark clean up to the hilt.

Grandpa had taught her that. They had practised together on the days Daddy had gone to market to barter. When there had been food, before the big hunger, he had impaled rabbits against their barn door. She had never been quite that good, but she had been learning on wooden targets. Daddy would never have let her carry a weapon. But he wasn't with her now.

Armed with her new knife, a water skin, and a small pouch of dried berries and venison jerky, she had left it all behind. Her heart had rattled around in her chest every step of the way, and she had wept, but she had to be strong, for Daddy. She had let the tears fall to the grass, hadn't once wiped them away, and had kept her course, trusting her legs to carry her away from the cabin and the smoking ruins. She hadn't looked back.

She had come to the forest after only a few hours of trekking across fields and meadows. They had crossed through one just like it when they had first landed on the beach of New Land, but Grandpa had been with them then. He had known how to read the sky, the stars, and their magic compass talisman. Billy had never wandered out of sight of a grownup before she had come to the cabin. And in all the long weeks she had been foraging for food while Daddy lay bedridden, she had never strayed more than a mile.

Yet the forest had stretched from one horizon to the other, a vast wall of greenery that towered over her, creaking and whispering in all its impenetrable mystery. She could have tried going around, but her gut—no, her feet—had known better. There was no way around. She didn't know how she knew, but she knew.

So here she was, lost amidst endless tracts of moss, bracken, bark and leaf litter. Her feet itched to go on, as though possessed of an alien will that would not bow to the weakness invading the rest of her body. But though they longed to go on, there was no fighting that weakness for her. The water skin had been empty for hours, and the berries had only made her gag.

Presently, she stopped and sagged over a hanging bough, gasping for breath in the humid fug. A single sunbeam cut down from the sky and lit the ground around her feet, its golden radiance alive with pollen and dust motes. Above her head, birds twittered under a baby blue sky, and higher up, she caught a trace of a whistling breeze. But it all seemed so far away, another world.

Her feet itched. She had to go on. If she stayed here, she would never get out.

She steeled herself, let go of the branch and put one foot in front of the other. She made it only two steps before crashing to the ground, sinking into a pile of mulch and brown leaves. The world revolved around her in a nauseating blur. Her head throbbed to the beat of her pulse, and for a few moments all she heard was a dull ringing. When it cleared, she managed to raise her head just a little, enough to take in her surroundings afresh.

A carpet of green and brown, woven together by twisting vines and embalming lichen, lay basted over everything, in every direction. Black shadow smothered any gaps in the foliage, and the air was alive with swarming insects, desperate to suck away the last of her body's moisture. The air was heavy and stank of rotting plant matter. It all looked the same. There was no telling which way would lead to bright open escarpments, which to killer bogs, and which led ever deeper into its eternal mass.

She couldn't even tell which way she had come any more. Yet still her feet itched. Still, she knew which way to go. It was almost as though a glowing line in the compost was drawn out ahead of her, cutting right through a thick screening of ferns and vanishing into the darkness. Her destination lay beyond.

But how far? A warning voice in her head told her that

if she didn't get up soon, she never would. But even if she moved now, she wouldn't get far. She could feel her senses withering, her mind numbing to reason. She could keep walking perhaps, but what if she ran into danger? By then, she might have become a gibbering idiot, walking mile and mile until her body gave out.

Daddy was counting on her. He was back there in the cabin even now, fading even more. She had to get back to him. Without her to bring him more food, he would starve. And if she failed … well, the Panda Man had promised he would die for sure.

She felt new life steel into her legs—just a dribble, but enough to push her to her feet. Mud and leaves clung to her face, but she didn't bother wiping them away. Her arms were like lead blocks. Instead, she staggered forward, following the glowing line that was at once not there, and yet blazing with the intensity of a bonfire before her eyes.

She shuffled on for a long time, how long she had no idea, with the endless trees slipping past and her dirt-caked feet plodding away beneath her. But just as she had known, she didn't last long. Soon she crashed to the ground again, and this time, she was too weak to even break her fall. A branch gashed her across the cheek, but she barely felt her skin tearing.

The awaiting bed of leaves was as welcoming as the softest mattress. Suddenly the forest seemed very far away, as did her thirst. All the worry about Daddy didn't seem so bad anymore. Even the itch in her feet had faded to a distant winking pearlescence in her peripheral vision. Silence enveloped her. It was alright; she would stay here.

The silence stretched on for what seemed an eternity. Then there were voices around her, unfamiliar and excited.

"What've we got here?"

"Poor thing! Sweet little angel's all alone, she is."

"Alone, indeed, my dear friend. All alone …"

She tried to lift her head, but all she managed was to open her eyes a fraction. Blurry faces loomed over her, studded with smiles full of yellow teeth, and a sticky stench filled her nose. Then she felt hands gripping her arms, and she was being lifted into the air.

They were laughing.

CHAPTER 5

Alexander stood before the wall-height window and glimpsed his own haggard reflection in the weathered glass. He had ascended close to the tower's peak, hundreds of feet up, climbing dusty stairs that hadn't seen another person for months. Rich finance types had once worked in this office, coordinating the stocks of people halfway around the world. Now it was all entombed in cobwebs, the computer terminals so much plastic.

Through the window, he could see for miles. Beyond the tower, London winked and sparkled under the afternoon sun. Forty years had given nature plenty of time to bring most places to rubble and rusted detritus. The other great cities in the north had suffered at the hands of warring tribes, and others still had been pulled apart by fledgling communities for materials. But here things were different; the capital looked much the same as before the End. The rising waters had flooded many of the low-lying areas, but some parts looked almost Saran-wrapped, preserved for all eternity, monuments to men and women long since vanished.

Many people had given London a wide berth. It was too large a reminder of what they had lost for most to stomach. And there was nothing for them here in any case. The city flooded more each year, its great river barrier stalled and useless, rotting the great bounty inch by inch. Already the food had been long looted, the clothes that had carpeted the streets had been hoarded by traders, and any motorcars people had managed to fix had once again become useless when the gasoline ran dry. Even the endless mountains of electronics were useless, their circuitry reduced to dust in the flash of the End.

But for Alexander, it held a special place in his heart. It embodied all they strived to save, and what they could be. So much knowledge, art, and culture lay hidden in its depths. They had chosen to make the council's fortress here for that very reason. Here they could be seen as the last twinkling jewel of the Old World, residing in the dormant heart of their forbears' domain.

Now a dark mark lay over it all. They were out there, somewhere, watching and waiting.

He wasn't going to let this happen. All their work couldn't come to nothing because of a few grudges. People had starved, but their sacrifice would live on in the Old World's legacy.

He bunched his fists.

How can they not see that it was necessary?

The mindless rabble could put an end to a lifetime of work. The darkness already had a foothold in the North.

"Twingo's been hit." Evelyn's voice washed over him

like a wave from behind, shattering the silence.

He turned to her. "How bad?"

She was breathless from climbing the stairs. She looked old. That had been surprising him a lot of late, just how old they were all getting. They weren't the young go-getters anymore. Soon Father Time would sweep them all away, and others would have to take their place. But there was still so much to do, so far to go.

Her wrinkled face creased further into a grimace. "It's gone."

He sighed, sinking into a nearby swivel chair, ignoring the great cloud of dust that puffed up around him. It creaked under his weight, but held, just. "I don't believe it. They were a tough bunch of bastards. Vandeborn and Bates kept the northerners away from our gates for years."

"It looks like they put up a hell of a fight. But it's all ash now. A lot of them are missing … They must have been taken."

Twingo had been a few miles away, a legendary trading post, a paradise for entrepreneurs and a nightmare for any unsavoury characters. It was the closest thing they had ever had to an army. With that gone, their last buffer against the north—and anyone else—was also gone. Hundreds of miles now separated them from their closest allies.

"They'll try to turn them," Evelyn said, coming to stand beside him. "The ones that they don't kill. We're going to be fighting our own flesh and blood soon enough." Evelyn was a woman who held her head high even at the worst of times, but right now her regal veil fractured, and her shawled arm wrapped around him. "For the first time in my life, I don't see a way we can win."

Alexander folded his hand over hers. He had no words of comfort left.

Who could have known they would end up here? Of all their accomplishments and victories, the thousands of dedicated people across the land that had fallen under their banner, precious little remained. All they had brought to bear was on the brink of going up in flames.

It hadn't always been this way. Once upon a time, when the echoes of the Old World were still fresh, they had been almost unstoppable.

FIRST INTERLUDE

The hammer came down on the chisel with a final clink, and the engraving was complete. Stretching some fifty feet across the sheer face of the rocky bluff, the Latin alphabet stood capitalised and proud. It had taken two hours of painstaking work to etch the letters, and finishing touches had delayed them twice as long.

James Chadwick stepped back, admired his handiwork, and wiped his brow. His critical eye picked out niggles and imperfections from start to finish, but he knew it would do; it was more than satisfactory. He had chosen his site carefully, within plain sight for half a mile around, yet sheltered from the elements. Fortune granted, it would last some hundred years before weathering began to blur its form.

He inspected it critically, trying to see it from the point of view of virgin eyes, those who might stumble upon it in the high grass, once the ruins of the Old World had crumbled to dust. Would they see what he saw—see the beauty, a window to a whole world of knowledge and truth? Here before him was something the people of the Old

World would have taken for granted: a key to the sumptuous bounty of the mind. Even if he and his kind failed to pass anything else down through the ages, here was something that might provide a window to a new beginning. This was one of many fail-safes built across the land, just in case it all came to nothing.

But that would never happen as long as he had a hammer to hand. Not as long as Alexander Cain drew breath.

"Crooked," Alex called from the ridge afar.

"It'll do."

"When they bow down before these letters in ages to come, you might think different."

James rolled his eyes and stared across the meadow at his silhouetted form. "When they make statues of you and me, we'll see who's worrying about neatness. It's all there."

"That it is." Alex rode across the meadow, his white steed parting the tall wheat until he was abreast James's chocolate colt. "There might be hope for us all yet."

"Even if we lost everything else?" James thought of the vast stores of books that lay in the libraries he loved so dearly, his childhood playgrounds; the vast treasure troves that lay locked amidst moss-covered underfunded public shacks.

"It's happened before," Alex said. "Mankind has lost all sense of itself time and time again through the ages. But no matter how far we're knocked down, we always find our feet again. It might take decades, centuries, maybe millennia, but we get there, if we have but the simplest tools." He planted his hands on his hips and surveyed the alphabet emblazoned on the stone rock face. "Cornerstones like this, they're all we ever really need."

James had heard it all before, enough times for it to roll off his own tongue and into the ears of countless young'uns who gathered to hear their oratories wherever they bunked during their travels. Yet to hear the words straight from Alex's mouth never lost its charm, that unique spark that seemed forever undiminished. He really was a relic of an older world, one gone from this Earth. Oftentimes, to hear Alex speak was to be at peace.

"You packed the capsule like I told you?"

James nodded, kicking the dirt mound at his feet. "Just like all the others."

"You're sure?"

"Do I look like an amateur?"

Alex reached down from his mount and clapped him on the shoulder. "Only in a certain light."

"You can be a real arsehole when you put your mind to it."

"Practice, my friend. Practice." His white mare wheeled around and headed back into the wheat stalks. "The sun's getting high. Better move. We have a long day ahead."

James nodded, but his mind was elsewhere, on the steel box at his feet, covered in a mound of fresh dirt. Beside the alphabet was a sizable arrow pointing to the very spot where it lay buried, filled with a few vital trinkets; the OED, writing implements and carefully wrapped paper, maps marking the sites of bank vaults they had filled with literature, poetry, philosophy and scientific texts, and sealed their heavy doors with thick films of resin. Such tombs of wisdom would last for hundreds of years, at least long enough to endure the ravages of any new dark age that may befall the world, with any luck.

Trails of breadcrumbs. That was the way Alex taught it. Start small, let those who sought the light come forth of their own accord.

Their lives were secret lives, under the reign of barons and feudal chiefs and blood feuds, the cruel stirrings of the Old World's remnants. After the End, the remaining populace had clumped into villages, clans, and gangs, and while many clung together in innocent hope of a peace, the strong had begun to prey upon the weak.

They lived under the radar, moved in shadow, and spread their message in stuttered whispers.

"James," Alex called. He was already some distance away.

James uttered a non-committal grunt, still eyeing his work. Alex was right; it was crooked. His lip curled at the thought of such shoddiness, and a moment of inadequacy brought with it a resentment he couldn't quite place. Then he was seeing it with fresh eyes once more, and a more chipper air fell over him. Mounting his colt and parting the corn stalks in pursuit of his elder brother's trail, he left the rock behind, forever marked by the words of man.

*

They rode hard for an hour or more, crossing endless wild meadows and young sapling forests that had once been cultivated farmland. The morning's engraving hadn't been their primary item of business today and had taken longer than James would have liked. Now they were in danger of being late.

The sun was directly overhead when wisps of campfire smoke appeared on the horizon. The meadowland ahead buckled into a corrugation of rolling grassy hills, and upon the peak of one, where the grass was downtrodden in many places, the tops of chimneys and thatched roofs came into view. They slowed their pace and waved to a few field hands returning home from nearby orchards, nestled in the lee of a valley. Though they received welcoming smiles in return, James saw Alex shift his rifle around from his back and under the duffle swinging at his thigh.

Reluctantly, he did the same, keeping one hand on the safety. Even among friends, firefights were still common over simple misunderstandings, even misrecognition. These were dark times.

But as they rode higher and their view of Newquay's Moon fleshed out into narrow alleys, rickety plank-walled huts, stables, taverns, and bunkhouses, James's apprehension melted away. Excitement squirmed in his gut as they rode into the centre of the square before the water tower, where the populace was gathering. The day's comings and goings stalled in a trice, and people came running. Any break in the monotony was welcome.

Already, he was searching their muddied faces while Alex

bade them all hearty greetings. He too smiled and waved, but at the same time he searched for one in particular. It had been hell being away from her so long. She had plagued his thoughts every minute of these long weeks.

He spotted her off to the left, sandwiched between a pair of gruff, filthy farm hands, a head shorter than the rest of the crowd. One moment all he saw was the ash blond crown of curled locks, and then the crowd parted some, and there she was. Eyes like polished steel, pale skin in perpetual blush, a jaw too rugged to be wholly feminine, but hardy and well-formed.

James almost forgot himself by waving to her. She was no classic beauty; her hair was matted from work and she was dressed in a muddied Old World tunic, the cheap product of factories that had once enslaved great droves in the East—clothes that had carpeted all the land after the End. But James was intoxicated. A beast once unknown to him clawed up from the depths of his subconscious, pulling a primal red blindness over his eyes. He wanted to touch her, feel that hair between his fingers, her skin on his.

But at the same time, there was something else, altogether different. It was a stoicism, a kind of peace that nothing else could bring. It was the looks she gave him. Beth Tarbuck was one of those people who brightened up the world just by having been born into it. If she had been born in the Old World, she would have been the sole desire of boys for miles around—not for her looks, but for her smile, her laugh, and the look in her eyes that only few people can give, one that can make someone feel truly understood.

She smiled for the merest moment, so fast James wondered if it had been his imagination, followed by a wink just as fast. Then her face was plain as the rest, filled with the same adulation as the rest of the crowd. Before he was aware of it, James had nickered his mount forward, drawn toward her. A wave of dizziness washed over him, the hand on his rifle forgotten. Hands were slapping against his legs and horse as people cried welcome, and he mumbled back, but in his mind, he was already over there with her, climbing down from the saddle and taking her in his arms. His chest felt swollen with something entirely unlike air; it was like soup, thick and expanding, filling him up. And elsewhere, other feelings stirred his flesh.

"James," Alex called. His voice cut through the haze, snapping the link between James and the golden tunnel separating him from Beth, and then he was blinking amidst a sea of faces, bombarded by a racket of voices. "Come on." Alex had already turned away. He hadn't noticed anything.

James cleared his throat, making a renewed effort to smile and shake hands with the traders, aides, mothers, and scavengers below him. But his eyes were still drawn to the left, to the very same spot, furtively stealing glances at her whenever he could.

All the while she remained immobile, the shadow of a smile lingering on her lips, watching him. When it proved too much for him and he once again made to inch forward through the crowd, she shook her head almost imperceptibly. Her eyes flashed.

Later, they said.

She turned in a flash of icy gold, leaving an impression of thick lips, grey eyes, and a smile to light up the world frozen in the air. When he looked again, she was gone. In her place were only the beefy paws of the farm hands being mashed together in great booming claps.

Drunk on the afterglow she had left in the air, even from thirty feet away, James made to carry on in Alex's image, but couldn't quite shake the stupor that had fallen over him. They reined up by the stables and James dropped to the ground, taking a feed bag from the head stock keeper with thanks and attaching it to his mount's muzzle.

"Glad to see you both, young masters!" cried Malverston, town mayor four years running. "*Elected mayor,*" he proudly announced at every opportunity, though no election had ever been held. He was an enormous near-spherical man with a grimy beard that ran down to his navel in tangled greasy spiracles. His beady black eyes latched onto Alex and James like leeches. "Always a thrill, always. What news of the world?"

James cringed inwardly at the exaggerated falseness, the grandiose antiquated exclamations. Malverston was full of them. He thought himself some kind of generous member of the gentry, a relic from the eighteenth century who was embarrassed to find himself of good fortune and chose to mingle with the commoners. But James knew better. They saw his kind all too often.

"As always, Mayor, there's plenty to tell and little time to tell it," Alex sang over the continued hum of the crowd. James hated these pleasantries, pretending friendships that were simply not there. Alexander Cain was no songbird, but a quiet, pensive soul. He would be a great man one day— they all said it, wherever they went. James would be lucky to be half the man he was when he came of age. Yet this eternal front he put on in public, the showmanship, it was all a lie.

But it was all part of the mission. That was the way they had always done things. And all things told, James was glad to endure a little falseness if it meant success. He had a destiny, after all, and he would do anything to see it realised. The world relied on the precious few like Alex and himself. If they failed, a new Dark Age would sweep over everything in a generation.

"And you, my dear Mr Chadwick! You're looking more strapping by the day."

James nodded and called on his practised diplomatic smile, honed to perfection over countless iterations. But his body seemed gummed up, his mind still on Beth. "Mayor," he stammered.

He caught a confused warning glance from Alex and shook himself, squashing Beth's face from his mind.

Malverston clapped, lest any attention waver from him, and laughed in great hacking gulps. "Good, good, fortune smiles on us all. My dear friends, I'm sure our guests are tired after their long ride. Let's give them some space and refreshment." He flicked a hand in the direction of the stock keeper. "Harry, give their horses a fair seeing to, won't you?"

The stock keeper's brow twitched, but he nodded. "Of course, Mayor."

"Good, good. We ran out of the jerky you brought on your last trip. We certainly have a taste for it around these parts."

"I'm glad everyone enjoyed it." Alex was still smiling, but James knew every inch of him too well for the micro expressions of distaste lurking under his brow to go unnoticed.

The partiality to jerky was chiefly that of the mayor, rather than the town. His subjects were lucky to receive anything but the occasional tinned spam or tuna when after a taste of the Old World. Newquay's Moon was a long way from any city of note, and so the scavengers had picked the loot left behind after the End clean in the Early Years.

"In time there'll be plenty more," Alex was saying.

"So what have you brought?" Malverston cried.

"Only good intentions, and an offer you'd be a fool to refuse."

A momentary fury flashed behind Malverston's piggy eyes. But then the flicker was gone and he was wearing his amiable smile once more. "Indeed, young master Cain? Please, let's get comfortable." He gestured to the largest building in town, the pantry around back overspilling with the goods brought by those looking to win his favour.

That was how power exchanged hands in the South-West. They relied on trade caravans and wandering allies for such luxuries, which carried a hefty premium. It was no surprise they had taken to Alex and James. They took to anyone willing to give a discount, regardless of their ulterior motives. Their affections and allegiance came down to how much you were willing to shave off your price. James and Alex had spent the last few months shepherding carts of goods into the area for far less than it was worth. They would ride into town and give a few sacks away for dirt cheap, then spend the rest of the day giving it away free to the surrounding area, flooding the market, devaluing even the finest Old World treats. If they could keep prices low, they might be able to shake the hold some of their competitors had over Newquay's Moon.

There were some sour people about, all bad news. The more leeches they could pick off this place, the easier it would be to gain a foothold.

The crowd began to disperse, excitement fizzing out. James always hated this part of opening negotiations with a frontier settlement. The everyman always ended up caught between squabbling fat cats.

They'll have all they want soon enough, he consoled himself.

Alex ducked his head close to James, dropping his voice to a murmur. "I'll give him the pitch. You stay out here. I don't want to crowd him. This one likes mano-a-mano. Play nice out here. Join us in ten."

"And if things don't pan out?"

"Then we'll be leaving pretty fast. Malverston's all for playing big daddy when the chips are in his hands, but if we ask him to play fair ... be ready."

He disappeared inside with the wobbling tower of gout and furs that was Malverston, and James was left alone by the stables, fighting back a grin. He admired Alex's guts. He had just walked right into the bear's cave.

Malverston was crooked, indeed, but they were going to give him the offer to join the alliance in any case. It would mean he would have to go straight—unlikely, but possible. Offering and risking things going south was still a hell of a lot better than usurping a kingpin. And if he refused … well, they would carry on with their plan.

Once these people no longer bowed to petty bribery, maybe they could sit at the table and enter a real dialogue. Too many resilient pockets of civilisation had succumbed to the ravages of a new barbarism that was sweeping the land; alone they would all fall in time, but together, maybe they stood a chance.

They'd get rid of Malverston and his slime, in time. But for now, they had to play along. For the time being, he held all the keys.

The South-West, notably Cornwall and Devon, had been so scarcely populated even before the End that, in some respects, little had changed.

Malverston had been a farmer once, rich in his own way. But then the End had come, and he had awoken to find all his neighbours gone. Naturally, he had claimed all their land and assets as his own.

Now, he was the wealthiest landowner for over a hundred miles, having somehow convinced everyone inside his domain that he, and he alone, held rights to its bounty.

That was just the way the dice had landed. It could have been far worse. So long as those who worked his land paid their duty to his inner circle, they were left in peace.

But that didn't mean things were fair. The town was Malverston's throne, and it didn't pay to forget it. By now, many of the locals were already filing back to their homes, the fields, or the tavern. James searched for Beth among them, but he knew he wouldn't find her. She never let him see her until she was ready. By now she could have hidden herself anywhere, fetching water or working the farthest orchards.

Fire stoked in his gut, squirming and tingling like a glug of fine whisky. He had to bide his time and wait for her to come to him, when the excitement had waned and they could be alone. He just hoped Alex could entertain Malverston long enough. He couldn't bear not seeing her— he would wither as a summer flower succumbs to a frosty night.

A little crestfallen, but still excited, he dawdled a minute to make sure a gunfight wasn't about to kick off inside. But no, from the mayor's house came only rancorous laugher, and the sound of plenty of drink being decanted.

James finally let his fingers fall away from the safety catch on his rifle, and slung it over his back. Then he returned to his mount, lifted the duffle bag off the saddle, and set off towards the nearest house. Before he could rap his knuckles on the door a second time, a milky-eyed old woman in a patched tunic opened the door with trembling fingers. Her face screwed up into a mask of wariness and suspicion until he touched her on the arm and said, "Mrs McKinley, it's me."

She snuffed, jerking free, squinting and pursing her

ancient lips at him.

He blinked. "Mrs McKliney?"

His heart sank. Didn't she recognise him?

Her squint persisted a moment longer, then her myriad wrinkles smoothed with delight, and she tugged him inside, a great croaking laugh storming from her lips. "Gotcha, sucker! I'm not that old yet."

He grinned and stooped into the gloom, taking in the dust on the mantelpiece, the halo of soot around the fireplace, and the musty odour of unwashed skin and stale urine. The flames in the grate were the only source of light, but still it was obvious nobody had visited in some time.

Anger flashed in the soft membrane behind his eyes. It was all too easy to forget the elderly, he knew that, but this was more than that.

She was clutching at his sleeve still, caressing it, her eyes swimming, searching his own. A crooning whine rattled deep in her throat, pining like a puppy. She squinted, inching closer, scrutinising his face through thick cataracts. "So handsome," she muttered, taking his chin between claw-like fingers.

"How are we today?" he slurred around her hand.

"Hip's killing me." A phlegmatic grunt welled in her throat. "Girls will eat you up in no time."

Beth's face flashed before his eyes. "I don't know about that."

She cackled, showing rows of brown rotten teeth. "We'll see."

James blinked in surprise when her fingers pinched his

buttocks. For a moment, he was aghast, disbelieving, then he smiled helplessly. He watched her hobble, and his heart sank at how far she stooped, how slow she moved.

She was tough, but alone out here … He could see her time was running out. When they had first discovered Newquay's Moon, she had been at the helm, a straight-backed pillar of strength who had held the wolves at bay since the End. This place had been her reason for being.

Then Malverston had moved into the area, and age had taken its toll on her energy. As she had slowed, the landowner's influence had grown. And one day, he had simply claimed the town for his own, rigging an impromptu election to pacify the populace. Since then, Alice McKinley had remained here in this hut, slowly fading.

James suspected he was one of few to ever visit. He was drawn to her door more than any other. There was something about her, some sliver of the Old World that seemed alive in her despite her filmy corneas and drooping jaw, some secret wisdom that had vanished from so much of the land since the End. He smiled as she tugged him to the grimy table beside the kitchenette and pushed him into a seat before bustling around with the kettle, struggling to light the stove.

He leaped up. "Please, let me," he said, taking the splint and bending over the cramped kitchenette. Once the flame had caught, he stepped back, for she was already flapping him away impatiently.

"I'm no coot," she croaked, her voice so faded it was barely audible. "Can light my own fire …" She wheezed, and he guessed she was laughing. "You're a good boy." She grunted, making tea with laborious unconscious dexterity, something James loved to watch elders do. Another echo of the Old World, a ritual of a world that had moved on. "You should stop visiting me."

"And miss your plum cobbler? You know how hard it is to find dessert out east?"

She laughed, a vibrant and lively sound wholly unbefitting her trembling, failing body. "Now I know that's the truth. All men are ruled by their bellies, among other things … Speaking of which, I saw you and Master Cain ride in. Those other fools out there might be young, but they're blinder than I am." She jeered, "There's something potent about young hearts. When they get after one another, their spark gets all over everything, hangs in the air." A ringing pause, then she said, "Who's the lucky girl?"

James's throat filled with putty. He mouthed wordlessly until she turned around with a tray laden with a teapot, cups and saucers, milk, and sugar. Seven billion souls might have disappeared from this Earth, empires emptied, civilisations cut short, but afternoon tea went on. A coy smile sat on her lips, threaded with muted pain as she sat.

"You knew?"

"You've had something growing inside of you since I first laid eyes on you. As much as I'd like it to be a crush on me, I can't say that's it." That coy smile grew wider. "There are some things that can't buoy a person up the same way. It's like nectar, fills you through and through. Even your *sacred mission* can't do that, am I right?"

He didn't answer.

She poured the tea, and they sat and drank in companionable silence for a long while. James kept a wary ear out for sounds of violence coming from Malverston's house, but outside, the town was all but silent. Though his trained ear listened as a matter of course, his head was swimming. Thinking of Beth's face, the way her hair splashed over her shoulders—just thinking about her brought her scent to his nose, notes of talcum powder and lavender. Somehow, amidst the mud and grit of the orchards and the packed-dirt streets of the town, she took care to smell like that.

Was it for him, that scent?

Alice was laughing quietly. James came back to the room slowly. "What?" he said.

"You're a bright young thing, but you're dumb as a bag of wet kittens."

"How do you figure that?"

"Because you're sitting in the dark, drinking tea with an old bat instead of out there wooing the knickers off your sweetheart."

James squirmed. His cheeks were glowing. "I don't know what I would say," he muttered.

He was used to being in control, expounding the wisdom of the Old World to those less fortunate. It had become almost second nature to stand in Alex's shadow, to be elevated by all that cold, logical knowledge. To get muddled up now with fleshy, hot, raw emotions was turning him around. It was all so … sticky.

"Say?" Her face grew sombre. "Speak your mind. Life's too short for nerves and tripping over yourself. Take her by the arms and tell her exactly what you're thinking."

He choked on his tea. "I … I …"

Her face smoothed, her eyelids fluttering. She put her tea down on the saucer and leaned forwards, milky eyes shimmering. "My darling, none of us have as much time as we think. If you don't take every chance you ever get by the balls, one day you'll wake up old and broken, and it'll be too late."

He didn't reply, just sat nursing his tea.

In the corner of his eye, he saw a smile return to her lips, threaded with a sympathy that was almost forlorn. "My, my, girls are really going to eat you alive. I hope Ms Tarbuck digs her claws in tight."

James started, his knee banging painfully against the table. "How did you know?"

She rolled her eyes. "This town ain't a big place, and all I got to do all day is squint out the window trying to see some goddamn thing. So far as I can see of anything, there's only one other punch-drunk doolally wandering around. She got that same look in her eye. Like I said, it gets in the air."

James rubbed his smarting leg, embarrassment forgotten. If she knew, what about Alex? Had he sensed something amiss? Somehow, James didn't like the idea of Alex finding out. He was liable to think James's concentration was slipping. And when anything threatened their *great destiny* or their *mission*, he was liable to start meddling.

He finished his tea and cleaned up Alice's house awhile, dusting, setting things straight, and replacing her woodpile from the stock out in the square. Then he kissed her on the cheek and headed for the door. "I'll visit again soon."

"Don't worry about me. I'm too old and no good for this world as it is. Don't need to go dragging a trailblazer like you down with me." Now that he was at the door, she looked so much smaller, so much older, a tiny thing gnarled in the dark.

He strode back to the table, leaned over and gave her arm a squeeze. "You're blind as a mule, too."

Her bitter frown melted away, and then she was laughing again, blowing stale breath over him. She pinched his chin. "Get out of my house, you little shit."

CHAPTER 6

The pigeons were everywhere. Perched upon every rooftop, fence post, and power line across all of New Canterbury. No matter how many times they were shooed and scattered, they circled back and blanketed the city all over again. It had been that same way for over a day now. Some people had started shooting them, but taking down even a dozen birds didn't make a dent in the flock, and ammunition was precious. Even up on the ridge to the north, overlooking the city, they filled the treeline.

Robert Strong scoured the hilltop for a full five minutes before breaking cover and stepping out into the high grass. Acrid columns of smoke rose from the series of craters spaced every hundred feet along the ridge: all that remained of New Canterbury's wind farm. He trod carefully around myriad chunks of charred shrapnel and made his way to the nearest smouldering hole. There was nothing left, not even a stump. The turbines had all been reduced to a medley of particulate glass and molten slag.

"I can't believe it's just gone," Sarah whispered at his side. Two heads shorter than he, she barely reached his shoulder. His fiancée's spectacles flashed as she turned in a wide arc, surveying the destruction. "All of it, just gone. How could they have done this?"

"Explosives. High-grade stuff."

"Nobody's had that kind of thing since the End."

"Well, they got it. There's some pretty serious stuff lying out there in depots and bunkers. All you have to know is where to look."

She shivered. "They're *farmers.*"

"They're angry, and they're desperate. People can do terrible things when they're desperate."

They were quiet for a while. Then she said, "The famine was a trigger. This is revenge. I wonder if the radio message was real at all. Maybe it was just some trick to lure the council to London, make us vulnerable."

He didn't reply.

They had struck without warning while Alexander had led the ambassadorial convoy to London. Most had sought shelter in the cathedral, shivering under the pews like whipped puppies. Others had barricaded themselves in their homes, sweeping their families indoors before nailing the windows shut. Others with the skills to scratch a living in the woods had fled the city altogether.

Only a handful had remained by his side. No more than half a dozen, out of eight hundred men, women, and children.

What they would do if they ran into any intruders was anyone's guess.

They were all looking to him. Nobody said anything,

but there was no mistaking the way they congregated around him. With Alexander gone and Norman in tow, and even Lucian absent, he was all they had.

But he had never expected this. At six five, his dark skin rippling with muscle, he had always been the brawn, not the brains. But, for now, there was nobody else.

Retreating up here hadn't been his plan. He had just needed to get Sarah outside. Since the massacre out at the enemy stronghold, she had barely said a word, just sat swaddled in a pile of blankets with every candle they owned ablaze, waiting for angry hordes to come bursting through the door.

He watched her carefully as she took in the sight of the wreckage. Her brow twitched each time she looked upon another smoking crater.

Had he really only proposed to her yesterday? It must have been; he had knelt before her not an hour before the ambassadorial convoy had left for London. The bombs had detonated no more than an hour later. Now, all that seemed like a hundred years ago. Neither of them had slept since then. He shook his head, trying to clear a ringing he knew would only get worse.

But there would be time for sleep later. Right now, they had to figure out what they were going to do in the short term.

Sarah turned to him then, and the look in her eye made him wonder whether she had read his mind. "They're out there, aren't they?"

"Probably."

"Why haven't they finished it? If they can do this"—she gestured to the carnage around them—"there's no way we'd be able to put up much of a fight."

"That's not true. We have some of the best snipers I've ever come across. I wouldn't want to be the one who tries to sneak up on this place unwelcomed." He managed to keep his voice level, but shame flushed his cheeks. That might have been true with the others around, but with the city scattered and most gunners either holed up with their loved ones or wandering the forest's nooks and crannies, they were all but defenceless.

He knew she could see right through him. The arch to her eyebrow only heightened his shame. He forgot how sharp she was sometimes. And, how strong. The sight of the Old World explosives had shattered the nerves of dozens of the toughest men this side of the Thames. He couldn't blame them; only a handful had seen such power. Only Robert and a few others had witnessed ordnance like that before, in the northern skirmishes during the Early Years. Yet here she was, standing right beside him, shaken, but not beaten. He felt a swell of longing for her, and wrapped his arm around her shoulder. "You're right," he said. "We wouldn't be any match for them, not like this."

"Then why not finish it? They must know what they've done to us. Our elders are gone, we have no power, our guards are all hiding behind locked doors… They've razed dozens of settlements to the ground in the last few weeks. Why spare us?"

He shook his head. "I don't know."

The wind picked up and skewed the smoke columns to the south, turning the horizon a dirty brown. They could now see clear across the ridge, with a full view of the treeline. The hairs on Robert's forearms stood on end. There must have been hundreds of pigeons in the trees, all cooing, all watching. At first there had been only a few. Then the explosion had rocked the city, and they had been arriving in a continuous stream since then.

"They're *everywhere*," Sarah said.

"Yeah."

"What do they mean?"

"I don't know."

She sighed. "I'm tired of not knowing, all this mystery. We can't live like this."

She stroked his arm in slow circles, and he inhaled sharply. They stood like that with the wind blowing smoke into their faces and through their hair until they were deaf to the pigeons' cooing and the sight of the wreckage had lost its edge.

Robert brushed Sarah's hair behind her ear and held her close. He couldn't believe she could be taken away from him. This was supposed to be their time. He had played protector for too long, putting the needs of others ahead of his own.

He wanted routine, excitement, and passion—and everything that came with it: lazy days between the sheets, mundanity, petty bickering, and dreams of the future. Not twenty-four hours ago, he had pictured them both old and weathered, sitting upon the porch of a home he had planned to build with his own hands, somewhere quiet where she could read her books and he could work on projects in the shed. Nothing fancy, just simple and real. He wanted it all. And now it could all be stolen from them.

Everything they had fought for, it could all come to nothing but flames, and death. He hadn't given up hope, not by a long stretch, but there were moments when all that seemed left for them was to decide what to do with the time they had left.

Sarah's fingers traced the defined contours of his forearm, circling higher. His eyes were drawn to the soft swelling below the nape of her neck as she took each breath. He kept stroking her hair as a stirring grew in his loins, and her breathing grew deeper. It seemed to take an age to meet her gaze, each of their heads creeping round until he stared down at her, and she up at him.

"It's dangerous out here," she said.

"Yes."

Her hand left his arm and reached up to his cheek. Her voice picked up a smooth bass. How she managed to look so alluring from behind those gawky glasses was beyond reckoning. "We should go back."

His hunger peaked, and their lips met in a blur of skin and muddied clothes. He dropped his rifle to the ground—if they were sprung now, then so be it—and held onto sense just long enough to check the ground for shrapnel. Then he was lying her down in the grass, and soon lost all hope of telling her skin from his. For a time, they pushed back the darkness.

SECOND INTERLUDE

James returned to the square, but jubilant clattering and laughter still emanated from Malverston's house. It didn't sound like it was going to be over anytime soon.

He wandered towards the edge of town and headed up onto the nearest grassy rise, looking over the surrounding lands. Newquay's Moon was set to the north of the remains of the coastal city of Newquay itself, on the northern shore of England's Cornwall peninsula. Up here, a few miles from the seagulls, sand dunes, rotting caravan parks, quaint cobbled streets, and cottages, the hills afforded a good vantage point in every direction. It would be almost impossible to sneak up on the town.

James loved visiting here. After some of the scant horrors of northern England, and the squabbling bands of proto-societies in the South, this county was a haven. It was hotter too, warmed by the Gulf Stream, and so exotic foodstuffs could be grown, with the right care and attention—on occasion they succeeded in growing things that used to be imported from the tropics, before the End. It was only from here that the British Isles could source fresh strawberries, tea, peaches, and maybe even a few miniature bananas.

Consequently, places like Newquay's Moon, though they looked dirty and hard pressed on the surface, had grown fat and wealthy on the profits of their labour. Coupled with the relative peace they had found, the persistence of some kind of law, and the lack of barbarous raiders prowling the countryside, James was sometimes at a loss to explain how it had survived. An island of civility on the edge of a country set to tear itself apart.

That was why they were here, now. They needed Newquay's Moon on their side before it was discovered. Because, eventually, somebody with truly bad intentions would stumble across places like this. And when they did, one of the Old World's last echoes would vanish to the sound of screams and trickling blood.

James took a deep breath of the coastal winds and surveyed the orchards in the valleys afar. Was Beth down there?

A cooing brought him back from scanning the rows of peaches. Instinct brought his arm up to shoulder height. A moment later a fluttering beat about his head, and a wood pigeon alighted upon his elbow.

"Morning, Chuck," James said. He took note of the other pigeons in nearby trees, perched upon rooftops, and circling overhead. They always managed to find him. "Mail?"

Chuck cooed. Tied to his leg, tucked neatly in a leather slot James had crafted himself, was a tiny scroll of paper. James tweezed it free and unfurled it, reading Lucian's sloppy handwriting upon it:

Come at once, need you both. L.

He frowned, tucked the scrap into his pocket, and looked over his shoulder. The door to Malverston's was still shut fast. He couldn't just go barging in on them; Alex's way was always a delicate one, and interrupting was bound to scupper his wily words.

But Lucian wouldn't have sent a message unless he had to. The others needed them.

A few years before, perhaps he would have gotten itchy feet. But he'd been in too many scrapes for a few words to faze him. They were always at the crux of some kind of crisis. Instead, he took a handful of seeds from a pouch at his belt and offered them to Chuck, who obliged by digging in.

What could be going on back home that was bad enough to send word all this way? Even if they rode hard, it would take over a day to get back. And that would put an end to their careful plans for Newquay's Moon and the surrounding villages.

Why was nothing ever simple?

He mulled it over. The possibility that they were under attack was something he held at the back of his mind with trained rigidity. If it were true, there was nothing he could do about it, and there was no sense getting worked up. It would only cloud his thoughts. And he had work here to do.

"I knew you'd come today."

James turned on his heel, and his heart leapt into his

mouth. Beth stood a mere arm's length away, her work tunic tumbling in the breeze. Her ash-blond carpet of hair sailed on the air. A basket of peaches was tucked under her arm. She had managed to get within only feet of him and he hadn't heard a thing.

Nobody could sneak up on him.

Home and the others evaporated from his thoughts with an almost-audible *poof.* He resisted the urge to pinch himself, at the same time holding his tongue until he was sure his throat wouldn't spasm. She joined him on the ridge and the two of them stood looking over the orchards in silence for a while, neither of them looking at the other.

"How's that?" he said finally.

She pointed skywards, to the birds passing overhead. "They always show up before you. Harbingers."

"I ought to watch that."

"Not exactly stealthy."

"Why not hang up a sign?"

He could feel her eyes moving over him. His skin buzzed as though she had run a hand from his scalp to his loins. "How long are you here?"

Lucian's handwriting popped back into the front of his mind. His hand hovered over his pocket. "Not long," he said grimly.

She nodded, turned back to look at the orchards. "Some people enjoy the company of visitors. If they ask when you'll be back, what should I tell them?"

His heart skipped a beat. "Depends on how our talks go with your good mayor."

"If you were to hazard a guess?"

"I can't think of anything that would keep us away for long."

"Oh? What could you possibly want with a dump like this?"

James stole a glance at her, smooth flushed cheeks highlighted against her alabaster skin. "It isn't all bad," he said. Before he knew it he was inching closer, unable to stop himself, his feet moving of their own accord. All thought of what it could mean for the mission, the politics, for her, all forgotten.

She too had turned from the horizon and was facing him. Her eyes danced over him, and he realised that it wasn't only her cheeks that were flushed. Her neck was blushing a vibrant pink, and her chest heaved under all that cloth. The air was filled with their ragged breathing, and as though caught by invisible hands, they began to fall towards one another.

The hill, the sky, the grass; all of it was gone, vanished. All that he saw was her dirt-streaked face, those stainless-steel eyes, and thick young lips. His throat tightened, his knees trembled, and despite all his long years of scholarly training, he stumbled closer, longing for nothing more than to fold himself into her, to run his hands over every inch of her skin.

He was going to do it. They were a foot away, then inches, then the heady well of lavender and talc blinded him, and finally the warmth of her breath caressed his cheek. He closed his eyes.

"Excellent!" Malverston's voice came crashing in through the purple haze that had fallen over James's mind. "People, come, come! We have word!"

James whirled to see the mayor's bulbous mass come crashing outside with Alex in tow, his arms held wide and his head thrown back with rancorous glee. A tankard of ale swung at his hip, and even from this distance, James could make out spots of food stuck in the knots of his beard. "Come, come! Great celebrations all around." A moment later, irate. "*Get out here!*"

In seconds doors all over town opened, and ant-like heads popped up among the orchards far down the hill. Then they were herding back to the square, as though drawn by the same magnetism that had almost clamped James's lips to Beth's, great thick clods of people that entirely destroyed the privacy the ridge had enjoyed only seconds ago.

Beth stepped away hurriedly and made to follow.

"Wait!" he said.

Her eyes warned him *no*. "You'll be back soon?" On top of the genuine concern of her frown, he caught the faint glimmer of feminine tease.

He made to persist a moment longer, saw the droves of townsfolk pouring into the square, then sighed. "You have no idea."

She winked, mischief written in the hitch of her brow, then a group of women running with their skirts held high passed. She melded into their ranks and was gone. James was left behind, lame upon the ridge, Chuck still hooting and pecking away upon his elbow. He looked at the bird, sighed once more, and then took after the crowd. "Careful, Chuck. She's clearly after you."

*

"Our good friends have made us a great offer!" Malverston boomed to his flock. He had taken centre position in the town square, standing atop the rickety frame the women used to scale the well for water. "Come closer, my friends, closer!"

James slipped into the crowd's ranks, drawing his slicker's hood close over his head. He needn't have bothered, for nobody even glanced his way. All eyes were trained fast on the platform.

Alex was making an admirable effort to keep his dignity, swaddled under Malverston's beefy shoulder. Though dwarfed by the sheer volume of meat hanging from the jovial mayor's frame, somehow he seemed the more significant of the pair—and it was obvious Malverston sensed it.

Malverston was red faced, and his voice took on a stentorian note, turning the crowd's attention him through force of volume. "Our good friends and I have come to an agreement regarding an endeavour I deem most profitable. Through my efforts—and their assistance—all the townspeople stand to benefit, in time."

James suppressed a smirk. He was too good to be true, Malverston, almost a caricature. It was difficult to believe anyone could genuinely be that conceited.

"Newquay's Moon will henceforth pledge its allegiance to Mr Cain's most excellent cause. In exchange for a fair share of certain commodities, we shall aid in their selfless efforts to save the treasures of the Old World. Between us, we will preserve knowledge that stands to be lost."

James tensed, but avoided meeting Alex's eye. What had he agreed to this time? Malverston would surely have tried to wrangle something extra, and most likely there would be hidden repercussions down the line. One thing was certain: there was no charity in this deal from either party. Newquay's Moon was a means to an end for Malverston, and another piece in their mission's puzzle for them.

But that was the way of things. They paid a price for progress, sometimes an absurd price, but every inch of territory counted. This is what it took to sow the seeds of a new beginning.

In many ways, it was hair-raising to see Alex on the front line. If anything happened to him, everything would fall apart. But there was no other choice, because nobody else could be trusted to do the job. Someday James would stand in his shoes. That was his destiny.

"We owe these wonderful people our thanks. They will haul this town and its allies to greatness, and riches of which we couldn't have dreamed are now within our reach."

The crowd stirred. James sensed hot and cold from the crowd, the buzz of muttering, a medley of starry-eyed hopeful imaginings from those totally under Malverston's spell, and smouldering dissent from those who lived under his rule out of necessity. Riches would indeed come to Newquay's Moon, but none of them would see it.

"I think we owe our new allies a round of applause. To the future!" Malverston thumped his hands together, and the crowd followed suit after some encouragement. His booming cries racked the square until the resentful patter turned to a full-blown ovation.

James clapped along with the rest of them. From the sweaty mass of bodies around him, he received a sharp poke in the ribs. He looked around to see Beth standing beside him, half hidden by a flurry of clapping hands. She offered the shadow of a coy smile, then she was clapping along with the rest of them. "Looks like we're going to be good friends," she said, using the cover of the racket.

"All thanks to your gracious mayor," he called.

"I didn't think you people would strike a deal with that slime."

"He has things we need."

"Things like the deeds to a few ten thousand acres?"

"Things like that."

"I thought you were all about freedom, and electing leaders."

He sighed. "If we can get a foothold here, we can change things from the inside. We can help you get rid of him in time."

"But for now, you're going to take his dirty money and hightail it away from here."

He smiled despite himself. *No room for quaint talk with this one.*

"For now, I suppose."

The applause died down, and Alex stepped forward to make his own additions to Malverston's speech. James's lips twitched into a helpless grin when he started talking, and he began wielding the crowd with practised ease. It was a skill he had had plenty of time to hone over the years, before audiences ranging from agoraphobic hermits to the backward backstreet scavenger communities in the ruins of the northern cities. The crowd's noises took on an attentive note, and the grumbling shifted to enthused muttering.

He didn't have to say much. "My friends, today is an historic point in our time. I hope in future years we can all look back on this as a turning point from the descent toward darkness which the End set in motion. Together, I believe we can reverse the fall of the Old World. Humanity has been struck down, but it is not defeated. There is hope in the myriad resources all around us—the time capsules left behind in the form of technology, and the knowledge hidden away in our rotting libraries.

"Things may seem desperate. As a civilisation, we are on the brink of ruin, fractured and alone. We have forgotten much of what once made us who we were. Make no mistake when I say, no matter what we do, all paths that lay before us will be difficult to travel. But we have a choice: we can choose to fight the creeping darkness, to take back what made us powerful and wise, to fight ignorance and cruelty and greed."

Malverston's piggy eyes twitched, but Alex continued. "All it takes is friendship. United, we can halt the decay of the bounty left behind."

James inhaled despite himself. Beth was pushing up against his jacket. For a moment he almost pushed her away on instinct, but then took note of the crowd, rapturously focused on Alex's every word. He glanced down at her, and risked stroking her face. A shiver ran from his finger all the way to the top of his head, tickling his heart as it passed through his chest.

"When will I see you again?" she whispered.

"I don't know." Lucian's note popped into his head once more. "Maybe a while. But I'll be back."

He jerked, holding in a yelp. A chill had jolted through his midriff. His nerves were raw, overloaded for a moment. Then he felt her hand tracing a path across his thigh. "If you're not, I'll kill you."

He swallowed. "Yes, ma'am."

Alex was still working his magic. "This unity will take time to set in order, and so for a time, we must part ways once more. But in the meantime, you can still make a difference, every one of you. You all have the power to change your own destinies."

"Indeed, indeed!" Malverston's boomed, smearing the nervousness that had crept into his voice by adding a sprinkle of jovial laughter. "With the help of a few key individuals, we can all move towards a brighter future."

Alex's face was neutral, but his eyes flashed with something akin to the humouring patience a parent would show a hyperactive child. "Yes, we can. But it's important to remember that we each have a path set out before us, and where that path leads is up to us. If we're content to wallow and shirk opportunity, to merely survive, then our last chance will slip through our fingers. But if we each act towards a common goal, then together, we can reap all that we sow. The power to save the world is in your hands."

Moments later, the crowd erupted into raucous applause of its own accord, no urging or bullying required. It was the same everywhere they went. People had been told by the neo-feudal lords who had first seized power that they lived under the dominion of a few, that only through servitude and fealty could they bear the brunt of the great fall to come, when the leftovers of the Old World were utterly spent. All it took was for someone to lift the wool from their eyes.

One day, James would stand where Alex stood. His fate had been decided from the moment they met, days after the End. Alex had been a spotty teenager, James a newborn infant. The first people either of them had seen since the End in a new, hostile, lonely world. They had been together since.

The mass grew tighter and people stepped forward, some climbing the platform to shake Alex by the hand, others merely wanting to be closer to him. Suddenly, the rotund mass of the mayor was all but invisible—James felt he might have been the only one to clock Malverston's thunderous face, blemished by jealousy and a stroke of fear.

Despite the surging, ebullient crowd, and even Beth, who was among the few to retain their composure, James kept his eyes fastened on Malverston, and felt a flicker of disquiet flash in his gut. There was danger there, bubbling beneath the surface. The mayor wouldn't forget this, he was sure of it.

But the crowd took no heed. They swarmed about him, and soon they were chanting. Alex's eyes glistened, shards of lapis lazuli set in a face brimming with dignified acceptance. He seemed set to shake the hand of every person in town. It was in these moments James saw someone else beneath Alex's youthful golden beard, and the spry body in its prime: an old grizzled messiah, the man he was born to be. In these moments, he was Alexander. *The* Alexander Cain.

The crowd was chanting, "Three cheers for Cain. Hurrah—Hurrah—Hurrah! *Hail Cain!*"

*

"Leave?" Alexander frowned.

They stood not far from the platform, their heads lowered and their voices low. The crowd was still abuzz, not far away, and Malverston still stood up on the platform, eyeing them watchfully. James showed Alexander the message from Lucian. He read it in silence, and for a moment, he was Alex once more, concern blossoming behind his eyes. "When did you get this?"

"While you were with Malverston. They're in trouble. We have to get back, now."

"We still have business here."

"They wouldn't send word if they didn't need us."

The concern in the older man's eyes quelled like a fire doused with a bucket of water. Alexander was back. "In time. We've come too far to abandon this now."

James cursed. "Something about all this doesn't sit right. It's wrong."

"We've done it a thousand times before. We have to compromise. Remember what I taught you."

"I remember!" James breathed. "This is different. *Malverston's* different. He's not just another land grabber, he's … he's evil, Alex!"

Alex's face flickered, but before he could answer, they were being hailed.

"Mr Cain, Master Chadwick!" Malverston called from the platform. "What chat requires such serious faces? Perhaps you're keen to leave our company?" His voice was facetious, but laced with suspicion.

"Our friends are in need of us," Alex called.

"Nonsense!" Malverston boomed. He spread his arms wide. "Now is the time for celebration. Certainly you'll stay! Or else all this was but a sham, don't you think? What say you?" A direct challenge. There was no mistaking it.

Alexander looked torn for a moment, his eyes searching his sockets, and for a second James thought he would decline. But then his shoulders sagged. "We would be delighted, Mayor."

"Excellent! Aha, prepare the hall immediately," he barked to his advisors. The townspeople began milling and making preparations, fear and uncertainty festering about them already.

Alexander lowered his head and turned back to James. "We'll leave tonight, as soon as he's assuaged. He's a dangerous man. We have to leave him happy, or this is all for nothing."

"I can't believe we're teaming up with that slime. What did you promise him?"

Alex squeezed his wrist. "Tonight."

CHAPTER 7

Norman hurried along the hallway, breathing in rapid bursts.

So much rode on this one meeting between the remaining powers of the South, but somehow he had fallen asleep leaning against the wall. He had dreamed the very same dream that had plagued him since Jason, the knife-wielding madman, vanguard of the enemy, had stolen into his home in New Canterbury and left his body a broken wreck.

In the dream, he had been lying upon his back in a rainstorm in the pitch dark of night, flanked by illuminated skyscrapers shining like beacons under myriad lightning flashes. Younger versions of Alexander and Lucian, and several others he didn't recognise, stood over him, yelling words that were muffled as if a pillow had been placed over his head. And once again, between their shoulders, peering down at him with a preternatural leer, a pallid young man with the face of a wolf, dark streaks under his eyes. And his words echoed back to him as though from the distant past. *"Remember, Norman. You were all there. Remember."*

He woke shivering. For the briefest of moments, he had been sure a thin layer of frost had covered his skin, evaporating as he leaped to his feet in fright. The dream seemed more real each time, as though it were merging with reality, and reality was slipping further towards the illogical blur of dreamscape. The figures he had seen on the lobby stairs kept coming back to him. Had they really been there? How could that be possible?

They had worn suits, had carried working smartphones—the Old World relics that stood proud in Alexander's office, beneath in New Canterbury's vaults, and peppered the ruins of almost all the Old World. There had been live electricity in those things, and he swore he had heard tiny scratching voices emerging from them, voices from across the sea.

What's happening to me?

He checked his watch, saw that the council was due to convene any moment, and any thought of his dream vanished from his mind. A few other stragglers trudged around him. As a group they lumbered towards a set of large, wooden doors ahead. A great buzzing wafted from within, thousands of voices. There was no mistaking the excitement and apprehension.

The air was heavy, humid and yet lacking in warmth. It made the already laborious task of breathing almost impossible.

"The cheek of it," a nearby man muttered to himself, his heavy green overcoat masking his features and contrasting against his twisted white hair. "Holding this meeting now, of all times."

He spoke to nobody in particular, but seemed to speak for the collective, as several others around him grumbled in unanimous agreement.

"We're about to be slaughtered, and they want to play politics. How about putting some effort into getting some food? Forget this rabble playing arsonist; we're all still bloody starvin'."

More murmuring.

So discontented were they that they failed to notice Norman beside them, for which he was grateful. It had been many hours since he had gone unnoticed. The buzz grew closer, the blending of a thousand different conversations, mixed with the racket of chairs scraping and the clapping of shoes on wooden floorboards.

Norman rubbed his chest absently, and they passed from the hall into an enormous room, the council chambers. During the Early Years, when the empty shell of London had first been surveyed by those looking to rebuild, Canary Wharf had become a meeting place, and the tower had been in service since then as the coalition had formed under Alexander's hand. This room had seen every major negotiation between every power in the South since the End.

"So few. So few have come," the farmer said. His gruff grumble had given way to an awed tremble at the back of his throat.

So few are left.

The chambers were housed in a hollow that had formed

of its own accord as the tower decayed in the first years; support struts close to the glassy pyramidal structure at the tower's peak had given way and carved a path of destruction through the spire's heart, cutting a channel dozens of floors deep before reaching the twentieth floor, where they had come to rest, along with many tonnes of debris. Under its weight, three whole floors had collapsed, leaving a cavern that filled almost the whole width and depth of the tower.

When they had found it, the cavern had been unstable and ready to collapse further, but they had cleared the rubble, strengthened the floors, and converted it into what it was today.

The result was a true wonder. There was no need for artificial light in here. Golden shafts of light lanced down a pyramid of glass hundreds of feet above and pooled before a parabolic bench that housed over two dozen elevated seats. Though these seats were closer in appearance to thrones.

Positioned upon each of the three floors in the chamber were thousands of chairs: designer stools, executive swivel chairs, ergonomic recliners, and unwieldy chic things of leather luxury, all poached from the tower's many derelict offices. The overall layout was that of an amphitheatre, centred on a large oval of open space, a polished concrete dais upon which the sunbeams glittered.

It was an embodiment of what they truly were: the dregs of the civilised world, fizzing lights in the dark, brought together under one spire for mutual warmth and comfort.

Despite any humble truths, Norman could never get over the fact that Alexander had a penchant for the grandiose. The chambers reminded Norman of Olympus.

There had been a time when the space had been so crammed with bustling bodies that the floor and walls seemed alive with endless beds of insects. Now, the council chambers seemed enormous in comparison to the paltry numbers in attendance, which barely filled the lower stalls, leaving at least five thousand empty seats in the higher tiers.

Nevertheless, he felt a swell in his chest at the sight of such numbers. To know that, no matter the odds, they were not alone, was worth taking a moment to appreciate. He thought for a moment of all of the hundreds who remained in Canterbury, missing out on such a spectacle. Without power, surrounded by the enemy, with their leaders all missing in action, the situation must by now have been grim indeed.

An unexpected desire to be back there with them washed over him.

Conversation was rife, still, and council was not yet in session. Around half the council members sat at the bench, all dressed in white robes, all shrivelled old relics of a world that had moved on. Some seats would never be filled. Their owners' bodies were spoiling under the sun upon the streets beyond their walls, but a few that should have been filled, were not. Including Alexander's.

The other stragglers made their way to their seats, and Norman craned his neck in search of someone he recognised until he spotted a familiar face beckoning him. Richard, apprentice to the master scholar John DeGray, raised his head above the sea of hair and sunburned necks.

"Where have you been?" Richard said as Norman squeezed in beside him.

"I ..." Norman made to reply, but in the next moment his mind thrummed with a ringing scream. A nauseating wave overwhelmed him; suddenly, the room was full of people, hundreds of bristling figures in expensive business suits. They were at once there and not there, sitting upon non-existent chairs and at invisible desks. In the moment he saw them many walked right through the seated council crowd.

The same things he'd seen on the stairs.

Echoes, he thought. Echoes of Before.

How did he know that? He had no idea. But he knew.

"Norman?" Alexander said.

Norman jerked and took a breath, and the Echoes were gone. In their place were all those expectant faces once more. He felt cold all over, a bone-deep shiver deep in his chest.

Just broken ribs huh? What the hell is happening to me?

"Norman?" Richard hissed.

"Huh? Uh, sleeping. I was sleeping." Norman leaned forward to peer down the row. The others who had travelled from New Canterbury in their convoy were bunched together; surrounded them were similar islands from the other settlements. Previous summits had seen a general mixing throughout, with no order to the seating. But that was not so today. Everyone huddled close to their own clans, those on the edges hunching their shoulders as though to ward off attack even from their last remaining allies.

Allie was sitting on Richard's other side. "Hi, stranger," she said.

"Hi, yourself."

Her face looked as though she had questions, but he shook his head minutely, and she held her tongue.

"Where have you been?" he said.

"The infirmary," Richard said. "Doing my best with the wounded."

"Where's Dr Abernathy?"

"Gone. The doc went out to Surrey a week ago, just before it went dark. Nobody's heard from there since." He shrugged. "I studied medicine from my master's texts. We even used New Canterbury's models to practice a few procedures. But I'm no expert. And"—he gave a wry laugh devoid of humour—"it's a little different working on a live patient."

Norman nodded. It was difficult to be heard or to hear over the noise, but he persisted. "It would be a lot easier if Heather were here," he said. New Canterbury's doctor had stayed back home to help the sick and frightened.

"She's best staying where she is," Richard said. "All the same, some people up there are going to die of eighteenth-century illnesses. Blood infection, gangrene, pneumonia, good old-fashioned shock ..." He shook his head. "We've got no shortage of people willing to pitch in and help, but I'm surrounded by poultices and herbs up there. A lot of apothecary merchants, nurses and midwives ... nobody who could use a scalpel." He sighed. "We've even tumbled back to the brink of chanting. Sometimes I wonder what's going on out there … whether they've started bathing in fox piss and hunting witches …"

His young face, peaky and pale from too little sunlight and too many years spent alone in DeGray's classroom, looked far older than Norman remembered it. Like Allie, the last year had changed him. Alexander's web of fluffy, artificial safety had been swept from under them all. The harshness of the world had rubbed the puppy fat from their skin and the wool from over their eyes.

Norman and Allie shared a look.

"Where's DeGray?" Norman said.

"My master was called away on urgent business with the council members. From what I hear, he's preparing a presentation."

"About what?"

"I try not to make a habit of prying. His temper …"

Norman couldn't help smiling. "Beat him at chess yet?"

Master and apprentice had played a score-and-ten times every day for as long as Norman could remember. To his knowledge, Richard had never come close to defeating John DeGray.

The shadow of a smile touched Richard's lips. "I have faith," he said.

"There are worse things to hold onto right now."

The buzzing was suddenly cut short by the groaning of the iron hinges set into the door at the rear of the chambers, behind the council bench. For a moment there was silence, then there was movement. Alexander Cain strode in, dressed in the full ceremonial white robes of New Canterbury, complete with a sweeping cape billowing out behind him. With an unreadable face, he approached the bench, his footfalls echoing in the terse silence that now hung heavy over the room.

Everyone stood. The sound of their feet clapping the white floor sent a deep reverberating boom through the tower's heart.

Alexander stepped up to his chair, the largest and most throne-like of them all, set a foot higher than the others, and sat while staring directly ahead. His eyes had become jewels that sucked all the light from the room bar that around his own body; when he inhaled, it was easy to believe that hats and crops of hair wobbled, as though drawn towards him.

In those few scant moments, the fibres of each isolated clan were gathered up by his gaze and twisted into a single rope. Suddenly the thousands of empty chairs seemed invisible. Before, they had been fragmented, a broken remnant. Now, they were one, united under the one most of them had bowed to upon altars, sworn fealty to, even prayed to at bedtime since birth: the Messiah. The one who would bring them back to dignity, their loved ones, and all they had lost.

It wasn't their custom to lower oneself to any man, but even Norman felt the queer urge to bow.

Evelyn Fisher's sonorous voice filled every cranny under the tower's vast glass-capped ceiling. "Ladies and gentlemen, please be seated and hold your tongues," she said, her usually haggard and dishevelled body ramrod straight. Norman was privy to a dazzling tessellation; thousands turned their heads in rapid succession towards her as she sat immediately to Alexander's left. Somehow, the silence deepened to something Norman imagined only the dead had heard before. She swept a final stern glare around at those gathered, then nodded, and the rear doors of the chamber slammed shut. "Thank you," she said after some time. "Council is now in session."

CHAPTER 8

Billy smelled lemons. Someone was brushing her hair, slow and steady. Her head was heavy, full of iron wool. Her tongue seemed too big for her mouth, and her eyes were gummed together. She worked them open while she tried to swallow, but the sides of her gullet seemed welded together.

"Time to wake up, darling." The voice was one she had never expected to hear again.

"Ma?"

"It's almost noon, clover."

Billy's heart ached at the sound of it. Through gummed eyes, she could see a heart-shaped face framed by short dark hair. The teardrop shape of her mother's face surrounded by a pall of bright light. She had always smelled of lemons.

"What happened?" she rasped.

"Shh, it's okay."

"No … You went away, Ma. I remember. You got sick …" She had starved and ended up not dissimilar from Daddy: bedridden, babbling nonsense, withering by the day. They had buried her in the bluebell patch by the reading tree. "Ma, we lost Grandpa. The monsters took him away. And now Daddy's sick too and … I'm all alone."

"You're not alone, darling. I'm here."

"Ma …" Billy smiled, and for a moment, she was okay. There was light everywhere, and she lay in the folds of something so soft it could only have been her parents' mattress. That meant Daddy and Grandpa were probably coming home from the fields. She had been in a bad way, perhaps ill, but now she was on the mend. She was home.

Then there was noise: muttering somewhere out of sight, excited and sibilant. She had heard it before, just before the darkness had consumed her in the forest. She had been near death, lost in the darkness, and she had fallen—Daddy would surely die now she had failed. And Ma? Ma lay under six feet of dirt, hundreds of miles away.

"No!" She made to sit up, but Ma's hand pressed down on her chest. "Calm, Billy, calm." Her voice was strange, deeper, half hers and half another's. Suddenly, she had dark streaks running under her eyes.

"You're not Ma!"

"No." The fair, motherly expression had become a hard stare. Ma's teardrop jawline now jutted out several inches more, square and trim. The cheeks had sunken, revealing sharp high cheekbones. "Time to wake up, Billy."

"*You!*" She struggled, but the strange noise was closer now, and she sensed urgency in the morphing figure's gaze.

"Stay alert, Billy. Stay safe. All is not as it seems," the Panda Man said.

"Where's Ma?" she cried, struggling under his hand. The

muttering separated out into two distinct voices. She had the sudden sense that the light and the face hovering above her was only a veil, and behind it something else was going on altogether. She could feel her body now, heavy and weak, slowly stirring. She fought to sit up. "Where's Ma?"

The face above her smiled, and suddenly it was Ma again, marked by the same pair of dark streaks under her eyes. But when she spoke, the voice was still that of the Panda Man. "Wake up, now. And remember, you have a job to do. Unless you want Daddy to end up like me."

*

"Daddy!" Billy was sitting up, gasping and cold. The Panda Man was gone, as was the pool of white light. Now she was surrounded by a murky, grey gloom. She was almost certain that this had been the reality hiding behind her vision of Ma all along. Her mind had retreated to a safe, happy place. An echo ran through her mind, a voice charged with urgency. *Be safe. All is not as it seems.*

She stopped, breath held in her throat. The whispering came closer. Before she knew what she was doing, she was patting around on the ground, ignoring her throbbing head, until her fingers ran across the rough canvas of her bag. She pulled it towards her, hugging it briefly before thrusting her hand inside for the paring knife, hidden in a side pouch. She ran her hand over the cold blade gingerly and pulled it out, invisible in the darkness.

Then before she knew it, something alien forced its way

up from the pit of her stomach, and she was coughing on her hands and knees. The attack lasted for only a few seconds, but in that time a coppery-tasting slime dribbled from her lips, and her ribs ached from the strain of such hacking contractions. Then it had passed, and she was gasping.

Daddy's cough had started like that. She shivered.

The voices were just outside now. Both had a rough-edged bass, overlaid by a high-pitched whine. Their accents were strange, nothing like how people spoke back home. She had heard people speak strangely before, like the tradesmen who had come south from Dublin or Derry, but these accents were very different. All people in New Land spoke like the monsters who had taken Grandpa.

"How can they's be all gone, eh?" rattled one, almost a screech.

A deeper rumbling voice answered. "I dunno, but they'd all been burnt to a bloody right crisp."

"That's the third this week. We're gonna run out of places to hit if we ain't careful."

Billy pushed herself up onto her hands and knees and began crawling back, away from the voices, blind to whatever lay behind her. The voices echoed metallically around her head. She guessed she was in some kind of backroom. Her hand met vertical concrete, damp and slimy, cold to the touch. She gasped and darted sideways, but met another flanking wall within a few feet. She had crawled into a corner.

"We ain't there yet," the first voice was saying.

"S'pose we do."

"Then we move on like always. They was gonna find us out sooner or later."

"I don't like all these stories they're telling about this ghost army."

"Don't be daft! They're just pulling your leg. It's one of them Chinese whispers they tell to people like you who are stupid enough to believe it."

The first voice, wounded, gave a grunt. "I dunno. It gives me the willies."

"Shaddap. I'm done thinkin' for the day. My dogs are killing me and I need a little … refreshment."

A pair of high-pitched giggles floated across the darkness. Billy's heart leaped a beat, and she squeezed herself as far as she could into the corner. For a moment there was silence, then there was a metallic squeal, and light flooded into her eyes. She held up her hand to shield her vision, and between her fingers she discerned two hump-backed silhouettes, one squat and fat, one tall and thin. They advanced into the room.

"Well, lookie here, Jerry. She's awake," croaked the first of the voices. It belonged to the squat figure.

"Indeed she is, Sammy," crooned the second. "Indeed she is."

The two figures grew closer until no longer washed out by the light flooding in, and their silhouettes fleshed out into detail. The squat one was at least fifty with tufts of short, spiky grey hair, a forehead greased with a forest of oily spots, and a flat nose that had obviously been stamped in some distant time. The taller figure was younger, pale to the point of translucence, with long greasy bangs framing a skull-like face. Though their bodies were very different in build, their expressions were remarkably similar: puckered and coy, tortured by poor nutrition and not enough sunlight.

Now that they had stepped from the light, Billy saw that they were both women. Both were dressed in stinking masses of rags with black plastic bags wrapped around their rotten shoes. Black grime streaked their arms and necks. Dried flowers and herbs hung from every scrap of their clothing; desiccated scraps and bunches bound with decaying twine, pinned to the lapels of their coats, woven into their sleeves, jostling upon their belts, and braided into their masses of matted hair. They almost looked like the swamp creatures from one of grandpa's storybooks.

"Don't be shy, honey," said Sammy, the short one.

Jerry, the taller, shrugged. "We won't bite."

Both of them giggled at that, and a look passed between them.

Billy pressed herself harder against the wall. In response, Sammy held up her hands and took a sharp step forward. She smiled and bent over with her hands planted on her lap, succeeding only in framing her rows of tiny, rotten teeth. "You look pale as a sheet, sweet pea. No need to go fretting. Jerry and I are friendly."

"Friendly, that's right," Jerry said. She was smiling too. "We're medicine men. Just without the danglies."

Sammy nodded. "That's right, child. We're healers, so

don't you worry. You're in good hands. What we got usually sets people back quite a price, but we couldn't leave a little angel like you to waste away out there."

"Nu-uh, not a little cherub like you."

Billy almost relaxed, but then another echo of the Panda Man hit: all is not as it seems. She looked again, and this time she noticed something: neither of their smiles was quite right. There was something else mixed in there, deep down—a certain ugliness that couldn't be hidden.

She palmed the knife's handle, but kept still, looking for a way out. But now that there was light, she saw that the room was long and narrow, and the only exit was the door through which the women had just entered. The women advanced slowly, one step at a time. Billy froze up, her mind blank, until they were within ten feet of her bag. Then she gasped and scrabbled against the wall, pushing herself to her feet despite the spell of dizziness that washed over her.

"Woah, there, little one, easy! Don't wanna hurt yourself," Sammy said. For a moment, she looked frank and genuinely concerned, but then something else seemed to take over; a flicker of shadow that sent her tongue prowling her upper lip. "You'll ruin that pretty face," she muttered.

Billy staggered left, trying to circle them. Her legs felt like lead, but her senses were coming back to her. Her legs shook a little less under her weight. She remembered the Panda Man's words clearly now. She had to get moving, soon. Daddy's life depended on it. And he had been right: all wasn't as it seemed. She wasn't sure why, for the women seemed friendly, but she sensed danger.

"What do you want?" she tried to say. What emerged was something closer to *Wwwaa-yurwhant?*

Sammy got down on one knee with her arms still splayed out in front of her. Jerry hung back a few paces, her expression stoic and unreadable, her gaze flicking back and forth between her companion and Billy, as though entranced by an entertaining show. "Nothin' at all, honey. Oh, look at you, all confused. How long you been lost out in the woods all alone? Where's your mummy and daddy?"

Billy inched along the wall, trying to ignore the pulsing in her head, as though her skull were full of sand, arid as their farm had become last summer after the crops had wilted to the ground. Her heartbeat throbbed the fleshy mass of her tongue. "Ma went away," she said. She hesitated, but Sammy's understanding little nod, coupled with that constant smile, teased the rest out of her. "Daddy's sick."

"So you *are* all alone? All the way out here?"

Billy nodded.

Both women uttered maternal groans and crept forth a little farther. Billy braced against the dripping moss lining the wall behind her. "I'm not supposed to talk to strangers," she said finally.

Sammy nodded with furrowed brows. "Clever girl. A good head you have there. But you're not well, honey, so come on over here and we'll get you a cool drink and something to eat."

Billy remained still, but her stomach betrayed her, bellowing explosively and folding in on itself at the thought of food. Sammy and Jerry glanced at one another and giggled. "Now if that isn't nature calling, I don't know what is," Sammy said.

"Nature, calling," Jerry said. Her voice was little more than a sigh, a little too high-pitched for comfort. "Come on, girl, we have all sorts to eat. Once you're fed and watered, there'll be time for shyness. Right now, I don't like all that white in your cheeks. Little peaches like you should be full of blush."

"Oh yes," Sammy said. "I agree. Come on, now. Let's get you plumped up."

Billy shook her head. She had craved the opportunity to talk to anyone from New Land since Daddy had gotten sick—anyone who could help her. She had rehearsed begging them to return to the cabin for her, and saved her Ma's pendant—the last thing they had left of her—to trade for medicine. Knowing that there were still other people who hadn't been burned to a cinder should have been a godsend. Even to be offered food instead of scrounging around in the dirt was something that would have sent her imagination into fits of joy not long ago.

They had rescued her from the forest. She would have died in there if they hadn't come along. There was no doubting it.

But there was something wrong with them. The greenery clinging to their clothes seemed suffused into their skin. It was almost as though they really were made of moss, had grown out of the mud and grime that coated them.

"I can't stay," she said. "I have to go."

"You're not fit to take another step, sweet pea," Sammy said.

Billy's grip on the knife was now so hard her fingers ached.

"You're not thinking straight," Jerry said. "Just come on with us and get a bite."

"No, I—"

"*Don't be rude, dear!*" Sammy hissed, lurching forward and seizing Billy's wrist. The motherly note to her expression had vanished. She looked Billy up and down critically. "Come on with us, now. There's a good girl. We had the good graces you haul you out of the woods. God knows what would have happened to you in there. Now come get some food. You're going to need your strength."

Jerry's face had morphed in much the same way. "And plenty of it."

"No, I have to go. Daddy needs me!" Billy cried.

Suddenly their faces were dark with shadows that hadn't been there a moment before. Sammy's face shot down from above, snaggle-toothed and snarling. "Your daddy isn't here now, is he? We're here. And it's only fair you pay a fair price for the kindness we showed you."

Jerry snuffled with piggy laughter and lashed out with a plastic-clad foot, kicking Billy sharply across the back of her thighs.

Billy cried out and tried to wrench free, but she was weak. They hauled her into the middle of the room. "Please, just let me go!"

Sammy wasn't listening. "I've been looking forward to

this for far too bloody long." She licked her lips, running her calloused thumb over Billy's arm. "But looks like it was worth the wait. Oh, she's *firm*."

Jerry crooned, stepping around behind Billy, out of sight.

"See, we made quite the killing out of that unfortunate famine," Sammy jeered. "Quite the killing. Before the End, when I was a nipper, people used to laugh at my line of work. They called me quack, hack, fraud—a witch!" Her face contorted into a snarl. "Usually fancy doctors in the pockets of the big pharmaceutical companies."

What are they talking about? Why is she holding on so tight?

Her wrist throbbed with fresh bruises. Jerry's ragged breath closed in behind, only inches away, brushing the nape of her neck. Suddenly she realised that something had gone horribly wrong.

Sammy cackled. "Now, people don't remember so well how things used to be. And all those fancy doctors and the big labs and pills—all gone." She made a gesture similar to flicking a fly off her arm. "Now people appreciate the power of *natural* remedies again."

"And there's quite a profit in it for those who still remember," Jerry squeaked.

"*Quite* a profit," Sammy agreed. "But we've run into a little snag. And lucky for us all, little one, there's something you can do to help us out there.

"See, I got this little blemish here. Take a look, see." She pulled her coat aside to reveal her left collarbone, upon which lay an angry patch of skin two inches across, vibrant red and capped with a seeping sore that made Billy wince. "We used everything we got on it, and still it won't clear up."

"Even dandelion root and burdock broth did nothing!" Jerry said with disgust. "There's a dark aura over this place. More of those evil things are popping up all over. Jerry found her first yesterday. Something in the air is eating us alive."

"Even our most powerful remedies are no match for that filth," Jerry said. "We need something a little stronger."

"What?" Billy squeaked.

Both the women were looming over her now, and their hot stinking breath washed down over her from front and behind. Sammy's grip on her was vice-like. Her froggy face creased into a drooling mass of lips, boils and folds of wrinkled skin. "The light inside you is strong." She frowned. "I never seen anything like it. Glowing. I got a little of the light, myself, and Jerry just a pinch. Both of ours blighted by all this bad mojo." She looked troubled for a moment, and began speaking with her eyes unfixed, almost to herself. "But we can fix it by borrowing a bit of yours. Only fair, wouldn't you say, for saving your life?"

Jerry uttered a formless squeak of excitement. "Don't you worry. You just keep real still."

Billy struggled and kicked, but they both had hold of her wrists and ankles, and were easing her down towards the ground. She thrashed and cried, but then her voice stopped in her throat as Sammy pressed her hands on her bare belly, and began to slide them down towards her belt. "Shh," she cooed, pressing her. "It'll be over soon."

"You can scream if you like," Jerry whispered into her ear. Her lips touched Billy's neck. "Nobody's gonna hear you."

Billy would have screamed then, if a single picture hadn't popped into her head: Daddy, lying back there in the cabin, coughing and hacking his way closer to the ground just like Ma. And then, suddenly, there was strength in her, lancing out from a secret place in her core. For a moment the medicine women froze, as though blinded by something invisible shining out of her. Then her hand slipped free, found her belt, and she took the knife in her hand. She swung it up in a jagged arc, and brought it down with everything she had.

A piercing shriek rang out, and Billy's other wrist was free. Sammy fell back out of sight, clutching her left eye, blood and a strange clear liquid spurting from between her fingers. "My eye! Arrrgh! I'm blind! Jerry, the bitch blinded me!"

Billy span around on the ground to face Jerry, whose face was frozen in a dumbfounded gape, and slashed across the knuckles of both the hands gripping her ankles. Jerry uttered a shriek of her own, so high-pitched that it set Billy's ears ringing. Before she knew what she was doing, driven by the strength that now thrummed in her veins, she sank the blade up to the hilt into Jerry's plastic-clad foot, and tore it out again. The woman uttered a whine not dissimilar to a howling dog, and toppled back out of sight into the dark.

Then Billy was on her feet, dragging her bag up with her

and running for the door. She emerged at the threshold and looked out upon a recess in a hillside. Below was the same forest she had been lost in, but she was raised high above the canopy. A trail led away, snaking down the hillside, leading to open fields stretching away to the horizon.

She uttered a startled *urgh* then, as another sensation suddenly filled her: the same itch in her feet that she had followed since leaving Daddy, an irresistible pull that pointed across the fields, into the unknown. She turned back into the darkened room, and gripped the heavy iron door, throwing all her weight against it.

Sammy, clutching her spurting eye, covered in streaks of blood from head to toe, scrabbled towards her, her face infected with hatred. The people before the End had been right: underneath all her remedies and talk of the Light Inside, she was a quack, a hack, and a witch. "*YOU BITCH, YOU BLINDED ME! DON'T YOU DARE CLOSE THAT DOOR, I'LL KILL YOU, YOU LITTLE SLUT! WHORE! YOU CAN'T DO—*"

The door slammed shut, and Billy pulled the heavy wooden log that acted as a lock down over it. It fell into place with a satisfying thud, and she stepped away as muffled screeching and pounding rang out from the other side. She turned on her heel, shaking uncontrollably. She stood for a moment longer before she fell to her knees and vomited. She felt dirty. The strange possessing strength drained out of her all at once, and she keeled over onto the ground. For a while, everything was dark.

She came to with a jerk some time later. She had been

dreaming, but already it was half forgotten. She had been standing in a street flanked by tall buildings, and the rain had been hammering down on darkened tarmac. She had stood to one side of a huddle of bedraggled people all bent over a twitching young boy. She could almost see his face under an unruly mop of black hair—

But the rest was a blur, fading fast. All that remained was a feeling, one of having touching someone, as if she had reached across a great distance and, somehow, bumped up against somebody.

But who?

When she felt strong enough to move again, she crawled towards the sound of distant trickling and found a stream. She rolled the last few feet down its banks and dipped her head into a blissful pool of water, drinking in great gulps, ignoring the taste of mud. Her stomach clenched into spasms as soon as the water hit, but still she drank and drank until she rolled up away onto the banks again, gasping and belching. She lay there in the cool sun-dappled mud and stared up at the clouds peeking through the oak branches overhead. She could feel the water doing its work inside her, diffusing into her body's parched tissues, clearing away the gunk that had been clogging her mind.

There was something in the sky, shaped like a bird yet quite unlike any she had ever seen. Its wings weren't flapping but rather stuck out to the side, and it was too far away—far too high in the sky, above the clouds. It flew a straight path until it passed behind the fronds of an ash tree, but though she waited, it never emerged from the other side.

She frowned, then blinked. Grandpa had talked about flying machines once. Had it really been there, or was she more tired than she thought?

Daddy had started seeing things when he got sick. Maybe she was starting to see things, too.

But no, it had been there. A strange certainty insisted: an Echo from Before.

An Echo.

Eventually she sat up and looked around as she filled her water skin. Everything seemed sharper, clearer. Every moment since she had entered the forest seemed distant and fuzzy, as though it had all been a mere half-forgotten dream. She wondered whether Sammy and Jerry had been as much a dream as Ma and the Panda Man, but then she caught a distant thumping on the wind, and realised they were still up there pounding on the door.

Thoughts now came fast. She formed a plan in the few seconds it took to steel herself to stand. She scrabbled back toward the door, and stood there listening to the pounding.

"*Bitch!*" Sammy cried. "*Let us out!*"

"*Sammy, it won't stop bleeding ... I don't feel so good.*"

"*Shut up, keep pushing. Girl, you let us out, and we'll make it worth your while.*"

Billy looked farther up the path and saw a wagon laden with vials and jars, all full of the same herbs and flowers. She approached warily and pulled back the canvas cover, and gasped as she revealed a bounty of dried meats, bags of grain, ripe fruits, a box of biscuits, and a loaf of granite-hard bread. She stuffed the meat and fruit into her bag, and sat in the dirt as she gobbled the biscuits. For a time she was deafened by her own satisfied groans and the racket of her working jaw. After, she tore the stale loaf apart through sheer violence and gnawed away until it was gone.

Already feeling new strength in her, she took in the myriad medicines.

Would any of them help Daddy? She had no way of knowing. The medicine ladies on the other side of the door would never tell her now. And she doubted the medicines would help in any case.

She took a thick blanket for cold nights, a full rusted canteen to supplement her water skin, and a man-sized filthy saucer-like hat to keep off the sun. Feeling far more prepared and bolstered against the elements, she returned to the door.

The pounding had stopped now. Sammy seemed to sense her presence; Billy could certainly sense both women, feel their weakness and their fear, and somehow, she knew both were now slumped on the floor. The sensation related to the itch in her feet spoke from the base of her skull: the women were like her—they knew things and felt things that other people couldn't—but they were also different, broken, black.

Then she felt something else: an absence. She could only feel Sammy now. Jerry's black light had winked out. Sammy, ever more afraid, spoke through the door. "I have something more valuable than anything you'll find out there in the world. The biggest secret lies in here. We may pedal bullshit remedies, but make no mistake, I have a piece of the same light inside of you. Nothing like yours, but Jerry and I got a sliver. It shows you things." A pause. "It showed us the truth … the truth about the End."

Billy paused, caught mid-stride. Before leaving home, she had never known there had been anything but the way things were. But seeing New Land, and the great ruined cities on the horizon, and the stories Daddy had heard from Grandpa, her eyes had been opened to the terrible truth: something dreadful had happened to the world, which was much, much larger than she had ever imagined. For a moment, she considered turning back.

But then the itch in her feet tugged at her heels, and she remembered the Panda Man's threat. Daddy's life depended on her.

She kept walking, heading away down the hill.

"Girl, Jerry's gone. You can't leave me alone in here with this … thing. Girl! You let me OUT!"

Much later, she heard a final echoing scream, coupled with a manic cackle, which brought her out in gooseflesh.

"The light won't protect you forever. One day it won't need you anymore. In the end, it throws us all into the darkness!"

THIRD INTERLUDE

A feast had been prepared in their honour. Newquay's Moon was prosperous even for the South-West, and James couldn't help boggling at the great bowls of Old World tinned goods and preserves: peaches in syrup, hearts of palm, dates, beef jerky, beans, corned beef. After almost twenty years since the End, even the hardiest of preserved foods were beginning to foul, but millions of tonnes still littered the ruined cities, and so the plenty had yet to pass. Besides that, there were great volumes of the truly imperishable goods left behind by their ancestors: hard liquor, sugar, salt, pickles, corn, and entire flagons of honey. There were also small mountains of the Moon's crops: fresh grapes from the orchards, tea, apples, fresh baked bread, potatoes, pies, gravy, and a few kegs of cider.

"What do you think, young master?" Malverston boomed at James as they sat at the head table, raised above the rest of the hall, such that they could see every nook.

James did his best to keep his smile uniform. "It's very generous, Mayor. Thank you for this honour."

They had been treated to such things before, but none

as egregious as this. There was simply too much. There was no doubting more than half would be wasted, and somebody, somewhere not far away, would go hungry because of it, perhaps for weeks. The whole town had been 'invited,' and more than a few looked intrigued and unsettled to enter Malverston's lair of finery and excess. They were still swaddled in ecstasy and frantic conversation for now, but later, once Alex and James were gone, James suspected many would see the darker side of their mayor emerge with a vengeance.

Malverston waved a hand dismissively and clapped a hand against James's back, such that he slopped cider all over the tablecloth. "Think nothing of it, my boy. It's a small price to pay for a man of my means, as I'm sure you're aware. It's the least I can do for those who will bring such prosperity to this place." He lowered his voice, folding several kilograms of arm fat over James's shoulder as he drew him into a confidential muttering. "Perhaps all this mumbo jumbo your master's peddling about the magic of books and sacred destinies can lift us all out of the dirt, huh? Maybe we can stop being bit players in a world that's being swallowed up fast. It's a land grab, these days, my boy— survival of the fittest never played so big a part in world affairs as right now. Between the two of us, I was never meant to be small fry. If you play your cards right, we could end up very close indeed." He shovelled a handful of grapes into his mouth. Juice running down his masticating chops, he gestured to the hall at large. "After all, a time will come when I can't manage my districts on my own. I'll need trusted friends to help me keep the peace, and keep people where they belong."

I should drown you in your goblet right now, for the good of all these people, James thought. The gross overabundance of food dug at him like a hidden blade.

Smothering the grating voice in his head, he raised his own glass. "I look forward to our future together, Mayor."

"Please, George. Call me George! We're going to the best of friends, after all, closer even than to your master—ah, here he comes, now! Mr Cain, you honour us."

Alex—or, rather, *Alexander*, appeared at the table, dressed in the same style of simple white robe that James had donned for the occasion. "Thank you, Mayor," he said. James's instincts had been right to recognise him as Alexander tonight; his chin was angled skyward, his eyes glazed, his countenance reserved. In times like these, he wasn't himself. He was what some were coming to call the Messiah.

And in his shadow, James enjoyed a title of his own, bathed in the reflected radiance of *the* Cain; James was the Chosen One. Alexander told his story wherever he went. Every speech, every public appearance, James was thrust forward into the limelight of Alexander's stories of what was to come. For one day those who survived the End would be dead and gone, and their children would be left behind. And James would be carrying the torch.

Now that Newquay's Moon was with them, they could use it as a hub in the South-West, and coordinate their forays from there. Malverston's lands, previously closed off to outsiders, would be free for them to scour for countless hidden cultural artefacts and scraps of technology. And, of course, they now stood a chance at saving all the books rotting in baths of mildew in the land's surviving libraries. But for all that, had Alex really signed a deal with this devil?

Sometimes, behind all his certainty of the mission, James had his doubts. Sometimes, Alex lost himself in Alexander, and forgot the very people he was trying to save.

Malverston glugged the full height of his flagon—a gratuitous pewter tankard befitting his penchant for the theatrical—with sticky runoff dripping from the knotted tendrils of his beard. He was a good way through his fourth serving before he slammed his fist upon the table, sending plates and bowls trembling an inch into the air, and roared, "Girls!"

A strain fell over the continued buzz in the hall, and James felt hundreds of gazes fix glances at him and the others at the head table. Then the slow beat of a drum kicked up, and a chorus of jingling bells heralded the arrival of a procession of women from a side door. Newquay's Moon was a healthy community, but it was still a small place, and young women were few and far between. But Malverston and his men were too drunk to much care about the gnarled, work-hardened hands of the orchard pickers; their lustful roars filled the hall, nonetheless.

James's stomach tied in knots at the sight of Beth Tarbuck's gyrating hips. Her face was obscured by a cyan veil just like the others, but there was no mistaking her figure, nor the unmistakable grace afforded to her by her youth compared to the other dancers. In any case, he had spent enough time admiring her form from afar to have known it anywhere. They paraded around the hall for a while, sitting in men's laps and twirling their hair, laughing and giggling despite the poorly concealed malice in their eyes, slowly making their way forwards.

Soon they were pivoting and undulating in a throng before the head table. Every eye fixed Malverston with a seductive glare. The mayor raised his goblet and gave a gargling wolf whistle, oblivious to the sneering lips that lay beneath those lusty gazes. James was pretty certain none of them were dancing for their own pleasure; most likely some unfortunate accident would have befallen their families had they had refused.

The drumbeat built to a crescendo and then the dance broke. Most townsfolk returned uncomfortably to their meals, and the dancers took to wandering the hall, entertaining the drunkest single menfolk with a laborious sense of duty about them, much to the tight-lipped chagrin of the women who had been spared public humiliation.

James glanced at Alex, who had watched proceedings with a vacant, reserved expression. It was all he could do to emulate the same plainness, and ignore the angry fire in his gut. He drank frequently, whenever a man groped or poked; each predatory cackle that rang out driving his teeth harder together. He suppressed a grunt when Malverston nudged him with a boisterous wink. "My boy, I see you eyein' up that one," he slurred. "What's up: got the lover's nuts?"

James blinked and jerked his gaze away from Beth. He

usually made a habit of being discreet—a necessity in politically charged pleasantries such as this—but in those last few moments, he had been staring.

Malverston bawled and slapped his knee in jubilation, landing spittle across James's face in a fine spray. "No sense being shy about instinct, son. Hunger like that shows you're a man. It's only natural. In some ways, all this apocalypse business was a godsend, allowed a little balance to come back to the world. You're too young to know anything much about before—"

I've forgotten more about it than you'll ever know, you sack of lard. They're called books.

—"but back then, there were all kinds of pansies with soft hands and expensive suits running the show, passing all kinds of mollycoddling laws. Women had the same place as men or close to it—they would've taken over completely, in time, I have no doubt—and all kinds of *defective* people with *conditions* were given taxpayers' money to keep them breathing. Backward, unjust nonsense." He gestured to the dancing women, his red cheeks glowing with inebriation. "Now, natural order has been restored. Don't you agree, Master Chadwick?"

James glanced at Alexander, seated a few chairs away, not only out of earshot but engaged in conversation with several of the dirty old men Malverston had named his advisors. He ground his teeth a little tighter. There was a lot riding on keeping the peace with the Moon. This alliance would save them years of struggling to win over all the towns and tradesmen between here and Land's End.

But right now, it was hard to believe it was worth it. And what kind of power were they putting in the hands of this monster?

James resisted the urge to grind the gout-ridden brute into his platter of fresh baked delicatessen and hold it there until the twitching had stopped.

"Yes," he said. The word seemed to lacerate his throat as he forced it out. "Of course. Natural order."

"I thought so. I've got a nose for good character." He tapped his bulbous, crimson schnoz. His gaze grew sly. "So you like the girl?"

James allowed his gaze to return to Beth, but made a point to keep his expression blank. "She's all right."

Beth and the others were making a long, slow pass of the head table, having extricated themselves from the clutches of the town's drunken scoundrels—though more than a few had been doused with sticky beer, and a couple sported knocks and scrapes that would soon blossom into handsome bruises.

"All right? My son, she's a stunner! Just ripened, fresh from the vine. One of my most prized assets." Malverston lurched forward with a vigour that seemed impossible for such a gluttonous wretch, and seized Beth Tarbuck by the hem of her dress. The other dancers flashed on by, their faces blank as James's, but for a moment, the entire hall stiffened. Beth flew into the waiting crook of his elbow, and he whirled her around to face James, pressing her cheek up against his.

They both looked upon James, Malverston's face twisted

into a gaudy sneer. Beth's eyes glittered with disgust, having for a moment become murderous marbles set deep in her skull. Then, she transformed into a voluptuous vixen and had looped her arm over the mayor's shoulder, turning her side askance to plant a wet kiss on his neck. She purred as one of his paws gripped her buttocks.

"What do you think, Chadwick? Not bad, eh? All this is the gravy that comes with seizing opportunity." He turned to her face, which looked almost too pink. James had never seen her in makeup before, let alone freshly bathed. He felt as though he could fall through some wall between reality and illusion if he looked at her for too long. Malverston's fat, ugly tongue snaked the entire length of her cheek, leaving a slimy trail from her chin to her hairline. "The fruits of hard labour are the most delicious," he muttered.

James's stomach turned over. Under the table, his hand twitched towards the pistol holstered at his belt. His hand was already on its way towards the safety catch when she shook her head. It was only a fraction, coupled with a flicker in her gaze, but it was there. Then she was purring once more, tracing her fingers along the nape of the mayor's neck as she prowled behind him, dragging her shining curtain of hair across his lap, his chest, across his face.

"She has spirit, this one," he said. He lurched forward once more and grabbed her by the throat, hauling her around to face him once more. "Almost has me forgetting to watch my back sometimes."

James rose an inch from his chair before he caught another warning glance. This time it came from Alexander, who seemed to finally have caught onto what was going on. He was nodding to the hissing husks that were Malverston's advisors, who clustered around him as though they could absorb his brilliance if they drew close enough, but still he beamed a warning in James's direction.

Beth gasped as she was hauled around between Malverston's knees, clasping at the knuckles of the enormous fist wrapped under her jaw. She choked out a seductive giggle. "Finally got your attention, m'lord? A girl could think she was losing her touch."

Malverston bared his teeth, running a finger along the exposed flesh of her flat belly where her dress had ridden up. "Creatures like this one are the last forbidden fruits in this world, Chadwick. They keen and grin, they give you a hell of a run between the sheets, but all the while you're a hair's breadth away from being stuck in the eye with a hairpin."

Beth's face paled, yet still she maintained her coquettish grin, running her finger over his chest. "What can I say? Men who can take a little play are hard to find. Real men."

Malverston gave a guttural growl. "Any man who looked me in the eye like this one would have eaten lead a long time ago. But these women, Chadwick, you just can't bring yourself to put them out of their misery. They're all backwards, diseased, rotten seed of the lowest families, but here I am bringing them into my house. Women, Chadwick. Women will be the end of us all." He dropped his fist, and Beth crumpled to the floor, rolling down the platform steps and landing in a heap of tussled hair and torn gown. She rose up gasping, red faced with bloodshot eyes, panting and wheezing.

Malverston waved his hand, and the drumming came to an immediate stop. The other dancers scrabbled forward and helped Beth to her feet before filing away through the side doors, leaving the rest of the townspeople still seated, forcibly maintaining the veil of good cheer, eating and drinking.

Malverston relaxed back and nodded to Alexander. "My apologies, those were bordering on private affairs. But I'm overwhelmed sometimes. All these people leaning on me to guide them, sometimes I can get a little worked up. You understand, of course, leader to leader?"

"Of course, Mayor," Alexander said. There wasn't a mote of contempt in his tone. "We all have our foibles."

"Foibles!" Malverston said. "Indeed, indeed. Mine is women, to be sure." His face darkened and he relaxed back so that only James could hear him. "Especially that one. I'd kill her if I didn't love her so much." Then he was smiling, stuffing pastry into his mouth and drawing James into a companionable embrace. "Now, young master, tell me, what's it really like, being a creature of destiny? What's it like living under the great Alexander Cain?"

James exhaled as Beth disappeared, and fixed his gaze on Alexander. He thought he caught an unspoken apology, but he couldn't be sure. It might have been wishful thinking. Because, in truth, he knew that if the mission had called for it, Alexander would have watched Malverston choke her to death right in front of them.

"There is no higher honour," he said.

CHAPTER 9

Lucian hadn't seen daylight for three days. They had kept the sack over his head that long.

Now, the world seemed impossibly blue, the sun a merciless garish ball of fire overhead. Everything was washed out, a glowing sheen setting everything ablaze so that he couldn't tell where the sky ended and the ground began. He had been walking all night, and they had given him a thin broth, a slurp of water and an hour of sleep before beating him back to his feet.

The terrain was even, gravelly, and folded like unmade bed sheets into endless hills and valleys. Prowling the wilds for over forty years had given him the surefootedness to avoid stumbling, but around him he had heard others scrabbling around on their knees and skidding in the scree, along with their pained cries as they were whipped and kicked by their captors.

Now he could see the extent of the convoy, stretching in single file away over hundreds of yards and beyond the next rise. Each of the shuffling figures was torn, marked by charred patches of skin, wrapped in unidentifiable ash-covered rags, gazes locked on the ground at their feet.

The guards were spread out on horseback, creating a tunnel bristling with leather whip-straps, iron pokers and gun barrels.

Lucian looked up at the guard who had lifted his head. Behind a few days' growth of wispy facial hair, Charlie's expression conveyed his thoughts at a glance. *Stay quiet, or else.*

Lucian looked down at the mud again, wondering why he no longer had his hood; most still wore theirs.

Maybe it was because they thought he would no longer recognise where he was. If that was so, they were right.

"Welcome to the club," said a voice at his shoulder.

He looked around to see a barrel-chested man in his sixties, grey bearded and, physically, a powerhouse, especially when compared to the rest of the prisoners. Most of them were little more than wisps, skeletons in motion. His face was so swollen it looked as though he was suffering from Elephantitis, caked along one side in dried blood so old it had become a sticky brown residue; and though he kept pace, he limped on a leg bound in rotten dressings.

Despite his injuries, the stranger smiled, then flicked his head down to indicate they should talk with their eyes on the ground. A brief silence passed as Charlie cantered his mount a little farther ahead, then the stranger huffed through a sharp bout of laughter. "I knew they messed me up bad, but I'd hoped there was something of my ugly mug left."

Lucian frowned.

I know that voice, he thought. He risked glancing again, and in a momentary flick of his head he scanned the stranger's swollen face once more. Yes, there was definitely something there he recognised. For a moment he couldn't place it, but then he reached further back into the depths of memory, and pulled up a name and face he hadn't thought about in many years.

But no, it couldn't be.

"Vandeborn?" he said.

Another grunt of laughter. "Ah, maybe I'm not so far gone, after all." A pause. "McKay, of all the people I could have run into, you're the last I expected."

Lucian gave a grunt of his own. "Same goes for you."

He dropped back, forgetting Charlie. To hell with the kid—if he wanted to beat him, so be it. He fell into step with Max Vandeborn, and the two of them enjoyed a companionable silence for longer than Lucian would have thought possible. For endless minutes, it seemed, there was no need to talk, for all that needed to be said was spread out before them. Their situation couldn't have been better illustrated by the endless procession of prisoners—all that remained of the free communities of the South.

In time, though, his lips began moving of their own accord. "How long has it been?" he said. "Twenty years?"

Max grunted. "Maybe. I thought longer."

"How's life?"

"You know how it is. People come and go, times are good and bad. Recent times, more bad than good, I guess."

It took Lucian some time to stem a belly-wrenching fit

of wheezing laughter. "Tell me about it."

They walked on, people were whipped, and the bloodied remains of a man whose body had given out was flung atop a pile of other emaciated corpses on the flat-bed of a wagon. Their laughter petered out and when they spoke again, their voices had grown sober and plain.

"What happened?" Lucian said.

"They hit us hard at sunrise. Burned us out, killed half, took half. That was then. They must have whipped a few dozen more to death by now. I haven't seen anyone from back home for over a day."

Despite himself, Lucian was disheartened. Max Vandeborn and Bill Bateman had always put the willies into even the most reckless con artists. They had lynched anyone who disrespected the rules of their house.

It was a blow to know even Twingo had crumpled like a house of cards.

He nodded. "Same story everywhere." He hesitated. "Bill?"

Max shook his head. "Took a knife to the chest."

"I'm sorry."

"Yeah. Me too."

"What are you doing here?" Max said. "Last time I saw you, you were quite the hot shit. I never thought you'd have let them take you alive."

"I could say the same to you."

Max cursed. "I should have died back there. God knows I've wished for it since. I even tried goading these pussies into sticking me. All my friends back home fell around me, and the others they took have been thrown on the wagons or left in the dirt, but I'm still here. I just can't bring myself to throw myself on the sword, just in case further down the line there's a chance to take a few of them with me. Anyways, it feels like it's almost out of my hands, like something's keeping me alive, wants me to see something before I'm put out of my misery."

Lucian's throat dried. "Funny, I thought the same thing."

"You saw Him too, then?"

"Saw who?"

"Your brother."

Lucian's chest tightened.

So it was true. James really was at the helm of it all. Despite all the signs, he hadn't been ready to believe it. After so long, it had been all too easy to think him dead. That the blackest mark in their history had never happened.

"So it really is him leading all this?"

"I've seen him with these very peepers, friend."

Lucian nodded, numb.

He changed the subject before his mind could linger. "Where are we heading?"

Max nodded to the sun. "We've been tracking north since we left the tunnels they had us holed up in. Straight as an arrow."

"How do you know?"

Max smiled. "Remember I said *welcome to the club*? I was talking about the hoods. I never had the pleasure of wearing one."

"Why?" Lucian said, looking once more along the long line of people, most hooded, some not.

"Took me a while to figure it out."

"Well?"

"The hooded ones they want confused, beaten. They're the ones they take away for torture whenever we hole up somewhere. They always come back … different. Or they don't come back at all."

"And the rest of us?"

"Us, we're the ones they line up to watch when they raze some other village or group of traders. They make us watch on our knees. See, I figure that's why we're here. We're not for turning. We're here to see everything we built turn to ash."

Lucian cursed. "We received a radio message. The council was gathering in Canary Wharf."

"Radio? A real transmission?"

"Apparently."

"Think it means somebody else is out there?"

"A lot of people are praying for it, like some magic pill that'll make everything dandy. But I wouldn't bet on it."

They kept walking. Charlie rode up a while and prowled alongside them, his eyes darting to Max—not, Lucian noted with satisfaction, without a note of apprehension about him—before heading up ahead once more. So that was why he had been hooded in the first place: Charlie didn't want James to know whom he'd brought along for the ride.

When Max started talking again, it was almost to himself. "Some men are born mean, and some are made that way. Chadwick was a fool, too kind for this world, but he was just. He could have made something out of the ash of the Old World, maybe even better than Cain could have. And now he's set on turning what's left into dust. What the hell happened to him?"

Lucian didn't answer. Finally, he said, "You're wrong. We're here for more than just to see the dregs of our lot fall. I think James has something more in store for us."

Max was quiet for a time. "Well, I suppose we'll see. We're going somewhere, after all. Many things lie in the North."

"Many," Lucian said, but his thoughts lingered on one place in particular.

FOURTH INTERLUDE

"I'm going to kill him." James threw himself over Beth, casting aside the peach vines and cupping her face. In the moonlight her skin glowed like marble, pale and bloodless. Her brow furrowed in intense concentration, and he could see an internal struggle raged behind her eyes. She shook her head, tearing her matted dress off and throwing it onto the dirt.

"No," she said. "Don't you dare."

"That was so stupid, aggravating him like that!"

"I had to. He expects it."

"You can't let him do that to you. It's inhuman."

"You can't change the way things are in the Moon, James. He holds all the keys. There's too much at stake to throw it all away for me."

James gripped her desperately. "Come with me. Run away!"

"I can't." She swallowed hard. "He'll kill my family. That how he gets any of us to do anything. If anybody hadn't shown at the banquet tonight …" She mimed holding flaming torch to kindling.

"That son of a bitch deserves to die." He gripped her by the sides of her head and looked down into the dark holes where her eyes would have been. "I won't let him get away with this."

To his surprise, she tittered, a weepy yet stubborn sound devoid of all humour. "With what?"

"Treating you like you were some slab of meat. I can't believe everyone just … just watched. Even me."

She sighed and sank to the dirt. Crouched there in her sweat-stained undergarments, hangdog and pale, she was more alluring than when her hips had been in full gyration before the head table. Here was the real Beth Tarbuck, breathing in the scent of ripe peaches and petrichor, wriggling her toes into the soft wet earth. The shallow imposter who had danced before him, even with all the rouge exposed flesh rippling under golden torchlight, had been but a twisted shadow. The ache didn't come from his loins this time, but his chest, so sharp it could have doubled him over.

"That was nothing," she muttered. "He behaved himself tonight, for your sake, I'm sure."

"What do you mean?" He crouched down beside her and, for a moment, glanced up the hill at Alice McKinley's crooked form silhouetted against the great gibbous moon. She had known Beth would be down here, even though Malverston had neglected to invite her to the festivities. She hadn't offered to accompany him, though he sensed it hadn't been for a lack of caring—quite the opposite. She gave the tiniest of nods and then vanished into the mass of

Newquay's Moon.

"He might have you believe that all that was in your honour, but there is no shortage of his little banquets. Every time he orders the whole town to turn over their finest food and cider, and he brings all his slimy friends from all over to sit at those tables and worship his great golden shlong." She sneered. "Know what they say about men with big feet? Well it ain't true. But men like him have to be compensating for something, don't they?" The sneer lingered on her face for a moment, then slid away like water off slate. "Believe me, most people around here never saw the other side of those doors before tonight. I suppose at least that part was for your benefit. And where there's a banquet, there's dancing." She growled and cast the torn remnants of her dress into the orchard.

James sat by her, seething but immobile. "Why do you all do it? He couldn't burn you all out, he needs you. Without the town, he's nothing."

She fixed him with a fierce stare. "You have no idea," she muttered, "no idea what he really is." She ripped her hair into its natural bramble-bush mayhem. She reached out and took his hands. He hadn't realised they had been trembling. "Leave it be. Anything you do will make it worse. That's the way of men like him. Anyway, you and Alexander care too much about your treaty with the Moon to tear it up over a field-hand's daughter."

James wanted to deny it, but found he couldn't. Instinct told him that the right thing to do would be to take his pistol and blast Malverston away in the attitude of Old

World chivalry. But all his long years by Alexander's side kept him lame and mum.

She was right. They needed Malverston.

He grunted, fumed, and then found calm again as he looked upon her marble cheeks. "It's not right."

She punched his shoulder. "What ever is? You've been with the *Messiah* too long if you think the world is any kind of fair."

James smiled, resisting the urge to rub where she had hit him. She had quite the right hook. "Things will get better now that we're involved. We have things he wants, but we and our partners don't deal with tyrants. He'll have to play ball and change, even if only on the surface. And once the region is civilised again—really civilised, with enforced justice—there'll be no room for his type."

She was quiet, staring off along the row of peach trees, towards the distant bulge of the faraway hills, and the endless silvered wheat stalks in between, dancing in the breeze.

James swallowed. His words hadn't come out right. They had sounded pre-prepared, mechanical and didactic. He had sounded almost like Alexander.

That wouldn't do. He needed her to know he cared. He needed to see her smile. "I promise it'll be better. Once he's gone, we'll even have schools, art, books. The Old World will be at your fingertips."

"I don't care about the Old World," she grated. "I don't care about books, all those grimy cities, or your precious mission. Things like that can never matter to people like me. All I can worry about is getting my weekly protection quota to Malverston's men, and trying to keep out of his bed as often as possible."

James felt his lips working, but he had no words left to offer. He searched deep, clawing at the bare innards of his mind. In the end what he managed to dredge up sounded pitiful and empty. "I will come back, soon."

She looked as though on the verge of saying something, but a rustling to their right sent them both scrambling to their feet. James fingered his pistol grip, and called out. "Who's there?"

A moment more rustling, then a tiny figure emerged from the peach trees. "What are you doing with her?" a harsh girlish voice hissed. "You get back, dirty pig!"

Beth growled like a cornered dog. "Go home, Mel. What are you doing out here?"

"Keeping dirty raping mongrels like him from taking you in the bushes. You know what Mum says, '*It's all any of them want from us.*'"

Little Melanie Tarbuck fixed James with a vicious glare. Despite the darkness, James could just make out the slingshot in her hands, and the tiny ball loaded into the string—it would cut right through his skull at this range. She couldn't have been more than eleven, but the weapon she carried was no toy, and she knew it. He had seen her cut crows clean out of the sky with it.

"Mel, go home." Beth's voice was infected with the same exasperated fury that siblings had reserved for one another since time immemorial, but she took the precaution of putting herself between James and the slingshot, nonetheless. That wasn't a good sign.

James cleared his throat as he noticed the string slacken some. She had really been fixed to brain him. He tried to keep his fingers away from the butt of his pistol, but instinct kept drawing them back.

"He's a friend, Mel. He's one of Cain's lot."

"I know who he is." Her face was set, far too old for her years. "You're the one who's been sniffing around our house every time they show up. Well you stay away from my sister. She's not interested in boys. She and I are just fine with Mum, just the three of us."

"Shut *up*, Mel. Get out of here. Go home!"

She shrugged. "Come on, then."

"Without me, you little nit."

Melanie's gaze remained even, cool. It was eerie, seeing a child handle herself with such detachment. She set him on edge far more than any of the great ugly gorillas Malverston used as his private militia. "You can't trust him. Men are all the same. We can't trust any of them besides Dad—and he's gone."

"He's not like the mayor's men. Cain's lot are ... different."

"That's how they get you. Mum says they try all sorts of things to get you to trust them, then they get you alone, then ..." She seemed to see the tattered remains of Beth's dress hanging about her under-things for the first time. She bared her teeth. "You get away. Go on, go, before I put this rock through your eye!"

"It wasn't him, Mel, it was me."

"Why would you rip Mum's dress?" Mel snapped disbelievingly.

"Because—because the mayor made me dance again. I—I … I felt his stink on me." In the moonlight her face had flushed a dark grey.

Mel paused, and for the first time her emotionless veil dropped. "Again?" she said. "After what Mum did … he promised he'd leave us alone."

"I know. He lied."

"How could you?"

"I did it to keep you safe."

"I don't need protecting. I'd split his head wide open if he came anywhere near our house."

Beth stepped forward and snatched the slingshot from Mel's hand. "You stupid little girl, you think this thing would stop him? You have no idea what kinds of things he'd do, what *I've* had to do to keep him away from our door …" Her voice cracked, and she pushed her sister hard enough to send her careening into the vines behind her.

She eyed Beth, wounded and downcast, then after a few moments took her slingshot back and stowed it in her belt. "What were you doing with him, then?"

"We were just talking."

James risked leaning around Beth, holding his hands out to the side. "I was making sure she was all right. You have my word."

She glared at him and said nothing.

He tried again. "I'm James. James Chadwick."

"I said I knew who you were. You think we're just a bunch of stupid farmers, but we all know who you are." Her brow flickered. "You're the one who sends the birds. Everyone's heard of your bunch. The one with the big mouth they call the Messiah. You … They call you the Pigeon Keeper."

James blinked. "That's right," he said. He took a step forward, around Beth. "We're here to help you, your sister, everyone in town."

"We don't need your help! We're just fine on our own."

James and Beth shared a look. "It's okay," he said. "I have to go, anyway."

Beth stiffened. "Now?"

He glanced between the two sisters. Mel was plastered to her side now; there would be no separating them. His time with Beth was over. "We have a situation back home we need to take care of." He hovered for a moment, wanting nothing more than to take her by the hand and ride with her away from this place. Instead, he nodded to the little girl, and turned to leave.

"What do you want with us?" Mel Tarbuck said.

He paused, and shook his head. "Just to help."

"Well, you should stay away. If you hadn't come tonight, we'd both be home." She took Beth's arm, and for a moment, James saw the little girl underneath. "My dad gave my mum that dress. It was one of the only things the mayor hadn't taken away from us … Now that's gone too." She glowered. "Just stay away."

James made to protest, but Beth flickered her eyelids

shut and shook her head minutely, squeezing Mel's hand.

A moment of awkward silence passed between them. Then the noise of the emptying hall was carried on the wind, and the sound of people tramping home reached their ears. It was time to re-join the crowd before his absence was noticed. He backed away. "If you need me," he said, "use the birds. They know where to find me."

Then he was moving through the peach trees, heading uphill. Some time later Beth's voice trickled from the darkness. "Stay safe, Pigeon Keeper."

Minutes later, he and Alexander were riding across open fields, unspeaking. What had to be done had been done, and despite the turmoil roiling in his gut at the thought of what Malverston might do to Beth, he put Newquay's Moon out of his mind, and turned his attention to the others back home.

CHAPTER 10

Sarah was in constant motion, flitting back and forth between the endless reams of rescued art, cassette tapes, DVDs, records, books and computer components, all perfectly preserved in vacuum-sealed plastic baggies. She checked each one, nodding and muttering to herself as she made her way through the myriad rows that filled the vastness of the catacombs. Decades of salvage work lay before them, the world before the End in miniature.

At least, that's how she and Alexander sold it. All Robert saw was a whole lot of useless junk, the leftovers of those dead and gone. The electronics were fried, little more than dust; the art was nice to look at, but he couldn't see the appeal of most of it—hell, he could have replicated half of it with a potato dipped in paint; and the books, well, he was never one for reading. Not that he would ever admit that to Sarah.

Robert watched her with fascination. He had never been here before. Precious few were even aware this place existed beneath the streets of New Canterbury. He had been charged with guarding the heavy doors by Alexander, but this labyrinth of halls and tunnels had never been for his eyes. Everything was too delicate to let a lumbering oaf like him inside.

"I'm not sure how I can help," Robert said.

She was flitting back and forth in a blaze of motion, checking minute details to which he was blind.

How did she keep track of anything amidst all this chaos? The mountains of Old World refuse seemed to stretch on forever.

She stepped away into the aisle, her gaze scouring the floor. "You're a tracker," she said, "so track."

"What?"

"Somebody's been in here."

Robert looked at the floor, bare brushed concrete, and cleared his throat. "How can you tell?"

"I can't, not for sure." She frowned. "But some of it is missing."

Robert couldn't help glancing away from her at the enormity of the collection. There were dozens of other halls just like it, each just as full. "I don't want to tell you your business, but are you sure you're not just imagining it? There's so much …"

"I know every item we catalogued," she said. He could see the hurt in her eyes. "Every one. They all have their own look and feel, their own imperfections, and their own place. And some of them are gone." She looked confused, but there was no uncertainty about that look. To her mind, at least, a very frugal thief was at large.

"I can't track in here," he said.

She scoffed, spectacles shining under the harsh artificial lights. Her eyes were magnified to enormous proportions by the thick lenses. "You're the best tracker we have. You sniffed out the office building where they …" She stopped, brows furrowed, and shook her head.

Where the enemy had been holed up. Where they slaughtered all those people, while we watched.

It had marked her, being exposed to the real world like that. She had been trussed up under the safe haven Alexander had created for too long. Too many of the city's people had. If he was right, they were all in for a hard ride, because things were about to get a hell of a lot worse.

"It doesn't work that way," he said. "There's no magic second sight. I can only read the ground when there's something that can be disturbed: bent blades of grass, snapped twigs, impressions in the mud, that kind of thing."

She didn't seem to be listening. "What would anybody want with this stuff?"

What do we want with it? Robert stopped himself from saying.

He stepped up behind her and gripped her shoulders, dwarfed by his hands. "We've been through a lot, lately. It's okay if things are getting to you. Even the toughest bastards crack if you put them under enough pressure."

She tensed, and slowly turned around to face him. "I'm not crazy, Robert." Her gaze had turned to ice.

"I didn't say that."

"You implied it. Like I'm losing my marbles, seeing things."

"We're all tired." He gently turned her around and started walking them back towards the surface.

We don't have time to chase relics. I have to check the perimeter.

But he wasn't leaving her down here. "Why don't we go back topside and get some fresh air? You probably put it all someplace else—"

She wrestled from his grip and stepped away. "Stop treating me like I'm made of glass!" she yelled.

He froze. His thoughts of checking in with the perimeter guard vanished. He said, "I'm not."

"Yes, you are. You have been since they started shooting the slaves. Like you think I'm going to fall apart at any point. Well, I'm not, all right?" Her lip was quivering, but her cheeks were crimson red. "You might get to play hero for some people, but I'm not some fainting damsel that you get to swoop in and save." Her voice cracked and she took a deep breath.

Robert swallowed, his cheeks flushing. She was right; he had been treating her like she was one of the princesses from a storybook—like she was weak. And he knew better than that. In his haste, he hadn't been paying attention, and he had forgotten what had attracted him to her in the first place. Beneath her prim librarian's exterior slumbered a mighty she-wolf. "I'm sorry," he said, "I am."

She didn't move for a while.

"You're sure something's missing?"

"I'm positive."

He watched for a flicker upon her face, but none

showed. "I believe you."

She looked up at him. "You should never have doubted me."

"I know. I'm sorry."

They stood still for a few moments, then she was in motion again. "It's just odds and ends, nothing specific. But I'm certain of it. There are things missing."

"What did they take?"

"A little of everything. And they have good taste, whoever they are." Her nose bristled with irritation. "Books, mostly. First editions, priceless articles. Some of my favourites. Irreplaceable. Besides that, some of the smaller canvases, some old film reels."

"No electronics?"

"I don't think so."

He paced up and down the hall a little. "You're *sure?* Absolutely sure?"

She shot him another look, and he held up his hands. "Fine." He looked down along the path they had just taken, and farther along to the very end of the catacombs, hundreds of yards ahead. "It's just hard to see how they got in through a sealed blast door. You and Alexander have the only keys, and I didn't see any disturbance in the dust outside. There's only one entrance?"

"I can't say for sure. Alexander started storing things here before I was old enough to read. But they were making vaults like this since the End. They got pretty good at it. I can vouch for him."

"But we still can't be sure. We know they've been

sneaking into the city for a long time, using the sewers. All they'd need is a thin wall to tunnel through, and they'd be in."

She finished up in the hall and returned to his side. "More of the same," she said. "Either there were over a dozen of them, or they've made more than one trip in here."

They returned to the surface slowly, and Robert kept his guard up the whole way. The fact that they weren't safe, even so close to home, inside their own perimeter, couldn't have been fresher in his mind.

"I don't understand it. They've been destroying everything they come into contact with. Burning it all up. Why would they steal those ... relics? They're farmers, they shunned what came Before."

Robert sighed. It was yet another mystery to add to the plethora of shadows already surrounding them. "I don't know," he said. "I suppose there's more to them than we thought."

FIFTH INTERLUDE

They arrived home past noon the following day. They had driven their mounts hard, too hard, and now ambled forth in a weakened shuffle. James recognised Lucian's shock of shoulder-length hair in profile even from half a mile away. He was standing at the fence post surrounding their farmland.

Crops were still a rare sight, outside of isolated oases such as Cornwall. Most of the country's arable land had become a hopeless chaos of wild plants and weeds; without tending hands and pesticides, the mollycoddled grains and other crop-yielding species whose genes had been touched by man's hand over the millennia had been pushed out.

Most had become hunter-gatherers when the canned food had grown sparser, living on hunted game, tubers, and wild berries. In the North, a small-scale extinction was already underway for the survivors of the End. They had sensed the cities' supply of preserved goods coming to depletion, but had seemed unable to muster the will to do anything about it. Now they were fading, leaving empty lean-to settlements and near-feudal villages blowing in the wind; yet more decaying ruins, beside those of the Old World.

But here, mile after mile of ploughed fields greeted the eye. All lovingly brought forth by their own hands, James's chief among them. When he had been a boy, he had tended but one lonely field of corn. Back then, only he and Alexander had truly believed in it, in beginning anew and seizing control of their fate.

Now, they had surplus every harvest, they formed the nexus of a growing network of trade routes, and they had dozens of pilgrims under their employ; those who had travelled from across the country to meet Alex and his ilk, seduced by his speeches, his wares of already-forgotten Old World knowledge and relics, and the grandness of the mission to save humanity.

Lucian held up a hand, and Alex raised his in reply. There had been reason enough to greet them, but it was obvious there was no emergency, and so James and Alexander climbed down from their exhausted mounts and walked the rest of the way.

A little while later, a small, scrawny figure joined Lucian's: little Norman Creek, who played with a toy airplane, passing it through the air in great sweeping arcs. They passed through the gateway in the fence and headed towards the stone courtyard at the end of the dirt lane. Lucian and the boy fell into step with them and they walked in companionable silence for a time.

Whenever they ventured out, there was never any promise of return. To be safe behind their own borders again never failed to bring about a reflective lull.

Families out in the fields waved, thigh deep in blossoming rapeseed, and it was all James could do to keep from puffing his chest. They had sowed the land well.

The cooing became audible soon after.

From all around them came the chorus of the wood pigeons: *Hoo-hoo-who. Hoo-hoo-who.*

There had been a time when James had kept a single, small coop with no more than a dozen birds. And until his education in Alex's classes had started in earnest, they had made good pets.

And he had discovered something very strange. The books described wood pigeons as having remarkable navigational abilities, allowing them to find their homes from impossible distances—even from completely alien territory. This second sight was thanks to tiny shards of magnetised material in their brains aligning with the Earth's magnetic field.

But after a while experimenting, James had come to a bizarre and disturbing conclusion when his birds always ended up clustered not around the coop, but around him, wherever it was that he happened to be. Sometimes, he would release them a hundred miles from home, then travel on with Alex to visit a wild clan to discuss joining the alliance.

And instead of gathering around the stone courtyard, the birds would appear in the sky over his head. They always found him. Nobody else, it seemed, shared this bizarre attraction. Even pigeons he hadn't raised, wild birds, seemed to share a certain fascination with him.

So far as he could tell from any book that he could find, there was no explanation.

One time, Alex had said that he had seen strange things happen to pigeons just after the End, when James had been but a baby. He had loved birds even then, he was told.

It seemed they shared a bond that no Old World science could explain.

"Yet another mystery to add to the growing mountain range," Lincoln often said.

Once James had opened his mind to all the secrets hidden in the millions of books scattered in the rubble, he had learned about the Great War long ago where pigeons had been used to send messages to millions of soldiers stationed in muddy trenches.

The idea had stuck fast in his mind. Imagine bringing word to and from the few others who still lived out there in the vastness of the world, conversing without the danger and rigour of travelling across the great hostile stretches between them, linking up the ragged clans out there in the wilderness in the same vein of the old ways of the written letter, or the fantastical magic that had been the telegram, the text message, and email.

And so he set about turning their kinship to his advantage, training them to disperse far and wide, covering all the land. Like telephone boxes.

Young Melissa Tarbuck had been right: wherever he went, people already knew him as the Pigeon Keeper.

"You got our message?" Lucian said finally as Chuck

alighted upon James's shoulder.

"We left as soon as we could," Alex said. His voice was tight. "Whatever's going on, it was important enough to bring us back from Cornwall." It wasn't a question.

"Yes," Lucian said.

"If we lose their cooperation, we could be set back years."

Lucian scowled. "I wouldn't have done it if I hadn't thought I had to."

Alex was quiet for a moment, then nodded. "Show me."

Norman watched them all warily, still playing with his model airplane. He followed in their wake, not really paying them any mind, just wanting to be a part of it like always. He was a strange kid, caught between the two schools of thought that had divided James and Lucian; he neither eschewed the Old World's bounty, nor did he grasp any sense of wonder or destiny. He was indifferent to it all, just a kid who liked his toys and reading.

Alex had little time for him. He had little potential, a poor asset for the mission.

But James accepted him for what he was: a good boy who adored his parents and might be made into a passable carrier of their torch, if he were but given the time of day and a little encouragement. He reached down to Norman now and ruffled his hair.

Then he turned to Lucian, and the two of them clasped arms as Alex hurried on ahead.

"What took you?" Lucian muttered.

"Later," James said. "Now, tell me what's going on?"

*

The courtyard was usually empty in the afternoon. Only during the Sunday communal meal were tables brought for everyone to eat together. Besides that, it was an occasional haunt for those looking to catch up, or rope an extra hand into field work for the day.

Today, the stone circle—around which their tiny oasis of thatched cottages stood, built with their own hands—was obstructed by a large wooden cart. Tied to it were a few oxen, mighty beasts with impressive flanks of solid muscle. Bulging sacks were piled high upon the back of the cart, covered over with torn blue tarpaulin.

Nobody manned the foreign behemoth. It sat unattended and alien in the centre of their homestead.

"What is this?" Alex said.

"He rode up yesterday morning," Lucian said, leading them away towards the stables. They rounded a corner and came into sight of a small gathering in the shade of the stable door's awning, the remainder of those James would have called his family: Agatha, more matriarchal than even the Early Years as she entered her sixties, even if she had begun to forget things; Hector and Helen Creek, Norman's parents, hanging back a little, their faces etched with worry; and grizzled old Lincoln, who had in the Old World been a naval engineer, and gone by the name Sir Oliver Farringdon.

Between their feet lay sprawled an odd creature, a shrunken man wrapped in an enormous mass of coats and underthings, all of them far too large for his lanky frame. His eyes bulged from their sockets, bug-like, giving his face an expression of permanent surprise. The remains of more food than a man could eat in a week were strewn around him. Even now he was still eating, chomping on fresh bread in great mouthfuls, not bothering to even tear it from the loaf.

"Who is he?" Alex said.

Lucian bowed his head slightly to keep them out of earshot. "At first I thought he was hysterical. We almost had him packed up and set to turn around before he gave us something to listen to. Said if we turned him away we'd all end up in the ground."

"He threatened you?"

"Thought so. Almost had his skin for it. But no … He meant all of us. As in, everyone." They turned a corner and Lucian lowered his voice. "I was sure he was just some nut, dumber than a bag of blind mice, then he spat something out that made us start listening. But you'll want to hear it from him."

James scowled, thinking of Beth. She could be in Malverston's clutches by now. Her, or her sister, or mother. He had managed to keep his focus until now—but if they had been called back on account of some wandering crazed hobo … "How could you do this?" he hissed. "Did the sun soften your head? Our work in Newquay's Moon is important. We were so close, Lucian, so close! And now— you've pulled us away to listen to some wandering madman!"

Lucian glanced between him and Alex, and his lips grew tight. "You'll want to hear him. I'm certain of it."

"How do you know?"

"Because, he came from Radden." A moment's silence stole between them all, and James and Alex shared a look. Lucian finished: "He said someone's calling you home."

Radden.

James shivered as an icy chill swept across his body, tautening the hair upon his crown and drawing his balls close to his body. He hadn't heard that word for a long time, not since he was a boy.

Radden County was in the far North, slicked along the length of the Lake District, where James and Alex had been born and lived before the End. To his knowledge, they were the only two from the entire region to have survived—two, from a population of over a hundred thousand.

By their reckoning, over ninety-nine per cent of the world's population had vanished, leaving an even spread of random survivors across the Earth's surface. That put an average of one human being per eight square miles the world over. In all of the British Isles, there couldn't have been more than five to ten thousand survivors. But even this paltry smattering paled in comparison to what had happened in Radden. It had been wiped clean. Since then, it had remained abandoned, unplundered, avoided as fervently as death itself.

A forbidden land.

James felt his guts tighten up. In the twenty years since the End, the idea of returning had never entered their minds. Alex himself hadn't even spoken of it since James had asked to know from where he had come, many years ago.

Now, Alex's face was a tight mask, eyeing the dirty slumped glutton under the stable awning. They approached the rest of the way in silence, and the man sat bolt upright at the sight of them.

"Sir!" he exclaimed, spraying gobs of half-chewed bread at their feet. He bowed his head and scrambled to his feet, taking on an obsequious stoop and pulling an ancient fedora from his head, holding it to his chest.

"It's all right, friend," Alex said. "You have nothing to fear from me. Speak."

Gerard bowed ever so slightly, gripping the brim of his hat a little tighter and flushing beet red. "All r'pect, sir, but I didn't come here for you." His eyes wafted among them until the others, even Alexander, had stepped away, and James alone was left in his gaze's path. "You're the Keeper? You swear on it, lest the End take you?"

As if to prove the point, a pigeon peeped into view from the guttering and dropped down onto James's shoulder, pecking at his duster. "I am," he said.

Gerard's brows flickered. "They tell it up North like you're som'in nigh on Odin: that you're double tall as me and have a face like granite. You could be any man from Adam, by Christ."

James shrugged. "I can't prove anything."

Gerard scrutinised him with a wry twist creeping into his lips. "No, it's you. Tall tales, they told, the usual bull shite … 'cept your eyes. They got them right. Green as a leaf in the summer sun." He paused, and sighed. "'Tis you." He stepped forward and looked hard into James's face. "'Tis indeed … I got a message for you."

James glanced at Alex, who was eyeing them with an unreadable expression. Lucian had loped to the side to join the others, looking unsettled and unsure. Norman huddled around his father's legs, tugging on his sleeve unconsciously. Even Agatha and Lincoln, though they held their tongues, looked troubled.

Nothing like this had ever happened before. They seldom ever had visitors, let alone a wanderer from the far North.

"What is it?" James said, swallowing uncertainly.

The man looked suddenly nervous, his eyes darting to the others. "For *you*."

"You can trust them."

He didn't look convinced. In fact, he looked wary. His eyes kept returning to Alex. "For *you*."

James sighed and nodded inside. The man seemed grateful and stepped into the gloom of the stables. It was muggy inside, and James trudged through hay until they stood beside a pair of dark steeds, the fug of manure and unwashed horseflesh filling his nose. They settled in the midst of shadow and he met the man's eyes again. "Well?"

The man was breathless. "You've been around that other one too long. Your path is set, Chadwick. You have a part to play."

James recoiled. "What are you talking about?"

"The other one. The meddler. The one who might undo it all."

"You're talking about Alex …?"

"Him. He's undoing things that mustn't be undone."

"We're fighting to take back what we lost."

"You can't! If you do, we could lose everything."

"We already lost everything, friend."

The man laughed hysterically. "You have no idea … no idea how far this goes, how small this world and its troubles are. But all the pieces matter, no matter how small, and you're one of them, Chadwick. Your path is set!" His eyes bulged from his head.

"I choose my own destiny, friend, and it's here, with them—"

The man took a step forward abruptly, and his babble halted. "I'm sorry to have to do this …"

"What?"

James realised, too late, that his eyes had changed. There was something else in them: genuine sorrow, but also something else—no, some*one* else; a young man stood behind the bedraggled figure before him, a beautiful high-cheeked grinning prince with dark streaks under his eyes. "Forgive me," he whispered, and before James could react, a pair of filthy spider-like hands were clapped around his head.

Pain arced in his skull as though a bolt of lightning had leapt between his ears.

He saw moorland, rugged heath and rolling hills, a single snow-capped mountain in the distance, all of it slathered in thick fog that poured into deep valleys and skated out across great glassy lakes. Towns were dotted here and there, great decaying things that had been old and dense with secrets long before the End had robbed them of life. He saw it all, every inch of plaster, heath, and rock in a single flash.

He had never laid eyes on that place before, but he knew it was Radden.

Then another bolt of lightning whited it all out, and he stood at the end of a stone tunnel stretching away into infinity. He was underneath the moors now, far down below where no gas line or rail tunnel could reach. Torches flickered, set high near the ceiling, and he was rushing past them at an impossible speed, hurtling around corners and along vast stretches, passing strange carvings, paintings, shadows of figures walking out of sight—some of them weren't quite human.

A cavern appeared ahead, and he hurtled towards it until it opened out, revealing a long wooden table. Sat in a rickety old chair with his feet up on the table, arms spread wide in welcome, was the beautiful young man. The streaks under his eyes were like slicks of tar. "I'm waiting," he said.

In a split second, James was being squashed, hurled, and rolled in ways a person cannot be rolled. The tunnel warped out of shape, groaning under some unseen strain, then the stone, the dripping dew, the flames, even the air, fractured, and he saw what lay behind it. He saw *between* the tunnel and other places, some light and some dark, some silent and some alive with countless whispering voices. All of them separated by vast distances, yet right beside one another, woven into a single tapestry, an intricate web tended to by—

James stopped spinning and rolling, and the other places vanished. Darkness once more, total dark this time. He sensed he was far away from his body now. Somewhere out of sight he could hear whimpering, fearful souls lost in the void—he could feel them, endless thousands, millions. And somewhere above it all, on a scale far beyond anything he could conceive, something swung back and forth. Back, and forth. Back and forth. Driving the clockwork of all existence.

Tick, tock, tick, tock.

The young man's voice spoke once more. "Hurry."

Then heat, the smell of manure, and a soft neigh close by. James was breathing hard, staring into the wanderer's eyes, which were now opaque, filled only with sorrow. His hands were covered with a smoking layer of frost, and James heard his hair crackle and a pinch of cold upon his temples as a film of ice evaporated in the humid stable air.

"What did you do to me?" he whispered.

"I'm sorry, mister. I did some bad things … bad things … He gave me a way to wipe my slate clean, but this was part o' the deal." He took a shuddering breath. "If I was you, I'd try to forget all this crazy. That's my plan." He swallowed. "But something tells me you won't get the chance."

James felt hollow, his innards thrumming as though his entire body had become a recently struck bell. He heard his own distant voice. "I think you should leave, now."

The man didn't hesitate, nor did he say another word. He trudged through the hay and disappeared outside.

James stood in the dark until the thrumming had settled, and strength returned to his limbs. Then he walked out into the sun, blinding after the total dark of wherever the man had transported him.

That was crazy. He didn't remember Radden, only imagined it from Alex's description. But what he had just seen had been no crude mental creation; he had seen every blade of grass and crumb of moss-covered mortar, smelled the dank fug of lichen and wildflowers, felt the moisture of condensing fog and salt-laden sea air on his skin. It had been real.

The others were waiting to one side where he'd left them, unmoving and watchful. Norman was caged firmly between his father's protective arms, his airplane hanging at his side. The wanderer's cart was already passing through the gate, barrelling down the uneven road at a reckless pace to the sound of hollering and cracking whips.

"What happened?" Alex said.

"Nothing. He's just some nut."

Agatha frowned. "Y'sure, James? He looked like he'd seen a ghost or somethin'," Agatha said. "Righ' scare on 'im."

"I'm sure." He shrugged, hoping his face wouldn't betray him. "He just babbled a while and ran out." James paused for effect. "He didn't say anything more?"

"Just hopped on his wagon and off he went," Lincoln

croaked, shrugging.

"How did he know you were from Radden?" Helen said.

Hector cleared his throat, nodding to Norman. *"Don't worry the boy,"* that cough said.

But she was heedless. "How *could* he know?"

"She's right," Lucian said. His eyes were fixed on James in a dead stare. Alex had fixed him with a look all too similar.

They see right through me. They know.

James was at a loss for words, mouthing openly. He thought he might end up standing there forever when Alex spoke up suddenly.

"You saw those sacks. He was a scavenger. Probably figured there was a whole lot of loot in Radden; nobody plunders No Man's Land. I found James in a cottage on the outskirts of the county. His parents were gone but there was everything there you needed to know everything about them. He was probably just trying his luck, seeing if he could gain some leverage over us, make a quick buck."

"How could he know some baby grew into Pigeon Boy, here?" Lucian said.

Alex's confident smile flickered. "You'd be surprised how many people know his name. And the wind can carry names a long, long way."

"Thanks to you in no small part," James said. He tried a smile, but Alex's face flickered even more, almost a twitch.

Is he mad at me? Did I just upstage him?

Nobody had ever come looking for someone besides the Messiah.

Nevertheless, the group visibly relaxed, the tension melting away. They watched the cart disappear into the distance, bouncing and jostling between the heads of wheat until it was nothing but a blur under the sun.

Lincoln and Agatha looked shamefaced. "Sorry to scupper the negotiations in Newquay's Moon," Lincoln said.

"T'was us who asked Lucian to call ya back," Agatha said.

"We didn't want to take any chances."

Alex shook his head. "It doesn't matter. We did what we needed to do. Malverston agreed to our terms. We have full access to their lands and the outlying provinces. They're even open to bulk trade with us, in time. It wasn't ideal timing, being pulled away, but … mission accomplished."

"You're sure?"

"We'll have to grease the wheels along the line to make up for bouncing from his preening party. But then again, it might just help us if he thinks he has one over us."

James thought of Beth again. He wondered if she and her sister were in hiding right now, whether they had left Malverston inflated enough to quell his mean streak. He nodded along with Alex, but couldn't bring himself to say anything. He wasn't sure how he felt. The vision was still buzzing in his mind like a swarm of locusts.

Lucian was looking at him. "The guy was really a fake?" He looked troubled. "Damn. He was good. He had me fooled."

"Crazy as crazy gets," James said. For a moment, as he

said it, he believed it. But he knew it was a lie; something had changed in him. Even now, he felt a strange sensation building in his lower body: an itch, an insistent prodding, pointing like an arrow away from the courtyard. He shook himself.

Lucian cursed. "He duped us. It sounds stupid but … he said some weird things during the night. Stuff about you being different, about you playing a part in some cosmic jigsaw puzzle. Babble, most of it, but there was something to it. It all sounded very … big. It was almost like he thought you had something to do with the End."

The family turned and headed inside, turning their attention to the deal with Malverston.

James leaned confidentially towards Lucian. "That's impossible."

"Stranger things have happened." Lucian gestured to the horizon, at the crumbling skyline of Nottingham, as though James could need reminding that, twenty years ago, over six billion people had vanished without a trace.

Yes, it *was* crazy. But so was everything about the world they lived in.

*

They sat down to a lunch of bread, cheese, and a stew of potato, mushrooms, wildflowers, and an exotic slurry of various meats—a creation of Agatha's which Lincoln referred to as *jungle stew*. By the time they reached the table, stomachs were growling audibly, and the mysterious traveller was forgotten.

For a time there was silence under the roof thatched by their own hands, and they ate as only people who know the dangers of real hunger can eat: methodically, savouring every crumb and drop with unwavering gusto. The wood burner beside the table was small, and when they had dragged it from the wreckage of an old barn conversion a few miles away, it had been little more than a bucket of rust. But Lincoln had taken it into his workshop and set to it with all the wisdom of the Old World, and his practised engineer's hands had restored it to shining beauty.

It warmed every cubic foot of air under the high roof without a hint of struggle.

James was forever in awe of Lincoln, and the few other professionals who had survived the End. They displayed true mastery—fonts of endless trivia and titbits of knowledge that books could never convey, that could only come from experience or be communicated between master and apprentice; things that were in true danger of becoming lost forever, if they had not already.

He had done his best to absorb the minutiae of his trade, but the majority passed over his head. He was a thinker at heart, not a doer. And Lincoln, though he had been among the founding members of the mission, was not taken to divulging his secrets; instead, his nuggets of invaluable skill seeped from him in dribs and drabs, often unexpectedly, and he grumbled like a man bothered by irksome children when pressed for a repeat performance.

Nevertheless, everything around them stood testament

to his abilities; he had designed and supervised the renovation of every line and beam of the homestead. It had been a quaint old farmhouse when they had found it; now, it was a monument to their mission. Without him, and the continuous pillar of maternal strength Agatha had provided each day, they would have been lost.

"Small favours," Alexander sometimes said. "The world may lie in ruin, but it'll be saved by small favours."

The others were out in the fields and wouldn't be back until evening, and so they enjoyed a companionable lull, filling their stomachs and resting stiffened legs. Hector helped Norman fill out a page of arithmetic sums, patiently crossing out mistakes—a little too often for James to feel encouraged of any progress. Norman's face was creased into a fierce frown of misery and confusion.

Finally, Lincoln smacked his lips and pushed his bowl away, steepling his fingers and leaning across the table. "So, Alex, put our minds at ease," he said.

Alex swallowed and smiled. "Like I said, Malverston's on board."

Agatha, sat beside Lincoln, failed to suppress a coy smile. "Sometimes I can't help but think he imagine us some kind o' foolish." She sighed in Lincoln's direction.

He hummed assent, and their eyes met. "Fools, indeed."

Agatha turned her gaze upon Alex, then James. "Wha' did you two have to promise tha' bag o' slime to win 'im over?"

Alex sat quietly, folding his hands before him, chewing slowly and swallowing with an audible *glug*. "We're going to teach them," he said.

"Teach them what?"

"Our ways, what we've learned about how to start over. We're going to start a school. Here."

Everyone jerked as though an electrical current had been passed through the table. James gaped and turned in his seat, staring into Alex's deadpan expression. "*What?*"

"How could you agree to this without consulting us?" Lincoln hissed.

"Alex, this is …" Agatha looked down at her hands.

Norman watched them all with wary eyes, his pencil poised above unfinished sums. Hector laid a steadying hand on his shoulder, but said nothing, his face taut as he exchanged a troubled glance with Helen.

Alex bore all this as though he were alone in the room. He smiled easily. "We should expect our first students by morning. Honestly, I can't wait to receive them. Hector, is the classroom ready?"

"It's ready." Hector's brow was so low it almost concealed his eyes from view. His hand had tightened on Norman's shoulder enough to make the boy wince.

Hector had taken up the role as general caretaker around camp, carefully maintaining the large building they had built specifically for learning—a wide open, high-roofed concrete shell crammed with the wealth of the Old World they had salvaged. They called it the Temple. Alex had mentored James under that roof for many years.

Hector had been trying to get Alex to do the same for Norman for almost a long. His efforts had been in vain.

Instead, Norman had been consigned to learning through the others in an opportunistic fashion, poaching titbits from each of them as they went about their daily lives. He enjoyed reading, but James had taken the liberty of perusing his reading list from time to time, and could only feel sorry for the boy; he made admirable efforts to read widely, but there was no coordination, no direction. The boy was a blind man feeling his way through an endless ocean of words and scripture, with nobody from the Old World to guide him.

He had done his best to guide Norman himself, but he was away too often, and was far from an authority. Agatha and Lincoln did what they could, but to fit in, Norman had to be invested with the zeal for the mission. The only one who could have done the boy justice was the only one who successfully ignored the boy's very existence.

Alex was too busy for the young man, too swept up in building their network of allies and trading partners. Since James had completed his scholarly training and taken to joining him on expeditions, Alex had made but the most cursory appearances in the classroom.

"Good," Alex said. "Then we'll be ready to receive them by morning. I trust you're all comfortable pitching in with the teaching?"

Helen leaned forward. "Just wait a second, Alex!"

"Why would Malverston ask for this? It's way out of character," Lincoln said.

Alex was impassive. "He's not a fool. He knows that the one who rules the masses is one who learns from history.

And if he can build a small army of people who know the Old World, he'll have everything he needs to lay the foundation of his own government."

Lincoln grumbled. "He's looking to stay in power … through education?"

"He underestimates us. He sees it as just a way of shushing the naysayers."

"So why does he need us? Plenty of people know the Old World." Helen held Hector's arm via a tight bunch of sleeve, waving him to keep his tongue. He looked furious. She, meanwhile, kept her voice level, though still she looked troubled, almost hurt. "We want him out of power, not to strengthen his position. All this time, we've asked to have our son taught, and we've sat quietly while you chased old first editions and dodgy salvagers. And now we're pulling out all the stops for *him*?"

"It seems we've made an impression on the town." There was no mistaking the note of pride in Alex's voice. "He's giving them what they want, but he's not thinking about how it'll change them, really wake them up to his filth. In the end, it'll undermine him. We might not even have to take any action at all, other than teach them all we know."

James had the urge to hold his head in his hands. He knew Alex had been up to something bound to sit with them poorly, but this was much worse.

None of them were convinced. That much was obvious at a glance.

Alex leaned forward, for the first time showing a hint of concern. "Look, we were always going to start schooling others, sooner or later."

"Yes, but God, Alex!" Lincoln said.

"Why them, of all people, to start? The most volatile political theatre we've encountered."

"On the contrary, they're the ideal candidates. They've held on to the old ways, mostly, in any case. They've just forgotten the value of what they know. It won't take long for them to remember. It's the perfect experiment. If it doesn't work, no harm to us; we'll have learned what doesn't work. If it does, Malverston's own people will dethrone him."

Hector stood up sharply, tipping his chair over in a fit of rage. His face was bright red and inflamed. He seemed to be struggling for words that were out of reach. He looked around at the others, looking for help, then down at Norman. For a moment it looked as though he would reach across the table for Alex, but then Helen's hand reached up to his shoulder and held firm. "And Norman?" he said. "He'll be able to participate in the classes?"

Alex's face was blank, then creased into an easy smile. "Of course, of course. I'm sure it'll be a great benefit to him." It was a skilful ruse, but in that momentary blankness, James had seen the truth: Alex hadn't given Norman a single thought. He wondered whether Hector had seen it too.

But if Hector sensed anything untoward, he made sure not to compromise his turn of luck. "Good," he said, his face poker-flat. He left the room in three bounding strides.

The others looked at their hands. Helen looked hurt, her

eyes flashing around at the rest of them. Then she set about packing away Norman's things into a knapsack, deliberate and slow. Norman sat with his head hung and his face pale, eyes wary. Once she was done, she slipped the knot tight and took his arm, standing to face the table.

"It's not fair," she said quietly. "You all know that."

Then she shepherded Norman out the door, nudging him when he turned back, his big eyes wide and confused.

The others stayed for a while, but not long. There was little left to say. Alex explained that they should expect their first batch of students at sunrise the following morning, and that was that. They departed the room slowly, lost in their own thoughts, so that James and Alex were alone.

James clicked his tongue. "I don't understand why you spurn him like that."

"What?"

"Norman. You've never given him the time of day."

Alex looked hurt. "I love him. I'd do anything for him, just as much as the rest of you."

"You know what I mean. You … you spent the first twenty years after the End preparing me for the mission. You gave up sleep and leisure, a wife, a family … You gave everything to make me what I am today because you believed that the future lay in teaching the young all we'd lost."

"That's right."

"Then why would you throw away a chance to teach another? He's here, right under your roof. He's a bright boy, and he wants to learn, so why haven't you done the same with him? Hector would give anything to have you take him into the classroom. Hell, anybody would. You're *the* Alexander Cain, now—"

"Careful. All that's for the stage, when we're out there. I'm just Alex, remember? I want it to stay that way."

"My point is that you're the biggest hope we have. You were born to lead people, so lead him. I don't understand why you're so keen to abandon him. Hell, you're bringing people from hundreds of miles away to be taught, but you can't bring yourself to sit at a table with a kid who has been right under your nose for almost ten years!"

"That's for political purposes. It's a means to an end. And in any case, I don't see you complaining about how I never had Lucian in the classroom. He's been around since the End, but he's never spent a single day with his head in a book."

"Don't dodge. Lucian chose his path. But Norman … You're so keen to abandon him. Why?"

Alex said nothing for a long time. Something not quite anger, but smouldering derision, lurked somewhere amidst his expression; some shadow that set his eyes askance. Eventually, he said, "He's blind."

James blinked. "Blind?"

"He only sees the world in front of his face, sees things for what they are."

"So do most people."

"Yes, but *you* didn't. You were a shining beacon in the dark, James, even before you could talk. You saw what might be, not just what you knew. I'd been grappling with the others for so long, trying to get them to act, to do something! I was alone. And then there you were, looking out at all those crumbling ruins, and you imagined, you dreamed. You had destiny! But Norman … he's just …"

"A boy?"

Alex sighed. He leaned back in his chair, brooding. "The boy has no sense of wonder. No destiny. I wouldn't know what to do with him."

"Teach him!" James paused, then he was speaking again before he knew what he was saying. "Or I will."

He hadn't meant to say that, but now that it was out, he knew he meant it.

How could I teach him? I never saw the Old World, either.

But if Alex wouldn't, he would try. He wouldn't leave the boy to devolve into one of the witless savages that eked out a life in the North.

Alex was looking at him strangely. "Is the reason you're focusing so much on this because you're afraid I'll ask you about what happened in the stables?"

James swallowed convulsively. He made to say something fast, desperate to curtail any opportunity to dwell on what happened. Already it was almost possible to pretend that it was all part of the mad blur between leaving Beth in the orchards, and arriving home. "What are you talking about?"

Alex didn't move, and yet his entire manner shifted. He had gone from companionable partner to cold stranger in an instant. "I know you, James. You saw something."

"It's all a joke!" James said. "I'm tired, he was crazy, and

I had a dizzy spell. He was waxing lyrical about all kinds of insanity, and I got swept up in it for a second, that's all."

"Just tell me. Please."

James laughed, leaning across the table. "For a moment I thought I saw moorland, and fog, and towns. Old towns. I thought it was Radden. I … I was sure it *was* Radden." He paused, then shrugged. "But it's just my imagination. I've never even seen the place. Anyway, it's all nonsense. Seeing other places, having visions, it's all bumpf."

Alex was quiet. Somewhere outside, some of the others were arguing. "Anything else?"

James shrugged. "There was a man. Some pale-faced guy with this big hyena grin on his face, and dark marks under his eyes."

Alex's face fell slack upon his skull, formless and drooping, like jelly thrown over a spear of rock. The colour drained from his skin until he was paler than the whitewashed wall behind him. But his eyes were the worst: haunted, sunken in his skull. "Dark marks?" he muttered.

James frowned. "That's right. But it was just heat madness, that's all."

Alex wiped his mouth with the back of his hand. "Yes. Yes, just madness."

"It was just my imagination," James said. "I've never seen anywhere north of Manchester. You know that. And so what? I saw some guy, a figment of my imagination. Somebody who looked like they'd misapplied mascara and—"

"—and looked a little like a wolf," Alex finished.

James stared. "How did you know that?"

Alex's brow flickered. "What did he say?"

"Alex …"

"What did he say?"

James sighed. "He said he was waiting."

Alex stood over what seemed an age, meandering his way around the room as though blind, steadying himself with chair-backs and upholstery. James's skin came out in gooseflesh, seeing him that way. He reached the door and turned around, looking more child-like than James had ever seen him. "And the frost?" he said. "Did you feel that too?"

James's throat closed down to a pinhole as he remembered the ice crystals that had evaporated off his temples the moment the man's hands had left his head. "How did you know about that?" he whispered.

Alex hung his head. He cursed under his breath. A long silence passed between them, and then he said, "We have to go."

"Where?"

"Radden."

James almost fell off his chair. "We can't! We just arrived. The students from the Moon will be here by morning. The others are up in arms." He flung his hands in the air. "And this is crazy! He was just a madman, like you said."

"No. He wasn't."

"How can you say that?" James yelled. He was on his feet. "There's no such thing as magic powers or psychic visions. You taught me that. Anyone with a mote of rationality knows that."

"James," Alex said, "look out the window. Does anything out there look like a world that subscribes to the rational? There's a reason the North is overrun with the Rapture sects, that the roads are overrun with zealots. It's so easy to think all this is God's punishment, or aliens swooped down and took everyone. It's just that crazy." He pulled the door open and stepped onto the threshold. "We have to go, as soon as possible."

"You're serious?"

Alex said nothing, just nodded.

"When?"

"Tomorrow."

James watched him until any doubt he was joking had dissipated, then said, "Fine, then I'm coming with you."

"Yes."

James realised he didn't have a choice, either way.

*

Later, one of James's pigeons fluttered onto the windowsill. He untied the scroll tied around its leg and read the fine cursive scrawled upon it. He recognised Ms McKinley's hand at once, and breathed a sigh of relief.

She had been the first person to ever reply to the endless messages he had sent across the land when he had been a boy, when he had been feverish with excitement, certain he could unite the world with a few handwritten greetings, and goodwill.

Since then, the messages they exchanged were the one thing James kept to himself. It was his little secret.

Today, however, his heart sank. The message ended with a shaking scrawl.

Looks like Malverston's tired of my meddling. I hear them coming. Be careful, you little shit.

CHAPTER 11

Canterbury cathedral hadn't known the ravages of the End. A few short years of vacancy had elapsed before survivors had once again sought shelter and guidance under its roof. Since, various groups had come and gone, but the transept floors had stayed swept, and the myriad spires had been well cared for. Like many other ancient buildings, the decay of time had left it almost untouched, especially compared to the modern homes that had all but melted into plasterboard sludge after a few short years.

The figures depicted in the stained glass windows, beauteous gilded things of dazzling complexity and splendour, stared out over the encroaching wild lands, untroubled and angelic.

It was the only place left anyone felt safe. And now Robert suspected even this last bastion was crumbling in the people's minds. A significant number of the city's eight hundred inhabitants had taken refuge here when the attacks had started and the wind farm had been destroyed. Most hadn't left since.

Robert had made the mistake of bringing some food—

food they couldn't afford to waste—hoping to ease their fears and quell the worst of the rumours. With so few men and their perimeter in shambles, it was all he could do.

Now they were upon him, hundreds of bedraggled figures, all soiled and hungry, demanding to be saved. Not long ago, these people had been his fellow citizens, his neighbours and friends. These were the people who had greeted him each morning and worked away in the fields beside him for years. He knew almost all of them by name and their everyday lives intimately.

But these creatures he barely recognised. Their wild, bulging eyes and bared teeth took up too much of their faces, and their reaching hands had become a wall of scrabbling talons. The racket was deafening, echoing under the high roof and smearing their voices into a riotous hubbub. Before he knew it, he was backing away towards the doors, and as a single dark mass, they followed.

Myriad questions bombarded him from every direction.

"Where are they now? How many of them?"

"What of our food stores?"

"Has there been word from the ambassadors?"

"They haven't gotten to the last of the grain, have they?"

"We haven't had power in days. When will the lights be back?"

"What are you doing to stop them? Why haven't you killed them all?"

"My children are hungry, you must bring us food! Where's Alexander?"

He backed up until his six-five frame was pressed flat

against the wall, and the maddening racket closed in an unbroken half-moon around him. Time and time again he tried answering, but could scarcely manage a few words before an uproar of protest silenced him; why was *that* question important, and not theirs? Frozen and powerless despite all his strength and stature, Robert felt like cowering for the first time in memory.

Then a single voice cut across them, one he knew but at the same time didn't recognise, so full of power and fury. "Be silent! All of you, shut up!"

It was a voice that usually carried a feminine breathiness, conveying peace and reserved consideration. It was one the city-folk were accustomed to hear subsumed into the susurrus of public socials, a dignified central component of any well-to-do congregation. Now it was rough edged and undercut by crass aggression. One would expect its owner to be wielding a freshly smashed glass bottle.

Sarah stood before Robert and her hair flagged out behind her in a forest of tangled ends. The blouse she had been wearing the past two days was spattered with mud and grease, and in her hand, instead of a glass bottle, were her thick-framed spectacles, almost opaque with dust. "I said *shut up!*" she roared.

Hundreds of voices died with her screech's ringing echo. The crowd shrank before her. Some fell back on their haunches, staring.

Sarah's form inflated and sank as she drew a single enormous breath. "How dare you?" she breathed. "How dare any of you?"

Suddenly, the crowd was not a crowd at all, but a gathering of scared men and women dressed in the same clothes they'd worn for days, their faces puffed from weeping and sunken with fatigue. There were no bared teeth now, only quivering lips. A few children whimpered, pressing their faces into their guardians' legs.

Sarah and Heather, the city's doctor, had entered through the barricaded side doors from the courtyard. Heather hung on the threshold still, her medical overalls in an unsettling state of disarray. She looked hangdog and almost grey with exhaustion. Like dandelions in a high wind, the city's elderly folk had wilted from the stress of being under siege. She hadn't emerged from her clinic for at least ten hours; he didn't think she had slept since before the attack.

Any other time, he was sure she would have been inundated with complaints of aches and ills, but right now, nobody seemed to have noticed her presence. All eyes were on Sarah.

Robert stepped away from the wall, and placed his hands over her shoulders. She twitched violently at his touch, and he thought she would lash out and strike him, but instead, she relented after a moment of tension. Then in a curious instantaneous transformation, she was Sarah again, a mere wisp of a woman, and the monster was gone. She choked. "How could you? Robert's trying to help us all, risking his life out there while you all cower in here, and you hound him like dogs!"

Shame fell over the room like a blanket. Eyes fixed on

far walls, floors, pews, and candle brackets, anywhere but her. The echoes died away and the cathedral was plunged into deep quiet.

Robert looked down on her in admiration. He hadn't known such power could come from something so small, yet moments ago, she could have toppled mountains. He squeezed her shoulders in thanks, and she gripped his hand in reply.

He cleared his throat. "The turbines are gone. Once the last of the gasoline is gone, our generators are going to die. After that, we'll only have our coal reserves. The lights won't be coming back on." He let the whispers whip through the room, but then continued in the most sonorous tones he could muster, before the panic could catch. "Our food stocks are thin, but if we work hard re-sowing, we'll pull through."

Mr Higgins, a senile, gentle old thing, stepped forward with his hands clasped. "And the others? What have we heard of our friends? Alexander? Messrs McKay and Creek?"

"No word." Before more than a shared inhalation could sweep the room, he hastened to add, "But that doesn't mean anything in itself. We know the convoy reached London safely, and that the council summit was due to begin. Alexander left with the others a little over twelve hours ago. So far as I'm concerned, that's no time at all. We should be prepared to hunker down for a lot longer. For now, we're on our own."

Sarah said, "They're still here, in the city. I know some

of you knew that." She stepped from Robert's reach. "We've been into the vaults, and things are missing. They're still amongst us, even now. We can't keep hiding in here, else we're just inviting them to keep inching closer. If we don't make a stand, then before long, they'll be pressed up against our doors and it'll be too late.

"I know you're all scared." She paused. "I'm scared too. I've never been so afraid—afraid of starving, of disease, of strangers coming to kill us, of the darkness.

"But the others are gone, and they might not be coming back. We can't keep waiting for them to save us, holed up in here like animals in a corral. We have to save ourselves."

What's gotten into her? She's always been so prim and quiet.

He felt a burst of pride. *Alexander always did choose his friends well. That man knows people better than they know themselves. I wonder whether he knew she had this in her.*

There was strength in the room, where only a minute before there had been only a wilted, listless darkness. Lethargy gave way to a single golden band of hope, threading every pair of eyes under the cathedral roof. Suddenly, he became aware that she had started something, and he hoped she was ready to step up to the plate, because these people were going to follow her, not him.

Then a voice rose up from the ether, and Robert's heart iced over.

"Fire!" The call came from outside. It wasn't a bellow intended to raise the alarm; it was the species of exclamation that escapes a person's mouth at the sight of certain mortal dangers. "Fire!"

Robert was the first to the door, forcing his way out as everyone rushed for the cobbled streets. He had barely emerged into the late afternoon light when he caught sight of the amber glow on the horizon. The conflagration had taken hold near the edge of the occupied portion of the city, reaching almost fifty feet into the air, furious raging flames billowing copious spires of black smoke, the kind that could only mean burning paper.

He knew what it was long before they came in sight of the building. It was the warehouse that most called the Library, a vast hanger that stored hundreds of thousands of volumes that they had painstakingly collected—those that hadn't yet been sorted for the vaults or sent as kindling for civilisation elsewhere. Countless antiques, first editions, rare finds and original manuscripts. All ablaze.

A wail swept over his head from behind, the cry of a mother who sees her child in peril. It was coming from Sarah.

She raced forward, but Heather was on her in a moment, grappling with the writhing librarian while crying, "It's too late! There's nothing you can do."

"No!" Sarah screamed. "It can't be. We have to do something. Robert, Robert, water. *Water!* Everyone, get water. We can save some of it, we have to."

"Sarah," Robert said. He had never felt so helpless. "It is too late. The fire's too high."

She screeched. "Do you know how long it took us—?"

"Yes." Robert didn't know how he kept his voice level, confronted with the raw pain etched into her cheeks, but he did it. He had to, for her. "I'm sorry."

She sank to the floor in Heather's arms, great hacking sobs shooting from her body. Her eyes were huge, enormous, bulging with bloodshot veins and tears the size of raindrops. Her mouth hung open in an inarticulate gape of terror and rage. Heather locked eyes with Robert and nodded toward the clinic. He nodded in reply; they needed to get her away before she did something foolish. He wouldn't put it past her to rush headlong into the pyre if it meant saving a single book.

The cathedral refugees were rushing toward the river with buckets and pails in their hands. Something had broken; they had been spurned into new life. They were going to take charge of their destinies. Perhaps now they stood a chance.

But it had come at a price.

"I'll kill them!" Sarah's shriek came from out of sight, over towards the clinic, but it seemed to pierce the bellowing flames, the crash of shattering glass, and the hundreds of hollering city folk. "I'll kill them all!"

Robert was left standing alone outside the cathedral, scanning the horizon for signs of approaching enemies. If they attacked now, there was little he could do but get to the clinic, and try to get as many running as possible. But it seemed the fire wasn't the opening salvo of a new attack; instead, he suspected, merely a symbol, a reminder that they were not alone.

Something was glimmering by his feet: Sarah's spectacles, one lens shattered upon the cobbles, the other cracked—each sliver catching the warehouse in reflection, burning down into a fractal infinity of roaring flames.

*

Something dark was on the move. It was far beyond the horizon, so far away she couldn't believe the world could be so large, but Billy could sense it. A long, thin, fuzzy-edged stain the colour of treacle, oozing across the land. She had first felt it a little over an hour before, a patch of shadow that could have lain under a wandering cloud, somewhere out of sight. But as her feet had carried her ever westward, toward the setting sun, the shadow had deepened and elongated.

Now, it could almost have been a snake, slithering across the unseen reaches of New Land—Enger Land, Daddy had called it. Enger Land. What a strange name.

Whenever she stopped, she slept. Each time, she dreamed, but on waking the dreams were already half forgotten. She was left with only muddled images. She had been standing in a street flanked by tall buildings, and the rain had been hammering down on darkened tarmac. She had stood to one side of a huddle of bedraggled people all bent over a twitching young boy. She could almost see his face under an unruly mop of black hair—

But the rest was a blur, fading fast. All that remained was a feeling, one of having touched someone, as if she had reached across a great distance and, somehow, bumped up against somebody.

But who?

She had been walking since she had left Sammy locked behind the storm drain door, and had avoided every tree as though they were hungry carnivores waiting to devour her. She was not eager to become lost to another forest any time soon. Instead, she had kept to the edges of open grassland, skirting bare rock outcrops and tracking ancient public walkways, past fallen farms, train yards, housing estates and motorways.

Just like back home, everywhere there were signs of Before—something Daddy, Ma, and Grandpa had kept secret from her until they had arrived in Enger Land. Though the rusting relics had been playgrounds since she could walk, she had never guessed there had been other people. She had only ever seen the three of them and a few passing tradesmen; all the stories, photographs, artworks and buildings had surely come from them.

But it wasn't so. Daddy had told her that Before there had been millions, all gone now, vanished. *Poof.* Into thin air.

Her mind still reeled. She couldn't imagine so many. And the world was so big, so very big.

She had suspected that it had been the fever, making him say those things, that all the wonders of which he told her were just dreams brought on by his sickness. But here, now, walking amongst all this, the rusted metal, crumbling homes, scattered precious jewellery, cooking utensils, photo frames, wires and the strange hulks of metal called *cars*, she had to believe it. It was all true.

And if that was true, maybe the Panda Man was real, too. It would be far less strange than the rest of New Land, the vast, unending graveyard.

The land had flattened of late. The rolling hills had given way to unceasing fields and meadows, the heather and tangles of knotted crops giving way to unbroken pasture—thousands of acres of grass that stretched toward the horizon, opening out in every direction. It was almost unnaturally flat, without a single rise or dimple in sight.

At some point she had passed a road marker upon a buckled green sign, the writing barely legible: *Salisbury - 4m*

Trying to ignore the foreboding she felt when she looked in the direction of that dark smudge afar, she pressed on, following the unyielding itch that arced down her legs, pulsing through her feet and into the ground. She kept on constant watch for others, but she was no longer desperate to see another human face, not like she had been before. In fact, she often found herself hoping she wouldn't find anyone, and that she would find herself inexplicably back at the cabin.

If other people in New Land were like the medicine women, she was better off taking her chances on her own.

Thoughts of Daddy were now ever present, a splinter growing in her mind. She had been gone too long. The Panda Man had sent her on a fool's quest into the unknown, and there was no end in sight; by now Daddy had either awakened to find her gone, in which case he would be angry—what if he tried to look for her? If he fell down the hill leading inland from the cabin, he would never make it back.

But the alternative was worse: he hadn't woken. And if he hadn't woken for this long, would he ever?

Slowly, her resolve dissolved, the edifice that Panda Man had set under her being eroded by dual images in her mind's eye: in one, Daddy clutched the cabin door, ghostly pale and spluttering bloody sputum as he toppled end over end towards the charred wreckage of the travellers' camp; the other showed him in ruinous repose beneath soiled bed sheets, his unseeing eyes staring up at the ceiling.

Soon, not even the fear the Panda Man had instilled in her, nor his promises that the task he had set could save Daddy's life, was enough to quell that all-consuming mental image. She had to be with him, even if that meant he was going to go away like Ma and Grandpa. The thought of doing what the Panda Man had asked, and then arriving back at the cabin only to find he had already gone, was too much to bear.

She was on the verge of turning back when the arch appeared.

One moment the endless grassy plain stretched away toward infinity, fringed by the ribbon where green met blue sky and clouds, and bordered only by distant streaks of ancient lumbering ash and oak. The next, she was facing a stone archway twelve feet high. It looked far older than anything from Before she had ever seen, half covered with creepers and ivy. The workmanship was jagged, but deliberate, the carving rough and ready. The stone was a mottled obsidian and flint colour, shining with slivers of igneous crystal and pyrite that swirled in complex vortices about its face. Atop it were patterns that looked like those Billy had seen at home but hadn't seen here in Enger Land—Daddy and Grandpa had called them *Celtic*—and at the very top, an inset carved symbol: a swinging bob upon a string. A pendulum.

She blinked, agape, and took a leap back. It hadn't grown up out of the ground, nor rushed up from afar; it seemed almost as though it had *slid* into view, as though she had been looking from the wrong angle before, and some trick of the light had hidden it.

But she knew it hadn't been there before. There had been so sign of it. And there was nothing else for a mile in any direction. She couldn't have wandered so close without noticing its presence.

Yet here it was, right before her.

At almost the same instant it appeared, the itch in her feet died, replaced by a sudden lack of certainty in direction and purpose. A lost sensation rushed in, almost nauseating.

She stood staring, all thought of Daddy gone from her mind. This was some other thing of the Panda Man's doing, some other bastardisation of reality and common sense. For a moment, she wasn't thinking of anything, then she realised that she was waiting for him to appear.

But nothing happened, bar a gust of wind blowing across the meadow as though only to amplify her sense of isolation. One of the pigeons that had been following her alighted atop the arch and bobbed along its ridge.

So it is real. Is that comforting, or not?

She couldn't decide.

She about faced, scanning the open expanse for a sign of pale cheeks and dark streaks, and that disturbing wolfish smile. But there was nothing.

And, somehow, she sensed that this wasn't *his* doing. This was something else. It felt different, somehow less potent. A shiver ran down her spine and into her limbs.

She considered ignoring it. She had been on the cusp of deciding to turn back. Daddy's face was hovering in her mind's eye again; even this apparition couldn't keep him from her thoughts now. She needed to get back to him before it was too late.

The pigeon strutting atop the arch fluttered down and alighted on her shoulder, bobbing and pecking at her pack in search of food.

She hesitated, then stroked its head. It was tame enough. Almost like a pet. That meant people.

"Get help, can't you?" she said, more to herself, stroking its head.

The pigeon cooed in reply, and cocked its head, an oddly human gesture that seemed to say, "Sorry, no can do."

She knew that was just her mind playing silly tricks, but the bird really *did* seem to have understood her.

She sighed. "You and your friends are following me. The least you could do is return the favour," she muttered. She smiled to herself. She was talking to a bird. It was good to be silly. It had been too long. "Go on, show me. Show me the way, birdie."

The pigeon cooed again, and this time took wing, flying through the arch. And as it did so, it quite perfectly vanished.

Poof.

Billy stared, blinked, and accepted what she'd seen. Too much oddity had already passed for disbelief.

The bird had disappeared just as the arch had blossomed from the ether: in the same impossible warping movement, sideways into some other space.

Enger Land is like the fairy tales Grandpa used to tell. All magic and spells. I wonder where the faeries and wizards are. Daddy said all that was make believe. Daddy was wrong.

The itch in her feet was gone, and she felt strange without it. It had been in her so long that to have it taken away so suddenly was like losing a hand.

But the birdie had shown her the way.

Daddy needed her, and she still intended to turn back—Daddy couldn't wait any longer; the Panda Man would have to find those men on his own—but not yet. The arch was too fantastic to ignore.

Billy stepped up to the stone arch that could not have been there and stepped through.

She expected to come falling out through the other side and find that the pigeon had been fluttering there, just out of view behind the archway the whole time. Instead, intense cold stole across her body, like a winter gale that reached down to her bones, and her skin contracted as ice formed in a thin layer over her head and limbs.

Then the meadow was gone, along with the blue sky.

She was in a murky gloom that was all too familiar. The half-light and clustered sunbeams had become etched into her memory, wrapped up with the trauma of her brush with death; she knew she was in a forest long before her eyes registered it.

Panic swelled behind her eyes.

She couldn't be lost under the trees again! Not now with the itch gone and Daddy fading by the second.

It had all been a trap. The Panda Man must have known that she was planning to turn back.

She cursed her foolishness. If she had only kept her word and seen it through, she might have saved Daddy. The Panda Man had promised, after all.

Now, she might have killed him and herself. She failed to stop a whimper passing her lips.

But it wasn't the same forest. That was obvious at a glance. The trees were bigger, bulkier, and much older, so old that the bark of their great trunks was like granite, and cobwebs thick and tangled as rope hung from the branches. The air, too, tasted old—not spoiled or foul, but prehistoric, so old as to have lost all life or discernible scent. From the tenebrous depths echoed a low, preternatural creaking.

And ahead, standing in the middle of a small clearing, was a low building that had long lost all paintwork or furnishings. She approached the hull of the structure, an iron-rusted brown-and-red husk with windows that had become opaque from weathering, blanketed heavily with moss and leaf litter.

A sign hung over the doorway. Though it too was rusted and covered with mud, to the point of being almost illegible, after squinting a few moments, Billy was able to sound it out.

Laurent's.

A few twisted metal stumps stood outside, which might once have been tables and chairs; but save for that, the building merely sprang up out of the forest, the only construction in sight bar the stone arch. She looked back through the arch, expecting to the see the plain from which she had come, but saw only the same tapestry of gnarled stone-like branches and knotted roots.

With a flutter of feathers, the pigeon dropped down onto her shoulder once more, and the two of them looked upon the strange building's carcass.

She tried to think of something to say, but after a full minute could only come up with, "I don't understand."

How could I? It's magic, like Grandpa said. Maybe the storybooks were all *true.*

And in the stories, there was only one way to go: forward.

Follow the yellow brick road.

Stepping with ginger care over the black soil, shuddering as the ice crystals on her skin melted into a cold glistening sheen, she stepped up to the door, which was coarse and jagged with a garish mauve patina. She reached out once, jerked back in hesitation, then took a deep breath and, holding Daddy's face in her mind, pushed her way inside.

The door squealed, and Billy's heart leapt, thundering

into her throat when a rattling impact exploded at her feet. She plastered herself against the wall, gasping.

A lump of dented metal lay before her, the bell that had hung over the door. Massaging her chest, she stepped into a thick mist of dust, waving her arms before her to part the great chunky motes.

There were tables and chairs of all kinds, the upholstery rotted and lank on the bare frames. Out back was a counter with a covered display case, empty, but with enough room for a large selection of foodstuffs. Scattered around the edge were tall boxes, each with a tray set upon it dotted with dark, lumpy dust. The entire space was empty and silent, a tomb.

She approached the closest tray and picked up one of the strange lumps, holding it up to the lesser murk shining in through the door. It was soft, some kind of plant matter, maybe leaves. She frowned.

Then, from behind her, a rough yet lilting voice, "Tea."

She whirled with a gasp and the tray clattered to the floor. The pigeon took flight in a fit of wing beats, and for what seemed an age, all she could do was stare, unseeing, and hold up her hands in defence. "Please, *don't!*" she screamed. Then she fell, tripping over the tray's spilled contents, and went sprawling.

A beat passed, then the voice came again. It sounded amused. "My apologies. I must work on my entrances." A pause. "Please forgive my rudeness."

Billy scrabbled to her feet and observed a bedraggled man dressed in a flowing purple trench coat, leaning back in one of the chairs with one leg crossed over the other. He sported a rough crop of stubble and his hands and face were dirty, but he looked cleaner than the medicine ladies. His twinkling eyes dominated his face, hooded by truly impressive grey eyebrows, so bushy and pointed they protruded half an inch up toward his hairline.

His expression was frank and friendly, but strange. Upon his head was perched a dog-eared hat, from which sprouted a long, wilted feather.

The man smiled. "Would you care to join me?" he said and gestured to a steaming teapot before him, around which were satellites of cups, saucers, sugar and cream, all spick and span, shining white bone china.

None of it, nor he, had been there a moment ago.

The wizard, she thought automatically. She sat without complaint, her pulse still yammering in her ears. She took a shuddering breath and tried to look unafraid. But her memory of Sammy and her sidekick, and the feel of their grubby, diseased hands running over her stomach, was still fresh in her mind.

"You look like you could do with a fresh cuppa," the man in purple said and clapped his hands together, a strangely androgynous gesture from a man with such a hardened, street-wise visage. He set about the cups and saucers with practised showmanship, setting them in a row and pouring golden liquid from the pot with dainty finesse, his back absurdly straight. He then pushed the cup across at her, and mimed drinking with a wink, his pinkie cocked skyward.

Billy drank. Liquid velvet trickled past her tongue, the flavour somewhere between tart tannin and sticky citrus delight. The steam wafted into her nose and she was overwhelmed by the scent of lemons—redolent and nectar sweet. Tears came to her eyes before she knew why. By the time she realised it was identical to the perfume Ma had worn, she was weeping in earnest.

The man in purple watched without concern and took a sip from his own cup, smacking his lips and sighing. Then he put the cup down and rubbed his hands together. "Good! Refreshments are done. Now, to business. I have plenty to do." He paused as though in afterthought and touched her arm. She didn't recoil. "Can you be brave a while longer?"

Billy put down her cup and turned her head away from the steaming vapour. It was too painful to smell; Ma could have been but a foot away. She wiped her tears on her sleeve angrily. "Yes," she muttered, her voice husky with pain.

The man smiled, a real, approving smile. "That'a girl. Things get stranger and stranger from here on. But bravery will pull you through anything."

Billy blinked the last of the moisture from her eyes and sat back. She had had enough of this freakery. The tea was delicious, like nectar, but it had set a hive of emotions buzzing in her head. Now she wanted to leave as fast as possible. "Who are you?"

He nodded, again with a note of approval. "No dilly-dallying. I can jive with that. Neither of us belongs here, after all. I bet you feel it, too, don't you? That little tug down in your belly that tells you you're not meant to be sitting here?"

Billy nodded, frowning.

How could he know that?

"Because I have certain privileges," the man said as though she had spoken aloud.

She gaped.

He laughed. "My darling, it's a pleasure." He took her hand in his scruffy paw and kissed it. The feather in his cap bobbed.

Billy took her hands under the table and swallowed. "I don't understand," she said flatly.

He arched an eyebrow, took a look around at the crumbled ruins of *Laurent's*, and nodded. "A fair statement." He shivered in disapproval, tutting as he took in the sight of the teashop as though seeing it afresh. "My, the place really has gone to shambles. Terrible management, you see." He glanced at her. "It usually looks a lot nicer, believe me. And there are more"—he licked his lips—"tasty treats. A shame. Good thing I had the forethought to order the tea." He grinned, a mischievous glint to his eye, and took another sip of citrus infusion.

Billy shook her head. "I don't ..."

"Understand. Yes, I know. Forgive me. I was sent on short notice." He pushed his cup aside and steepled his fingers, leaning across the table. "Please, bring me up to speed. It's so hard to keep track of everyone's minutiae."

Everyone?

Her mouth worked of its own accord. "Daddy's sick. I was taking care of him, looking for food. Then a ... man ...

appeared. I think he's a man. He might be a … a wizard, like you. He said I had to find two men who I've been seeing in my dreams or Daddy would die. Then I knew where to go. I just knew. I got lost in a forest, two old ladies tried to kill me, and then I found the arch. Now, I'm here. And I have no idea where to go." Saying it all aloud scared her. It was all silliness of the strangest dream. Suddenly, she felt very tired.

When she said the word *wizard*, the man in purple chuckled indulgently, in good humour, the way grownups always did when she said something they thought childish. Yet at the same time, she thought she might have caught a change in his eyes—for the briefest moment, they might have flashed a shade of violet.

"I apologise on behalf of my colleague. You're being bounced around quite a bit, aren't you?" he said in distaste. "But it's the only way to get you to where you need to be. If there were any way to have you safe and sound right now, it would already be done. But our hands are tied, and things are set in motion." He shrugged. "We're improvising."

"Who is *he*?" She didn't say Panda Man; she suspected it would only make her sound silly, like a baby.

He held up a finger. "That is a very long story, and one you will hear in due course. But not now. You need to get where you're going, and find your mystery men. You'll be safer with them. Then we can start setting things right."

She leaned forward. "I was safe with Daddy! Why would you take me away from him so I was in danger, then send so far away to make me safe again?" She shook with anger, rising out of her seat, but his hand on her shoulder forced her back down.

"You were not safe," he said slowly. "I promise you that. Things might be okay for now, but soon enough, all manners of people and things will see you. Your light is sparked. Soon, they'll all come for you."

"Light?" She swallowed. "Sammy talked about the light. I thought she was a crazy lady."

"She was. But the light is real. Real as mud." The pigeon flew in through the open door and alighted on the man's shoulder. "These guys are evidence of that. They're following you by now, I bet?"

She didn't deny it.

He nodded. "It'll get worse fast. If we don't get you to Cain's lot soon, you'll be exposed. And if Chadwick gets you ..." He shuddered. "The truth is that you're cleaning up our mess. If things had gone to plan, you and Fol would be busy gathering the others by now. But Fol couldn't wait. He never waits!" His lip curled. "Things should never have been allowed to go this far. I told him about meddling with this world!" He gaze had grown distant and his expression sour, as though he was speaking more to himself than her. Then his eyes cleared, and he shook his head. "The thing is, this world is patchy. Some places are bright, some dark. Our reach is limited. You probably noticed ..." He pointed down at her feet. "You suddenly felt lost, I bet, hmm? Places like Salisbury—where you just came from—they're dark. My colleague can't see that place. That's why you're dealing with me."

Why am I seeing you at all?

He nodded sagely. "A fine question. Like I said, all I can say is that you'll get your answers, in time. First, we have to stop Chadwick."

"Who's he?"

"He's a problem, that's who." He shook his head. "A spiteful shame, he showed such promise. He could have put things to right long before you were born, if things had played out different." He shrugged. "But that's not the way the pendulum swung." He reached into his pocket, rummaged for a moment, then brought out a mildewed scrap of folded paper and pushed it across the table. "Here, this should get you to the next leg of the journey. You'll see your Panda Man again soon."

She took the paper and unfolded it, revealing an ancient-looking map, drawn in what seemed to be charcoal and ochre. The outline of New Land was the same as Grandpa's maps, but this one was bare save for a few markers that brought her arms out in gooseflesh: a winding path that led from a perfect miniature drawing of the cabin, to dark trees—she guessed the forest where she had become lost—then on to the arch.

"That's where I have to go?" she said.

He nodded. "Just follow the yellow bricks," he said.

She smiled despite herself. Then, something about his words percolated into focus. "I never said I called him Panda Man," she said.

His eyebrows shot up past his hairline. "No?"

"No."

"Hmm. How strange," he said. Then that mischievous little grin blossomed on his face again, those enormous eyebrows twitching.

Billy returned to the map. She was in the process of folding it carefully away when, quite suddenly, a young woman wearing a black apron strode into the room and approached the table.

Billy gave a yelp of surprise. She hadn't seen a woman who didn't look mean enough to slice her up since Ma had gone away.

She watched in fascination, but the woman didn't pay her any mind, almost as though she didn't see her at all. She walked right up to the man in purple, and bent over him to murmur in confidence. "Our time is up," he said. "I have another appointment."

"With who?"

"A lovely young woman who's quite forgotten her own name."

His companion cleared her throat.

The man in purple nodded. For a moment he seemed much, much older; it was the heavy accepting nod akin to those Grandpa had given when facing grave news. He dismissed her with a flutter of his eyelids, and the woman stepped back towards the counter. She didn't even glance in Billy's direction.

The man climbed to his feet and sighed. "I can't stay. Busy, busy, always so busy." He tapped Billy's pocket, where the map sat. "Take care of that. And when it fails, follow your feet."

"You're going?"

"I must."

"Tell me more first!"

"I'm afraid there's no time."

He straightened his hat, adjusting the feather. "Give my regards to your Panda Man." He said the last words with a certain relish, as though they amused him immensely.

Billy was standing too. She almost stepped to bar his way, but knew it would be futile. But he couldn't leave. She had so many questions—and here, now, she wasn't alone. "Why all this for me?" she said.

"Because you're a special one, Billy. There's a great many things lying ahead for you. A *great* many. That's why we're going through all this trouble to keep you safe." He patted her shoulder. "It was a pleasure. Now, I must go."

"Will I see you again?"

"Probably." He shrugged. "But it might be a while. And … far, far away from here."

He turned, and addressed the woman. "Shall we?"

The woman nodded stoically.

The two of them headed towards the counter, in the direction of the back room.

The man in purple turned and winked. "We'll have a real chinwag another time." He flicked his eyes to the ruin around them. "Like I said, it's usually much more impressive." Perhaps Billy saw that same violet twinkle in his eyes, then. Perhaps not. "Take care, Ms Peyton," he said, then he and the woman walked out back, and Billy knew they were gone.

She wasted no time in leaving, and made her way back to the arch. She braced against the cold she knew would come, and threw herself through the archway. She knew what to expect, but still she cried out when the ice enveloped her, and bright blue daylight suddenly flooded her eyes. She stumbled, almost at a running pace, and staggered to a stop upon the endless flat meadow.

She turned back to look behind her. She was almost unsurprised to see that the arch was gone.

Had any of that really happened? It had been a mere moment ago, but now with the wind on her face and the smell of fresh grass in her nose, it seemed so silly. And all this seemed too *normal,* as though there were no space for magic.

Then she saw the pigeons. They were everywhere now, swooping overhead in great circling flocks and lining the boughs of the distant trees from edge to edge. Her guts trembled.

There isn't much time, she thought. But the voice in her head sounded suspiciously like that of the man in purple.

The itch in her feet was still absent, but now she had the map. She unfolded it and followed the path laid out. The next stop: a strange collection of stones, some vertical and some laid horizontal atop them, all arranged in a wide circle. If she was reading the map right, it wasn't far.

She put her back to where the archway had been, aligning the map in her hands to the path so that it was directly ahead, and started walking.

"Just follow the yellow bricks," she muttered. "Hang on, Daddy. I'll be home soon."

*

Norman grunted as somebody pinched his arm.

Allie muttered in his ear. "You were leaning on me."

He blinked. He hadn't been aware of anything. "I was?"

"You were moaning."

"Guess I fell asleep."

Concern flashed across her face. "Are you sure you're okay? If you're not up to this …"

"I'm fine."

She nodded slowly. "That dream again?"

"The same." But it hadn't been. There had been somebody else there this time, someone new. A young girl with fire-red hair had been standing behind Alex, Lucian and the others. And again, that same cold stabbing into his skin like broken glass.

He shook himself and turned back to the councillors at the bench. He sensed everyone holding their breath as Evelyn steepled her fingers. She cleared her throat. "The council recognises Alexander Cain and Agatha Shute of New Canterbury."

Norman focused on Agatha, her thick cataracts and blank expression only more obvious than usual, amidst the composed dignity of the other councillors. Several times already she had looked confused, but Alexander had leaned across and assuaged her each time.

The dementia was growing worse. It had held at a steady gradual decline for a long time, but it seemed the trauma of conflict had finally tipped her into a downward spiral.

Between her, Alexander, and Evelyn, they comprised the original trio, the old guard.

More for appearances than anything else. We need a little old school right now.

Evelyn pointed toward two people to her left: Rush and Oppenheimer. Both were the rugged sort, and their ages were impossible to tell, lost somewhere between sixty and ninety. Beyond them sat a woman in her late forties, fat and slouching, her pudgy eyes observing the room with reserved coldness.

"Geoffrey Oppenheimer and David Rush of the market communities in Norwich and Southampton. Maria Thompson is a temporary representative of a recently discovered federation of villages to the far east."

Oppenheimer and Rush nodded curtly. Thompson didn't respond, her toad-like eyes dark under her prominent brow.

Evelyn continued the introductions, naming representatives of Bristol, the districts of Cornwall, Northampton, Oxford, Ashford, Bath, and Gloucester. All of them were absent. Of around twenty seats at the bench, only six were chaired.

"Doctor Dennis Abernathy of Exeter, and"—she cleared her throat—"Mr Oliver Farringdon are both stranded elsewhere."

Six of almost two dozen. That's all that made it. Christ.

"Thank you all for coming," Alexander said. His voice boomed in the vast expanses of the council chambers. All eyes fixed on him, including those of the other council heads. "It's been a hard year for us all. But I'm heartened to know that despite everything that's been thrown our way, we still sit here, now, together.

"But we can't afford to forget our situation. We have to decide what we're going to do, and fast."

Everyone glanced around at one another, their faces blank.

It's like they're hoping a grand solution is going to leap from the ether and dance before them.

Alexander continued. "For now, we're safe here. But as you know only too well, we cannot leave, and London is now a gauntlet. Just gathering here has cost us … we've lost friends." He cleared his throat, his eyes flitting to the empty chairs. "We haven't much time."

Evelyn nodded. "First order of address: the hostiles that have emerged in the wake of winter's peak."

The room's attention narrowed. Now they were getting somewhere.

She gestured to the room. "None among us are unaffected by this scourge. At the rate the threat is growing we, our allies, and all future hope for our way of life, face extinction. Already, they have destroyed many of the outer baronies. The web we've woven is coming undone."

"It's all so much smoking char," Oppenheimer growled.

Murmurs of acknowledgement and anger filled the room.

Alexander broke in. "New Canterbury bore the brunt of the earliest attacks. We've been dealing with them for weeks."

A grumble. Everyone turned to Rush, the Bristol ambassador, a harried red-faced man with a bird's nest rim of hair surrounding a bald sunburned crown. Over a hundred had set out as part of his convoy. Less than a dozen had survived. His piggy little eyes were haunted. "Where did they come from?"

Alexander shook his head. "No telling. One day one of our scavenging parties came across starving refugees by the coast, larger than any group we'd seen for months. On End Day we found a man beaten half to death on the edge of New Canterbury. He told us about others close by, watching the city. He didn't survive. The one who brought him in, Rayford Hubble, was murdered soon after." He paused. "To my knowledge, that was first blood."

Everybody looked around. There were no objections.

"They started this," Marek called from the forward rows. "Animals. Yellow cowards. That's all this is, a mob of criminals." He was on his feet, stocky shoulders bunched.

Evelyn waved him be seated.

He hovered a moment, but relented under her imperious glare, grumbling.

Oppenheimer, looking frail and red-eyed, spoke in a near whisper. "He's right. They're thugs. They are just using all this hunger and sickness to hit us while we're down. That's how it's done in the North: no leader, no plan, just blood and taking. Power changes hands like the tides up there." He had been hunched over like a wounded animal, but now he unfurled in a fit of decrepit rage.

His voice swelled like a kettle approaching the boil.

"There can't be more than a few dozen of those cowards. They're preying on fear, but pitched against what we can bring to bear, they're nothing." He stabbed the bench with a skeletal finger. "We take our guard and a dozen other able-bodied, full armour and combat armament. We'll hunt them down like rats and end this."

The other councillors visibly tensed.

"He shouldn't be up there," Richard muttered. "He's in pieces. Emotionally involved."

Allie huffed in mock laughter. "Everyone's emotionally involved."

"Look at the poor old goat. He's in tears."

"He has every right to be. So do most of them. Oppenenheimer looks like he's about to snap."

"And Agatha … look at her. She doesn't even know where she is." He sounded dismayed. "This is cruel. She should be back home."

Allie grunted. "Along with the rest of us."

"Quiet," Norman said.

They glanced at him and fell silent.

Evelyn was speaking in a placating tone. "Mr Oppenheimer, we all appreciate you've experienced a loss, but I beg you keep composed."

Though soothing and quiet, her voice could have cut glass. But Oppenheimer was heedless.

"I've stood in their valleys. They're using low-calibre rounds, single-shot rifles. Old things, probably relics that in the Old Times fired nothing but buckshot. Bunch of vultures looking to chip away at all we've built until there's nothing left—we've stood for it long enough. Let us end this, now!" His voice built to a throaty old-man bellow toward the end, and the chambers rang with its echo for several moments, leaving an awkward silence in its wake. His face streamed with tears.

Nobody broke the silence. All eyes once again settled on Alexander.

He spoke after laying a hand on Oppenheimer's shoulder for a long, measured moment. It was enough to bring the old man's tirade to an end. "If that were so, Geoffrey, we would be out there right now. You have my word on it. But it is not so. Yesterday, we discovered the hideout from which they launched their attacks on New Canterbury. Cleared out, abandoned, but enough to give us plenty of information.

"They're slavers. Wherever they go, they pick up the strong and those they can use as leverage. The rest, they kill, and then they burn everything. If they have that kind of power, they number far greater than the dozens. There are hundreds at the very least. With slave labour to swell their ranks, we may be facing an army of thousands."

"*Thousands?*" Rush hissed. "There's been no such force since the End. We can't face something like that!"

"Let him finish," Thompson croaked, her froggy eyes bulging. "I would hear the rest, Mr Cain."

Alex nodded his thanks. "They've been scattered, razing the weakest settlements. Now they're moving on to cities, still in small groups, relying on guerrilla strikes. But if they want to challenge us, then they'll need to regroup. Then, we'll see what we're really up against."

"Like I said, a handful of nuts," Oppenheimer cried.

Alexander's face tensed. "Maybe you're right. But if *I'm* right, we could put a weapon in the hands of every man, woman, and child, and still they'd wash over us like floodwaters over a pebble."

"How sure are we of all this?" Thompson said.

In answer, Alexander drew the crowd's attention to the front of the crowd, close to Marek. From the masses ambled John DeGray, his rotund figure casting an apple-bellied shadow across the far wall. Grey and grizzled, encumbered by an armful of documents and dusty notes, his ruddy face looked upon the room with professorial dignity.

He cleared his throat and pushed his glasses along the bridge of his nose, completing the picture.

Norman felt his heart sink. This was Alexander's comforting authority figure?

He was a scholar in a warzone.

The chambers slithered with unsettled shuffling. Only Richard looked stoic; when John started speaking, the young student leaned forward, enraptured.

Norman couldn't help thinking it would be a long time before John DeGray surrendered his black king chess piece to his sole student.

"The council's reckoning is sound. The numbers support the stated estimates. According to our records, the British populations stood between fifteen and twenty-five thousand. In the wake of the famine, an optimistic estimate may be ten thousand, maybe less."

"Then all this talk of a slavering horde of thousands must be so much blither," Thompson cried. She gave a titter, bristling in indignation, as though the whole summit were nothing but a waste of her time. "We know nothing of the rest of the world. For all we know, Britain alone still harbours life. If this *is* true … it would mean the majority of the known surviving human race stands against us!"

"Yes, it would," Alexander said, his eyes glittering jewels.

The exasperated smile on Thompson's face wilted.

The room erupted into a rumbling hubbub, and it was some time before the council even tried to restore order.

After looking out across the bobbing heads a long while, Norman became aware of Allison's hand clutched in his own, cold and clammy.

"Nothing like an old-school lecture to hammer home the facts of life, shit and all," Richard said bitterly. Suddenly, he didn't sound half as enthused.

*

A thud sent dozens jumping in their seats. Agatha's hand had slammed down on the bench, her misty gaze suddenly sharp, yet confused and angry. "Malverston can't ge' away wi'this. We have to move against him, now! For the sake of the mission!" She blinked and her face softened, looking around at her fellow councillors. "Oh, my … you're all so *old*," she muttered. She sounded hurt and afraid.

Alexander rested a hand over hers and leaned in close. They whispered in collusion a while, and her shoulders relaxed some.

"Who's Malverston?" Allie said.

Norman shrugged as Alexander returned his gaze to the crowd.

Agatha looked lost and sad, like a child lost in a vast bustling crowd. But soon that milky stare had returned, and she was gone again.

The room shifted, everyone uncomfortable in their own skins.

Thompson called them to silence. "What else do we know about them?"

Alexander gestured to DeGray.

John looked startled, cleared his throat and flipped a page or two in his chart. "Well," he said finally, "not a whole lot."

"What about weathering the siege?"

"Communications will be our greatest problem. We may stand a chance of relying on our reserves for weeks, if not months, but our respective homes … they will have to take it upon themselves to organise a defence."

Norman felt a twinge of unease as he thought of New Canterbury. All they had was Robert and Sarah. How would they cope with being charged with the fates of eight hundred? Worse, eight hundred accustomed to being led by the great Alexander Cain.

Robert was a silent type, a protector, not a politician.

A scowl emanated from Richard's direction.

"Looks like DeGray's lecture is getting cut short," Allie said.

Marek was on his feet again. "All this talk of cowering in the dirt is giving me a gut ache," he snarled. Beside DeGray's soft flabby form, Marek looked stark and primal. "Grow some balls, the lot of you. We need to talk offence."

Richard tutted as forlorn cries of *"well said"* and *"hear, hear!"* rose from the crowd. An obsequious grimace crossed his face, as though feeling his master's embarrassment for himself.

He really thinks all this is just academic, Norman thought. *As if the two of them can ride it out on the sidelines like Old World reporters. This war's going to steamroll him flat.*

"The council does not recognise unelected speakers," Evelyn hissed.

"Enough with all this posturing, you crooked old fools!" Marek bellowed. "We've got our backs to the wall, our friends are being burned alive, and you're playing dress-up with your noses in the air. Get your heads out of your arses, and let's talk brass tacks!"

The room was struck rigid, the low murmur frozen out of the air.

A muscle jumped in Alexander's jaw.

Norman winced despite himself. For any emotion to show on Alexander's face at all meant below roiled a great ocean of fury.

All we have left are appearances. This veil of normalcy, of officialdom. And Marek just shot it to hell.

The silence stretched on a beat too long, as stark reality rained down upon them. Norman saw something else entirely before him now: a bunch of scared idiots pretending to be something they would never be: a nation, kindred—

Then, a throaty roar akin to a lion's rose from the rear of the room. "Brass tacks it is, then!"

The heavy doors had been thrust ajar, and a small group of men stood in the doorway, framing a skeletal, ancient man with a goatee that came down to his chest, and the beaten barrel of an old hunting rifle slung over his back. He looked too fragile to bear its weight, but his back was unbowed, and his eyes twinkled with the fire of a much younger man.

The chambers fell quiet in an instant. Alexander rose to his feet and hurried from the bench, abandoning his magisterial dignity. Despite the ugly atmosphere, a warm smile dominated his face.

He embraced the twig-like shadow of a man at the rear of the chambers. Many in the crowd rose to their feet, craning their necks, mouths ajar.

"Finally," Norman said.

Trust the old bastard to leave it to the eleventh hour to poke his head in.

"Who is that?" Allie said.

Evelyn spoke over them all, answering for him. Even her icy tone had melted some. "The council recognises Sir Oliver Farringdon of London."

"Handle's been '*Lincoln*' since the Big Curtain, if it pleases the council," the old man growled. He sported sideburns and a grizzled shock of white hair to complete the

King of the Jungle appearance. His voice was tired but hearty, in an *'I've been through this a thousand times and I mean to go on a thousand more'* kind of comfortable familiarity.

"Give him a top hat, and he'd look like the Abe, himself," Richard said, awed.

"That's the joke, honey," Allie said.

Evelyn's voice had sprouted a tone of grudging fondness beneath its icy veneer. "The council recognises Mr Lincoln." She paused.

Jesus, it's almost like she's got something caught in her throat. Her, of all people.

"We had word you and your party were stranded at City Airport. We …"

"Struck me off, dear madam?" He gave a bark of laughter, a sound that almost picked Norman up off his seat. "Nonsense. It'll take more than a few shield-beating natives to take me down."

Alexander had yet to take his hands from the old man's shoulders. They spoke in hushed tones, but the silence in the chambers was now so deep that everyone could hear.

"Good timing."

"Looks like it. Impeccable as ever, if I do say so myself. What did you do, sing *'Gloomy Sunday'*? You know you can't hold a C-sharp for shit."

They were walking down the aisle, flanked by Lincoln's companions. They were heading for the raised circle before the bench, carrying something wrapped in a thick blanket.

It seemed the chambers could have quieted no further,

yet they did just that; milky-eyed Agatha had stumbled from the bench. Having sat through the proceedings in near silence, staring up at the dust motes dancing in the sunbeams, she now made a beeline for the men by the door. There were tears in her eyes.

Lincoln approached her with solemn grace, and bowed deeply. He took her hand and kissed it. "My lady," he muttered.

She giggled like a schoolgirl. "Ye old dog," she said. She didn't sound more than eleven years old.

Lincoln straightened and turned to Alexander. "You've been taking care of our good mother, I trust?"

"I'm forgettin', Oliver," Agatha said. A change had come over her, a brief clearing of the clouds. "But I'm still in here." She blinked tearfully, taking no notice of the crowd. "I probably don't have long … It's good to see you."

"And you, my lady."

The mission's three original councillors, together again.

Norman swallowed. An immovable lump had lodged in his throat.

They had raised him after his parents died, that night he got the scar on his forehead. He'd lost his memory of his mother and father, in any case. These three were all he'd ever had.

Before he knew it, he was on his feet. He heard Allie's protests only distantly, passing through the crowd as though in a dream. He didn't even bother with his cane; the pain in his ribs was dull and distant. The crowd's stares glanced off him, failing to penetrate.

So this is what it's like to be one of them.

They spotted him from afar, and the same expression shone from each of their faces: relief.

They must think I'm stepping forward to meet my great destiny. Rising up at the last minute, and all that. Why not? Let them have it.

A voice in the back of his mind cleared its throat. *Isn't that exactly what you're doing? Like it or not, you're involved now.*

"My boy!" Lincoln cried, gripping him with his iron-hard workman's hands.

"I … I … you're all here," Norman said.

"Always, darlin'." Agatha smiled, caressing his arm. "Must be damn awful, seein' me every day and knowin' I don't see you back. For the both o' you." She glanced at Alexander.

They said nothing, didn't need to. Norman's chest ached.

Lincoln was looking around expectantly, searching the crowd. "Lucian?"

Norman shook his head. "They have him."

Lincoln's brow furrowed, but his lip twisted in a smouldering grin. "Well I'm not weeping yet. If anyone's going to pull a miracle out of his arse, it's that one." He turned to his men, who were lowering their strange load onto the ground. "Shall we?" He gestured to the bench.

Norman smiled and made to return to his seat. But before he could take a step, he was jerked back. Looking down, he found three hands clasped around his arm.

"Where d'you think you're goin', sugar?" Agatha said.

"Now's your time, stud. Great destiny, and all that," Lincoln growled.

Alexander said nothing. His eyes said it all.

Norman felt himself nodding. What choice was there?

They headed back to the bench. Norman took a seat beside Lincoln, both of them to Alexander's left. With two more chairs filled, the councillors' bench didn't look quite so bare. He tried not to wonder whose seat he was sitting in right now—were they trapped, or rotting somewhere out in the city?

He kept his eyes resolutely on the table, trying to ignore the pressure of hundreds of stares from the audience.

Cross your fingers for me, Allie. This could go badly.

Lincoln grumbled as he eased himself down, laying his rifle down on the bench with a reverberating clatter.

"How did you get here, Mr Lincoln?" Evelyn said.

Lincoln clapped his hands together and rubbed vigorously. "Well we were pinned down over at City Airport, just like you said," he roared. "And, boy, they didn't want us there. Rounds going over our heads every other second. I thought we'd be blue and bloated by sundown."

His companions, who were all young dirty men, had stepped back from the package and stepped to the side. They were wiry and strong, gaunt-faced and stoic, but there was no hiding their exhaustion. Each of them was liberally covered with odd scrapes and bruises, charred by hot shrapnel, and half-blinded by dirt.

"But?" Alexander said.

Lincoln shrugged. "Well, boys and girls," he said, addressing the room at large, "would you believe an old goat's tall tale?"

"Stop playin', Oliver. I have minutes before I git back to droolsville," Agatha said.

"When they stopped shooting, we came out and saw their banners all over the city—they wanted us to see. They were marching north." He barked, and slapped his knee. "Praise God for small miracles, folks, because they're gone."

By the time Lincoln finished, the room was on its feet, cheering.

*

"They'll be back," Evelyn said. Even her icy crispness couldn't quite stamp out the celebrations.

People hugged and cheered. From elsewhere in the tower echoed laughter from the wounded and those tending them on the higher floors. Norman spotted Allie and Richard embracing, and he smiled.

He would have given a whole lot to be up there holding her, then. Mystery or not, good news was good news, and he'd seldom had opportunity to celebrate of late. He'd have liked to do it with her.

He settled for a hearty pound on the back from Lincoln and a shared smile of relief with Alexander.

The jubilation died down and eventually they were all seated again.

"It seems the knife is no longer at our throats," Alexander said. "Perhaps we have a little time to prepare. If they are gone, we may stand a chance of communicating our plan to all of us who remain."

"For the grand finale? The big showdown on horseback?" Thompson snorted. "What is this? *The Lord of the Rings*?"

"It is what it is," Norman said. He blinked, surprised that he had spoken. Yet he found that the words came easy, and the pressure of all the stares afar failed to rattle him. "We've been suffering too long to go on wittering. We're in the shit, and we have to dig our way out. Marek's right: brass tacks, and now!"

The crowd bustled with cries of assent.

"Braah, he speaks the truth!"

"Leastways, the young'un sees sense."

"The Chosen One's got a tongue, after all. Hear him, every'un!"

That last cry had had a rough and gravely sheen, but had a touch too much of Allie and Richard's voices to miss.

He thanked them silently.

Lincoln growled appreciatively, and his eyes twinkled with amusement as he turned them upon Evelyn and Thompson.

Evelyn shook her head with a tired sigh. Thompson scowled in turn and put her hands up in mock surrender.

"What is this you've brought before us?" Evelyn blustered, jutting her chin in the direction of the package in the centre circle.

"Ah! A treat for us all, and no mistake!" Lincoln said. His voice was suddenly excited, the kind of mindless enthusiasm of a young boy.

Norman knew that tone. Lincoln always sounded that way around machines. Especially Old World machines.

He leaned forward in his chair, along with hundreds of others as Lincoln clambered from the bench and shuffled to the leader of his companions, a young oval-faced Arab in his late twenties.

Latif Hadad. If Richard was the world's last scholar to the last professor, then Latif was the last apprentice to Lincoln, the last engineer. He sported a threadbare baseball cap, and his copper skin was aglow, making him achingly handsome. He dismissed the other men with a flick of his head.

They fell back and took seats close to the front, leaving Lincoln and Latif hunched over the embalmed object. They stepped either side of it and, with a nod to one another, gripped the protective blanket and pulled it away. Underneath, a large cardboard box had been stuffed with sleeping bags, hay, rucksacks and spare clothing. Nestled amidst the wad of padding with almost religious care was a block of metal around fifteen inches square.

A HAM radio.

"The message you received, it was from this?" Alexander said. He sounded unlike himself, distant and awed.

Lincoln looked pleased by the gasps echoing around the chambers. "The very same."

Norman leaned forward. He couldn't bring himself to

look away from the cobweb-strewn metal box, covered with knobs and switches. Ringing silence had taken the place of the restless whispering, as though the crate were warping space into a black hole that sucked in the light, sound, even fear.

"It works?" Thompson said. It sounded as if her throat had narrowed to the width of a needle. "Really works?"

By way of answer, Latif leaned over with reverential care and flicked a large red switch on top of the radio.

A screech like bear claws on a chalkboard filled the room, one that made Norman want to sink his teeth into the bench. Everyone was covering their ears and groaning, mostly with discomfort but also with disappointment. Latif, wincing, flicked it off again.

"Mr Lincoln?" Evelyn said.

The old lion grumbled. "I've spent the better part of forty years trying to fix communications equipment. Our only chance of reaching the wider world, and perhaps those stranded in the North by highwaymen, lay in establishing radio contact. But all I could ever pick up was that same scream, covering every frequency."

The Blanket, Norman thought.

Lincoln continued. "As far as we can surmise, radio and microwave bands of the spectrum are useless for comms, and there's been no sign of the Blanket decaying."

Norman had heard stories of people going crazy listening to the Blanket's wailing, searching for hidden messages.

"The whipper-snapper can barely keep his mouth shut

since we found it, so why don't I hand this to him?" Lincoln said.

Latif stepped forward with a courteous bow. "The Blanket is fractured," he said. "A little over a fortnight ago, we were on a salvage run to the dockyards, gathering spares and backup components for our generators in anticipation of the siege. We knew we were pushing our luck staying so long after the recall order, but we thought we could make it—and we wouldn't last long if we lost power—"

Just like New Canterbury. Despite Latif's spiel, Norman's mind conjured an image of the darkened city after nightfall, surrounded by a horde of black shadows perched on hilltops, predatory eyes glinting in the starlight.

"—by the time we knew they were after us, we were surrounded. We lost Hicks and Carmichael before they pushed us back to the airport. We set up in one of the hangers and sealed it off." He shrugged. "We dug in, and held them for a day or so. But we're tinkerers, not military men. Sitting so close to all those Old World air birds … We explored during the lulls. I think we all wanted to keep looking when the bullets starting flying again. We were boxed in, after all. We got into some deep, dusty corners; that's the only reason we found the hatchway."

"Hatchway?" Alexander said. He was leaning forward with brimming intensity.

"It was some kind of door. Secret, like, built into the wall. You'd have to know it was there to find it … or be a hell of a nosy so-and-so. That's when we got our first surprise: there was a service elevator inside, which lit up ready as you like. There was power."

He paused and knelt down, tinkering with the dials, consulting a dense scrawl of biro on his forearm. "They hadn't attacked for an hour, but they were coming back, and we didn't have a lot of help, so what the hell? We went down. It was a treasure trove, all kinds of delights." He rubbed his hands like a child faced with a room of honey jars. "Aircraft, motorcars, comms equipment, a few tonnes of stored sundries and foodstuffs, barrels of purified water, enough linen to clothe an army, enough weapons to arm one, and a truckload of these." He gestured to the radio. "It was all perfectly sealed, all ready, all whole. The lights came on right away—some fancy power source must be hidden down there somewhere, but we couldn't find it."

Agatha leaned forward and made to speak. For a moment her milky eyes filmed over and Norman thought she had slipped away, but then—though it only seemed through sheer force of will—she cleared again. "Somebody wen' an' repaired all tha' after the End and stuck it down in the dark?"

"No. There was no sign of the damage we usually see in transistors and other advanced circuitry. It was all fresh off the production line, never used."

"How'sat possible?" Agatha glanced at Lincoln. "Billy goat 'ere searched high an' low for summat like that years before you sat on your mum's teat."

"The whole place must have been shielded somehow. We dug into the wall and found some kind of lining, though I couldn't tell you much about it. We've never seen anything like it. It almost looks like there's some kind of integrated circuitry woven into it on a molecular level—"

"Mr Latif, we're short of time," Evelyn cut across him. "Forgive my bluntness, but what's your point?"

"The point is somebody knew about the End before it happened, and planned for it."

Norman shivered as a full-body chill worked over his skin, as if a bucket of insects had been poured over his head.

Alexander slowly leaned back from the bench and steepled his fingers. "Are you sure?"

"Positive," Lincoln said. "There's a bombshell to be going on with. *Somebody knew.*"

*

Charlie grimaced at the pigeons flapping around his head.

Dirty fucking rats with wings, shedding feathers and shitting everywhere, all day.

Once this was over, he never wanted to see a bird ever again.

Wood-smoke and a sickly charred smell—one he was unsettled to find he was growing used to—clogged the deep meat of his nose.

Jason's voice trickled like black, boiling tar in the back of his mind. "It's the fat under the skin. Like bacon." He had been grinning when he said that, an ugly sight that made Charlie's skin crawl. "That's the smell of barbequed bumpkins. Don't it give ya the jones to slit more throats?"

Charlie pushed the sick feeling rising in his gut out of

mind, watching the man with the emerald eyes crouched on the other side of the fire. Hooded and taciturn, he had hung his balaclava on a post to air in the wind. Every second longer, Charlie's stomach grew only more unsettled at the ruined face, the shiny masses of scar tissue and exposed cheekbone.

From far away his father's voice spoke to him. "How did you end up with this crowd?"

He shook himself as the grey-haired murderer flashed before his eye.

The bastards killed you, Dad. That's how. I have to make it right.

And he would. If he had to burn a thousand backward hamlets and trading posts to get a shot at tearing down the edifice of those who had beat him, kicked him like a diseased mongrel, he would do it.

"So why the stomach ache, Charlie boy?" the voice of his father muttered.

He wiped his hands on his trousers. They were still sticky from clearing the last village—

From hauling slices of little boys and girls, cooked medium rare.

"Shut up!" he hissed aloud, through grated teeth. He squeezed the nauseating thoughts deep down in the shadows.

Emerald eyes shifted to him from across the campfire, and Charlie blushed despite himself. A few pigeons alighted on the hooded figure's arm, and he caressed their delicate feathers. "Don't forget what they are, and what they've done. Stay focused," he said.

Charlie looked away from the working, bare jaws. "I'm fine," he muttered. "It's nothing."

Those eyes locked fast upon him, magnificent burning gems that could have set Charlie's clothes ablaze. Charlie had spent more time with that monster Jason that he thought he could stomach and watched him do things that would haunt him in the night for the rest of his life. But no matter how much Jason disgusted him and sent his skin prickling, he could never match the fear that bubbled up in Charlie's gut when those eyes turned on him.

In those moments he felt himself shrink, turn to transparent brittle crystal. Those eyes scared him because he knew he could never hide anything from them.

A thousand retorts welled up on his tongue, but he bit them back. What would be the point?

They lapsed into silence, filled only by the crackling of the fire and the pigeons' fluttering. Charlie looked down at his hands.

Would they wash clean, or had they been forever stained?

Every now and then a cry of pain reached them from the valley below, where the captives were fed slops and flogged in equal measure. That was their life now: move from place to place, raze anything standing, kill those who fought back, and take the rest to join the others in the nearest ravine or riverbed, slowly breaking them.

Lucian was down there now. Maybe it was him crying out.

Charlie grunted.

Probably not. The bastard was tough.

He felt those eyes on him again, pressing into his mind like a spoon into jelly. "Your prisoner is still alive?"

Charlie shrugged. "For now. You should have let me kill him when I first got my hands on him." But he knew he didn't mean it. He hadn't lied back in the bunker: just killing the son of a bitch would have been unsatisfactory.

Still, he wanted to be angry at something. The rage felt good. "What do you want *him* for, anyway?"

No reply, just soft muttering to those damned pigeons.

"I'm talking to you! I'm here to get even, to hurt them the way they hurt me, took away everything. So tell me, just when are we going to stop playing around and end this?"

But the man with the emerald eyes wasn't listening. The pigeons had risen into the air in an explosion of wing beats and wheeled away. A frown had settled low over the hooded figure's gaze, dark and forbidding. "Do as I ask," he said at last. "Keep him alive. Let him come to us."

"But—"

"You'll get what you're owed when the time is right."

Charlie scowled. He nodded to the sky. "What happened to your friends? They get sick of you?"

His words fell on deaf ears. That frown had deepened into a mask of disquiet and, maybe, confusion.

Was there something out there even he didn't know about?

CHAPTER 12

"The point is academic," Evelyn said. "We haven't time for this."

John DeGray stepped forward without warning, his face twisted with indignation. "I beg the council reconsider. We must hear more of this!"

"Mr DeGray, the wolves are breathing down our throats, and you'd have us waste yet more time on this curiosity?"

"You're damn right! This changes our understanding of history and all of reality as we know it. Think of the implications—"

"Mr DeGray, please take your seat."

"I'd hear more o' this," Agatha chimed. "I got precious seconds left o' clarity, and I'd spend 'em learning' some God's honest truth."

"There isn't time!" Evelyn cried. She looked to Alexander for help.

Alexander drummed his fingers on the bench. After an uncomfortable pause he said. "The Chair speaks true: we haven't much time. But every detail counts. Please continue."

"As it pleases the council," Latif said. "It didn't take us long to start fiddling, unpacking things, rooting around. We expected them to drop a grenade or two down the shaft from up top any moment, so why not enjoy ourselves? I checked the radio and got the Blanket on every channel, just like I expected, and then … just twiddling the dials, I came across something else. A signal.

"We risked going back up top. They were still out there, so we needed runners to get the message back home. We drew straws …"

"And sent half a dozen men to their deaths," Lincoln growled matter-of-factly.

"We've been stuck there ever since. And then earlier today … they were just gone. In the meantime, we've learned …"

Latif stopped there with abrupt finality. He looked like a man resisting the urge to vomit up something vile.

Norman's mind worked at a furious pace. The other councillors' faces were masks of concentration. Between them he was sure he could hear the distant clanking of a thousand mental cogs. It was a strange thing, to be speaking of hidden messages and conspiracies of the Old World, with the threat of being torn apart by savages so imminent. But here they were.

"Why have you brought this before us?" Thompson said.

Agatha giggled, but it was a harsh sound, grating and derisive.

And I'm the one with dementia. Stop being such head-in-the-sand chickenshit, that tone said.

"Ain't it obvious?" she crooned. "They brought it back so we could hear the transmission. Right, wrinkles?"

"Right you are, madam," Lincoln said. "You're in for a treat." He nodded to Latif, who consulted the biro on his arm and nodded in reply. Lincoln flipped a final switch and stepped back.

Norman braced, ready to throw his hands over his ears. He blinked when something quite different came rattling from the Old World speakers: a tiny, scratching, broken voice.

He body jerked of its own accord.

There's a man's voice on the radio.

Others seemed caught in the same breathless revelation. Eyes were wide and unfixed throughout the chambers. Those aged enough to have seen the Old World had the light of nostalgia in their eyes, while those who had only heard stories of the big Before gaped open-mouthed—all the bedtime stories were true!

"*—on? … Ga'darn thing, just work … Wait, the light, it's on!*"

An odd clicking, a solid thump, and then a grunt. The voice went on, though it jittered and thrummed, thin and watery despite its gruffness:

"*Arghright, here goes: Broadcastin' from Milton Percy radio tower. We bring werd from Dunburgh Alliance of t'eh Far North. We're seekin aid, to send a warnin' to those where the lights is still burnin in the South.*"

The voice was strange, thick as custard and stuffed with rolling vowels. Norman had heard an accent like that from only one person, someone who had spent his earliest years in Old World Glasgow. He'd heard it from Lucian.

The broadcaster was a Scot.

He blinked and leaned forward even farther, determined not to miss a word.

"Beware the comin' darkness. All manner of crazy folk, leagues of the bastards. They came w'tout warning, and they killed all they touched. Our cities are flamin, our dead rotting in the sun. They came from everywhere, after t'eh hunger of t'eh winter jus' gone, on t'eh prowl for revenge from us who won't forget the ways of Before.

"We know they've gone south aways for a good while, that they're moppin' ye's up like flies. It's given us a wee time to prepare, but we can't win alone. We need ye's. We'll be makin' a stand, to the last man if we have'tae, but we'd not do it before we had every'un we could on our side. If anyone is out there, please, come outta the shadows.

"A break-off group's got us messengers pinned down here, at t'eh broadcast site, but if ye could spring us from their hold, we could raise t'eh alarm elseplace—we cud bring all we've to give to yer lands, and stan' beside ye. If we don't stop them, they'll have all t'eh lights go out fer gud.

"Please, ye must come. Our coordinates are fifty-four degrees, thirty minutes, thirty-six-point-five seconds north; three degrees, twenty-seven minutes, fifty-two-point-nine seconds west. Please, ye mus' help."

Another click, a groan. An electronic whine, then,

finally, so distant as to be almost part of the white noise. "*Please.*"

Then static. Latif lowered the volume to a distant hiss. "He repeats himself, over and over," he said. "The messaging is circling."

"Looping," Lincoln said. "It's looping."

"Whatever. It's been the same message playing for almost two weeks now."

"He was …" Norman began.

Alexander nodded. "Scottish. We've never wandered farther than Northumberland; the North has belonged to the rapture cults and highwaymen since the End. But it seems the people of Scotland have themselves a shadow of civilisation just like ours."

"Sounds like they're up to their ears in shit, too," Agatha said.

"That it does," Lincoln said. "But the fact remains, there are others. We aren't alone after all."

At that, there was finally the beginning of a faint spell of muttering in the crowd.

Can't blame them, Norman thought. *It's like Columbus finding the New World.*

"To plague the Far North and us at once, their numbers must indeed be enormous." Lincoln paused. "So many … How could chaos bring so many together, hunting for blood?"

Oppenheimer, wilted and frail, looked more sorrowful than ever. Heavy rings sagged under his eyes, and his skin was almost translucent.

Look at him; he's too old to lose a daughter, let alone face this. They're all too old for this.

"All it takes is a loon with a pitchfork to make the first strike," Oppenheimer muttered. "Once the frenzy starts, there's no stopping it."

"I don't think we have all the facts just yet," Evelyn said in guarded tones. "There's always a man behind the curtain. Or woman."

"Can we send a reply?" Norman said.

Everyone looked at him, most blinking in surprise. It seemed the concept hadn't occurred to them.

Lincoln was looking at him appreciatively. "No. Latif and I have tried. The Blanket holds on all other frequencies, and the message broadcasts constantly, keeping the cleared one occupied."

Norman's stomach sank. A few grumbled in disappointment.

Alexander cleared his throat and changed the subject. "Coordinates. He spoke coordinates. Mr DeGray, could you enlighten us?"

DeGray stepped from the crowd, ashen faced and sweaty. He fumbled with his satchel of notes as Latif turned up the volume once more. The message looped around, and this time John scratched them down. He then struggled with his satchel, eventually producing a large map of northern England, which he held out horizontally for all to see. "They're transmitting from somewhere sandwiched between Allerdale and Copeland. A district of Cumbria called Radden."

Alexander, Agatha and Lincoln started visibly. They each recovered fast, but everyone in the room must have seen it.

The hairs on Norman's arms stood on end.

What now? More secrets.

"Curse all this talk o' Radden an' the North. Like I said before, James, git on with it and go satisfy yer curiosity. We'll wait for Malverston's goons, don't you mind," Agatha cried.

Thompson looked concerned, and sat beside the old lady whose eyes were once more cloudy and distant. Rush reached over towards her hesitatingly, but drew back when she turned her filmy gaze upon him.

Agatha shook herself and looked down at Lincoln, Alexander, and finally over at Norman. Her brows twitched constantly.

Old, Norman expected her to say. *You all look so old.*

Evelyn spoke up hurriedly. "What are we going to do about this?" Her voice had lost all trace of its commanding tone. It was a sincere question, flat and true.

"I should think there's only one course of action," Rush said. "We have to contact these people as soon as possible, take a force north to liberate them."

Thompson started. Her gaze said it all: she thought him mad. "Just hold a bloody minute, there! We can't be doing any such thing."

The others tensed. Norman sensed dozens of others in the crowd wittering their disapproval, the remainder decrying their assent. The councillors remained stoic, but

Norman sensed a fracture among them.

Careful, now. Keep your cool. Sides are being drawn. Pick carefully.

He glanced at Alexander, who spared him a momentary flick of the eyes before training his gaze firmly on the radio.

He's relying on you. They all are.

Norman tried to grease his throat without swallowing too hard. Still, the click of his Adam's apple seemed deafening.

"Why the hell not?" Rush said.

Thompson blustered with such severity that her froggy face wobbled like jelly. "We're about to be overrun by people waving the heads of those we love on their pitchforks, and you'd have us march what little strength we have on some fool's errand? Worse, to spring a bunch of strangers from a siege that could be just the same, if not worse, than this one?"

DeGray cleared his throat. "The world as we know it is changed by this message." His podgy cheeks were flushed as he eyed the radio. "I advise against haste."

Agatha squeezed a cross pendant hanging around her neck. "Bloody thing's like Pandora's Box," she muttered.

"It's not fair to ask anyone to risk their lives again, after all they've been through," Oppenheimer said. He looked so far away, so defeated, that for a moment nobody looked ready to put up a fight.

Then, Lincoln cried, "I never took one of our councillors for a yellow belly!"

The others started, and Norman suppressed a groan that

almost spilled from his lips.

Unlike the rest of them, Lincoln hadn't watched Oppenheimer's family fall to the tarmac in pools of their own blood.

"Oliver," Agatha mumbled, "hold ya tongue. Nobody's yella. He's right. We've all lost somethin'. We can't go nowhere on account of some voice from a box."

"The first voice to come out of any box for forty years!" Lincoln said. "The very fact that these people even know what a radio is means they're the kind of people we need to touch base with. We saw the banner. They're gone! We must make contact, immediately, while there's still time."

John DeGray, a man who had ensconced himself safe in his classroom for so many years with only his single student to contend with, seemed on the verge of violence. "This is one of the greatest discoveries we've made since the End." He licked his lips, and his eyes flickered. "We must … We must be brave. We must act!"

Evelyn closed her eyes a moment and looked around at the council afresh. Norman hoped she wasn't going to ask him what he thought. In fact, he was hoping the others had forgotten he was there at all.

It's all too big for me. Let them not see me.

"Mr Cain, what have you to say?" Evelyn said.

Alexander had watched it all play out in silence, his jaw set hard as granite. Now, his trance visibly wrenched to breaking point, like the branch of an ancient tree. He dragged his hands along his face, stretching the grizzled skin.

He looks tired, Norman thought.

And old, said a voice in his head that sounded like Agatha. *So old …*

From the fizzing in his gut, Norman realised that was more frightening than anything else.

"These people are our kindred. They may be our only hope. I know some of you must be doubting whether we could make contact, or what good it would do if we did, or even whether this message is an ancient relic recorded years ago … something we've just now stumbled on by accident.

"The fact is, we don't have time for doubt. Mr DeGray is right: we have to act."

A brief silence followed, then he pounded his fist on the desk lightly. "We'll vote on it now. If we go, we'll muster everything we can bring to bear and march on those coordinates. Then, whatever happens, happens."

"And if we decline?" Thompson said warily.

"We prepare as best we can, then hole up, and wait for whatever's coming."

"That won't be enough," Oppenheimer muttered, pale and sunken.

"No," Alexander said, "probably not. But if that's what the council chooses, so be it."

"Surely you can't expect us to make a unilateral decision like this on gut reaction!" Thompson said.

When Alexander turned his gaze on her, Norman saw a coldness he had seen only a few times before. This was the Messiah beneath the flesh, without his draperies of bravado and diplomatic aplomb. "You were elected to lead your people and sit on this bench in their stead. There's no time to debate, and no way to relay the news in any case. We act now. Make your decisions, and prepare to vote."

Norman's hands had grown clammy, and a mote of panic rattled in his chest. He couldn't help glancing into the crowd at random, hoping to find a comforting face. He found only blank, shocked stares.

They expect me *to be in on this? I'm not ready. I don't even represent anyone.*

But you do, said a voice deeper down, close to the bubbling black tar of his subconscious. You represent them all, whether you want to or not. Alexander, and all his stories, have made sure of that.

He swallowed hard. Agatha and Lincoln each gave a minute nod of encouragement. But Norman couldn't bring himself to make eye contact with Alexander; the pressure was too great—any moment it would char his flesh, burn him up and leave the chair a smoking ruin.

Evelyn cleared her throat. "The council calls a vote, regarding the matter of the distress call intercepted by Mr Lincoln and Mr Hadad. All those in favour of mounting a rescue expedition, raise their hands now."

It was all happening too fast. Eight hands stood between them and their fate.

Alexander and Agatha were the first to thrust their hands in the air, in the name of New Canterbury, staring stonily ahead. Lincoln followed in short order, his face grave.

Norman was appalled to see a frown had appeared on Agatha's face as she looked at her own aloft forearm. She was slipping away. They had to settle this, fast.

Evelyn's decision was next. Marek stepped forward from the darkness and took a low bow. "I think I speak for the tower when I say we'd be fools to ignore a sign like this," he growled. He reserved a single extra moment to send a glance of derision in Thompson's direction, then sank back.

Evelyn's hand was held high a moment later, and the tower-folk stomped their feet in unison, a thrumming, powerful sound that injected the will of five hundred into her wrinkled fingers.

Faltering all the way, Rush's hands joined theirs. His brows were furrowed, and he avoided the gazes of Thompson and Oppenheimer on either side of him.

Thompson folded her arms across her chest, looking around at them all with disbelief etched onto her face. Her bulging eyes were red with moisture, and her lips had paled to a thin white line.

Oppenheimer was moments behind her, leaning back onto his bony behind. The husk of a man, and father, looked over at the remainder of his people in the crowd, and the empty seats where his family should have sat.

Rush's vote makes four yeas against two nays. Looks like my vote doesn't count for much anyway.

Norman sighed with relief.

Then the bottom fell out. Rush put down his hand. A hollow, wounded sound escaped his throat, then he too sat back and folded his arms.

A lump of warm lead the size of a billiard ball lodged in Norman's throat.

Spoke too soon. Now it's all down to you.

Yea, and they went.

Nay, and they had a hung vote. That meant hours of back-room politics, and sermons of passion. They didn't have time for any of that.

But to say yes meant maybe condemning thousand to their deaths. It would be on his head—deaths met either on some foreign battlefield, or in homes burning in the wake of an army marching under a pigeon sigil.

It was too much. And so many eyes pressing in on him!

Wait. Wait. It's all too too fast.

He needed to think.

No time to think.

He needed help.

You're on your own, squire. Time you faced up to it.

He couldn't. It wasn't his place.

It's your place alone.

Why?

Because it's your destiny. It's what Alexander drilled into their heads, because the son of a bitch always knew that eventually something would come along that was too big for him, and when that happened people would need someone to look to with blind faith. Not a leader, but a hero.

But I'm no hero. I'm a mess. When I'm not sucking air with ribs that feel like chunks of broken glass, I'm hallucinating ghosts from Before.

But did it matter? Did the truth actually matter? Wasn't the idea of a hero always more powerful than any man, no matter how great, could ever be?

Shit.

"Mr Creek?" Evelyn's voice split off into myriad crannies until a thousand separate echoes whispered his name. "Mr Creek, the deciding vote falls to you." For a moment he thought he saw a pleading twitch amidst her icy brow.

Norman took a last look into the crowd and he found Allison. She nodded with such vehemence that, compared to the council's subtleties and vagaries, it carried real power. His hand rose into the air as though yanked on invisible wires.

"It's settled, then," Evelyn said. "We go."

PART 4

THE LAST TRUMPET

"This is the way the world ends
Not with a bang but a whimper."
— T.S. Eliot

CHAPTER 13

Lucian grunted, gritting his teeth hard enough to set his gums bleeding. The sentries' leather whipping straps had gotten to know the flesh of his back well of late. By now the breadth of his shoulders felt hot enough to smoulder like last night's campfire. But he wasn't going to give them the satisfaction of knowing just how bad it hurt—that he wanted to get down on his knees and squeal, just like dozens who did just that every other minute, somewhere along the miles-long trail of slavers and captives.

"Keep it moving," Charlie growled. "You're slowing up, my friend. A guy could think you're getting near quitting time."

Lucian ignored him. Stumbling beside him, Max Vandeborn grunted something that sounded suspiciously like "little prick".

Along the whole throng of ragged bodies, held aloft by the mounted sentries, were long hollow poles, fluttering from which were blood-red flags. Upon each was a hastily painted white symbol, one that by now played Lucian's heartstrings like a harpsichord. The white pigeon sigils glared just as much as the real pigeons that hovered overhead and alighted on people's shoulders.

More people had been appearing for the last few hours. At first it had been only small groups, sometimes only twos or threes being shepherded by a single guard. Then there had been staggered clumps, then wispy threads strung out over a hundred yards. Slowly, those threads had thickened, multiplied and lengthened, until now ribbons of marching hangdog figures linked up with the main drag like capillaries converging on a vein.

All of them laboured north under the sigil.

"So many," Vandeborn muttered. "I didn't think there were even this many left."

Charlie grunted somewhere out of sight. "You'd be surprised what you can find if you push hard enough."

Up ahead, someone crumpled to the mud, falling flat on their face in a stupor of blind exhaustion. Nobody dared try picking them up; they'd all learned that the punishment for that was to be beaten until they were lying right next to the fallen. An exasperated guard shunted the muddied figure to the side of the path with the base of his pole, and the droves of feet marched on.

Hundreds of bodies lay in their wake, strung over endless miles.

"How long are you going to keep marching us like this? You won't have any of us left if we go much farther," Lucian said.

Vandeborn guffawed. "Wouldn't put it past the sick fucks to have it as their plan all along. March the lot of us into the ground, then keep the strongest for house-slaves. Men can be cruel. Just read your history. It's the same story, over and over. All that crap about civilisation was just a phase … a spark in the shadows."

Charlie laughed openly. He was within shooting distance of genuine humour. "Don't you worry now. Won't be long."

As though to illustrate his point, he pointed to a sign that had appeared from over a hilltop ahead.

"No," Lucian whispered.

"What?" Vandeborn said.

Lucian didn't reply. He wasn't sure he could even if he'd tried.

The sign was old, beaten and so weathered that the paint had been stripped away completely. But the raised lettering was still there, and Lucian read it with mounting terror:

WELCOME TO RADDEN COUNTY

Welcome home, James, he thought.

SIXTH INTERLUDE

James's frosted breath twirled upwards in the cold night air as he saddled his mount. He took his time, moving with calculated smooth movements, lest he make a single rattle or chink of metal on metal. His head ached, fuzzy with exhaustion, but his vague stab at sleep had ended only in frustration.

That strange moorland the traveller's hands had zapped into his head had hijacked his mind's eye. Whenever he had dropped towards the warm miasma of sleep, the strange vision had become animated, spooling to life before his eyes like an Old World clockwork music-box. He'd flown over heathland, past cragged iron-grey peaks and the haunted remains of clusters of towns and satellite villages, hugging the rugged terrain. Each was wreathed in thick fog that slugged across the low-lying moorland, sheathed obsidian-black lakes from view, and made islands of naked rocky bluffs—they thrust through the blanket of land-cloud along the myriad ridges, as though the Earth had grown teeth.

Despite his efforts, his tossing and turning, he had been trapped with the flickering film reel behind his eyes.

He should have been thinking of Beth. He was worried for her, and a dull ache had already taken up residence in the fibrous meat of his heart.

Then there was the animal part of him that throbbed blue agony from his loins, calling out to the ruddy-faced angel who had put her hands on him and set a fire down there that would take days to die down.

One way or another, he knew she should have been the sole cause of his insomnia.

Yet still the staring images played out, etched onto the backs of his eyelids. He knew it was Radden. There was no merit in doubting it; the certainty nested inside him like a cold perfect sphere, unblemished and impenetrable.

Then there were the tunnels. They had come again after he had abandoned any hope of sleep and taken to padding the icy flagstones in his room, looking out over the moonlit wheat stalks that were growing lush and tall under their hands' tending love.

Reaping time would come soon, and they would be kept busy for many weeks with the grinding, the bagging, the storing and the trade—trade that would see dozens of caravans trail across the vast emptiness between them and the rest of their tenuous fledgling alliance. And when that happened, they would scarcely have time for anything else, least of all the schooling Alexander had prostituted them out to deliver.

But for now, all that wheat just lay swaying in the crisp night air, and their pupils-to-be were miles away.

He thought he would find that comforting. Instead, all

it did was bring yet more mental images. This time it wasn't of the ancient weathered landscape that had birthed him, yet he had no memory of—but still could somehow see— but instead the tunnels he had flown down so briefly when the traveller's hands had rested over his ears. He had been flying along them once again, and had come rushing up on that final room with shocking speed, and he could have sworn he was actually flying. His stomach fluttered, and the deceleration as he came rushing up upon the room's single occupant was potent.

The young man had been there once again, his hands splayed out in welcome. "*I'm waiting*," he said, just as before.

Then the visions had died, the mental images vanished, as though a thought bubble had popped somewhere in his head.

In that moment a new sensation had come: a strange impetus in his feet and lower legs, an itch. And before he knew what was happening, his legs had carried him to his wardrobe, possessed by a will not his own, and stranded him there staring in at his things. He had begun to pack clothes and supplies, then, not sure why he was doing it but certain he had to. Once he had finished, as though satisfied, his feet had then carried him out to the stables, stopping along the way with foot-tapping impatience until he'd picked up the saddle before him.

He was alone in the courtyard, checking the restraints and tying a bedroll to the back of the saddle, his brows pulled over his eyes in a deep frown. Still his feet itched, pointing away along the path leading to the road. Despite the darkness, the way they pointed seemed lit up like a great glaring beam.

He had business out there. And it couldn't wait.

Bathed in silver moonlight, in the silence of the courtyard with his friends and family sleeping peacefully not far away, something that felt like grinding gears spooled up deep in his head. Then, despite his disbelief, he raised his leg onto the first stirrup. He was sure he would have climbed on had the voice not sounded from close by.

"Looks like I'm not the only one who can't sleep." Alexander's voice was calm, but confused. He was silent a moment, and James could sense his own form—which was surely a mere fuzzy silhouette in such low light—being scanned. "Going somewhere?"

James sighed and fell back onto the cobbles. "Go back to bed," he said.

"Can't sleep. Nothing unusual about that. All the years I've spent haunting the library until the early hours, I never knew I had a fellow insomniac." His tone was conversional, but James wasn't fooled. Alex was a master of distraction; James knew he was just filling the silence until he could get a better hold on the situation.

"Just go back."

Alex stepped from the shadows. In the low light his big, frank eyes—those eyes that had won over angels and ogres alike—twinkled like shards of quartz.

"There's a lot to talk about. We didn't get a chance to go over what was said at dinner. Let's step inside. What do you say?"

The rhythm of his speech was one James recognised all too well. The falsity that was Alexander Cain had appeared in the courtyard, standing where Alex had stood only moments ago.

"Don't even try your charm on me. I'm immune."

Alex smiled, and the persona evaporated. Now his brother stood before him. "Where are you going?"

James looked off along the path that was, at least to his eyes, lit up as though with beams of midday sunlight, then turned back to Alex, standing amidst the darkness of dead night, while nearby an owl hooted balefully. Even closer someone gave an explosive snore and rustled in their bed sheets. "I—I don't know," he said.

"Then won't you come inside?"

"No."

Despite the darkness, he saw Alex's arched eyebrow.

He shook his head. "I have to go. I can't explain why. I just have to."

"And you don't know where?"

James blinked. "We both know where."

Alex was still for a moment, then ran a hand through the thickness of his beard. "You really saw something? And now you're going to follow these … What? Flashes? Visions? You're going to follow them off into the night?"

"Don't say it like that!"

"How am I supposed to say it?"

"Not like it's completely crazy at least."

"Isn't it?"

"You've said yourself, nothing's impossible. The End proved that."

Alex scowled. He gestured as though to expound something forceful, then curled his finger back into his palm, and let his hand drop again. "Fine. But can't it wait until morning?"

"No …" Even now the itch in his feet was throbbing, rising up his legs. Soon, he knew, it would be maddening. "It has to be now."

"And what is it you plan to do when you get wherever you're going?"

"I don't know! I don't know any more than you. That's why I have to go. I have to find out."

Alex mouthed in the gloom while James swung up onto the saddle. The silence was one other men might have filled with appeals like '*What am I supposed to tell the others?*' or '*We need you to help with the reaping!*' but Alex only watched.

He watched right up until James had swung his rifle up over his back, taken the reins up into his hands, and begun trotting a few paces from the courtyard.

Then his silence finally broke. "They'll be here tomorrow."

It was the tone that made James turn: guilt.

He wheeled his mount around to face Alex, and suddenly the images of Radden and the young man with the streaks beneath his eyes were gone. "Not Malverston's men?"

Alex's throat worked up and down. "They'll arrive by

midday."

James mouthed wordlessly, giving Alex time to step forward and take the reins in his own hands.

"How could you not tell me they were coming so soon?" James barked. "Were you planning on letting us know when they appeared at the bloody fence with their knapsacks and writing pads?"

"Malverston's unstable. He hasn't got long left, and he senses it. He's going to hold onto whatever he has for as long as he can, and he's trying to cement his legacy."

"So he needs heirs who know the Old World." James heard his own voice as though from far away. He felt as though a great weight had suddenly been tied around his ankle.

The itch in his leg was still there, but dulled now. And even if it had been raw enough to send him screaming, he couldn't have moved from the courtyard. Alex's shame alone, a thing he had seldom seen so naked and true, was enough to keep him rooted to the spot.

"Just give me a day," Alex said. "Help me talk the others around, get Malverston's men settled, get something going. If we can pull this off, we can have the Moon. The mayor's time is almost up. All we have to do is give him the comfort of the lie, stoke his fantasy of a council of dedicated followers maintaining his empire after he's gone. We both know those conniving bastards under him will tear each other apart as soon as Malverston's gone. Then we can move in, and start doing some good."

"Hark who's calling those slime balls conniving," James

said. His heart sank. "Alex, we can't keep doing this. I don't want to play dirty, even if it means getting a leg up on the mission."

"It's the only way we're ever going to make a real difference! That's the real world, James. We don't live in some storybook. Dirty politics have been a part of every society since the dawn of civilisation."

Maybe we're better off leaving civilisation in the dust, in that case, James thought.

"Give me a day," he said. "That's all I'm asking."

James hesitated, but Alex seemed to sense he would relent in the end. He'd already relaxed, and his shoulders had dropped.

James shivered in the chill of the night air. Now that the moment of flight had passed and he had grown still, the cold was beginning to seep through his thermal layers. For a summer evening, it was freezing. Thinking of it brought back memories of the ice that had formed on his head when the traveller had taken his hands away.

James climbed down from his mount, which snuffled as though in protest and dug at the cobbles with its hooves. "You don't seem all that sceptical," he said. "I expected you to tie me to the bed."

Alex pulled a face, but James couldn't place the expression. He took his mount by the reins at its snout and led it back toward the stables, and they walked beside one another. James waited for his reticence to wane.

"You said you were cold after," Alex said finally. "That there was ice where he'd touched you, when you saw whatever it was he wanted you to see."

"Yes," James said carefully.

Alex sighed. "It's called the Frost. At least, that's what we call it. A cold that fills you up so deep it feels like you could never be warm again, right down to your bones. For just a moment you feel hollowed out, almost like you're not real at all. And you see things, things in a deep, dark place …"

James shivered again, a full-body shudder, and this time it wasn't from the midnight chill. "You've felt it?"

"Everyone who survived the End felt it. You did too, though you must have been too young to remember it."

He'd been only a baby.

"So you believe me?"

Alex looked as though he was going to shake his head, but then he gritted his teeth and nodded. "I do."

James thought of the young man again, those dark shadows, his low voice. *'I'm waiting,'* he'd said.

Did Alex know about him too?

He thought about asking, but bit his tongue. Perhaps that was a step too far from good sense.

They reached the stables and Alex helped him loosen the saddle on his mount.

"Why me?" James said. "Why would that guy come all this way to make *me* see things of all people?"

A wry smile leaped to Alex's face. The quickness of it told James it was an automatic reaction. "Because you're special."

He offered no more.

James didn't ask for any. He was used to people saying

that. They had been his entire life. Alex and everyone else expected him to carry on the mission when the elders had grown grey and turned to dust.

Except, now, maybe there was some deeper truth to it.

And Radden? What about that? There's something special about that, too.

He looked at Alex, concentrating on stowing the stirrups in the dark, and made to ask him that question. They were both of that place, after all, but only Alex had any memory of it. What made it so different?

But it didn't seem right to ask him, here in the dark. He wouldn't get a straight answer, he sensed it.

Alex was right. It could wait until morning.

He had already begun preparing himself for a long night of restlessness, battling that irresistible urge to leap forth towards the fences and out into the world. Only moments ago it had been white fire, searing to the point of being blinding.

But now, curiously, he was astonished to find it gone. There was no certainty, no illuminated path, no itch. Nothing.

It seemed whatever possessive force that had infected him was satiated for now. It had got what it wanted.

In its absence, thoughts of Beth came flooding back, and fell upon his heart like a pile of masonry.

He made a promise to himself as they left the stables and headed back toward the courtyard: he would deal with this insanity in Radden, and then he would put an end to Malverston's reign. And he meant it: *he* would put an end to it, not some common wasting disease that would take him while he was most likely in a bliss of mead and snuff. He didn't deserve that.

Alex was silent as they walked back towards their bedrooms, his head low, his dark lips drawn so tight that they reflected slivers of starlight. James was surprised by how scared that silence made him, because maybe, just maybe, Alex was more afraid of Radden than any of them.

Now why might that be?

CHAPTER 14

Robert woke to the sound of distant rattles and popping. He rubbed his eyes with bunched fists, feeling like the world's biggest toddler, and started groaning immediately. Everything hurt. The kind of nebulous, woolly pain that comes with a twenty-hour sleep deficit drifted around inside his skull.

A day had passed. Endless hours of scouring the forests and meadows around New Canterbury had yielded no sign of the vagrants. They had melted away into nothing. The night had set eight hundred exhausted souls fit to tremble themselves into the nuthouse, but as twilight had fallen, something had changed in the folks locked up in the cathedral. Men and women who had only hours before been dull-eyed sheep had stepped forward with their hearts on their shoulders, ready to pitch in and stand watch and protect their families.

Hope had turned the table.

Over a hundred people had set up a tight perimeter around the inhabited part of the city, armed with every scrap of metal meanness their armoury had to offer. As the amber glow of approaching dawn had crushed out the pitch dark of starless night, they had started barricading the streets, pushing rusted motorcars and hauling sacks of grit, piling whatever Old World detritus they could find into walls as tall as a man.

By then, somebody had told Robert to go lie down. He must have needed it because he didn't remember anything after that, nor who had wrested his weapons from him and led him home.

Now he groaned. His head was throbbing and his muscles screamed in protest. His mouth tasted like a cat had taken a hearty dump down his gullet, and a great beast roared in the pit of his stomach. He groped the sheets on the other side of the bed, hoping to feel the warm softness of Sarah's belly, but found only uncreased linen.

"Sarah?" he called.

No answer. The heavy fog of dusty silence.

Weak, yellow morning sunlight lanced in through the open window, pooling on the floor and setting the dusty Old World carpet alight. He swung his legs out of bed and groaned again before struggling to his feet and padding across to the windowsill. The distant rattle and pop was louder here, coming from afar.

For a minute, he leaned against the frame and massaged his aching head, looking through slitted eyes at the silhouettes still patrolling the nearby rooftops. It seemed the vigil had been kept at least this long. Perhaps the blind groping panic had passed. He glanced back at the bed, wanting nothing more than to climb in and pull the covers over his aching head.

Then something clicked in the back of his mind, and he bolted upright, sending his head crashing into the window box ceiling.

He knew that sound. The popping and cracking came in bursts, followed by the ring of stark silence in repeating intervals. And on the brink of audibility, preceding each bout of rattling, there was shouting.

Gunfire.

He ran for the stairs. The rickety old house rumbled and creaked on its foundations to the beat of his thundering steps.

*

He hauled on his boots and duster, and was pounding the streets before he had time to lose his balance. Once he was hurtling along the cobbles, however, he wobbled a moment, caught off guard by how weak his body had become.

I'm getting lazy. It's this place. Food off the stove, running water, electricity. A sham of Old World suburbia. It's been enough to fool us into thinking we don't need to be ready. The body is just a machine, and badly kept machines run down.

He grabbed a lamp post and regained his balance, then wobbled off once again, heading for the nearest sentry outpost.

Goddamn cobbles are going to break my ankle. All this used to be so easy. Christ, I'm old.

The three-storey Victorian red brick apartment block

appeared up ahead. He burst in through the doorless entryway and took the stairs to the roof four at a time.

Gunshots still buzzed afar, the whip crack of small-arms fire, probably pistols and .32 rifles. It was coming in volleys, each preceded by that same barking voice. He could now tell it was far away, beyond the borders of the city in the fields, but that did nothing to quell his hammering heart.

He reached the rooftop and stopped just before the doorway. "Passage," he called breathlessly.

A voice came from just beyond the threshold. "Password?"

Robert felt a moment's relief at how calm the voice was. Maybe they weren't as defenceless as he'd thought. "Creek."

"Alright." The sharp click of a firearm hammer being lowered.

He stepped out onto the roof and nodded to the trio perched close to the ledge on their haunches.

His relief evaporated almost immediately.

They each flicked clumsy salutes, holding onto their weapons with grim determination. Weapons too big and heavy for muscles used to suburban chores. Weapons they hadn't known how to fire only hours ago, let alone hit anything.

Robert had tried to assign at least one veteran guard to each team, but there had been too many volunteers and little more than two dozen guards. And if he had made the teams larger, they would lose any semblance of stealth. He had been forced to put guns in untrained hands and leave them to make do.

It hadn't seemed so very foolish at the time. How tired he must have been to become that deluded. He couldn't afford to let himself get in that state again.

Mr Higgins was by far the oldest of the three, a grizzled stick insect of a man with a clump of frizzy white wool for hair. "Mr Strong, sir, you're awake," he bleated.

"I am."

"Maybe I could suggest you go back to bed a while longer. You were in quite the delirium when you left us."

"And you don't look so great now," one of his young companions said. Robert thought his name was Mark Pegg, but it could have been Danny Succo. He couldn't have been older than sixteen, and he cringed when Robert turned his gaze on him.

The other young man, himself twenty at most, was pale, his eyes fixed on the street.

"I'm fine," Robert said.

They all fidgeted at the bass of his reverberating impatient tone.

Two boys and an old man, sweaty-faced and shy because they're afraid of … What, being reprimanded? Or are they afraid of not being up to scratch?

The fact that they worry means they're not *up to scratch. I need soldiers, not farmers and children.*

But that was all New Canterbury had to offer. Ironic: the city was arguably home to the most powerful man in the known world, was the crown jewel of their order; yet, of all the alliance strongholds, it was also the most defenceless.

He looked at their holds on the rifles again, awkward

and unsteady, as though each barrel were in fact a great twelve-foot lead pole.

Could they even fire those things if a parade of these monsters came stamping up the street?

He suppressed a sigh of anguish. The spell of optimism he'd felt before was now a distant memory.

The hissing firecracker-burst of gunshots came again, and he turned to the city in search of the source. Higgins and the boys didn't seem perturbed. "What's going on?" he said.

"First try-outs, as ordered," Higgins said, puffing out his chest.

"We helped pick from the long list," Mark/Danny said, giving Robert a fawning approval-seeking smile.

Robert's heart skipped a beat. "What are you talking about?" he said.

The three looked at one another uneasily.

"Your orders, Mr Strong," Higgins said with care. "The ones you asked to be relayed."

"What orders?"

"About forming the militia."

Higgins's face fell slack when Robert surged forward and seized him by the lapels. Mark/Danny looked ready to faint, while the other lad had taken to once again scanning the streets.

"I want you to think very carefully about what you say next," Robert breathed. "Who gave those orders on my behalf?"

The corner of Higgins's mouth twitched as though he

thought for a moment Robert's outburst was a joke, or a test. But Robert had fixed him with a gaze honed over a long childhood of hard lessons in the far north, where you killed your dinner, and often had to kill again to keep it.

The gaze had been a gift from his father. Pa had been in the ground almost fifteen years, but now Robert heard his voice bubble up from the black ooze of distant memory. *"It's all in the eyes, boy. You kin hold a gun to some men's heads and get nothing' but gab for yer trouble. But you get your killer's stare down pat, and you kin make a man do anythin'."*

It had been a long time since he'd used that stare, but some things you never forgot, especially things that had kept you alive.

Higgins stammered, "Your fiancée, Mr Strong."

Robert dropped him in shock, and Higgins crumpled to the ground. In his haste, Robert hadn't been aware of holding the man a foot off the ground.

Then he was hurtling down the stairs again. They shouted after him but he didn't hear what they were saying, then he burst out onto the streets and kept running, bounding across the cobbles.

*

The firing squad was spread out along a thirty-yard stretch, each member facing a humanoid target made of sandbags, lashed twigs and spare rags. Holding small-calibre pistols that were dwarfed even by the women's hands, they each took aim, their faces screwed up in concentration, and waited for the signal.

"Fire!" Sarah called, and a host of waspish explosions sounded in quick succession.

The targets leaped on their fixings, quivering and throwing off puffs of sand and showering splinters into the high grass.

Each member of the squad then carefully put on their safety catches, handed the gun to the next person, and then made their way to the back of the lines strung out behind them. In all, there must have been sixty or seventy people.

"Better," Sarah said, a satisfied smile crossing her face as she stood with arms akimbo. She even managed to keep composed when Robert thundered into the clearing and gave a wordless cry that brought deathly silence down heavy over the congregation.

Despite a mounting medley of disbelief and fury, he had to admire her for that.

He didn't stop his barrelling approach until he towered over a foot above her, staring straight down into her naked eyes. They hadn't been able to find replacement glasses for her yet. She looked strange without them. Squinting to compensate, furrows had appeared in her peachy face, making her look more severe, waspish and older.

For a moment he was inarticulate, strangled by his outrage, then he growled low so nobody else could hear. "Have you lost your mind?"

He was using the same stare that had made Higgins a jabbering ruin. In truth, he wasn't prepared for a fight. He expected her to crumple into a mass of nerves and apology.

That's what I think of her, when all's said and done. Nice to know I'm just as chauvinist as Pa underneath.

But she remained with her hands resting on her hips, maintaining her gaze. She didn't even flinch. She didn't answer, just waited for him to go on, for his mounting rage to spill over.

He could feel the stares of the others pressing hard into his shoulder, but he ignored them. "Do you have any idea how dangerous this is? Putting guns in these people's hands? Giving orders in my name? Bringing them out here with no guard, no scouting party, no perimeter—I can't believe it!"

A glimmer of hurt flashed behind her eyes, but she held fast. Her arms dropped to her side, and she leaned closer. Her voice was low, but he was taken aback by how calm she sounded and ... how cold. "I'm giving them something they haven't had for a long time, the chance to stand on their own feet. You said we haven't got enough guns on the streets to put up a fight, and you're right. I'm correcting that."

Robert made to retort, but she sliced the air with her hand with such viciousness that his words stopped in his throat.

"No!" she breathed. Her voice shook, a moist thrumming deep in her chest. "No! I will not sit and wait for them to come marching in here and kill us all. I will *not!* And the only way we can even the odds is if we take these guns out of your precious armoury and actually use them. It's dangerous, sure. And no, there's no extra hands to stand guard. For all we know, they could be getting ready to charge down here right now and slaughter all of us.

"But how is that different from sitting at home? We haven't got any chance. We all know it—we can smell it. Even if every person in the city were a seasoned soldier, they'd still overrun us. So what's the harm? At least we're doing *something*, even if it's all just smoke and mirrors. Maybe we can take a few more of them with us when they finally stop playing with us."

The icy glimmer lancing out through her pupils cut a great wedge off his momentum. And she sensed it.

Before he could move, she leaned over to peer around the bulk of his arm, and nodded to the queues of waiting volunteers. "Next up, take aim! Go on, now."

The hissing of dozens of feet traipsing through grass sounded behind him. "No!" he cried. "Stay where you are. This is crazy." He turned and was shocked to find that only a few remained unmoved, watching uncertainly; most of the volunteers had moved into position before the targets, raising the pistols and squinting along the sights.

"Remember, calm, smooth. Squeeze the trigger, don't pull. Squeeze."

A chill ran through Robert. How long had it been since he had been the one saying those same words to her? It couldn't have been more than twenty-four hours. How fresh and frail she had seemed then, a lamb set to turn to jelly at the first sign of trouble.

She couldn't have had time to become a good shot herself, not in the few hours he'd been asleep. Her authority was an act; a clever act, but an act, nonetheless. Yet she was pulling it off with a cool assurance that was smooth as any of Alexander's speeches. He could feel the others respond to it, eased by her confidence. The fear had made them her puppets, and they were glad for it.

"Steady, now. Take your time. Ready to fire."

Two dozen hammers were pulled back in quick succession, and Sarah muttered to him, "It was now or never. You needed to rest. You still need to rest."

"You're giving doctor's orders, now?"

"No, but Heather's behind me on this. She's teaching whoever wasn't fit to shoot how to fit field dressings, tie a tourniquet, whatever might help us hold out a little longer."

"More than that," Heather said. "I'm tired of hypochondriacs looking to hold my hand." She bristled. "God, that's awful. But it's true. I've been living for this city, but I'm done. I want to really take back some bloody control." Her equine face seemed firmer, hollower. "Put me to work," she said.

Sarah was smiling. "I plan on it."

Robert gripped her arm and muttered, "You didn't even ask."

"If I'd asked, you'd have said no. There would have been no discussion, no debate, nothing. You would have sent me back to babysitting, and that would have been that." She folded her arms. "I did what I had to."

With that, she leaned to the side once again, and said, "Fire!"

The gunfire filled the air with splinters. Then silence once more. The pigeon flocks at the distant treeline burst into the sky, wheeling in a wide circle before coming to rest in the canopy once again.

He blinked, turning full around to face the targets. There had been a few misses, but most of the targets had taken hits to the torso and abdomen. A few sported ragged holes in the stalks that stood in place of neck and chins.

But it was the ease of it all that really struck him. There was nothing nervy about these people anymore; they passed the weapons between them and reshuffled for the next squad without comment, without thought. They were a long way from combat ready, and they'd never have the time to get anywhere near it, but he was staggered by how far they'd come.

Were these really the same jabbering, hopeless idiots who had accosted him in the cathedral last night?

Sarah had done a real job on them. A better job than he had by a country mile.

They came here because they heard I gave the okay, but they're not stupid. None of them are looking at me now. They're all looking at her. The same way they used to look at Alexander.

He shivered. What had happened to her?

They torched the things she loved most: her books. Her babies. Her life's work.

I wonder if they know how big a mistake it was, burning that warehouse. They've made their biggest enemy out of a librarian.

Despite all the eyes pressing in on him and his lingering anger, he almost laughed.

He was impressed. He hated to admit it, and there was

no doubting they were still amateurs, no matter how good Sarah's hold over them—they would be no match for even a handful of trained combatants—but he hadn't been this surprised in a long time.

Maybe this could be their saving grace. If I underestimated them, of all people, so could the enemy. We could use that.

Careful … Wishful thinking can bite you in the arse real quick.

But maybe, just maybe, we could use this. Maybe we stand a chance, after all.

He took hold of Sarah's arm and leaned in farther still, so close their noses were grazing. "You're forming a militia, Sarah. That means these people are going to get in sticky situations real fast, and most of them are going to die. Are you really prepared to have them all turn to you and point fingers when it hits the fan? Because if you survive, and I have to stress the *if*, they'll blame you. In their eyes, every drop of blood spilled will be on your hands."

Her eyes burned into him. "We're already in a sticky situation, Robert. Most of us are going to die either way."

In that moment, he realised he had never wanted her more. He held her gaze, and for a time, he could have sworn they each emitted beams of pure willpower from their eyes, beams that made battle in the scant inches between their faces. He was in danger of losing. Then he licked his lips, nodded slowly, and grunted. "Alright, fine. We'll do it your way."

"Good." Her face was flushed, full of anger and sweat and blood.

Oh God I want her. I knew this was in her all that time. That's the truth of it: I always knew. Those idiots have unleashed what was hidden under the librarian, under the schoolteacher. The real Sarah.

"Now show them what the hell they should really be doing," she crooned. "They're going to kill us, our friends, our children. Show us how to kill them back." For just a moment, he saw an image behind her pupils, a writhing union of naked flesh.

How could he be thinking about that now?

Where there's death, there's sex, my friend. Eros and Thanatos.

He turned to stand beside her, and folded his arms across his chest. "Again," he called.

But nobody moved until Sarah gave the nod. "Take aim," she said.

CHAPTER 15

The cooing was driving her insane.

Billy hadn't noticed when the pigeons swarming around her had stopped being a curiosity and became a plague. Dozens swarmed overhead and, although the treeline was blurred by the haze of distance, she wasn't fooled by the shadow of the canopy. They would be waiting there, too.

Why would they follow her? For her whole life, birds had pounded their wings to escape her whenever she had tried to play. Grandpa had said it was because people ate all the stupid birds who stuck around.

These pigeons were different. It was almost like they were being drawn to her, like the magic *magnets* Daddy had shown her with their invisible pulling and pushing. She wished they would go away. The cooing was slowly loosening all the screws in her head, letting everything rattle around in there like it would all fall out one ear if she wasn't careful.

But at least she wasn't alone. The bigness of the plain she had been walking over since the Arch was too much.

She had never seen a place so flat, so vast and empty. It wasn't just that there were no other Enger Land people here; it was that there weren't even any trees, nor bushes or thorns or thickets. Just tall grass for mile after mile, growing right up to her elbow in most places. There weren't even any animals to graze it short.

The birds were company at least.

Time was tricky now. She'd forgotten about night and day, and hours and minutes and seconds now seemed like funny, odd, formless things, just noises in her head that didn't mean anything. At some point there had been night; then it had been day again. The sun had coasted through the sky, but in her memory, it all seemed a blur.

A while ago she had seen another ghostie. It had been another skybird, way up above the clouds, pulling a pair of white puffy ribbons way across the big blue. She had watched it carefully to make sure it didn't disappear like the last one—she knew in her bones that if she looked away then back, it would be gone, just like all the other ghosties. But it had vanished anyway, even though she kept her eyes on it. All it took was a single blink, a tiny moment of darkness. And when her lids had come up again, there was no skybird and no ribbons. Just clouds.

She hoped all this would stop soon. Life was so much simpler before they left home and came to New Land.

No monsters, no sickness, no hunger, no ghosties or Panda Men, and *no stupid birds*!

But she tried not to think about that anymore, because every time she did she realised that things would never be simple again, not like before. It wouldn't be like before because Ma and Grandpa had gone away, Ma taken by the same coughing that was taking Daddy even now, and Grandpa by the monsters in the night—the ones that had come with their knives and curses, looking for food.

They could never go back now.

A part of her never wanted the walking to stop. At least now she had somewhere to go, something to keep the thoughts and memories from crowding in. The itch in her feet was strong; a pair of thrumming, invisible hands gripping her ankles and driving her forward through the grass, irresistible and tireless.

But the ache in her heart would never fade, that deep black hole only home and family could fill. And of that, all she had left was Daddy, lying back in the cabin with the spittle drying into a grimy crud on his lips, just like it had with Ma in her last lingering days, when her face had gone an ugly shade of purple and she hadn't woken no matter how much Billy had screamed and shaken her. Thinking of Daddy like that made the few bites of jerky and beans in her stomach roil and bubble, climbing her throat.

She was two people. One wanted to keep walking, but the other pined for the fever-warm bed sheets laid over Daddy—even if that meant lying coiled beside him until the sickness leeched into her own body and took her away as well.

She hadn't seen the man in the purple coat again, and somehow she knew he had made his only appearance—or at least his last for a long time. But now, she heard a voice she had hoped not to hear again, coming from nowhere yet right beside her.

"Keep moving, Billy. You're almost there. So close now," the Panda Man said.

She shivered. "I don't want to do this anymore," she moaned under her breath, not thinking about what she was saying. Her mouth leaked words like a dripping faucet.

"So close now. Keep moving."

"Can't stop anyway. Feet won't let me ... Have to keep going ... Want Daddy ... Why, why, why ..." Her own voice was only a hum, as far away as the fuzzy horizon, because there was something else besides the grass now. A thick, long road littered with the twisted wreckage of thousands of motorcars snaked its way across the landscape, cracked and overgrown, washed away in chunks hundreds of yards long by mudslides and foliage.

But Billy only registered it obliquely, somewhere deep behind the glare of the grey smattering of great stone slabs ahead.

She took out the map and looked at the winding red path scrawled over it. A luscious waft of lavender and tea leaves swept from the ancient frayed paper as she traced her finger along the route, westward away from the Arch toward the blown-up caricature of the strange stone circle now before her.

She held the map in her hand. It felt better there, promising that the way ahead was the right way. The only way.

As she drew closer, her chest started tightening. The

stone circle was old. Very old. As old as the vanishing Arch, maybe. And just as tied to the itch in her feet, the Panda Man, the ghosties and the Light, all of it. A place where power thrummed in the air. Things hid there, she could tell, hiding just out of sight in the same way the Arch had; *between* spaces, in such a way that one might think they would come into sight if they could only turn their gaze through that extra impossible dimension.

She thought of the sign she had seen so many miles behind her, beaten and weathered, but still legible: *Salisbury - 4m*

Now she remembered something else, a brown sign that had hung just below it. She had read that too without knowing it, and her mind had squirreled it away for later. Now a key had been turned, and that memory had popped free. She read the vivid memory as easily as the map in her hands. *National Heritage Site - Stonehenge*

That was this place. She knew it.

"Stonehenge," she whispered, working her mouth around the words, tasting them.

Yes, that was it. It fit.

"You're just full of surprises, little girl," the Panda Man said. She could have sworn she even heard the wet slick of his parting lips this time, but when she turned her head, there was nobody there.

She kept walking, and the stones grew larger. The itch grew stronger until it reached into the pit of her stomach and climbed her back to paw at her matted hair.

There's so much else *here. I just can't see it.*

She wondered whether other people who didn't have the itch—Sammy, the medicine woman, had called it the Light—would have felt it, too.

Whatever it was, the air was dripping with stories, whispers of things past, elsewhere, and those yet to come. And the Panda Man was with her every step of the way, though she couldn't see him any more than any of the rest of it. Like all those hidden treasures, he was hiding just out of sight. But it didn't bother her anymore. It was just another step on the path back to Daddy.

And taking these steps felt right. It was a funny thing to hold a candle inside her that muttered this secret truth, but she knew the candle told no lies. If she took a single step in any direction from true, it would be bad. And not just for her.

I don't care about that. Or anyone else. I need to get back to Daddy. And if the Panda Man won't let me go until all this is done, then I'll do it as fast as I can.

But all the same, her mouth fell open and her pace slowed to a crawl when she passed the first of the great grey stones. The ones on the outside were arranged in a wide, incomplete circle, rough rectangular blocks three times as tall as Daddy. Some had yet more horizontal stones on top, bridging a pair of the ringstones. Inside the ring were a few more scattered here and there, most standing but a few lying on their sides. All were covered in thick dewy moss, and the far side seemed half-buried in mud and detritus carried by the plain's high gales.

She passed under one of the capped ringstones and was

momentarily reminded of the Arch. These stones were far lighter, different altogether, but they were kindred, touched by the same *otherness*. The itch was unbearable now, a searing scream that set the skin of her legs on fire and climbed her spine in undulating waves. The air buzzed with something that made the hairs on her arm stand on end, and even the greasy locks on her head crackled and started to float into the air.

Finally, she came to stand in the centre of the broken ring, turning in slow circles, blinking slowly. Enger Land had buildings much bigger than this—she had seen more than she could count in the distance since she had left the cabin—but this seemed larger than even the thin, shiny spires poking up above the old ruined cities. Its nakedness, and the weathered ruggedness of each block, made it all seem more impressive.

The Old People Daddy had told her about from Before hadn't built like this. They had used bricks and plaster and metal and glass, just like Daddy and Grandpa had on the farm. Stones like these were older, even. The bigness of time and all the people who must have come this way before her was all too much.

Last week I thought it was only me, Daddy, Ma, Grandpa, and the weekend traders in all the whole wide world. It seems like forever ago.

"Getting them to build this thing was a real arse-ache," the Panda Man said. And this time he was there, standing right in front of her with his hands thrust into the deep pockets of his black overcoat, looking up around at the stones just like her. He rolled his eyes. "All they had to do was haul a few stones, follow the blueprints. The *whining* I had off those lazy savages, you wouldn't believe." He grinned and laughed at her, as though they were sharing a private joke. "And after all that, they went and started worshipping the damn thing, flocking from far and wide like it was something sacred, something special and new and unique. If they only knew about the others …" He shook his head and turned to her. "You made it."

Billy could only blink. The thrumming was still up around her head, turning the space between her ears to dancing mush. It was hard to think.

The Panda Man gestured around him. "I'm sorry you had to walk so far, but there was no other way."

"No other way for what?" she said. Her voice sounded muffled and far away, as though from beneath a heavy blanket.

"To show you things you need to see, and to get you where you need to go." He cleared his throat and beckoned her farther into the circle, breathing deep, like he was drinking in the strange buzzy static. He looked stronger here, his eyes sharper and more alert. But it was more than that; he was more *there*, more solid.

Suddenly her annoyance pierced through the static veil, and she bunched her fists. Daddy's face floated in front of her eyes. Then she was yelling. "Why did you have to pick me? Where are you taking me? Who was that other man? And the archway? And why are all these silly birds following me? And when can I go home?"

His brow creased in annoyance, and he flapped his hand impatiently. "Questions, questions, they'll only lead to more questions. Try not to get too bogged down in the many and various weirderies of this freak show."

"But—"

He gave an exasperated sigh, his shoulders dropping. It was an odd sight to see such childishness from that wolfish predatory face. "Fine!" He counted off his answers on the fingers of one hand, holding each digit in the other hand as he gave each answer. "You're special. To a place far from here for starters—then, if we can put a lid on this shitstorm, a whole lot farther. Him: sometimes a friend, sometimes an enemy, most of the time a colleague, and all of the time a pain in my bloody backside. The Arch is another tip on the iceberg I'm trying to show you, so don't bother asking. The birds follow you because you're marked, just like He is—was."

"Who's He?"

"What did I say about questions leading to questions?" He held his arms wide. "There, you happy? Time's a wasting'. We have to get on with the great dance of destiny, weave the threads of the great Web, serve the Pendulum's swing, and all that jazz," he added with an ironic theatrical twirl of his hand, rolling his eyes once more.

She crossed her arms. "Fine. But you didn't answer my last one. When can I go home?"

The Panda Man hesitated. "In time," he said with a winning smile. He really was a beautiful man, like Prince Charming. But it was just a sheen, a pretty wrapper laid over a Big Bad Wolf.

Daddy had a phrase for it, for the wagon-men who came through on the farm road to trade potatoes and barley for cloth and tools: *Wolves in sheep's clothing.*

He had covered his pause fast, recovered like a practiced showman. But still, that pause had been there.

He was a liar. She knew that without even thinking about it.

But I knew that already. I'm here because he said Daddy would die if I didn't, and that's all. Stop asking silly questions and do whatever he wants, then go home and get to Daddy.

He must be so sick by now.

A mental flash of pale see-through skin, cracked bleeding lips and skin turned blue. The sound of rasping breaths. A whimper.

No, no. Daddy's fine. It took Ma but Daddy's fine. I just have to get back. Get back now!

"Fine," she snapped, and looked up around at the ringstones. "What is this place?"

The Panda Man looked pleased. Was it because she was curious or because she hadn't asked more about going home?

It didn't matter.

Hurry. Hurry.

"This is an outpost," he said. "A meeting place, a temple, a looking-glass, and a doorway. It can be whatever we need it to be." He gestured all around. "Special places like this are all around. Most people could look their entire lives and never find most of them—only people with the spark of

Light like you can even get to them—but we need places like this to keep eyes and ears in this world—keep our foot in the door, so to speak.

"You had to deal with my colleague because you went into a dark zone, a place I can't go. Once upon a time, I could see every inch of this thread of the Web, but things have gotten so damn brittle." He looked troubled for a moment. "Things are going downhill fast now, for everyone. That's why we're here. We need to act."

Billy listened impatiently, tapping her foot.

I don't care about that. Just let me go home.

The Panda Man huffed, sensing her exasperation. "I forgot how little you people can care for the Pendulum's swing, blind as you are." He cocked his head, and for a moment, she saw that same old predatory leer, like he was a wild dog fixing to gobble her up. "So small … like bugs on a windshield."

She blinked, waiting. Maybe he really would gobble her up now.

And if he does? There's nothing I can do. "So get on with it." *That's what Grandpa would say.*

She waited, and then he was holding out his hand and that leer was gone. "Come on, take my hand. Let's go for a ride."

"Where?"

"You need to see some things to believe them. And no matter how much *Daddy* and *Grandpa* told you about all those people walking around Before, I bet your little mind just can't wrap itself around numbers like that. Hell, I bet you don't even believe them. Not really. How could you?

"So, here's me offering a little enlightenment. Take the hand." He waggled his fingers, then stepped forward and grasped her smooth, uncalloused palm.

As soon as her skin touched those alabaster spider-leg appendages, cold unlike any she'd ever felt bolted up her arm and crawled across her neck and head in a creeping wave, then the world was gone. The stones, the windswept grassy plain, even the pale blue sky. All of it vanished with the coming cold, and total blackness took its place.

She was rushing headlong through some other space outside all of New Land, all the vast emptiness through which she'd been wandering. And yet somewhere in all that aberrant nothing, she felt the others. All the others.

Every single human being who had vanished all those years ago. She didn't know how she felt them—it wasn't sight or touch or hearing, but a melding, an extension, of all three—or how she knew who they were, but she knew.

They were screaming. Each writhing body and wailing voice blurred into a stabbing, maddening medley of misery that sent her stomach turning over and her heart hammering. She was flying over the top of an endless wriggling carpet of their tortured bodies.

Oh God, there are so many. So many people. There can't be so many, can't be. More than lots. More than hundreds. More than thousands. Numbers can't go that high—what comes after thousands? So many!

"You see?" The Panda Man's voice, hollow and icy as the frost gnawing at her bones, sounded from beside her, though she could see nothing in this inky void she was flying through at such an impossible rate. "This is why you hauled your sorry little behind so many miles. You had to see it for yourself. Language is a fickle thing when it comes to this kind of heady crap."

Oh God, Oh God, there are so many SO MANY. Make it stop, please take me away, take me back, please don't make me watch—

The Panda Man spoke on, audible despite the billions of wailing voices and her own screech of agony. "Would you have believed this without seeing it? Would anyone? *Could* anyone?"

All that screaming. The racket, the sticky chaos of all those moving limbs. The smell of them, the trapped festering stink of myriad unwashed droves. She would go mad if she stayed. It would only take seconds, and then she would be cuckoo, loopy-loo. It would all go away.

Just take me home let me go back go back now I want my Daddy please let me see him just for a second please help DADDY!

A moment passed when even all those wailing voices seemed nulled by the strength of the Panda Man's reticence. Then he said, "I brought you here to show you this because you have a rare opportunity to make big changes, and not only for those poor bastards trapped here. For everyone."

They're trapped. Taken. Chained up like animals and put to work.

But for what? And by who?

She didn't know. But behind all the pain and confusion

and darkness, she felt something bad: evil. That was the only word for it. It was just a distant echo, a fingerprint, but even that was blinding, nauseating. It would swallow her up if she concentrated on it too long.

I can't do it. Take me back—take me back now!

The Panda Man's droning voice went on calmly. "You can help everyone, right a balance bigger than all of us, more than this one petty little corner of reality. But I had to show you this because it can only be your choice. If you want to go back to your Daddy, I can't stop you. But he will die, and the sickness in him will work its devilry on you just the same."

Tears should have been trickling into the corners of Billy's eyes, but here things were different. Not real, not quite. But that did nothing to dull the ache in her chest.

Daddy couldn't die. Not now, not ever. Without him, what would she have? Who would she be?

"And when you're alone, you'll choke your last breath, looking out across the sea, trying to spot that little farm you all left behind, where the bones of your mother lie buried. And then things will just go away, that'll be that."

Billy was weeping, but felt no tears on her cheeks. Here, in all this darkness, there were no tears. Just pain.

"Or … you can roll the dice and take what I'm offering: a chance." Another pause.

The Panda Man laughed, a noise so absurd amidst all the hurt that it cut like glass. "When you hear it put like that, I suppose it's not a choice at all. But we all have our little parts to play. The question is, are you going to play yours?"

Billy could feel herself slipping away, towards the abyss of insanity. All those voices, all that pain, all that endless darkness. There was something else, too; an evil thing behind it all, and a great swinging behemoth to which all these stolen people were chained, holding up—

They're holding the swing, the swing of the Pendulum. What Pendulum?

I don't care, I don't care, let me go, let me out! Daddy!

She couldn't abandon Daddy for this craziness, she couldn't.

But the fact was that, right now, that seemed a distant flaky nonsense, here amongst all the woe and penury, the grand scale of all, and the irresistible hold of the Panda Man on her wrist.

"What do you say, Billy?"

Let me go home, let me go, let me go!

All that screaming. All those people. All those years they had been trapped here holding up the swinging pendulum, a great obsidian shaft, the source—

"What say you, Billy?" His voice had grown stentorian, huge and ringing and cold. Her wrist would cave under the pressure of his grip. They were still flying over that endless carpet of writhing Vanished, screeching in contorted torpor.

Let me go.

Daddy's image was fading. The darkness, the pain, the Vanished. The Pendulum.

"What say you, Billy Peyton?"

Let me go, just let me go back to before with Ma and Daddy and Grandpa before it all went bad. Please let me go back, let me be happy, let me go!

But it would never stop. She knew that just as clearly as she knew all those people were really here hidden in the world behind the world—that it was all really here. She couldn't unsee this, unknow these terrible truths.

And now amongst all that woe and evil, fear, and craziness, she glimpsed something new: thousand-mile-long, black, furry legs, eight in all, leading to a hairy, bulbous thorax and abdomen, snapping fangs and eight diamond-studded eyes fixed on her. In the Spider's eyes was every story ever told, every dream ever dreamt, and every star in the sky—whole galaxies turned amidst the eternal orbs.

Another moment and there would be no return. Her stomach roiled like lava, and the anchors tethering her to sanity were popping lose, tearing nebulous chunks of memory and feeling loose at they went.

Twang, ping, snap!

This was it, the end.

The Panda Man's voice came a final time, inhuman and alien and deafening. "WHAT SAY YOU?"

Then she was screaming. "YES! YES! I'll do it. Just make it STOP!"

Then it was all gone. The Spider, the Vanished, the Pendulum. All the darkness and cold. All gone in an instant.

Warm air caressed her skin. Grey stones and rustling grass lay under a glittering sun and an infinity of pale blue sky. A pigeon cooed nearby.

But she felt no relief because something was different now. She had changed something, signed some ethereal contract.

Sold my soul. But to whom? The angels, or the devil?

Daddy's face flashed before her once more and shame filled her gut.

I'm sorry, Daddy. I'm so sorry.

A sigh whistled beside her and she jumped, almost surprised to see the Panda Man standing beside her. Somewhere behind that wolfish, victorious grin or his face, she saw regret. "I'm sorry I had to do that. Such things aren't meant for your kind. If I hadn't been sure you were so special, I would never have taken the risk. But I had to show you the truth."

"The truth?"

"This world never ended. Everyone is still alive and kicking—literally. They're just elsewhere. All part of a master plan to royally screw up all the worlds of the Web. And if you come with me, we can bring them back. You can save them all, Billy."

She didn't know what to say. But the words came anyway, without her help. "I don't care. I don't care about the dark or those people. I only care about Daddy." She swallowed, wiped the tears from her eyes—here, back in all the realness, the tears were real again—and stared him hard in the eye. "If I help you, will you leave me alone? Will you let me go back to Daddy?"

"Yes."

"Will you make him better?"

A shadow crossed his face. "I can't do that."

"Then let me go now."

"Billy, please—"

"No. I don't care. I want Daddy. He might go away any time. I was stupid when I listened to you and came all this way in the first place. I'm going back now. I'm not scared of you anymore."

She turned on her heel and made to walk away, but the Panda Man's voice made her freeze. It wasn't the words so much as the tone, so far removed from usual. He was begging. "If you go now, we all fall. Please, Billy."

She turned back to him slowly. "And Daddy? If I go back?"

"You'll see him awhile. But even if he recovers, what's coming will mean his end, and yours, just as surely as it'll spell it for everyone else."

"And if I go with you?"

He blinked. "I can't say. Nobody can see what is yet to come. If he's strong, he may live."

Fresh tears stung her eyes. "And we might be okay?"

"Maybe. I make no promises."

"Then why are you making me go?" She stamped. "Why did you bring me away from him?"

"Like I said, I'm offering a chance. Nothing more."

The stones and the Panda Man swam before her eyes as the tears piled up behind her eyelids. The patter of the teardrops falling to the grass joined the gentle whisper of the wind and the incessant cooing of the pigeons. Then, she was nodding, nodding despite the ache in her chest and the bubbling fear in her belly. "Okay."

He nodded slowly. "Okay."

"What do I have to do?"

He held out his hand once more. She winced at the thought of touching those fingers again, of the creeping cold they had brought, but stepped forward anyway. She made herself.

He smiled, but it was anything but comforting.

The moment she touched him, rain splashed down around her, and night swooped up to envelop the sunlight. Tall buildings sprang up all around, the very same from the half-forgotten dreams. She had tumbled into the dream world for real.

Once more the ragged cluster of people surrounding the twitching boy. One of them was the blond man she had seen before leaving daddy. The boy on the ground bore a striking resemblance to the other man she had seen.

It was all playing out before her all over again. This time, though, she knew the Panda Man was with her. He had something about him, not a smell but something like that.

"Why am I seeing this?" she said.

The next moment, he was beside her. She was a little worried that he didn't startle her.

Am I getting used to the silliness? That can't be good.

The Panda Man gnawed on a hanging fingernail, shrugging. "It's all part of your *big journey*. The ones running the show are big fans of melodrama."

She waited, bearing the jibe.

He continued. "It's important, that's why."

"Like me?"

He guffawed. "*Him?* No, not like you."

"Then what?"

The Panda Man gestured to the groaning lad, who bled steadily from a ragged cut on his forehead. "All this, all you've ever known, is just a scrim on top of … well, your language is too rudimentary to describe its scale and grandeur. In time, you'll see what I mean. This place is just some backwater nowhere. But at the same time it's vital, some kind of cosmic high ground." His face screwed up. "Excuse the purple prose, but in the words of the Solstice Scrolls: *All-Where is a web woven from the Pendulum's silk, and as with all things it has its ends; ends which can be moulded by those who take hold of them.*"

"I don't understand."

"I know. Don't worry about it. All you have to know is that this world *has* to stay safe, in balance. It's already been stretched thin by what you call the End. You've sensed them, haven't you? The darkness moving over the land?"

Billy swallowed, watching the twitching boy. He looked as if he was in so much *pain*. "Yes."

"If they aren't stopped, the show's over for everyone. And this idiot"—he pointed to the boy—"is one of the few people who can make a difference. So before we can start our real work, we've got to go save his sorry backside."

She blinked, suddenly exhausted by his words. "What real work?"

"One thing at a time, Billy."

Then the boy, the streets, and the rain were gone, and she was back at the Henge.

"Just help them," he said. "You'll know what to do."

"How?"

"The same way you got here."

The itch, the Light.

She felt her lip twitch. She didn't want to feel these things anymore or be pulled around like a puppet on strings.

But I have a choice. That's why he brought me all this way. All this funny magic can poke and prod, but it can't make me do anything. I can choose to go home to Daddy.

But if I go, we all go away. Me and Daddy will get sick, then everyone else … They go away because of the bad things that are going to happen. Attishoo, attishoo, we all fall down.

She swallowed hard. "Where do I go?"

He gave her a look that made her feel like he was looking inside of her, peering down through her eyes all the way to her toes. His eyes narrowed a tad, then he gave a small grunt of satisfaction. "You're in luck. We have an express service bound for your destination due to depart inside of a minute." He tittered. "I think you've walked far enough."

She shook her head. "What?"

He laughed more good-naturedly. "Just amusing myself, at your expense." He reached forward to grip her shoulders and turned her about-face, such that she was looking through the nearest of the ringstones.

The sun rises through this stone. On the morn of a summer's eve, the sun rises through its eye.

What did that mean? She didn't know. But the thought had arrived fully formed, just popped into her head like somebody else had spoken in her ear, only in her own voice.

But there was something else about this stone. She was looking at the grassy plain through its centre, but it was blurred, shimmering as though she was looking at its reflection in the surface of a running brook.

Another door.

"Radden Express, all aboard!" the Panda Man hollered. She hated that laugh, hated him and his ever-flipping mood.

She bunched her fists, wanting for all the world to mill her arms in a barrage of punching blows and beat him into the ground. But it wouldn't do any good. She would do what he wanted, then she would go home.

And maybe, just maybe, she and Daddy would be alright.

"What do I do?" she said.

"I think you know."

Step through.

She sighed, looked once more at him, and then stepped forward towards the ringstone. She paused and turned back to look at him over her shoulder. "Who *are* you?" she whispered.

He smiled, and for the first time, there was nothing scary or troubled about it. It was just a smile. "Call me Fol," he said.

She blinked.

Is that a weirder name than Panda Man or not?

She decided she didn't know as she stepped forward

through the ringstone. A sensation of being bent through an impossible angle, and she was appalled to realise it was, by now, a familiar feeling. Then the plain, the sun and the sky, the grass, the pigeons, Fol, and the ringstones were gone, and she was flying once more. But this time, it wasn't through darkness, and the moment of terror that filled her up at the thought that she had been tricked, that the Panda Man—or Fol—had sent her back to that void of torture, was replaced by open-mouthed wonder. She was flying. Flying over the world like a birdie. But she was moving faster than any bird; the ground was zipping past so fast it was only a blur of green and brown, mixed in with spots of grey and twinkling glass she guessed were cities.

Her stomach exploded with butterflies, and she was falling. She tumbled head over heels with a burst of that strange cold biting at her fingers and toes, and crackling in her hair. A rugged landscape of heathland, old broken towns, lakes and mountains rushed up to strike her in the face.

Then came a jolting impact. She saw stars, her head swam with soup-thick nausea, her back sang with pain against a hard floor, and a puff of dried leaves leapt into the air around her. She saw blue sky through a thick layer of fog hanging over her head and felt moist soil under her fingers. Thick ancient petrichor filled her nose.

She had landed.

But where?

Lucian took another lash of the whip across his shoulders with a resigned grunt, ignoring the burn in his hamstrings, and pushed his way over the lip of the sharp incline. Uneven ground pockmarked with rabbit holes passed underfoot, and a high wind was kicking up, turning to an unforgiving gale. They had been climbing for almost an hour, trudging uphill on legs barely strong enough to hold them on even ground.

He dropped back aways, hoping the rear security would be more lax and he'd have a chance at escaping. But they weren't fools, and a line of sentinels on horseback trawled at the very tail of the mile-long ant trail of prisoners, waiting to pick up any stragglers who weren't yet too weak to abandon on the wayside.

He thought for a while that feigning exhaustion would get him left behind. All he had to do was wait until they were out of sight, then run for the treeline, and make his way back south.

But those who keeled over were trampled by their fellow prisoners, many of whom were lost to catatonic stupors of hunger and fatigue. Worse, the guards rode their mounts' sharp hooves right over the torsos of the fallen, maybe to make an example, maybe for their own amusement.

Probably both.

Hundreds had been left behind on their journey. They were close to their destination—they had no clue where they were going, but a sense of closeness, of finality, pervaded them all. It seemed the guards wanted the rest of them alive.

And now, Lucian could see why. The ridge he had just crested overlooked a slight rolling valley, more of a dimple in the carpet of black rock and withered heather. He was looking along the furrow lengthways. Nestled within was a sprawling huddle of rawhide tents, interspersed with open fires and surrounded by palisade wooden fences.

Amongst it all were those already interned at the prison camp. He had never imagined there could be so many people in all the land. There were endless masses of them, an oozing myriad filling every inch between the tents, clustering in lumbering stoop-backed huddles around the glow of the fires. Filthy, stick-thin, harrow-eyed people marked by red welts from the lash.

A hand closed on his upper arm. "Come on, McKay," Vandeborn said, tugging him forward. He was still in the game, his barrel chest not yet hollowed by the long trek, and Lucian was glad to have at least one ally. And, unlike Lucian, Max had learned to keep his eyes on the ground and follow the flow of the convoy. He was a big, proud man, but he wasn't an idiot, and he wanted to live.

And here, everyone had a role to play. Theirs were *grovelling simpleton number 1000*, and *whipped dog number umpteen-and-one*, respectively.

Lucian couldn't bring himself to do that. A self-destructive itch poked its head up every time he lowered his gaze and tried surrendering to his captors' will. He was marking himself a prime candidate for public execution—plenty of examples had been made on the road, and there was still plenty of time for another—and he sensed that notoriety was something altogether a bad idea for another reason: Charlie had remained close to him all the while, within sight and earshot. He was a prized, secret cargo for the boy, at least in his mind; a morsel wrapped up in his handkerchief to savour later.

"Keep your head down. Keep moving," Vandeborn hissed. "We're almost there."

"We're there, alright." Lucian took up the plodding pace once more, and together, they made their way from the ridge and descended into the prison camp.

As they grew closer, he began to pick out more detail: the fires were in fact open-air smithing kilns, and the milling droves weren't clustering around them for warmth, but rather to heat old, blunted blades and sharp implements, readying them for reshaping. Farther away, showers of sparks coughed up above the tent posts where he guessed they were being hammered by others strong enough to wield a hammer.

They were forging weapons of war. Thousands of hunting knives, machetes, axes, pitchforks, even rough-hewn scaffolding poles whittled to sharp spears. And these were only the hand-to-hand weapons. He sensed that elsewhere, close by, were a great many firearms. The guards posted all around carried theirs with careless ease, indicating a plentiful supply.

Yet, peeking above all this, the thing that grabbed his attention the most was Charlie's gaze. He could feel it moving over him, as it so often had since they had started the long walk, pressing into the nape of his neck as though searching out the perfect spot to put a bullet.

The boy had plans to make him suffer, and he meant to make good on his promise for revenge.

But he wasn't up to it. Not yet, anyway. Anger had carried him this far, led him to this dangerous place— holding a secret captive amongst myriad others. Lucian was more valuable to them than any of these others by a mile-long stretch, a potential political prisoner.

Lucian would never have negotiated to save the life of another if it were him back home and someone else out here. But he knew fools back in New Canterbury and Canary Wharf who would. He couldn't live with himself, knowing they might have to sacrifice some vital strategic advantage in exchange for his sorry arse.

"I don't get it," Vandeborn said. "They're up in a fit about you all hogging food when the famine hit the hardest. They started the burning and killing to stop all that happening again. Sons of bitches would still get a bullet in the face from me, but I can wrap my head around where they'd be coming from." He grunted and glanced up momentarily from his feet, frowning at the camp ahead. "But I don't get this. None of these people are part of this. None of them wanted it. They're just ordinary folk." He paused as they passed under the nose of a skull-faced guard of almost seven feet, his skin a sickly yellow, a cruel soul if Lucian had ever seen one.

"No," Lucian said. "It's them that are behind all this. The ones holding the guns, and the keys." He grunted, not quite managing a laugh. "But the real kicker is that I'm betting bastards like that don't even know why they're here. This is just what they do. In the Old World, they would have been the rapists, the murderers, the psychopaths and the autocrats. But here, after the End, they're the perfect engine to blow this all out of proportion. I'm betting it all started amicable enough, with a real heart and message. But now …"

"Snowballed. That pigeon banner, the sob story about the starving women and children who died because of your mission, it's become just some vehicle to let the mental cases kill for the sake of killing. All these monkeys would have been rejects their whole lives, cut loose by their families and neighbours, turned away by every place they came by. Crazy breeds crazy, and nobody wants a madman around. But here, they're somebodies. Gods, even. They have power, and they take what they want and nobody can stop them."

Lucian was listening carefully. He had gotten the ball rolling on the conversation with great care, but here was the crux. He needed to know where Vandeborn's mind was. How far he had gotten on his own. "Right," he said, baiting the way ahead.

"But, there has to be something else going on," Vandeborn said. "The pace of all this, the pattern of attack, this place … it doesn't add up. They're like dogs circling in for the kill, and that just ain't how mobs play out.

"They should have been sloppy, sudden. They should have made mistakes. Hell, a mob on some revenge kick wouldn't have stood a chance against Twingo. But these guys, they're thinking. There's a plan, and it wasn't hatched by no committee. There's a man behind the curtain."

Lucian suppressed a smile.

Thank God somebody else has a head on their shoulders.

"There always is," he said.

"Any idea who it might be?"

Lucian kept his gaze on the ground. They were passing the first of the tents. Not only did he not want to risk being overheard, but he needed to keep them both focused on the here and now. "No," he said. "But we'll get to that soon enough."

"Oh yeah? You got plans to break out of dodge?"

"Yes."

"That's what I like to hear." They passed by a tent with an open flap, and they caught a glimpse of a small mountain of assault rifles within. Almost all were in varying states of decay and would never fire again, but there were so many, and at least a few of them would get a few dozen rounds off—though they could just as likely explode and kill the poor saps pulling the triggers. If even half these tents stored similar loot, they were in big trouble. "We've got our work cut out for us. These guys are serious." He cursed. "I never was any great fan of Cain, the mission, or any of the lot of you. We looked after you because you brought in the trade. But right now, I wish we'd paid you a little more kindness. Maybe we wouldn't be in this mess."

"It wouldn't have made any difference. We started this."

"What are you blabbing about?"

"Don't play dumb. You're not as stupid as some of those starry-eyed fools who come trooping around New Canterbury trying to spot the *Great Cain* and his little band of disciples. You know we've got skeletons in our cupboard, just like everyone else. And the famine sent them all marching out to bend us over for just desserts."

Vandeborn managed a laugh—a coarse and wheezy snort. "They got you, alright. Laid out flat over the kitchen counter with your skirt up over your head."

"Nice image."

"Take mind-candy where you can get it, mate."

"I'm not complaining."

Vandeborn shook his head. "You're alright, McKay."

"Yeah, well, you're still the same arsehole you always were."

The tents were thick all around them now. Up ahead, the ant trail was coiling up into a mass of milling, stupefied prisoners, all staring around at the other inmates. Written on their faces was the acceptance of doom in a mouse's frozen stance, in the moment before the cat's jaws go to work. Before anyone could find a spare moment to squat or fall prone in the mud, before Lucian and Max had even come within a hundred feet of the main body of them, blunt blades and whetstones were being hauled out from the nearest tents.

There was no sympathy on the faces of the other prisoners as they dumped the masses of iron and steel at the feet of so many hundreds of bedraggled figures, most of whom weren't even strong enough to lift their arms.

There was no room for sympathy here. Anyone weak enough for compassion wouldn't last long.

"So what's the breakout plan, chief?" Vandeborn whispered as they bent and hauled up an armful of rusted meat cleavers.

Lucian grunted. "Keep our heads low for now. Scope the place out. And the others. We'll need as many on our side as we can."

"That it? I could have spat that shite out. I meant a way to do any of that. How are we gunna get *out* of dodge?"

Lucian nodded over his shoulder, but kept his gaze low and his body moving. The guards watched them all closely, watching for stragglers, for weakness. And then there was Charlie to worry about; he wouldn't be far away, even now. "Up there. See the tent?" He took his small pile to an empty furrow between two smaller tents and set to work with the whetstone, ignoring the guards posted every few dozen feet. Showers of sparks sputtered into the mud.

He tensed despite himself as Vandeborn glanced in the direction he'd nodded, but the big guy was subtle enough, and he relaxed again.

The valley lay at the foot of a sheer cliff, rising several

hundred feet straight up to the edge of an old cluster of Victorian buildings. He sensed a large Old World settlement beyond the lip of the incline, and he had an inkling that he knew which. This place looked a lot like how Alex had described his hometown. He bet that up there was Radden.

Perched upon the very edge of the summit was a tepee-style tent, a crumpled cone of beaten, black leather. A small sliver of smoke trailed into the sky from within.

"There's our man behind the curtain," Vandeborn said. He struck an ornamental katana with his own whetstone and a cascade of sparks burst forth like a Catherine wheel. "What do we wish for when we get up there?"

I'm bloody lucky I'm not alone on this. I might actually stand a chance at getting up there.

But if he did? If they got up there and confronted whoever masterminded all this? And if it really was James running the show? Even after all that had happened, even if the lives of everyone he'd ever known were riding on it, could he really bring himself to kill his brother?"

Vandeborn was watching him closely. He cleared his throat and muttered, "One thing at a time."

CHAPTER 17

"**T**his is crazy," Allie said.

"Really, bloody crazy," Richard muttered.

Norman shook his head. "That ain't half of it."

Richard grumbled under his breath as he scooped up armfuls of maps, books of censuses and inventories, and a hastily scratched out transcript of the summit proceedings. "And yet I wouldn't have it any other way. Once more into the fray, dear friends, and all that." Glancing over at John DeGray with hungry eagerness, he set to stumbling through the crowd, squawking for people to stay clear. He left a trail of paper and dusty volumes in his wake.

Norman watched him go with mixed amusement and regret. He was still reeling from sitting at the councillors' bench. Watching the young fool skitter across the tower's dusty marble floor in aid of his master, he felt a slick of bile grease his throat.

Many people under the mission's banner had made their beds, and had no illusions about lying in them. But starry-eyed youngsters like Richard, raised to believe in the unassailable *goodness* of the mission and their elders' past deeds, they were all setting out to march to their dooms.

None of them have a clue.

Most had already volunteered for roles they thought best suited to their experience, and fractured into myriad sub-groups, each tasked with a different aspect of the fledgling expedition.

That was all there had been time for. A fledgling plan. No ironing out creases, no trimming the fuzzy edges.

If things went to hell, they would all go together.

Norman paused with a wordless cry, gritting his teeth. Cold had clamped down on his skin with sharp fangs.

It's happening again!

He fought to keep hold of the here and now, but he felt himself slipping, as though on sheet ice. The Echoes were all around: suited men and women, tourists encumbered with shopping bags and cameras slung over their necks, even the odd sweat-covered intern scrabbling with trays of coffee. All oblivious to their eventual fate.

Was this some freakish journey behind the curtain of the End's mystery, or had he really lost it?

What do you think, genius? If everyone weren't so distracted, they would have carted you away already.

No, it couldn't be real.

But then the cold intensified—painful gnawing cold that couldn't be thawed in a thousand years. He looked down at his hands and almost gasped aloud. Trails of vapour streamed off his knuckles, the kind that rises off melting snow.

Either it's real, or I'm in real trouble.

He concentrated on breathing until it had passed, and he felt warmth steeling into him again. He couldn't afford this, not now. He had to be strong.

Like we have a chance, anyway, said a traitorous voice in the back of his head.

He resisted the urge to slap himself.

No! At least we're doing something, *now. Anything's better than cowering here and waiting for death.*

Evelyn had banged her gavel and disbanded the council without pomp or ceremony, and everyone had drained from the chambers as one. Most of them would never be together again, that much was certain. People were going to die. A lot of people.

For the vast majority, the task now was damage control. If they could scramble enough resources, barricade any remaining dwellings, put enough guns in enough untrained, shaking hands, some of them might pull through.

Meanwhile, a small breakoff faction prepared the expedition that was blue-skies whimsy at best, and at worst a kamikaze dash of insanity. Norman was surprised just how many had volunteered to make the journey north. Radden was only a word to almost all of them—and an oft-avoided subject even to himself—and yet there was scarcely space for them all in the tower corridors. In fact, they were clamouring, desperate to get close to Alexander, Lincoln, John DeGray, and Marek Johnson, who had adopted the roles of de facto generals of a coalescing, ramshackle regiment.

Though he stood to the side, his ribs safe from the squeezing and buffeting of the crowd, Norman knew he was one of those generals. Eyes were moving over him constantly now, and he felt a magnetic, expectant tug drawing him forward.

It's because of what I started in there. Now that I've spoken in the chambers, sat at the bench, I've triggered what they've been waiting for all this time, ever since I was a nipper. They've all been waiting for me to pick up a staff and march them into the desert. The Chosen One.

He shivered.

Him, a leader of men, in what could be the last, most foolish cavalry charge in all of history.

I'm a cripple. And they're looking to me.

Despite an atmosphere so thick with imminent doom that it could be carved up and used for sandwich filling, he laughed to himself, a full-throated bawl that sent a few onlookers blinking in alarm.

Well, fine, he thought. If that's what they need, who am I to say no? It's all I might be good for at this point: play the role, be the bobble head they all need. Even if I'm fit to drop at the first sign of trouble, even if I'm a tongue-tied loser who couldn't string a speech together to save his own sorry skin.

Allie was staring at him hard. Her cheeks were flushed. He knew she wasn't thinking about any charge upon the Scottish Highlands.

He sighed. "What's wrong?"

"You're not going."

"I have to."

"No, you don't!" She seized his forearm in a death grip to belittle that of a falcon's talons.

He bent his head low. "Look, you know what's happening. You know what they all expect. And I know you've been told the same stories about me and Alexander since before you even came to New Canterbury. So don't stand there and play innocent like it's all some big, unfair punishment from Mummy Evelyn and Daddy Alexander. I'm a part of this now. I don't like it, of course I don't. So do me a favour and help me figure out how the hell I'm going to mount a horse, instead of standing there complaining!"

His voice was shuddering with the outburst, his breath stolen by an explosion of pain in his ribs. He grunted and fell against her, and she caught him with a wordless sob.

"See! See! You can't do this. It's madness."

"Don't," he muttered, wiping his lips with the back of his hand. "Don't." He met her gaze, saw the tears in the corners of her eyes, and had to look away again. Strings were plucked deep in his chest. "I'm sorry," he said, squeezing her palm.

Not long ago, her hands had been like the rest of her, wrapped in the softness of youth, pudgy and flushed and rounded. An image flashed in his memory of her naivety and fury at the famine's harsh reality, and the speed with which she had spread gossip throughout New Canterbury.

All of that was overshadowed by the young woman before him now. Her face was pockmarked by half-healed cuts from working the fields to save the last of the harvest, and streaked with the blood of those in the infirmary. Her hands had become wiry, roughened by blossoming, cracked callouses.

It all stirred only more violet, gushing desire inside him, accentuating her femininity. Neither of them had bathed since leaving home, yet he could have stood close and breathed her in for all time.

His pulse began racing, and then he was pulling her away from the masses of people, ignoring the screaming protest from his ribcage, pulling her along in his wake. He didn't stop until they rounded a corner, and then there was only heat and hands, and her lips on his.

*

They emerged from a disused storage cupboard some time later. Oblivion loomed, with only hours to prepare their last stand, and dispatch orders to the mission's kingdom. Their last bastions of strength could have been crumbling this very moment.

Here he was, one of the only men in all the land who could make a difference, and he had chosen to spend a wad of those precious moments canoodling in a dusty old cupboard.

Bloody right I did. All these fools should be doing the very same thing.

He couldn't help but feel sorry for them all as he led Allie by the hand back into the mayhem.

Order was forming from chaos. Norman could hear more activity outside, preparations for the myriad journeys to surviving settlements. Emergency rations were being raided and divvied up, the river assaulted with every pail and bucket. Tents, bedrolls, cooking pots and firelighters that hadn't seen action in years were being hauled from storage and shaken out in the wind.

Norman pulled Allie still farther into the masses, passing droves who now saluted him in a manner so casual he felt invested by unseen power, as though their faith hardened his bones and buoyed him up so he floated two inches above the floor. He didn't welcome it—didn't want to become that, one of *those men*, but the sensations came nonetheless.

They neared the centre of the mass as Lincoln spread his arms for silence, and though he was frail and brittle as a rusted girder, a bubble of silence with a twenty-foot radius slammed down over the congregation. "It's settled, then. Those who'll make ready the tower and elsewhere in the capital, rally to me. Sign your names with Latif Hadad and report to my workshop for instructions. Hurry, damn it!"

A swirling vortex of bodies oozed from the body of the crowd, swarmed Latif in a whirlwind of noise and scribbling and then vanished outside.

"Those with tactical knowledge or experience, join Professor DeGray. You will be our eyes and ears and our brains. Every decision henceforth will be made by majority vote from those who step forward, with veto power invested in the remaining councillors. Step forward, now."

Another more solemn sub-group slunk from the crowd

and stood before John and Richard: wizened combat veterans, academic types, terrified bibliophiles, and those with bodies lame but minds sharp all trailed forth. After a few quiet words from DeGray, and the distribution of key materials from Richard's bulging satchels, they too disappeared, heading for the tower's upper levels.

The crowd was thinning. Norman dragged Allie steadily onward, receiving more attention all the while. Salutes came in an endless blur, interspersed with the occasional bow or a grabbing hand from someone who just wanted to *touch him*, feel that the Chosen One was really among them.

And why not? He was the Chosen One. It was a lie; a falsity to which everyone was at least subconsciously aware. But what of it? That didn't make it any less real.

Lincoln continued. "Those willing to journey to the outer settlements, I ask you report to Evelyn Fisher and Alexander Cain. I will not sugar coat this. Most of you will be volunteering for certain death. But you may save lives by giving forewarning. There is no shame in refusal. I would sooner we all die than order the sacrifice a single pound of flesh.

"But you must also know this. We stand as one, or we die apart. Ladies and gentlemen, together we carry the Old World's flame. Today, that flame is dimming. I ask you step forward, one last time, lest it go out forever."

This time the entire crowd moved forward as one—heaving masses that numbered in the hundreds, maybe thousands. People who, on their own, might have been snivelling, crumpled wrecks, and accepted their fate without a fight, had been turned into true soldiers by words alone. The sheer volume of their echoing footsteps boggled comprehension—in all his life, Norman had never heard such a thing.

They would stand and fight for those they loved.

Norman came to stand beside the other generals not a moment too soon, for a stillness charged with appreciation that *this was it*, that *the lines had been drawn*, fell heavy over their shoulders like a smothering blanket. The dreary hopelessness had been washed out, and the air seemed almost runny, it was so light. But was this worse, the sheer finality of it all?

If we pull through, we'll be scarred deep, a remnant of all we've built. And if we don't … then that'll be that. The Old World will be truly gone, a rosy figment in the imagination of a few outcast undesirables.

Homes would burn, the knowledge and wisdom of mankind would slip into the void of unknowing, and darkness would run free over everything. And how long would that new Dark Age last? A decade? A century? A millennium?

How long would it take for the next renaissance to revive that spark? Was there even any certainty it would *ever* happen?

Norman's chest quivered at the thought of it.

How different all this could have been. If Mum and Dad had shacked up with somebody else, I might have accepted the world winding down, teetering on a knife-edge, in exchange for a little peace. I could have been happy living off some small patch of land way out where nobody ever bothered with. It would have been so easy to live, marry and bring up a few kids, love them and protect them, and die unaccomplished. I could have been buried in an unmarked grave, forgotten and uncelebrated. I could have done that.

Hell, right now that seemed like downright bliss.

But fate hadn't swung that way. He had been dealt another hand.

And amongst all his doubt and misery, there rested a nugget of truth that would never yield: he loved them, and this life. He knew that now—all the times he had been lauded a hero, all the times he had shied away and swallowed that great lump of hatred and fear in his throat, he had loved them; the homes they built and memory of the Old World they kept alive by their very being.

Allison now stood in front of Alexander. During the few moments their lips had parted in the cupboard, they had come to a decision. She would return home to New Canterbury, and do all she could. It was where she held the most sway, and could conjure the most comfort. Her gift of the gab could finally be cashed in fully.

But Norman wouldn't be going home. She had cried, even beat him on the chest in weak sobbing slaps, but she hadn't fought his decision. In the whites of her eyes, he had seen anguish squashed by acceptance, and something else. If he had been a romantic, he would have called it love.

As things were, he was ready to call it pride. She nodded to him now, and he was sure his feet lifted yet another inch off the floor.

If only none of this had happened. What might we have done? What would our children have looked like?

Lincoln spoke a final time, and all thoughts of what might have been, vanished.

"Those who wish to journey north to Radden in search of aid, step towards Norman Creek."

Only a hundred remained in the corridor. Every one of them stepped up.

Norman breathed a sigh of relief.

Good, they look strong, determined.

Most of all, he was relieved to see fear in their eyes. He had learned that was the true sign of strength: fear that threatened to tear the soul and send a person insane, overcome by sheer force of will, a refusal to give in.

He couldn't help but feel they belonged to him now. He could almost feel the weight of their souls in his hands. He took a deep breath, not knowing what he would say, but trusting his body. "Thank you," he said and was relieved at how strong he sounded.

Almost like Alexander. Well, not quite, but maybe something sank in, after all.

He could feel Alexander's eyes on him, above all the other thousands of stares. And though he would never forgive him for what he had done to his life, he met his gaze and nodded.

He would see the job done.

Then he was speaking again, not by choice, but because the Chosen One had taken control. "We leave as soon as we're ready. Make your preparations, and say your goodbyes. We ride for Radden."

Just like that, it was over. The council disbanded, the corridors emptied of bodies like a tub emptied of water, and silence fell over the chambers, maybe for evermore.

CHAPTER 18

"Fire!" yelled Sarah.

The answering bellow of two dozen pistols kicked up in perfect unison, and the long row of humanoid dummies lined up before the New Canterbury militia disappeared in a mist of woodchips and powdered straw. Some of them were cut clean in two, the obliterated heads and torsos toppling to the ground.

Each of those wielding a weapon flipped the safety catch without instruction and adopted two-handed poses, the weapons' noses pointed into the dirt. There were satisfied smiles aplenty.

She's done it, Robert thought. They're actually landing hits.

Heather had taken to the front line herself. Her target had been sheared off at chest level. The good doctor's face contorted into a snarl.

They were still amateurs, but they were fast learners. Already they seldom missed, even if they were only shooting at near point-blank range. But at least it was something. Guns were no longer alien to them.

And that was about as good as he would have ever dared hope for.

But it wasn't them that instilled the triumph coursing behind his eyes. It was Sarah.

The librarian's metamorphosis was complete. Somewhere behind the stiff posture and cold-steel glare, he could see the dim echo of the woman he had torn kicking and screaming from the massacre on the hill not two days before. In that short time she had shed the pall of softness that a lifetime behind bookshelves and teacher's desks had afforded her.

But it was only that. An echo.

The woman before him now was capable of ordering a volley against live targets. There was a hunger in her eyes, a hunger for blood. On a usual day it would have sent his bowels itching with concern and fear; the juxtaposition of that emotionless glare with her soft pale face was alarming.

But this was no ordinary day.

"They're getting better," she whispered, keeping her eyes on them. She nodded emphatically and twirled her finger to indicate that those next in line should take position.

While guns changed hands and the dummies were put back into some kind of humanoid form, Robert let a smile pass his lips. "They're much better," he said. He tried to inject as much encouragement into his voice as possible.

She looked pleased under the icy sheen that had formed over her body. "You think we'll be ready?"

To face off against what's coming? Never in a million years.
"You bet."

"Really?"

He looked her in the eyes. It was crucial he have hope, because he could see that she needed bolstering, even propped up by all her fury and lust for revenge. Even book burning wasn't enough to turn her into a stone-cold killer. She needed a kick in the pants.

He sucked as much doubt from his gaze as he could muster and forced a toothy grin. "They won't know what hit them."

Her face glowed, and she was on the verge of replying when a cry rang out behind them.

Robert turned to see one of the boys on Higgins's patrol racing across the open meadow, slinking between denuded fences and bushes in a scatty attempt at stealth. He reached them within the minute, doubled over with his hands on his knees, and said, "Coming … Someone's …coming!"

Robert didn't wait. He lifted the boy off the ground and ran with him, bounding back towards the city.

*

"Don't shoot!"

The hooves rattling upon the cobbled streets of New Canterbury had in times past brought forth crowds of gabbling locals, eager to welcome whichever weary traveller had wandered into their midst. The world had been a shade lighter then.

Now, the city could have been deserted. Nothing stirred, and silence pressed on the ear like a buffeting wind. Robert watched the lone rider canter towards the cathedral, rifle held above his head in a clear sign of surrender. It could have been a trick—maybe the son of a bitch had a bomb strapped to his chest.

But that didn't ring true to their style. And life was too short to keep tiptoeing around the first sign of trouble. He waved for Higgins and the boys to stay where they were, caught the eye of a few other sentries perched in their own hiding places, and received nods of encouragement from each. Then he descended the stairs and kicked the door open, back pressed flat against the wall.

"Who goes?" he said. His heavy voice made the rotting wall thrum and sent a cascade of cement dust raining down over his bald head.

"Name's Arnold. From the tower. I bring word from the council of Cain's mission."

Robert needed no more. If he was lying, then he'd be blown away in the next moment, and they could go back to their business. He was tired of this piddly shit, creeping around.

Sighing, he stepped out and approached the rider, his rifle trained on the newcomer until he was only a few paces away. Then he slung his rifle up over his shoulder, and the two of them nodded to one another. There was a hardness there, and a harrowed callousness in the rider's eyes, that removed the last traces of doubt from Robert's mind.

"Well, Arnold from the tower, speak your piece," Robert said.

"You're Robert Strong." It wasn't a question.

"Yes."

"I was told you'd be in charge."

"I suppose."

I'd call it holding onto the reins of dear life, but who's keeping tabs?

"What's your situation?"

"I'm the one asking the questions, friend. For all I know, you're of them."

"I'm *not* one of them." Arnold's eyes burned into his, and Robert saw and a flash of something almost like an instant replay—an echo of something terrible. No man could fake that.

Robert had read the eyes of many men in countless face-offs. No man could fake remembering the screams of children. And now he was close, Robert could see Arnold had flecks of dried blood on his face.

"No, you're not," he said. He turned over his shoulder, scanned the empty streets, trying to see it through Arnold's eyes. The cobbles were bare, every door shut tight—some nailed and boarded, others bearing windows bricked in. If tumbleweeds had been native to cities, they would have taken over this one in great swarms. "We're holding on," he said. "They were here not long ago, and I thought we were through. They stole, took things … They were playing with us. Then they just …"

"Left."

"Yes."

"Same story everywhere, it seems."

"Everywhere?"

Arnold's eyes flickered. "They're getting ready."

"For what?"

"The last big push. We haven't much time."

Robert took a step closer. His rifle was forgotten on his back. "Tell me everything."

*

Arnold spent the better part of fifteen minutes laying it all out: the siege and the carnage, the summit, the radio message, the final scrambling preparations, and the march on Radden. Robert's guts twisted up at the mention of the journey north.

Fools. What good could they possibly do, now? They think they're going to go skipping off to the far North for a wee chat with the Scots and find all the firepower we need waiting on a silver platter?

They don't know the North. Not like I do.

"And Norman's leading those idiots?" he said finally.

Arnold's brow twitched. "Mr Creek, yes."

He's not ready for that, not by a long shot. I don't think he ever will be. I can't believe anybody would follow that beaten sack of nerves anywhere.

"When do they leave?"

Arnold looked encouraged for the first time. "They're waiting on a few, sir."

"Who?"

"Well, I can't speak for most, but I was sent for one of them."

"Damn you, who?"

"You."

Robert blinked. He had known that was coming, of course he had. Yet to hear it spoken aloud now sent alarm bells ringing all across his head. Things had just been settling down; he had just been getting a handle on the situation.

Because, of course, he would go. He might hate it, might curse the names of anyone accompanying him, but he would go. He had to. He was the only one with any real experience of the lands north of Manchester.

Damn.

It had looked as though maybe, just maybe, he would have been able to keep them together long enough to hold out. Maybe even a few of them could have pulled through. The militia could have made a real difference if they had but another day to prepare.

And now he was going to be plucked from their midst. There was nobody else he could think of who had the mettle to stand as leader, nobody …

"Don't worry yourself, the city will be fine."

Robert fixed him with a sharp look.

Arnold was unperturbed. "Most of your ambassadorial convoy are returning."

"Who?"

"I'm told that Agatha Fisher, of the elders, will be in authority. The convoy will be headed by Allison Rutherford."

Rutherford! She was in charge?

She was a girl. A chatty Cathy at best.

What happened to Alexander? Or even DeGray?

And Agatha Fisher … She was a doll, a wonderful woman in her clear spells. But the dementia had taken a good strong hold of her now. She would be a burden if anything.

There was nobody. No leader—

Sarah.

She could do it. Even a handful of hours ago it would have been ludicrous, just asking for strife and bloodshed, but not now. Somehow, he knew she would never be the same again. They were all listening to her now; they looked in her direction before his despite all his stature and experience. Even rumbling, grizzled old men had lost any patronising tones. And, of course, the city's children adored her, would throw themselves over a cliff-edge if she but asked.

He didn't like it, not one bit. He'd sooner leave the city unguarded than single her out and make her such a target. But her newfound strength had left him so taken aback he was willing to believe she was capable of anything.

He had looked into her, just as he had looked into Higgins and Arnold the rider, and he had seen who she really was. And though he now had to face the fact he had never really known her at all before now, he knew he was wholly in love with that woman, the one who had been caged under those spectacles and that inch-thick sheen of soft-voiced pleasantness.

A hell-cat who could tear the balls off a seven-foot grizzly bear.

Even as he thought it, a distant flurry of whip cracks sounded out in the fields. She still had them at it, even with him having raced away to the city with the threat of impending attack a very real possibility.

"Fine," he said. "I'll go."

Arnold took the news without comment. Robert suspected the man had been instructed to expect nothing else.

The cheek of them all. That's Alexander's doing, no doubt. They can't put all this on me. And I know they will. They'll turn right around to me as soon as I get there, and expect me to go right along with whatever suicide mission they've concocted. Hell, I bet they'll be waiting for me to lead the charge.

"We haven't much time," Arnold said impatiently.

"Make time." Robert was walking back along the street, his eye catching slivers of light shining out from barely cracked doorjambs and curtains just parted. The city was slowly waking in the presence of the visitor, crawling from its shell and blinking in the sun. But he didn't have time to play den mother to them now. He was heading back towards the meadows. "I have to tell my fiancée."

*

She said only one thing in reply. "We're having our wedding, Robert."

He swallowed despite himself. "I'm coming back, Sarah."

He expected that to have some effect; he was even braced to lean forward and take her forearms in his hands as she softened. But her rigid frame didn't yield an inch, nor did her eyes thaw a single degree. In fact, she folded her arms over her chest and cocked her hip. "I know you are," she said. Her tone of voice said, *If you didn't, I'd raise you from the dead so I could kill you myself.* "But I'm not talking about when you come back. We're going to have that wedding, or you're not going anywhere."

She sounds like my mother. The thought ricocheted through Robert's mind without any help from him. He didn't even remember his mother, not really; she had died when he was very young. But now, as he dwelled on it, murky flashes of a stern-faced, foot-tapping woman swam up from the inky blackness. He could hear her voice even now, eerily similar to the nasal honk Sarah developed when she was stressed, like now.

It would have been funny if he weren't so mortified.

The militia were milling at a safe distance, occupying themselves with a sudden fascination with the city skyline, and plans to relieve the sentries who had now been posted on the rooftops for almost fourteen straight hours. Nevertheless, occasionally one of them would give the game away, and glance in Robert and Sarah's direction. They couldn't quite make enough noise to cover Sarah's exclamations, and an uncomfortable tension had settled over the meadow.

Robert wanted to move them away to a more private spot. Leaders couldn't be seen to have any weakness, especially not the domestic kind. But the thought of suggesting it made his insides shrivel.

Sarah took a step forward so that her chest pressed against his navel, and she stared up at him at a sheer eighty-degree angle. Her eyes radiated twin hairline beams of focused energy that he was sure cut through the back of his skull and cleaved the clouds in twain high above. "We *are* going to be married before you set foot out of the city. I don't care if the entire place burns to the ground around us. I don't care if the very last things I see in this world are your monkey shoulders squashed into some rotten Old World tux. I'm marrying you, Robert."

He considered resisting, considered voicing the sheer ridiculousness of what she was saying. Dozens of people they loved and would call their friends were relying on them, and thousands more needed them to stand fast. The rush to the finish line was almost upon them, and they were being called upon.

And they were going to hold it all up to tie the knot?

God alive, she'll be the end of me.

But she was right. The suddenness with which he agreed struck him hard.

If they were going to sacrifice everything, they deserved it. It was true, they were being called upon. But the vast majority of the people for whom they were set to give everything would forever be unknown to them.

How could they ask any less than to put their own affairs in order?

He swallowed, and his throat emitted a sharp crack that echoed out over the silent fields. "Yes, ma'am," he said.

CHAPTER 19

All the commotion could have fooled one into thinking things were bound to fall apart, that the centre couldn't hold, things were going awry, and a load of other poetical jazz. But the truth was that the plan was sublime in its simplicity.

The brains would stay in the tower; the muscle would act as runners.

The rest would march north. They were travelling light, with no wagons, extra sundries or foodstuffs to weigh them down. They were taking saddles, bedrolls, a small sack of food apiece, water canteens, and their weapons. There would be no leniency for those who couldn't keep up. People were going to be left behind.

Some would die of exposure or stupid accidents before they even arrived in Radden, of that there seemed little doubt. But the hundred riders all stood fast, and said their goodbyes: some stonily, some weeping and beslobbered; others holding their loved ones trembling, white-lipped, their eyes fixed on the middle distance.

Norman had been relying on Robert to lead the charge.

He balked when the messenger dispatched to New Canterbury arrived back and announced that Robert would be delayed for 'personal reasons'.

"But *why*?

Arnold, the rider, moved restlessly on his saddle as he trotted for the stables. "Part of getting the son of a bitch to come at all was on the condition that I leave his business out of this."

Norman cursed and set to wandering the tower, easing his aching chest as things came together into something resembling an organised force. They were sending as many of the wounded away as they could, though dozens were in too serious a condition to even lift.

What went unsaid was that they were moving the wounded because they were too stark a reminder of what was to come. Morale was all they had left to keep them going. It was hard to stay brave and chipper with a hundred screaming, bloodied friends and family lying riddled with holes on the sixth floor.

Now that decisions had been finalised, everyone was itching to move. The time for sentimentality had evaporated, and they longed to take the steps that might just save them.

Behind the discussions on the best route to ride north, which weapons to take, what they would do if the radio transmission turned out to be a genuine distress call—and what they would do if it was something more sinister— Norman's stomach tap-danced, as he wondered how he could ride north on a few fractured ribs without doing himself serious damage.

He was well on the way to healing, but this kind of exertion was plain stupid. If Heather had been there, she would have surely had him laid up to rest somewhere. The very idea of her signing off on him traipsing away into the unknown with a hundred burly men was enough to get him laughing—exactly what somebody with broken ribs didn't need.

But he had to keep that to himself, even if it was killing him inside. Even if he ended up a cripple for the rest of his life. Even if riding north killed him. That was his lot.

John DeGray and Richard had formulated several strategies and contingencies in short order and had given a crash course on the terrain they would be covering. Norman had expected that they would cover a little politics and negotiating tactics; Old World libraries were full of that kind of academic spiel. But they hadn't said a word about it. Instead, they had done something that would have been funny, had their faces not been so grave and fearful.

"We're going with you," John said, his rotund bulk emphasized by a glum slouch. He sounded resigned to it, as though he were relaying orders received from a higher power.

Norman would sooner have taken Oppenheimer's daughter. The professor was lithe as a two-hundred-pound boulder and on a good day was bound to fall off his mount at the sight of uneven ground.

But it wasn't DeGray that troubled Norman the most. It was Richard. He didn't look resigned at all, but eager and excited, like a younger sibling pacing around the feet of his elders, itching to be part of the football game.

It's like the attack on New Canterbury all over again, the night Ray was killed.

Neither of them had any place out there in the wild lands. They were too insulated from the grotesqueries of the world. It was a strange thing, to have people so senior in their order be so naive and innocent, but that was a by-product of the Old World way.

They belonged in the classroom, cataloguing the books and records brought back from the wastes, laboriously passing that knowledge on to the next generation.

Yet they seemed set on Radden. The fear in their eyes indicated they knew they would probably not come back, but that they also knew the expedition would go to ruin without them.

Norman didn't want to admit it, but he couldn't ignore the fact that Richard had saved his life during the New Canterbury attack. He would be dead if Richard hadn't pulled him from the crossfire.

Might as well accept it, their faces said.

What could he do? There were more messed up things about the expedition anyway.

Things are backward: those in the lead are broken, nervous wrecks, and the hundred at our command are holding things together. This is going to be a weird couple of days.

He kept walking, trying to ignore the creeping frost biting at his fingertips and stabbing at his earlobes. He couldn't fade away to that dark place, not now. Not again.

He sensed that if he sank back into the shadows, he might not be able to get back.

And what then? He might be lost to that alien place, between worlds, in that non-space where all those Old World people bawled. Or, the alternative: he really was crazy, and would spend the rest of his life a vacant drooling idiot.

Shaking his head, trying to ignore the edges of Echoes slithering in his peripheral vision, he kept on walking until he left Richard and DeGray behind, and was walking at random through the crowd.

He didn't stop until Alexander appeared amongst it all, the spider at the centre of the vast web—

Spider. At the middle of it all, there's always a spider, spinning the web of reality under the Pendulum's swing.

Norman blinked away a mental flash of eight enormous, arachnoid eyes, and approached Alexander. They fell into step on a parallel path, so as not to arouse attention.

"Be honest," Norman said, hating the tap of his cane on the ground. "Just once. Tell me, did you think this time would ever come? Really believe that I could do what you promised them?"

Only a beat passed before Alexander answered. "No. I didn't."

Norman nodded. He expected a swell of rage to twist his hands into claws. But he didn't feel a thing. In fact, he felt relieved because he knew that, finally, what Alexander said was the truth.

He had earned that. It was a small victory, but it was

more than he had had before.

"Then why?" he said. "You didn't need me. They always looked to you like you were a god."

"I'm just a man. No matter how many people believed in the mission or in me, it could never have matched the kind of belief that comes with something greater."

"But I'm just a man, too."

"It doesn't matter. They were taught to dream of a man who they didn't see before them. But all they need is faith in the idea that the *metamorphosis* was possible."

"You played with my life for an idea."

"And I'd do it again."

There it was. It had finally been said.

Would it really have been so hard to tell it like it was a long time ago? Couldn't he have respected me enough to tell me that I was expendable, just another pawn? I knew it, and he knew I knew.

Still, it had finally come out.

He stopped and turned to Alexander. "Thank you."

Alexander's eyes softened for a moment. "I'm leaving within the hour."

Norman flinched. "*What?*"

"I'm leaving."

"To go where?" he hissed, gripping Alexander's arm.

He stumbled a tad and his ribs screeched in unison, but he ignored the pain. The Echoes drifting in his peripheral vision faded, and the cold numbing his fingertips was suddenly gone. He had been shaken back to the here and now. But that didn't detract from the strength of his grip, nor the panic boiling in his gut.

Alexander's gaze remained cool. "Away from here, before I get anyone else killed."

"What are you talking about?"

"You saw what happened when I went after Oppenheimer. They're after me. All of this is because of me. Maybe if I go, this place stands a chance."

"Without you, we definitely don't stand a chance."

"I've done all I can—all the damage I can. It's you they're going to look to now. I might be able to warn a few others."

"You can't be serious. We're all staring death in the face instead of running for the hills because we believe in your mumbo-jumbo about saving the world.

"I know this … revenge kick, or vendetta, or whatever it is—it might make sense if I could remember just what the hell happened, but I don't, because of this." He pointed to the scar at his hairline. "You don't want to tell me? Fine. You want me to play 'good dog' anyway? That's fine too. But I am not going to let you run for the hills and let all these people burn so you can save your sorry skin."

Alexander's expression hadn't changed at all. "I don't care what happens to me. If I stay here, I'll make the tower a giant bull's-eye."

"What would be the point? They're gone. They wouldn't know you weren't here."

Alexander looked up at the surrounding skyscrapers, his face screwed up against the sun's glare. "They're still watching. They'd never give us too long a leash. I bet they could have overrun this place long ago, if they wanted. All this is just a game to him, to teach me a lesson."

Norman's heart skipped a beat.

"Him?"

A dark frown crossed Alexander's brow, and he looked away from the distant spires. They had reached the stables, where a small pile of goods had been laid out. He threw a tattered brown cloak over his back, slung a leather knapsack upon his shoulder, and took up a long staff.

Sometimes this messiah complex can be a little hard on the nose.

"They won't understand," Norman said helplessly. "None of them will."

"I know. But I still have to go. It's your job to keep them together."

"I can't. I don't even know if I can get on the back of a bloody horse."

"Yes, you can. I believe in you."

"You just said you never believed in me."

Alexander looked at him afresh, all the way up and down, and Norman was surprised to see a lack of that certain disappointment—something bordering on disdain—that he had always noted behind his eyes. "I do now. You're … different."

Norman couldn't help laughing. "You sound surprised."

They headed toward the main gate, Alexander now a mere amorphous pile of rags, unrecognised by the crowd.

"What do I tell them? They're going to notice that you've up and disappeared."

"That's why I have to move fast." He nodded his cloaked head to the catwalk above the gate, and the klaxon sounded. The gates squealed open and the guards trained their rifles upon the streets, but amidst the heavy preparations, not many people seemed to notice.

Alexander turned back to Norman, adopting a pronounced slouch to hide his face. "The other councillors know I'm leaving. But you're right. The others won't understand. Keep this under wraps as long as you can."

"*What do I tell them?*"

Alexander shrugged. "That you'll have to figure out for yourself. Use your head. You've got a good one on those shoulders."

Norman scowled. "Fine. Get out of here."

Alexander laid a hand on his shoulder. His grip was hard, painful. "Radden is a strange place, Norman." Suddenly, Norman sensed fear in him.

Is that why he's really leaving? Because of that place?

In that moment, Norman could have believed it. Alexander's haunted eyes shuddered in their sockets.

Alexander grunted. "Get the job done, and bring them all back safe."

Norman swallowed. "Go." He had no idea a single word could taste so bitter.

Alexander Cain's gaze lingered on him a final moment, then the Messiah turned, and left his kingdom in his wake.

SEVENTH INTERLUDE

The early hours of that morning were the longest of James's life. As the moon slunk behind the gnarled branches of the skeletal forests, and dark of night gave way to the pale blue of coming dawn, all thought abandoned him, and the floor warmed with his pacing steps. So many times did he pass back and forth over the same diagonal stretch of his room that he began to feel like a caged animal, some feral feline trussed up in the gloom, afraid and confused and alone.

Eventually, the sky grew pale, and all manner of twittering songbirds that roosted in the farmstead's eaves were in the full swing of their morning chorus. Dew nestled on the flourishing crop-heads, and the troops of hired hands that were fast becoming family were already appearing along the long gravelled road.

Yet to James, it was all a bad joke—a pretty, membranous shawl pulled over a nightmarish ghoul. The tug of the visions plaguing his every waking thought was visceral, almost painful, as though at any moment it might disembowel him.

He had almost immediately come to regret letting Alex talk him out of leaving in the night. He had returned to his room on legs itching to be in the saddle, and flashes of torchlit catacombs and great expanses of weather-beaten moorland tortured him from the shadows.

He made for the kitchen once the flagstones of his diagonal path had reached body temperature from his pacing, and he spent what might have been another hour striding back and forth before the long farmhouse table before Alex made his appearance.

James wasted no time at the sight of him. "Well?"

Alex held up a hand to hush him. He looked no less tired than James felt himself, skin drawn and translucent, hair ruffled, and clothes creased in great folds. "*Just* ... hear me out."

James felt that he might explode, but through enormous effort brought himself to the table and took a deep breath. Fingers drumming the planks, he nodded jerkily and gestured for Alex to go on.

Christ, I'm like an addict. All twitches and nervous laughter.

Alex took some time before speaking. His eyes wandered the walls as though seeing through to the bedrooms of the others and reading their slumbering faces. "We'll both go. But they can't know about this. They won't believe it."

"But you do?"

I'm not sure I believe it, myself. Why the hell hasn't he beaten me over the head and put me in a straitjacket already?

Alex looked disturbed, as though angry at himself. "It's

crazy, James."

"But you do believe me, don't you?"

Alex licked his lips, his unkempt golden beard catching stray winks of refracted morning light. His eyes searched him up and down. "Yes," he said finally.

"Why?"

"Radden." He looked shaken, as though giving voice to his thoughts had given them power and reality. "You can't know about that place. I know you can't." His eyes flashed with something haunted. "You were just a baby."

James let him stew a moment, but then the pull of the will infecting him took over. "I don't know what's going on. I'm afraid, Alex. But I know I have to go." He hesitated, then stammered. "It can't wait. Will you come with me?"

"I will, but you have to give me—"

"I can't. I can't wait."

Their eyes met across the silent kitchen, and Alex nodded slowly. "God damn it all," he muttered. "Alright."

*

They were almost saddled up when the procession of mounted riders passed the farmstead gates and came trotting up the mile-long road. James cursed aloud and heard Alex groan in annoyance.

"Perfect," Alex spat.

"What is it?"

"They're here."

It took James a moment to realise who he was talking

about.

Malverston's lot, he thought. A thousand trilling alarms were tripped inside his head.

That meant waking the others. That meant their clean getaway was marred beyond repair. What could have been a clean break into the heart of the macabre was about to become an awkward, sticky dance.

James swore continuously as the group approaching covered the last hundred yards to the central square. He hadn't known anyone could hold so many curses within them.

Then everything fell through the floor, and a nest of butterflies was loosed upon James's insides. Because though the riders were mostly those he expected—vapid, fox-faced men with puckered eyes and yellowed skin—sandwiched between them was the last person on Earth he would have bet on.

Riding with an iron stare and straight-backed dignity was Beth Tarbuck.

*

James didn't think; he reacted in the only way befitting the situation. He hid. He hid badly, scurrying behind his mount, ignoring the fact his own legs would still be visible amongst the horse's.

No. Nobody's luck can be that bad. No, no, no ...

Alex cursed under his breath, his hand raised in welcome, face drawn into a plastic grin. "James," he said in a perfect calm monotone.

"What?"

"Get the others, now. Full alert. I want as many guns on them as we've got."

James didn't wait another beat. With a twisted retinal ghost of Beth shimmering before his eyes, he scrambled away towards the stable door and dove for cover, slinking into the nook between the stables and the utility shed, spluttering cobwebs from his lips and pushing through slicks of leaf-mulch and accrued detritus.

Behind him, diplomatic greetings were exchanged from afar. The rumble of hooves upon packed earth rattled the stable wall, amplified by the hollow space inside so it sounded as though a hundred riders approached instead of a dozen. Then he sprinted around the back of the compound, keeping low to the ground, ignoring the cold bite of dew quickly soaking into his trousers and shirtsleeves.

He scrambled through his own bedroom window and burst into the corridor, picked up his own rifle from the umbrella stand beside the door, and pounded upon the door frame with the butt. The brass fixings sang a high-pitched ditty, and he heard the others burst from their beds throughout the farmhouse.

He called out one word, and it was enough to bring them running: "Malverston!"

Lincoln appeared first, brandishing his old hunting rifle, hair askance in a nest of salt-and-pepper thickets. His eyes were foggy with sleep, but they had all been drilling for attack so long that his body was moving on automatic, taking him away along the corridor at a tactical creep, pressed fast to the wall, finger ready on the trigger, disappearing away toward the roof space.

Agatha and Lucian were next, both fully awake and poised for action, their eyes darting amongst the shadows before looking on James and demanding to know the situation with the strength of their gazes.

"They're here," James breathed. Their eyes hardened across the hall from one another, and they slunk back out of sight for a moment before reappearing simultaneously, clad in boots and slickers, .9mm pistols at the ready.

James listened hard, straining against the roar of the background silence, and picked out distant voices outside. They sounded calm enough. He nodded to the others, and they in turn headed off to their own defence posts, vanishing into the stone and hardwood of the house.

Voices outside were growing louder. They should all be in position by now.

Last to appear were the Creeks.

No surprises there, he thought. Then he checked himself. It wasn't fair to expect too much of them. It was no secret that Helen and Hector weren't cut out for this world; they needed a little hand-holding. If he hadn't been sure they needed the cover of an extra gun, he would have preferred they stay out of it.

But things might be about to get ugly, and never mind how jovial Malverston had been last time they had met. The man was sharp, and he'd had time to think—the biggest danger to them of all. He could always have changed his mind about gathering the Old World's treasures by playing nice.

But why Beth? What could be the purpose of sending her?

His stomach crawled as a thought far worse occurred to him: maybe she had *requested* it, wheeled her way here, for him. Could she have been so stupid, just to be near him?

He had to think it might be so.

Embarrassment and unreasoning feckless anger burned his cheeks as Hector peered around the door at the end of the hall and caught his eye. James waved him on impatiently, and Hector fawningly dragged his way out in the direction of the library.

Where he won't get in the way, James thought, fighting a sudden hysterical urge to laugh.

Hector had left the door ajar. James cursed and made to dive back for his own window, but a frightened whimper rippled along the corridor, and he hesitated, gazing at the Creeks' bedroom door. Cursing the man, he crept along the corridor and peered in, pushing his finger to his lips. He caught sight of Helen upon the bed, doe-eyed, with her arms locked fast around the black shock of hair upon Norman's head.

The boy looked afraid—an unreasoning kind of fear, aligning with his mother's trembling. It was obvious he knew nothing of what was going on.

James did his best to inject as much calm and assurance as he could muster into a single nod, ignoring the unbroken, glassy sheen to Helen's eyes, and closed the door.

He hurried back to his room, slithered out through the window, and returned to the crawlspace beside the stables, the acrid odour of fear crawling into his nostrils, wafting up from the folds under his shirt.

Alex's voice had grown louder, but was still peaceable enough. He was standing his ground, just where James had left him, that same plastic, diplomatic smile on his face.

The band of mounted Mooners had come to a halt before the first cobbles of the square, lining up along the border between dirt and stone as though they had piled up against a solid wall.

James took a moment to pick out the others in their hiding places: Lincoln in the roof space just below the thatch-line, Lucian in the recess in the floor leading to the cellar, and Agatha amongst the water tank's maze of pipes. Then he took a steadying breath, settling down to listen.

"What difference does it make if we're early?" the closest of the Mooners bawled. He had a nasal, simpering voice; James guessed from having his nose broken a few times, probably from being such a greasy little worm.

He pulled a wide smile that was more like a silent snarl, showing a mouthful of yellow misaligned teeth.

"No problem, traveller," Alex called. "You surprised us is all. Surely you know we can't have just anyone approach our home without raising the alarm."

"Don't think me a fool, Cain. I see the guns pointed at us. I see them well."

Alex was unperturbed. "Just as I see the revolver you

have under your duffel there, traveller." He let that sit for a moment, and James was satisfied to see the sneer drop from the man's face. Then Alex said, "What do you say we get a little friendlier?"

The gathering of Mooners shifted upon their mounts, each puckered face squinting at the golden-haired man, calm as a monk before them, so effortlessly in command of the situation.

"Come now, surely Mayor Malverston would hate to hear our first meeting ended with any unpleasantness."

"We're here to learn, Cain. Learn the Old Ways. But don't think for a second any one of us wants anything to do with you or your ilk," the lead rider said, sneering.

Not the most diplomatic right-hand man.

This idiot was bound to start a firefight wherever he went.

Something of what Alex had said before came back to him now: Malverston was a cruel and greedy man, but Newquay's Moon could have had far worse. Swathes of towns in the North that otherwise might have flourished had met sticky ends because of a handful of barbaric leaders. And it seemed that amongst Malverston's inner circle of slithering serpents, there was no shortage of would-be tyrants.

What had Alex agreed to? They were getting involved in a situation that could get bad fast. When Malverston met his end—and he would, soon—these were the men who would fight over his corpse. And the worst part of it was that none of them were the kind to fight tooth and nail; that would have been over in seconds, and a single victor would emerge to claim his prize, if only to play King of the Hill.

But these men were of the weasel variety, pale-faced and insidious. Their battle would be one of backhanded politics, multi-layered schemes, and subterfuge. In their bid for power, these men would poison that quaint little town like an oil slick poured over an ocean reef.

"To learn the Old Ways you'll need a civil tongue for starters. Any leader worth his salt doesn't ride up to an ally's—nay, a teacher's—home with a loaded gun pointed at him. I'm sure you're not one of those people, are you, traveller?"

That sneer appeared on the pallid rider's face once more, but it was faded now, on the brink of embarrassed anger. He was quiet a moment, then a barely-audible *click* rang out from under his duffel, and he relaxed back a tad in his saddle. "Renner," he said.

Alex nodded. "Mr Renner, it's a pleasure to receive the scholars of Newquay's Moon. If you'll dismount and follow me, we'll get you settled."

All was silent for an absurd, awkward stretch. James momentarily wondered whether everyone would start shooting then, and the courtyard would vanish in a hail of shrapnel. His finger tightened on the trigger, and a single rivulet of sweat danced down the groove of his spine.

Then Renner slithered down from his mount, waxen face tight and ugly. He stepped out on to the cobbles and extended his hand. James was sure he could see a slick of dark slimy something clinging to his fingers, even from this far away.

Alex nodded, that same plastic smile on his lips even now, and took the hand in his.

Renner flicked his head, and the other riders trotted forward into the courtyard, eyeing the place as though it were a gold mine ripe for the plundering, their piggy eyes eating up every detail with predatory relish.

James took a deep breath and, though it felt wrong, eased the safety catch back on his rifle, and stepped out slowly from the crawlspace. None of them expressed surprise at his appearance, and he made a note not to underestimate them. Seconds later, Lucian, Agatha, Lincoln, and Hector made their appearances, and in moments they were all united in the middle of the courtyard.

He tried not to focus on Beth, and she in turn was making a noble effort to ignore his existence. Keeping his face rigid and eyes devoid of emotion, standing in line with the others, he gestured toward the stables.

A medley of emotions raved in his guts. On one hand, his escape to Radden had been foiled, and a bizarre sickening itch in his legs was begging for him to break away and sprint for the fences. On the other, there was this whole mess Alex had gotten them into. On any other day, the snivelling group of men would have brought his stomach out in blooms of butterflies all on its own. He wasn't fooled by the peace talks; these men were bile-spawn.

Then there was Beth. She was here, really *here*—now, amongst everything else. It was too much. The idea of her getting caught up in any of it, of her being hurt, was too much to bear. And the fact that he sincerely had to resist the urge to run the other way for the sake of some vision hurt the most of all.

He suppressed a tired sigh, one not of physical exhaustion, but a soul sigh.

Why did things always have to go to hell together?

Once the Mooners had disappeared into the stables, and Lucian had gone to stand watch over them, Agatha, Lincoln and Alex all ducked their heads together.

"Anything sensitive, anything valuable, anything we don't want them seeing—hide it!" Alex hissed.

The other two, each twenty years his senior, nodded without hesitation and made haste towards the farmhouse. Alex was left standing with a hand buried in his beard, fingers stroking and pulling at knotted strands. He spotted James, and his eyes flickered. "I'm sorry," he said. "It'll have to wait."

James nodded. He couldn't muster the energy for anything else, not even a scowl. His face felt as if it had turned to stone.

He slouched back toward the house, slinging his rifle up onto his shoulder. He didn't see the boy until he had almost stepped on him, lurking in the shadows.

Norman had been standing in the doorway, clutching the frame with both hands, watching owl-eyed as the stoop-backed sallow men loped past one by one. Now he fixed his gaze on James and whispered timidly, "Does this mean I can get teached too, now?"

*

The Mooners had made themselves at home and were lounging on the benches of the kitchen table by the time James was done helping Agatha and Lincoln. Between them, they had successfully hidden every scrap of paper, every weapon, every map and shred of the Old World under their roof. All of it was pushed under floorboards, behind cupboards and into crannies in the cellar: anywhere the sly serpents wouldn't be able to get their grimy hands on it.

They were honour bound to teach these men the very knowledge they had hidden, in time. But they would do it in their own way, and they would do it slowly. With luck, they could do it slow enough to keep from teaching them much of anything at all before Malverston's time came to an end.

Then this sham of a *school* could end, and the scrabble for power could be allowed to play out. Then, finally, they might just get what they had wanted in the first place—free reign to carry out the mission's work in the South-West without fear of the noose.

Lincoln and Agatha cornered him in the cellar, and in harsh whispers he laid everything out straight.

"What's going on with you and Alex?" Lincoln said. "Come on, now, lad, there's no sense hiding what's in plain sight."

"He's not hiding anything," Agatha hissed. "He was going. North." She turned her gaze upon him, glazed with the thinness of coming old age, and sighed. "Radden?"

He nodded, his throat too tight to form words.

The two of them looked at each other. A bolt of concern passed between their eyes. There was no mistaking it; they thought he was crazy.

Hell, who wouldn't? He would have thought the same if the roles had been reversed.

"Listen," he said. "You have to hold things together here while we're gone."

Lincoln laughed. "Hah! Surely you're not still going, boy?"

James said nothing, waiting until both their faces had grown graver still, then become incredulous.

"I have to," he said. There was nothing to add. He had no more to give.

It was that simple.

And, to their eternal credit, they both started nodding. The incredulity had faded to something altogether deeper, as though they had both remembered something—or, rather, admitted something to themselves that they had buried long ago.

"Well," Lincoln spat with a haggard sigh, "s'pose it was always going to be you. Always were different. Just fits that you're the one to get some crazy spirit call."

James swallowed. In truth, he would have liked either one of them to lunge forward and seize him, to rain parental scorn down upon him and forbid him from going, to save him from this madness. But instead, they both nodded quietly, over and over, until finally they went back to their work in silence.

Lucian accepted it without a trace of resistance at all, just gave the usual grunt, and muttered in resigned agitation, "Just another day in the life of the Chosen One." He spared a moment to lay a hand on his shoulder, and leaned close enough for their foreheads to touch, even though they were alone, as though he were afraid of his sentimentality being overheard, and muttered, "Be careful."

After that, he needed only to make a moment's eye contact with Alex in the corridor. It was settled. They would turn tail, and ride north, away from the very thing that would decide the future of their life's work in pursuit of a vision.

Vision.

Urgh. Even the word made him feel fake. It was thin, absurd. It was just too crazy.

But that didn't change a damn thing. He had to go.

Now, standing in the kitchen among the wolves who had entered their den, the strange itch in his legs was no fainter. He was being called, and it was time to go. Even if it meant hating himself for evermore.

The men talked constantly, bickering and hissing at one another, forming ever-shifting tenuous alliances, double-crossing without a moment's notice. Each face was twisted by a malice not born of hardship or loss or sorrow, but of an inner ugliness—the kind that made every bit of them seem green and translucent and sticky, clean-shaven and decked out in finery befitting Malverston's inner circle.

Sitting to one side, staring ahead at the wall and sipping from a cup of water as though she were the only person in the room, was Beth. She didn't clock James as he entered from the hallway, but he knew she had seen him, sensed a tightness grow about her, some inaudible buzz hanging over her head.

For a moment he was paralysed by fear and anger and bewildered helplessness, then he noticed that all of the men, especially Renner, were staring at him with slanted eyes.

Mustering every shred of energy left in him, he clapped his hands together and addressed the room. "If you'd like to follow me this way, we'll get you all set up!"

"We're waitin' on your woman to fix a brew," one of them drawled, casting a calloused talon in the direction of the stove, where Helen was clutching the sideboard as though it alone was keeping the men from devouring her. Her eyes watched the kettle as though begging it to boil faster.

"They'll be time for that later," James said, squashing a swell of hatred. "We'd like to get started as soon as possible."

Grumbling, but canny enough not to be seen to be unwilling, they all followed him to Alex's classroom.

Before leaving the kitchen, Renner took a moment to halt the group and turn to Beth, grumbling down at her as though she were a whipped dog. "Stay, girly," he said, a sick glint in his eye. "We'll be back for you later."

"S'right," said the man directly to his right. "Back for you all night. Maybe you'll get lucky and we'll all give you a little attention."

They all roared with laughter and filed into the corridor.

James stood frozen on the threshold. What he felt was beyond anger. The look on Beth's face, stony and resigned, was enough to convince him that she hadn't volunteered for this. Far from it. He couldn't tell what the reason was, but he knew it was something far worse than that.

Her veil broke for a single instant in which her eyes flicked to his, and it was enough to solidify a single unbreakable certainty.

Before all this was over, he was going to strangle the life from each and every one of those men.

He ached to swoop down on her, to take her into his arms and shield her from their hungry stares. But now wasn't the time; not now, not in front of either Malverston's men, or the others. For now, at least, their secret was secure, and with that came at least some semblance of safety.

If they didn't know they were involved, at least they couldn't use her as leverage against him.

Through sheer force of will, he turned away from her and followed the procession of men into the corridor, leaving Beth alone with Helen in the kitchen.

They reached the classroom, which was large but still nowhere near fit to accommodate a dozen grown men. The men each sneered visibly, as though they had caught their hosts out in some act of great incompetence. In short order they were seated on the floor, cross-legged like infants, staring up and waiting in silence for the lessons to begin.

James was pleased that neither Lucian nor Lincoln was visible, though they were both hiding only inches out of sight beyond the window, weapons at the ready. At the slightest sign of trouble, all dozen men would be lying in a heap on the floor.

Agatha was ready at the blackboard and was about to begin when Renner spat, "What's this old biddy doing, staindin' up there like she's Queen of the Hill?"

"Ms Fisher will be delivering your instruction for the day," James said.

There was immediate uproar. A few of them even kicked their chairs over as they leapt to their feet, cursing openly and gesticulating obscenely, red faced in moments.

Renner quieted them after a while by adding his own gutteral growl. "Ain't I ever going to be taught by no *woman*. We came for Cain, and I expect him to give over every goddamn word of his sacred little oratory himself."

"That's not going to happen," James said, staunching a pause of hesitation. This was the danger point. If they wouldn't play ball now, they were in trouble. He was going to have to push them. Steeling himself, he added, "This is your lot. Take it or leave it."

Terse silence.

Renner slowly licked his lips, his eyes darting between James, Agatha, and the open doorway. James could see the conflict there: the unwillingness to appear weak, the desire to saunter away from a bad deal, and the knowledge that he wasn't getting anywhere near Malverston's throne without this deal.

Staring straight ahead, he lowered himself down onto his seat. The others looked disconcerted, blinking, but followed suit, slinking behind Renner. A muscle in Renner's jaw jumped, and he set his eyes dead ahead, staring at Agatha with open hostility, but he stayed silent.

James backed out of the room with a silent nod to Agatha. She gave him a momentary half-smile, picked up a pointer, and turned to the blackboard. "We start with the Greeks—" she said, and then the door was closed behind him.

He gasped—Alex was pressed against the wall parallel to the door, ear pressed to the wall. His face was drawn, tired.

"I hate this," James mouthed.

Alex nodded.

They both headed for the kitchen, and all the while James fought the urge to break into a run. The gnawing itch in his legs burned like a hot knife imbedded deep in each heel. If he didn't satisfy its hunger soon, he might never stop screaming. But first, he needed to see her.

*

Beth gasped as she was planted fast against the wall of the stables. "James!"

"What the *hell* are you *doing* here?" he hissed.

Her stony exterior persisted a moment longer, then her eyes twitched, as though caught in a sudden struggle. Her bottom lip quivered, though she seemed to be making every effort to stop it. "They took her."

James, braced to scorn her for giving into desire, felt his cheeks fall slack. "What?"

"They took Melissa." Her gaze grew angry and her eyes

wide as a redness fizzed up behind a thin veil of tears while her brows furrowed above. She teetered a moment on a shuddering precipice, then crumpled and pushed away from him and hid her face as the shuddering cries came in earnest.

James let her go and watched her stumble in the shadows, wiping her eyes fiercely.

"They came to the house after you left, took down the door." She was spitting with rage now, though her voice was still porridge-thick with tears. "Mum and I couldn't stop them. They would have killed us all right there and then."

A bolt of panic thrust up from James's gut. For the first time since the traveller had laid hands on him, the itch in his legs was gone.

No! Malverston knows!

Beth seemed to sense his thoughts and shook her head. "They don't suspect. It's not because of you." She choked. "It's because of me."

"Because of what you did at the banquet?"

She nodded miserably. "He showed up himself after they had taken Mel away, said I'd showed him up for the last time. Can't tolerate some slut facing up to him—even if I am his favourite." She rubbed her eyes with a venomous scowl and slouched back towards him, burying her head in his chest. "He's breaking me in, James. I have to be a good girl, or they'll do the same to her as they did to me. I'm his goons' plaything until George is happy the debt is paid."

James swallowed. His throat cracked like a rifle shot. He needed several attempts before he could get a single word out. "I'm sorry." Then, before he could hesitate, he muttered, "But I can't stay. I have to go. There's something I have to do. Something important."

She met his gaze and he saw something he had never expected to see from her: plain, unveiled hurt, childish and raw. "What?" she said.

"I'll be back soon."

"James …"

"The others won't let anything happen to you."

"You have no idea," she said, shaking her head. "No idea what I am to these men. I'm less than a whore, a plaything. I'm meat, a punching bag, one rung below the mangy dog they all kick under the table. You … you're going to leave me with them." Suddenly the childish pain was ripped back under the hardened callous of her sombre gaze, and she nodded as though understanding him anew. "Fine."

James took hold of her shoulders again and held fast even when she tried to shake him off. "Listen—*listen!*" He placed his forehead on hers and whispered, "I *will* be back, as soon as I can. And I don't care if I have to tear up every treaty we have, we're going to get her back." Then, his voice shaking with red nauseating fury, he said, "And you … they're never going to bother you again. I promise."

Hating himself a little more every second, he untangled himself from her and stepped back. "As soon as it's done."

"What?" Her stare was like a cold lance slicing his cheeks. "What could be so important?"

Sinking in his heart. Another swell of self-hatred. "You wouldn't understand."

She looked at him a long time and nodded, but a small

part of the twinkle in her eye had faded, and he wasn't sure he'd ever see it again. "Okay," she said. "Go."

He stepped back out of the alley, backing away so as to keep her in his sight just a little while longer. "Be safe. Stay with the others." He tried a smile and his chapped lips split, bleeding bitter blood. "We will get her back, Beth."

Then he stepped around the corner before he could become trapped there in front of her. But the image of her that remained scarred on his retinas wasn't one he had hoped for: a young woman, alone in a dark alley, lost in a strange place, looking more alone than ever.

CHAPTER 20

Billy smelled soil, wet and earth-rich, thick like soup, filling her nostrils. She opened her eyes and stared up at a sky the colour of naked granite, lifeless and bleak. It was a struggle to move, but she hauled herself onto her haunches and shook a harsh ringing from her ears.

A moment ago she had been standing in the ringstones of Stonehenge with the Panda Man standing over her. Now, she was alone and the flat, endless plains of Salisbury were gone, replaced by woodland that even at a glance seemed ancient, even more so than those hallowed ringstones. Here the air was dense with stories, hidden amidst the amorphous growths of bark.

She was very far from Daddy now. She could feel it.

And that itch in her legs was full awake, radiating its will up her body in brilliant, irresistible pulses. She gave in to it, resigned to whatever she had been sent to do, allowing her limbs to be pulled about by the alien power inside her.

All around were Echoes of things past, moving indistinct and blurred in her peripheral vision, replaying snippets of long-forgotten lives over and over. She ignored them, placing one foot in front of the other, keeping Daddy's face centred in her mind's eye.

Just do what the Panda Man said. Then me and Daddy will be together. Just us, all safe and alone. No monsters, so sickness, no secret mission. Just us.

I get to go home as soon as this is done. He promised.

The old forest passed by, the mulch of eons running underfoot, and in time she came to the treeline. Beyond was a landscape as barren and grey as the overcast sky, cast iron in tone and stripped of all vitality by ceaseless whistling gales. Twisted heathland, muddy bogs, black lakes, foggy moors and looming cragged mountains met her gaze, stretching away to where land met sky, with no change in sight.

She paused a while to take it all in, knowing that somewhere out there was what had been calling her since she had left the farm and Ma's graveside. That had been only a few days ago, but it could have been a dozen lifetimes.

"I'm coming, Daddy," she said.

She was about to place her next step when total blackness blotted out the sky, and scratching canvas enveloped her head. Rough hands capped by long, tapered fingers gripped her own, and pinned her arms behind her back. Even through the bag was over her head, she smelled the rank odour of rotten breath seeping in, gouging at the back of her throat.

"Look at what we have here," said a high-pitched, chilling voice. It seemed to alight on her body like treacle, dripping off her shoulders, burning like acid. "A wanderer, all alone in the woods. We can't have her getting lost, now, can we, lads?"

A murmur of amused agreement rang out from all around, and suddenly Billy realised that she was surrounded by Bad Men, laughing and treading closer.

No! No, I have to go!

The itch in her legs burned impotently, and she made to run on its direction before she was lifted into the air and her shins pinwheeled uselessly.

I can't stop. I have to go. I have a job to do.

DADDY NEEDS ME!

As that thought ran through her head, a snippet of Daddy's face flashed up as bright as the sun. His skin was the colour of moss, his lips chapped and torn to shreds, his eyes a pair of flint shards. His breathing was pitiful, little more than a shudder.

Hurry, the Panda Man's voice uttered from somewhere far away, yet right beside her.

Her heart hammered. Not only because of that image or the Panda Man's voice. It was the other voice, the one that had spoken from the other side of the bag on her head.

She had heard that voice before, the night Grandpa had gone away forever. It was the other voice—the one who had chased them through the woods in the night, and then taken Grandpa away from her. The voice of the monster.

She kicked and screamed too late, for her hands were already being bound, and her back pressed firm against the feverish heat of the monster's chest.

"Welcome to Radden, little girl," he breathed.

Billy whimpered as men laughed and snorted all around her in the pitch darkness, and she was carried away in the monster's grasp. "No," she whispered.

*

"I should have listened to Dad," Robert said to the wind.

Dad had always told him to stay away from women.

New Canterbury, trussed up and boarded with myriad barricades, could have been any one of countless abandoned settlements. Any sign of the sparkling glory it had displayed by night under Alexander's reign had long passed.

He hadn't been up to this. He had given it everything he had, but he wasn't cut out for leadership. Too much politics, too much hand-holding. His place was in the field, where surviving was the task at hand, not keeping good face with the locals.

He shifted uncomfortably, pulling at the tightness of the starched shirt straining across his chest. The smell of mothballs filled his nose, wafting up from the lapels of an ancient tuxedo that was redolent of mould and decay. Below, in the lee of the hill overlooking the northern spur of the River Stour, preparations were being made.

Ignoring the sheer blind absurdity of what they were doing, droves of men and women flitted back and forth from their homes, bringing all manner of hoarded Old World knick-knacks and long-forgotten odds and ends. A mottled red carpet had been laid out on the grass, populated by rickety chairs and stools from the cathedral. From God-only-knew-where a group of struggling young men had brought out a white archway woven from cheap lengths of balsa wood and placed it at the head of the procession. All around, people were placing bouquets of wild flowers and tied bunches of grasses, even bringing the potted plants from home to fill the empty spaces.

Agatha's crooked form staggered back and forth upon a small, raised plinth before the arch. She had arrived only half an hour before, but upon being told of the coming ceremony, she had leapt from her wagon and demanded to perform the union. Robert didn't know if she even recognised him or Sarah, yet Agatha had insisted, pining over their youth, clearly lost to some long-distant past.

Now she was dressed in her long, white elder's shawl, sporting a vicar's collar to boot. In her hands was the King James Bible from which she had given service in the cathedral for as long as he could remember. As he watched, she muttered her lines in preparation, her eyes milky and faded.

She had been a great woman once, a leader of Alexander's original band. And this tiny old crone was all that remained of her. He would have given anything to have her back at the height of her power, when the End had been fresh in people's minds, and the fires of hope burned bright in the hearts of a few.

Things hadn't seemed so bleak, even when life itself had been tougher. Things had simply seemed more possible back then.

Not like now. The city had fared poorly under his lead.

But how would the city cope without even him? If he was really going to go gallivanting into the unknown, he had to know they would stand if the attacks started again.

A trail of people on horseback was approaching from London, weighed down by enough ordnance to turn a small city to cinders. Norman's troops, come for their trail-hunter. Come for him.

Still, his mind remained on his leaving.

This turmoil, however, wasn't one born of doubt, but of dread. Because he now knew Sarah would come forth if he left. She would rise to take his place.

She wasn't the same woman she had been. Infinitely stronger. She had put him to shame of late.

"Should've beaten it into me a little more, Dad," he said, turning his eyes on the cloudless sky. "With a big fucking stick."

*

Lucian waited for Max to duck his head back into the tent and nod the all clear before turning to the others. A group of around a dozen had been brought into the fold, a dozen out of legion. But he couldn't afford to trust the majority. He'd had to use his gut to choose only those he could be sure wouldn't break under pressure, and those he could use. Most were moribund, fragile sticks after so long in the labour camp—only these precious few had kept strong through luck and bargaining and tooth-and-claw.

He had ended up with a troop of the biggest, ugliest and

meanest men he'd ever seen. In any other circumstance, he would have given them a wide berth. If these men had come loping into New Canterbury one evening, he would have shot them all on sight.

But they were a means to an end. And he had every intention of meeting that end.

"Now's the time to walk if you have doubt," he said. "We're all screwed either way, but if we fail it'll be a bullet in the ear before sundown. So walk now if you're not itching for it, because you'll just slow us down."

He waited. Nobody moved an inch.

"Fine." He turned to Max. "What do we have?"

"Few knives, hammers, and suchlike. And this." He pulled a single stunted pistol from the inner folds of his myriad sweaters, the barrel spotted with rust, puny and pathetic in his dinner-plate-sized hands. "Might as well throw it." He looked at it in disgust. "Might get one shot off, if it doesn't explode. I wouldn't dream of holding out for a second."

"Keep it." He turned to the others. "We'll make do. That means getting close. You've all seen the cliffs. We're going to have to get up there and into that tent on the top without being seen. And once we're in—"

A crack nearby sent them all ducking back into the masses of spent ammunition and twisted scrap yet to be smelted, holding their breath. They had each slipped away from work in turn, and it was only a matter of time before they were missed. If they were found, it was all over.

Lucian ignored the stink of festering sweat and shit

wafting up from his own body, and waited until he was sure the noise had been innocuous. He was about to signal them to emerge from hiding when a ruckus kicked up outside, passing the other side of the tent—several sets of footsteps, both regular and staggered; the sick laughter of little boys torching ants with a magnifying glass and the unmistakable cries of a child.

Lucian warned the others to stay put with a sweeping glare, then crept to the entrance and peered through the hairline crack in the canvas. He wasn't surprised when Max joined him regardless.

Boots thumped past over ground whipped to muddy pudding, over which floated filthy masses of rags, masking bodies shuddering with the brutish guffawing of black souls.

"Look at 'er squirm, *yuk yuk*!"

"Haw haw! Ain't no way out of for you, missy."

Lucian twitched despite himself, sensing the twisted expression on their faces, which remained out of sight—in his mind's eye he could see the hunger in their eyes.

"*Yuk yuk*! Come here, let me cop a feel and see what's sprouting under those drawers."

A thump was followed by the gurgling *oof!* that only comes from a man utterly felled by a blow to the jewels, then the patter of small feet splashing toward the tent.

Lucian braced to confront whoever approached, and behind him, Max snicked back the hammer on the rusty pistol.

The pattering ceased mere feet away from the tent and a harsh cry rang out, strangled and terrified. Lucian couldn't resist peeking once more and caught sight of a small creature, almost black with dirt, face curtained by greasy locks of fire-red hair and inset with enormous white eyes.

Their gazes met and Lucian's heart jumped. It was a girl, a young girl, no older than ten. She skidded to a halt, carving twin gouges in the thick mud, and was yanked back by the grubby hands of a sneering man with no front teeth. Men and women of all walks of life, united only by a common sneering malice, were close behind, enormous and looming, cackling like wicked, cartoonish giants as they surrounded the girl. One of them slipped a bag over her head and lifted her kicking into the air, while another man came limping into view, rubbing his shin.

"Serves you right, fool," one of the women cried.

The limping man snarled and made to lash at the girl, but he and the others were frozen in place by a new voice, high-pitched and silky-smooth, one that sent alarms trilling in the primitive part of Lucian's head. "Put her down. I have plans for that one."

The girl was dropped in a heap into the mud and hauled up again by her collar, jerked forward and away. Just before she passed out of sight, she glanced once again into the tent, and Lucian cursed under his breath. Then she was gone.

What followed was the owner of the high-pitched, chilling voice. Both Lucian and Max were stilled. The man's appearance only amplified the alarms in Lucian's head; he had been in enough scrapes to know some men were born killers, and there was one of them. He was short, almost as short as Lucian himself, but every pound was solid, lithe muscle, built for deathly speed and dexterity as opposed to brute force.

"Jason," Lucian muttered.

"Huh?" Max said.

"Jason. His name is Jason."

"How do you know?"

"He led them in New Canterbury. The people who put a friend of mine on his back for days, and slit another's throat."

He was sure this was the man who had killed Rayford Hubble that night, and broken Norman's ribs like toothpicks. Even that old Irishman they had found beaten half to death out in the forest—the ferocity of those wounds had the stink of this predator's work.

"Who is he?" Max said.

"The Rottweiler let off the leash." Lucian cursed inwardly. They would have to deal with him, too, if they were going to scale the cliff and take James down. Yes, there were thirteen of them. But that man ... somehow, Lucian didn't relish the thought of taking him on without an entire regiment behind him.

Jason passed by, his lupine face pulled into a snarl, and vanished after his underlings and the little girl.

Lucian turned back to the others and waved them forward. "We don't have a lot of time. Soon there are going to be too many of them. All that smoke coming over the hills ... There must be thousands by now. As soon as we're done forging for them, they'll march south. And then it'll all be over."

The faces around him looked ready, their shoulders bunched and rippling, and the fists clenched until bone-white.

Lucian nodded. "Alright. As soon as we get a chance, we move."

CHAPTER 21

The setting sun turned red as arterial blood behind a thin veil of clouds. The light was low, yet gave life to every surface, every line, every speck of dust. Another golden inner light seemed to leak from the trees, the earth, and the hundred unwashed faces upon the red carpet were illuminated with anticipation.

Norman would have said a few hours before that his life couldn't have been much stranger. But now, standing here at the front of the crowds in an ancient itchy suit with a velvet pillow in hand, he had to admit he would have been wrong.

Only moments after dismounting, he and the other riders had found fine clothing thrown over their travel cloaks by the people of New Canterbury. Despite vehement protest, Norman and the others were shepherded toward the fields where the wedding court had been erected.

Robert himself had greeted Norman, then Allie and Agatha, who had dismounted from the first wagon. Robert had laid out his terms clear and fast: he would come, but first he was going to get hitched.

Norman had been flabbergasted beyond response, but there had been little he could do. By then he had already been pressed into his suit, they had been standing on the red carpets, and Agatha had vowed to carry out the ceremony.

In any case, it didn't matter. They needed Robert. And Norman knew this was a deal breaker.

Better to just get it over with.

And though he didn't want to admit it, a part of him would have given anything to have this: one last normal thing. It was only right. It was what they were fighting for, what they were all set to die for.

So here he was with one eye on the sky and the failing sunlight as people stood from their seats and a ramshackle band struck up the traditional wedding theme, playing instruments taken from the precious repository from Alexander's great time capsule of a house.

The crowd turned to catch sight of an ocean of spilling white cloth, pooling from an Athenian figure of feminine curves, and trailing for yards behind. Sarah Clarke was hidden by no veil. Her eyes had never seemed so large, free of spectacles. No doubt she couldn't see, but her face was unpuckered and freshly washed, radiant with fierce determination, taking each step as though pulling herself towards her fiancé with a rope binding them together.

Allison led the bridesmaids. Norman expected to see her smiling giddily, in keeping with her longstanding reputation as chief gossip of New Canterbury. But she was different, now—older, more demure. A dignity had come from the trials of the siege in London.

She had aged in soul by two decades, by the blood of Geoffrey Oppenheimer's children. She still smiled, but it was a happy and content smile, one of a woman relishing the here and now.

Sarah seemed different, too. Norman hesitated to call it coldness, but certainly she was tougher and more imposing. The rosy librarian and schoolteacher was now concealed by a shield to which men and women would rally.

Then there was Agatha standing at the altar, more present than Norman remembered seeing her, but a shadow of the great woman she had been before the dementia had taken her.

All the city's women were standing tall. Compared to them, Norman and the city's menfolk were cast in shadow.

The bride swept by along the aisle and Norman met Sarah's gaze. The last time he had seen her she had been gabbling and starry eyed, newly engaged. Now, she was another woman altogether.

What the hell happened here while we were away? What have they had to do?

He didn't want to know.

She smiled and he winked back. That was all that needed to be done.

Then Allie was passing and his chest swelled up until he was sure it would crawl up past his teeth. "You're next," she purred as she passed and he held back a laugh, caught by a fit of sudden good humour despite everything—and that was why this was worth it.

Sarah reached the mocked-up altar and turned to face Robert, who had turned a bizarre milky white despite his charcoal-black skin, and was covered in a layer of dripping sweat. Built like a bulldozer, the macho-man of New Canterbury had been tamed. He was shaking visibly. Sarah in turn looked nervous, but between them they seemed to shine, holding back the doom incumbent upon them and the city with some force.

Agatha cleared her throat. "Dearly beloved, we are gathered here today ..."

Norman stepped forward with the velvet pillow held out before him and tried to keep his eyes off Allie while Robert and Sarah's smiles grew wider until they were both identical jokers, and the rings lying on the pillow were taken.

Never thought I would be best man at a time like this.

Robert squeezed his shoulder and Norman stepped back, taking in the crowd and remembering with visceral impact just how much he loved this city and these people. He came to stand beside Heather, scarcely recognising her.

She was withered and work weary, a shadow of the long-faced doctor who had saved him from the edge of death not long ago, when Jason had crippled him. "You look well," she whispered.

Agatha was announcing the conclusion of her part of the spiel and the "*I do's*" were commencing. Robert and Sarah were holding hands, staring not at but into one another, blind to anything else. Yet it wasn't a gushing, sickening puppy romance—rather a furious and desperate vehemence, like two people gripping one another amidst the roiling of a coming maelstrom.

Norman nodded. His broken ribs troubled him still and the ride from London had them crying out in blinding pulses, a bad omen for the long ride north. But he owed every breath he took to Heather. "How are they?" he muttered, nodding to the city's people.

"Crumbling, afraid. We've lost almost everyone we could rely on." She cocked her head at the altar. "Except those two. They're holding us together, getting us ready."

Norman flexed his aching chest, ignoring a phantom truck—another Echo of the myriad that now appeared everywhere—turning a corner on a faraway street, and nodded. "I know you've given everything, but I need to know you're with us to the end. When it comes …"

"I'll do everything I can, Norman."

"Thank you."

"Are you ready to lead them?" Her eyes were on him. "You never wanted any of this. Of us all, it's most unfair on you. None of the rest of us were forced to live this life."

"It's done now."

"And?"

He turned to her. "I'm ready."

"I pronounce you as joined under God," Agatha said, her face amused and fond and alive. "You may kiss the bride."

Heather nodded. "Just remember that it's your life."

This was never my life, Norman thought.

Heather gripped his hand and her fingers' chill stole into his. "Ride safe."

Under the bloody sky and golden rain of falling autumnal leaves, Sarah and Robert's lips came together, and two became one.

*

There was no reception, no after party, no honeymoon. The attendees trailed back to their homes in silent procession, and the riders from London returned to their temporary camp before stripping off their moth-eaten tuxedos and preparing to go.

Those who were going to stay—Allie and Agatha included—began moving supplies to the city larder from the wagons, and bade their goodbyes. The newlyweds were left alone at the altar for the little time it took to prepare, and whatever occurred there nobody knew or cared to know.

Norman was soon once again ready to saddle up, with his troop of volunteers in front of him.

Richard and John were at the very front, their faces drawn and nervous, but their gazes set and diamond hard. Beside Norman huffed the bulk of Robert's black Shire horse, Obsidian, awaiting his master while standing a head over the other mounts. All had rallied to Norman, but there was no doubting who was going to lead them north—to what black rump they would fix their gaze the whole way there.

Then Allie was in front of him, held by the arm by Agatha. "I may be old 'n' crazy, but I know two people steelin' to ignore each other so's they don't have to say their last goodbyes," she drawled.

Norman was astonished to see her still lucid. It seemed her body had rallied against the dementia for this one last hurrah, sensing the end. "I've seen wiser people 'n' the both of you do the same when they knew something bad was coming and they sure as all Heaven regretted it once it was too late. So here's me doing you both the biggest good." Her eyes twinkled. "Make nice, and make sure you get your behind home safe, Norman." She sighed, held his chin, and shook her head. "So old, we're all so *old*. How did things go so wrong?" A note of simple sadness touched her brow, then she tottered away toward the cathedral.

Norman was left alone with Allie and the two of them shifted uneasily. Minutes ago they had been all side glances and coy smiles; but now, face to face, knowing that this could be the last time …

"I …" he said.

"You come back." He was startled by the cutting power in her voice, and the fact that she was meeting his eyes dead straight.

She's so different, so much *more* than she was, Norman thought.

So have you, said another quieter voice in his head. *In time, maybe both of you could have been real leaders, somebodies.*

"You come back to us. I don't care what you have to do. You bring them all back."

He struggled for a few moments, wanting to touch her,

to brush her hair behind her ear and feel warm skin on his—perhaps the real world couldn't touch them if they held on tight enough.

But if he gave in now, he would fall into her like a black hole, and they wouldn't be able to pry him off with a crowbar.

And so, against the raving want of every mote in him, he took a step back and swallowed. "I will."

Her eyes and nose had reddened, her round face young and glowing with pent-up hurt, shaking with the effort of keeping her hard stare. She sniffed wetly then turned and was gone in a blur of rosy cheeks and auburn hair.

Norman forced himself not to watch her go, keeping his gaze fixed on the floor until he was sure she was gone. By the time he pulled himself into his saddle, Robert was beside him, walking tall and powerful as a bull elephant. He leaped up onto Obsidian's back, took a single cursory look at the men and women ready to follow him unto hellfire, and said, "I'm ready."

They filed away from the city as darkness fell and the few streetlights afforded by the city's reserve power popped to life, without any grand speech or salutation to push them onward.

Norman fell to thinking of the long years he had lived here and taken it all for granted, hating his great destiny and his poor lot in life, all the while forgetting how fragile all this really was.

Before he knew it, they were cresting the northern hills and the last flames of day were sinking below the Earth, and

Robert stopped to hold up his hand in the direction of the dismantled altar—where, upon the windswept grass laden with shadow, a lone figure dressed in white was waving.

*

The sea roiled all along the base of the chalky cliffs. Each wave crashed upon the rocks with the roar of a lion, and together with the banshee wailing of the wind it was easy to believe the devil himself surfed ever closer just over the horizon.

Alexander fought the gale with his brow bearing the brunt of the high wind, keeping fixed on the way ahead, treading through the beaten grass lining the cliff edge. Beachy Head had changed little since his boyhood: that famous sheer cliff face thrusting up from the waves of England's southern shore. Southampton was close and, on occasion, he caught sight of a wisp of smoke trailing skyward from that direction—the fires still burned, it seemed. But he tried to keep the smoke to his back, unable to stomach the sight of it.

The cliffs had been his destination since leaving the compound at Canary Wharf. He had no idea why; they had simply possessed his mind's eye. He had only known that he had to get himself away. He had done enough damage. He had felt eyes on him from inside the gates and out, watching. James finally had all his chess pieces in place, ready to put his final play into action.

Isolating himself wouldn't forestall the attack, for things

had gone too far now, but what else was there for him to do?

But no matter how much he had tried to convince himself all the way through the wastes, the same thoughts had plagued him.

You just wanted out. You needed to get away from your demons and the real world. Dress it up all you like—you ran away.

And that was the bare truth. He knew it despite speaking over himself.

So he tried not to think. He concentrated only on putting one foot in front of the other, feeling the cold slowly work its way through his long billowing cloak and into his bones.

He was an old man. He realised it with a gravity he'd always been too busy for before. His joints were stiff with the slight cold despite the summer sun, and his balance had wilted from a once-thoughtless silent dance over ground to a bemused unsteady shuffle.

Where did all the years go? asked a voice.

Into New Canterbury, answered another. *Into the council and books and classrooms and vaults.*

And now James is holding a match to all of it.

His heart lurched and he went back to plodding, pushing away mental film reels of libraries ablaze, London darkened by the coming legions, and all those he had brought together crying out upon flaming pyres.

One foot in front of the other. One foot, now the other. Just keep going.

That way he could almost believe it was all academic, a fairy tale, just some trifling what-if. He carried on that way until the cabin came in sight.

For a while he registered it only as the sole human constriction in sight and his mind was preoccupied with a fitful childish rage against it and all man's creations blighting the land—maybe all the doubters had been right, and it would have been better to let it all fall back to dust after the End. Suppose he was the very evil he had set out to counter: the decaying force that would send what remained of civilised life crashing to the ground.

He had accepted there would be prices to pay for his mission's success a long time ago. He had known there would be grudges and that people would suffer and starve and die if their work was going to make any real headway. Those sacrifices would have to be made. And he had considered them a small price well worth paying, considering the countless future generations that could benefit.

But now everything was clouded. It could all have been for nothing. And so many could have suffered along the way under his unfeeling heedless influence. Was he the tyrant, and James the liberator after all?

The same taunting voice in his head again. *That was always the way of it. He tried to tell you, but you wouldn't listen. And you've made yourself an enemy nobody can stop.*

He pushed those words aside with a literal jerk and blinked to shake himself free. The cabin was closer. And now he could see a thin, pale sliver of smoke was coming from the chimney. Somebody was inside.

He had wandered very close, closer than any measure of sense permitted. And now he was treading the muddied ground under the guttering, against all instinct, numb to common sense.

He now craved company more than anything, even if it meant death at the hands of his host. Anything was better than being alone with his thoughts. He pushed open the door and peered into the gloom, at once recoiling as a stoppered puff of stale air swept over him, redolent of sickness and the sour stench of human waste.

Yet still he stepped forward, drawn by the flickering darkness thrown about by a tiny hearth fire set against the far wall. The unmistakable profile of somebody bedridden shuddered in shadow close to the doorway. From within came a voice no more than a broken whisper. "Billy? Billy, is that you? Please, let it be you."

Alexander stepped inside and came into the single room under the cabin's tin roof, askance and frugal and rough-sawn. A sunken skeleton clothed in blue-tinged skin lay amidst a mass of blankets, staring up at him with enormous, unfocused eyes. Alexander frowned. He had heard that kind of accent before, from the old man they had found beaten in the woods around New Canterbury. He waited a moment, then said, "Never thought I'd meet another Irishman."

The man trembled. "My daughter. My Billy. Is she with you?" A weak and desperate anger flashed upon his sallow cheeks. "What have you done with her?"

"Nobody around, friend. But maybe I can help. What's your story?"

The man blinked. "It's a long one. And I'm near the end of it."

Alexander dropped his satchel onto the ground with a thump, slid off the hood of his robe and squatted down onto a stool beside the bed. "Well, that makes two of us. I'm Alex."

The man made to speak, but then bent double and choked his way through a hacking fit of dry, wrenching coughs, sputtering droplets of blood onto the sheets and whimpering all the while. The smell of faeces intensified. He collapsed back, gasping, and Alexander leaned forward to set the sheets straight. He rinsed a sponge in a nearby basin and squeezed a few drops of water into the man's arid mouth.

The man sputtered and wheezed.

"What?" Alexander said.

"Don. My name's Don."

"Don." Alexander gripped his shoulder.

"My daughter. My girl. Billy." His bloodied eyes darted sideways desperately, searching the room in delirium. "Billy!"

"There's nobody but me."

"Where is she?" Bony fingers gripped Alexander's arm. "Where?"

"Tell me, Don. Tell me what happened and maybe we can find her."

A weeping splutter. "Like I said"—another gasp—"it's a

long story."

Alexander lowered himself back onto the stool. "I've got time."

EIGHTH INTERLUDE

James would have never expected that Alexander would follow him so far without protest. Yet they had been riding well through the day and not a word had passed between them. Cambridge, Corby and Nottingham had slid past, and they had stopped by a few friendly homesteads to rest and feed the horses, not talking and not planning. Then they had gone on.

Slowly the land changed as they went farther north and the buildings grew sparser, the roads more overgrown and potholed.

They began keeping one eye on the horizon and the other on the shadows as the sense of being watched became too obvious to ignore. There was no doubt they were being watched. Homes, apartment towers and offices were fewer and farther between, but they still pockmarked the sapling woodlands sprouting up everywhere, and lights were on in more than a few. But they wouldn't dream of wandering close to these places.

James had nothing but bad memories of the North. Every time he had journeyed beyond Leeds in the past, things had gone from bad to worse, and somebody had always ended up hurt. That it had usually been the other side to suffer losses had been blind, dumb luck.

Prowlers inhabited this wasteland, preying upon those taking the chance to pass through. Anybody who wasn't at the top of their game would either come out the other side chewed up and penniless, or they wouldn't come out at all. The mission could have all the luck in the world and unite the entire South under a single leadership, but they wouldn't touch this place, not for a long time. This would be the great unending desert at the periphery of their lands for ages to come.

It was a lot to ask of Alex, coming all the way out here on a whim. Hell, less than a whim. The whole thing was built on a crazy vision from a drunken stranger. They were risking their lives, and the alliance with the Moon was in direct jeopardy, not to mention Beth ...

He shook himself. He wasn't going to think about that. He couldn't afford to be distracted, because they were getting close. He knew they were getting close because he was almost delirious with the intensity of the itch in his legs now, and in the corners of his eyes were twinkling lights like those before a migraine. Somewhere at the back of his mind he could hear that alien voice whispering incoherent words.

But for the time being he had to keep straight and strong, keep guiding them north. Alex had kept quiet thus far, but how long would that last? And if he started mumbling and spouting all the crazy going on in his head, he was bound to turn them around right now and march him back home in a straitjacket.

In any case they couldn't stop. Their pace might have been their only reason for not running into trouble thus far. If they lingered anywhere too long, they were bound to attract attention. He could only hope their luck held out.

So he kept mum, and they kept going. Sheffield passed by at the far reaches of sight, a blitzed shell, the site of a thousand skirmishes and stand-offs between rival clans. Soon it too was gone, and they left even the scant suburbia behind. In its place was true countryside, rugged and untraversed and eternal.

As one day became two, and two days dragged into a long tiring week, the flatlands buckled into rolling hills, then sharp valleys and exposed rocky bluffs. Mountains crawled up over the horizon, the serrated teeth of some fallen behemoth. In time the first road signs for Radden County started dotting the roadside.

CHAPTER 22

Billy's face exploded into a slab of stinging flesh. The calloused hand striking down from above belonged to the sneering monster who had dragged her from the leaves. He had ordered the others to shepherd her through a campsite full of hot metal shafts, spluttering fires, and cowering skinny people before herding her into a large beige tent at the base of a cliff. Then he had shut them out and rounded on her, as though she were a delicious dish, the two of them finally alone.

"What do you want?" she said.

His jeering superior face darkened with sudden anger and he slapped her across the face again, harder this time. "Quiet," he hissed. "No talking."

Then his face was smooth and untroubled once more, and he set to walking about the edge of the tent while she cowered on the floor, holding her stinging hot face in her hands and trying to hold the tears in.

Her legs itched and her mind's eye was full of pictures of outside—though she had never seen this place before, she knew every part of it, could feel every clot of mud and the rough outline of every pebble between her fingers.

Because it's the place the Panda Man wanted to go. This is the place I was coming to. Why would he want me to come here? These are Bad Men. How can I do anything to stop Bad Men? I'm just … I'm just Billy.

She searched the edge of the tent for Fol's signature smile and dark billowing coat, but he was nowhere to be seen. The one time she wanted to see him, and she couldn't have been more alone.

"You're not of this place," the man said. "You speak some kind of tongue from aways."

She didn't say anything, just crawled up tighter in a ball and cradled her cheek. Her face was slicked and dripping with tears and snot. She had been so close to doing whatever it was she had to do, so close to going home. And now she was stuck here with this man—no, he wasn't a man. She could see no trace of a person behind his eyes.

The way he looked at her made her feel sick. Grownups did funny things sometimes, things she didn't like and things that seemed downright silly. But they were almost always good and clever in the end.

This man was different. He was like the medicine ladies. He wore the same sneer Sammy had smeared over her lips as she had reached for the buckle on her trousers; the hungry leer of a starving dog.

He was a monster, the monster.

"Let me go," she whispered.

The monster tensed. From his belt he brought out a curved knife longer than Billy's arm, and the amber glow of the fires filtering in from outside sent stars of reflected flames winking off its edge. "I said no talking."

There was no doubting now that this was the same man who had attacked their camp and chased her and Daddy and Grandpa through the night. He was the one who had taken Grandpa away. She had listened to him attack Grandpa in the darkness, beating with his fists, stamping down from above …

It really was Him.

A bottled surge of anger filled her up and overflowed despite her shuddering throat. "I know what you are. You're a Bad Man!"

He laughed, a ringing high-pitched chuckle that again reminded her of the kind of thing she expected from a hungry wild dog. Somehow his laughter was more chilling than any scream of fury. Her skin puckered in goosebumps and she tensed against a shudder propagating along her spine.

She remembered the little knife she had taken from the medicine ladies, tucked into her belt. She let one hand fall from her face and slither down to her side now, and her chest ached with relief when she found a slight bulge there at her hip. It was still there. But it was so small compared to his, little more than a potato peeler. He would gut her like a pig before she could break his skin.

"You're right about that, squirt. Bad man." He dragged out the latter words into a tuneless song, *Baaad man*. He stopped in front of her and lowered down on his haunches so that they were looking each other in the eye. "You talk funny. Where you from?"

She blinked, lowered her face behind her hands so his glaring blue eyes couldn't burn her skin, and bit back a whimper. She sensed the anger building inside him; the air was charged with it, but she kept still and kept her eyes off the knife.

I want to go home. I wanna go home, go home! I want Ma and Daddy and Grandpa, I want to go home!

The monster was quiet a moment, then shrugged like it didn't matter. "Fine. You're not a talker. I don't need that. I can get all the fun I need elseways." And Billy's heart almost exploded in her chest as the knife began a slow arc up from his side toward her.

She told herself to reach for her dagger, commanding her fingers to reach under her tunic and grasp the handle. But her arms were frozen with fear, her body stupid and unresponsive.

She couldn't do anything. She was just going to sit here and let him come.

Oh no. No. It can't happen to me, not me—why am I here? Why? I should be at home, I should never have come—help!

She groaned like a whipped animal and sunk toward the ground, waves of nausea and terror running through her body. She was shaking all over, and it all seemed silly and fake, but she knew she was definitely here in this stinking tent with a man who was about to kill her.

The monster whispered, "Beautiful skin. Hold still, I'm going to carve a pretty picture …"

"No, wait! Help!"

Nonononononono, please. DADDY!

With a jerk, she knew she had left her body behind. Despite the knife being only inches away from her face the whole world fell away and darkness took its place. For a moment she was spinning and floating just as she had when she had stepped through the Arch from the Henge, and then she thumped down on familiar floorboards beside a familiar bedframe. When she opened her eyes, she was looking down at Daddy, gaunt and wilted like a summer flower visited by Jack Frost.

"You're just like your mother," he wheezed.

*

Alexander dunked the sponge in the basin of stagnant warm water and rinsed it out with one eye on the quivering Irishman. They had just got to talking and Alexander had been settling into a story like so many others he'd heard over the last year about going hungry and watching the world wilt and the crops die. Don and his family had come across the sea.

He was captivated. They had brought in the old man back at New Canterbury, but there had always been the chance that he had been an expat living in England when the End hit. But this … this man was too young to have known the End, barely out of his thirties. He was a native of Ireland itself.

So others really were out there. After all these years, he finally had solid proof of it.

And if Ireland was still dotted with survivors like Don claimed, what did that mean for the rest of the world? The End had left perhaps only one in a thousand behind, but the world's population had been in the billions. If that was so then maybe the small circle of ten thousand souls left on Earth he had estimated all this time was far larger. Perhaps their true numbers lay in the millions.

He was so enamoured with a snowballing flight of imagination—the kind he hadn't felt in years, like those that used to drive the fits of passion in his youth that had forged the mission's heart—that he didn't notice Don's eyes glaze over.

By the time Alexander stooped forth from the stool, the Irishman was in the grips of muttering delirium, speaking incomprehensible tongues. Even in the short time Alexander had been with him, though his spirits seemed buoyed more by the moment, his body was fading. His lips were now a stark blue and his skin had the rubbery lacklustre appearance of a corpse.

The man with the sickle was on his way, there was no doubting it. Alexander couldn't guess how long he had, but it wasn't long. A day, maybe. Hours, probably. If Heather or one of the doctors from London were here, then maybe they could do something to save him, but there probably wasn't another person for miles around.

In any case, Alexander had seen enough cases of Tuberculosis over the years to know it at a glance. There wasn't a whole lot their medicines could do but make him comfortable. And that was all Alexander could hope to do, even if the only way he could accomplish it was through one last friendly chinwag.

Alexander leaned over him now and let a stream of the warm water drip down onto his forehead, splashing away the greasy sweat and bile and mucus, but still Don muttered feverishly, jittering beneath the sheets with his eyes rolled up into the back of his head. Alexander picked out only every other word, because that word was always the same. "Billy … Billy … Billy …"

*

"Daddy."

Billy stood in a whirlwind of blurred shadows. It was the cabin, but it was all far away and distant, blurred as though she were looking at it through shattered sooty glass.

Like the tornado that took Dorothy away from Kansas. I'm just like Dorothy. But this place is dark. There's no Oz.

No, there was no Oz. Just Daddy. He alone was in focus right in front of her, glowing despite the lack of light. She knew it was him, but she was terrified by how different he looked. He looked just like Ma had before she had gone away, shrivelled up like a prune with his hair brittle as the teeth of a broom. The dark patches under his eyes reminded her of the Panda Man—yet these patches weren't sleek black, but a blue so vivid that it could only have been painted on.

"Just like your mother," he repeated, shaking his head. His voice was no more than a whisper, as though the real

Daddy was deep down inside, trapped under the weight of all the dead flesh she was looking at. "Scatty as you like, but always there in the end."

"Daddy, I'm sorry," she blubbered. She stumbled forward and felt as though she was passing through something solid just beside the stool, a thickness that blacked out the world for a moment until she passed out the other side. She shook herself and continued on, falling across Daddy's lap. She let out a sigh as the feverish warmth of his body enveloped her, and she curled up in a ball, crawling up until she could loop her arms over his shoulders. She didn't care that the sheets were wet or that he smelled like the meat shed after a hot summer day. She didn't even care that the world around them was dark and fogged, without floor or sky, and all this might be a fairy tale happening only inside her head. She only cared about the feel of his hands slipping up to stroke her hair away from her forehead, the calloused fingers like sandpaper on her ice-white skin.

She moaned soft and slight, resting her head on his, sinking into the folds of the sheets with him. It had all happened so fast, losing Ma and Grandpa and the farm, and she had come so close to going away on the Panda Man's orders and never seeing Daddy again—not even saying goodbye.

She held on to his throat so tight he gripped her arms to ease her off, but his eyes were soft and swimming. *Big old bear eyes,* Ma had called them. He kissed her forehead. "My girl," he sighed. "You have nothing to be sorry for. I'm the one who owes the apology."

"I left you, Daddy. I left you all alone and I don't know why. You don't understand. He made me, promised that you would get hurt if I didn't go and there wasn't time … There wasn't time—"

He placed a finger reeking of bed-sweat up to her lips and shook his head. "No more. I understand."

"No, you don't understand and I'm sorry I didn't come back."

"Billy. I understand."

She blinked. "You do?"

"I do." He frowned and looked away for a moment. "I don't know how, but I do. I'm seeing it all now like I was there. The strangest thing I ever saw." He gasped. "Billy, you stupid girl, what you've done … Those women in the forest." His fists tightened around her shoulders and his sunken lips tightened to a solid white line. "That man … thing… whatever he is, pulling on you left, right and centre like you were his puppet." He spoke as though seeing it all playing out in front of him like a film reel in fast motion, and she waited for the finale. He stiffened at last and she swallowed as he breathed, "Billy! That knife … oh, Billy, no."

"It's okay, Daddy. I'm here now."

"No, Billy. No, you're not here."

She pulled away and blinked. "What?"

"You're still right there in that tent. It's all just … on pause."

"How do you know?"

"I don't know." He frowned, looking off beyond her at the clouded wall of nothing. "I just do."

"But I *am* here." She reached out and touched his chest, pressing her palm flat against the slick pale skin. "We're together, Daddy. And I'm never going away again." She rested her head on his shoulder and sighed again, closing her eyes. "It's over."

A moment lasted when she was with him and it didn't matter that anything beyond the bed was fuzzy and in darkness, nor that she could feel the back of her mind being stretched, as though she was being tugged back to somewhere far away by a hook attached to the back of her head. She was with him.

Then his hand touched her shoulder. "It's not over, Billy. You have to go on."

She shuddered. She was slipping back and away despite wanting to hold on to him. She could feel the rough canvas floor of the tent pressing into her knees. Her stomach fluttered at the thought of that knife so close to her throat. But she didn't care. She wouldn't believe it. This was real, it had to be.

"Billy. You have to keep going."

She pushed her head tighter against him and her voice was muffled. "I don't want to!"

"You have to. It's important. I don't understand what that man has you doing—and I'd give anything to have you a million miles away from all this, back home eating the first berries from the bushes behind the barn … But I know that you're different. I always knew, but nothing like this.

Something special. You've got to keep going even after me."

"I will, Daddy, I will. I'll keep going until I get home for real …" She paused, and frowned. "What do you mean *after you*?"

His eyes were swimming still, but now a very un-grownup sadness squatted behind them. "My time is up, Billy. There won't be anything to come back to. You have to keep going."

"Don't be silly, Daddy. You're here."

"Not for long, Billy. I'm sorry. I've done all I can to stay in this world. It's time for me to join your mother."

"No!" She gasped, her heart jumping up into her mouth. "Daddy, you can't go. You can't leave me!"

"No choice. We walked the path together as long as we can."

"I can't leave you alone!"

"I'm not alone, Billy. I have company. He'll see me off."

"But I can't leave you."

"You don't have a choice. Your time here is up." His eyebrows raised, he shrugged. "All this is weird stuff, Billy. I never believed in other worlds and ghosts and magic. But here we are." He laughed, then spluttered with a groan. "Just in time for me to know that you'll be fine. And you *will* be fine." He cupped her face in both his big rough hands once again and looked at her as though breathing her in, drinking up the sight of her. "My girl. My little girl. Just promise me one thing."

She sniffed. "Okay."

"Never come back. Don't ever look for me. Just keep

going."

Tears burst from her eyes onto her cheeks and she shook her head, holding back a cry.

"Promise me!"

"But, Daddy …"

He held onto her face, keeping her before him. "Do it for me. It's all for nothing if I don't know you'll be okay. And if you keep going …" He smiled. "You'll make a difference. A real difference. There are big for you."

"I don't understand."

"Neither do I. But you're too important to give up now."

"Okay."

"So you know what that means. It means you're not going to sit on that floor and let some arsehole bleed you out on the ground for kicks. You're going to get him first."

"Daddy, that knife. It's so big. And he … he's a monster."

"He is. But you're my daughter." A single tear trickled into his beard. "And like I said, you're just like your mother."

That tug at the back of her head was suddenly stronger, and she was slipping away from him. Suddenly, the cabin went from foggy blur to complete darkness, and the bed began to ebb and fade.

Daddy gripped her hard, but there was no pain, and suddenly his hands seemed cold and distant. This was it.

No, it can't be the last time. I won't leave. I can't!

But she was going anyway.

Daddy was talking fiercely. "Don't think, Billy. Don't hesitate. Hit first, hit hard."

The bed was gone. Now Daddy's hands were gone and he was whizzing up away from him.

"I love you, Daddy!"

Daddy sounded as though at the end of a long metal pipe. "And keep running."

"I love you!" she bawled.

His face shrank away and his body faded until all she could see were his smiling lips and soft brown bear eyes. "Run as fast as you can," he said.

Then the darkness was gone and vertigo gripped her in a spinning, wild moment before she was thrown back into her body on the ground in the tent. Time had crawled while she had been with Daddy, and the world had moved not an inch during the long minutes she had spent in the cabin. But now it was all snapping back, spooling up like a winding clock. And now shadow was falling over her. Her heart lurched.

For a sickening moment, she saw the huge, curved knife snaking through the air toward her throat, and the wicked glee in the eyes of the monster as he bent to work on her, and she thought she really would freeze. It was all about to be over.

But then Daddy's echoing voice came from the ether between the spaces. "Stick him!"

And then her hand was moving at her belt, so fast she had no idea what it was doing, somehow reaching out to full extension before her in no time at all. She closed her eyes and waited for the pain to start.

Nothing touched her. No pain.

Instead her arm thrummed with impact and an ear-splitting scream of pain and fury rang out.

She opened her eyes to see the monster reeling back from the paring knife in her grip, his hands held up to a gouge cut straight through the meat of his cheek. He fell back against the canvas and toppled over, staring at his fingers as though unable to believe he was seeing his own blood.

Then she was on her feet, running. This time, she wasn't going to stop. Men and women were coming from all directions to answer the screams and already they were pointing at her and giving chase. But she wasn't worried. The power of worlds was in her legs, and she knew she could beat them.

As she left the tent behind, a screech washed over her from behind. "BITCH! YOU *BITCH!* I'll make you bleed good for this, you hear? I'LL BLEED YOU GOOD, WHORE!"

By the time she reached the trees, dozens pursued her. But her legs were like air under her and she flew without thought over the uneven terrain. And as she ran, though her heart ached and she knew she would never see Daddy again, she laughed.

From far, far away, one last echo of his smooth lilting voice reached her. "That's my girl."

CHAPTER 23

Alexander jerked when Don emerged from his muttering stupor. His eyes had been rolled up into their sockets and he had been throwing his head from side to side, but suddenly he was back, staring at Alexander just as before, weak and pitiful. "Huh," he muttered.

"What just happened?"

"I saw my daughter. She's far away. Holy Mary, she's far away. But I got to say goodbye." A weak smile touched his lips.

Alexander smiled and nodded. "I'm glad."

Those sombre eyes flickered. "You don't believe me."

"It's not for any of us to say what's possible."

"Don't give me that shite." He choked his way through a brief laugh. "And don't you dare treat me like a kiddywink just because I'm dying. I sound crazy, right?"

Alexander smiled again, but this time he meant it. "Batshit."

"There we go. Wasn't so hard, was it?"

"You'd be surprised. I've been pretending to be somebody else so long, I've lost track of what it's like to tell the truth."

"You were some kind of chief, I suppose?"

"You could say that."

"Yeah, you got that way about you. You can see it in a man's eyes." Don tried to sit up but sank back again, hacking a thread of spittle onto the sheets in front of him. He didn't bother to wipe it away. "But I don't care if I sound crazy. I saw my girl, and I know she's going to do great things. She's got a place in this world, and that's all that matters. I can go be with my wife."

Alexander leaned forward. "How can you know? Really? Because I've known things. I have thought I knew them with every fibre of my being, and in the end, it turned out I didn't know a damn thing. And a lot of people ended up hurt or dead along the way." He was stooping over Don now, ignoring the stink and the rattling wheeze coming from his chest. "So how can you *know*?"

"I can't tell you. I just know. Might just be approaching the end means a man hears the whisper o' God. Men near the end can afford to hear." He grinned, showing yellow, rotten teeth. "Who're we going to tell?" He sat there a while before continuing on, looking at Alexander anew. "I know you."

Alexander blinked.

"I've seen you before."

"I think I'd remember meeting an Irishman."

"No. I've *seen* you every night after I close my eyes since we came across the water. And I think my girl's been seeing you as well." He frowned. "Just who are you?"

"I don't understand."

"That makes two of us."

Alexander sank slowly back onto his stool. "You have seen me in your dreams?"

"Easy, boy. You're not that pretty." Another nicotine-yellow grin. "Yeah, I seen you. You and few others. Spotty images, little film reels. It was like something was trying to speak to me, let me know it was important, somehow. I thought it was the sickness until my girl told me she'd been seeing the same."

"What did you see? Besides me, what did you see?"

"Man just south of thirty, black hair, eyes that look like somebody's told him Christmas ain't coming ever again."

Alexander swallowed with a rifle-shot crack.

Norman. Was he talking about Norman?

"And?" he said, licking his lips.

"Some other guy, young as well. But this one was different. Tall, dark clothes, black patches under his eyes like he'd had a fight with a bottle of mascara, and lost."

This time Alexander couldn't hold it in. His jaw fell ajar and he surged forward. His fists bunched around Don's collar of their own accord and suddenly he was breathing down his scrawny pale neck. "What did you say?"

"What's got into you?"

"Please, tell me! You saw him?"

"Clear as I saw you. In some old city with a big church on the river."

Canterbury. They're not hitting London, they're going for New Canterbury first.

But it was crazy. Don couldn't possibly have seen anything real. Could he?

He's seen us. And he saw that … thing. The one with the dark eyes.

Don shook his head, looking past Alexander's shoulder. "It was all on fire. And all around you, all of you … them. Those monsters who've been prowling the woods, taking people north, burning up anyone who fights back. They were all around you."

"They're coming? You're sure?"

"Bloody right they are."

"How long?"

"Can't say. I'm no bloody mystic. But they're coming for the lot of you. And my Billy is a part of it."

"What part?"

"I don't know. But without her, you lot are fixed to lose. It might not be in the here and now, maybe not even this big fight you're fixing for. But if your paths don't cross, some very bad things are going to happen."

Alexander let him down gently, breathless. "I'm sorry." He put his hand to his forehead and paced the cabin. Don watched him all the while, and it irked him. "You don't look all that concerned."

"Your paths will cross. You can't fight destiny."

Alexander laughed. "You can try. I know somebody who's been fighting their destiny all their life."

"Well you can't fight this kind. You believe me, you'll want to watch out for my girl—for the sweetest angel you ever saw. And they are coming."

Alexander ran a hand through his hand and cursed.

This wasn't possible. It was crazy.

But so much crazy had ruled the way of the world since the End. Even the End itself … They might have become used to it, but the very idea of it, all those people … It was all crazy.

I left for no reason, he thought. *I've left them and James is coming anyway.*

I knew he would, but I ran.

And now I have to go back, before it's too late.

He turned back to Don and sighed. "Son of a bitch," he breathed.

"Don't mention it, mate," Don said. "Now," he said and sat up. This time he struggled against his failing body and balanced on his bony arse. "I need a favour."

"What?"

"I need a hand getting up." He was leather-skinned and barely alive, but sitting up, and his eyes held a distant ember. "I've got a date with my wife."

*

Don hadn't been able to drag himself outside since Billy had left—it had taken all the strength he had to make it to the fireplace and throw a few more logs into the pit. When the fresh air hit his face, he gasped, overcome by the sheer freshness of it. He had been breathing the same stagnant air for endless hours. But the crisp seaside breeze flowing up over the cliffs was like sweet nectar, glacial and rich.

Alexander grunted beside him, hauling Don's moribund body from the interior of the cabin. All Don had left of his old life was in there; all his possessions, but he didn't feel an ounce of regret at leaving them behind. He was quite content never to see any of it again for the rest of his life.

Seeing as his life was bound to end in the next few minutes, it would all work out just fine.

They staggered out onto the grass of the cliff edge and Don cried out. His legs had seized up and were useless masses of dead flesh under him, the tendons shrunken and immobile, the muscles dried up as though with rigor mortis.

Christ, I could be dead already. My body's way ahead of me.

What would he have done if this guy hadn't come along?

Suffered. I'd have suffered in that bed by myself. I wouldn't have had the strength to end it.

"Thank God for you, mate," he wheezed. "You're an angel. I swear it."

Alexander grunted beside him. "I'm no angel, Donald. Believe me."

"No, no, I mean it. I've got nothing left but a chance at a little dignity. I get to make this date with Miranda because of you. So thank you. Thank you."

A pause, then a sigh. "Don't mention it."

It was only a short distance to the cliff edge, where the long, windswept grass gave way to a jagged edge, then the stark bright blue of the evening sky and the aquamarine of the English Channel.

Though his chest felt as though it was full of razor

blades, Don closed his eyes and took in a deep breath.

"This isn't a good idea. We should get you back inside," Alexander began. His grasp had grown stiff and hesitant.

Don gripped his wrist desperately. "Don't you dare chicken out on me, now," he growled. "You see this through."

They paused a moment and he felt Alexander's eyes on him. "Alright."

"To the end?"

"To the end."

Don squeezed his thanks, too weak to even nod.

Alexander looked around at the bare cliff-side. "Where?"

Don took a breath to brace himself and pointed to the very lip of the cliff. "There."

Alexander didn't move for a long time, and Don didn't have the strength to urge him. He could only wait and focus on dragging air into his burning lungs, which crackled like old paper bags with each inhalation.

Not long now. Just keep breathing. This is the last stretch.

Eventually, they started shuffling again and the cliff came closer.

They kept going until they were a few yards from the precipitous edge, then Don stiffened and forced himself to look at his new friend. "Here's good."

"You're sure you want to do this, Don?"

"I'm sure."

"We could go back. I could try for help …"

Don clapped his arm despite all the pain and the gathering darkness in his peripheral vision, and he laughed.

"Don't sugar-coat it now. I'm glad. I get to choose. You gave me the choice." He reached up to Alexander's shoulder, each inch he raised his arm feeling like a thousand-foot climb, and squeezed. "Thank you."

"It was a pleasure, Don."

Don nodded. He made to go, then turned back. "What will you do?"

Alexander's eyes twinkled.

"You're going back to your people, ain't you?"

"Yes."

"I told you things are going to get bad back there."

"That's why I have to go back. Even if it's just to die with my family."

"Why?"

"Because none of this would be happening if it weren't for me."

Don nodded. He tested his strength, loosening his grip and taking baby steps away into the grass. When he was sure he could stand on his own, he held out his arms to keep his balance. Though every joint felt like it were made of glass, and his feet might shatter any moment from the strain of bearing his weight, he took a decisive step back. "Good luck," he wheezed.

Alexander nodded solemnly. "Go to your wife."

Don turned away smiling, and ambled his way painfully to the cliff edge. In moments the wind was striking him full across his flank, icy and angry and primal, and he was staring hundreds of feet straight down. The sea roiled upon the rocks below, a foamy mass of bubbles. He longed to feel the sea again, just one last time, to run on the beach with Billy. He had lived so long without any kind of silliness—the kind of life-giving stupidity that made it all worthwhile. He should have done more things just for him, for the just because, instead of spending so many years slaving away, trying to control everything.

"You were always too serious."

Don looked sideways and felt like he was melting into the ground. Miranda stood at the pinnacle of the cliff edge, her hair as healthy and shining as the day he'd first met her, waving like a golden flag in the sea breeze. She wore a simple white summer dress, spotted with blue flowers. Her face was full and impish, pink and soft and spattered with freckles. It was the woman he had known before the sickness had touched her, not the desiccated remnant he had buried in the dandelion fields behind the farm.

The woman who had married him when all he had to offer were a few potato fields in the middle of barren nowhere. The mother of his child. His Miranda.

"You're here," he said.

She smiled, serene and coquettish. "You look terrible," she said, her voice sultry and smooth, warm and comforting like fresh butter on hot bread.

He wheezed his way through a laugh. "I don't feel too good, love."

"The same sickness that took me. It was my fault."

"No."

"Yes. The same sickness that was in my veins."

"We were careful to keep Billy safe. But somebody had

to take care of you."

"Don …"

"It's not your fault. We can't choose the cards we're dealt."

She stepped light and dainty through the grass and folded against him, resting her head in the hollowed crook of his shoulder, like she had when they had been young and brave and indestructible. His skin puckered into gooseflesh at her touch, yet her body seemed made of air, light as fluffy down.

Can she really be here? She's been dead months.

He didn't believe in an afterlife, never had. Yet that didn't matter a bit, looking at her now. She had come back to him.

"You did well," she said, sniffing and breathing deep as the ocean air swept over them.

He sighed as he swayed on his feet. The darkness in his peripheral vision was growing thicker, narrowing his view of the world as though he was looking at it through a telescope. "I failed. I failed you all."

"You didn't fail anybody. We owe you everything. You never gave up. Lesser men would have crumpled into the ground or turned to drink or run out of their family. But you stood. You're a good man." She wrapped her arms around his chest. Though he felt no pressure there, he groaned and sank into her.

"I tried," he muttered.

"You did more than that. You made sure Billy had a chance."

"She's lost, Miranda. I lost our daughter." He was almost weeping now.

"Sshh." She pressed a long manicured finger to his lips. "She's here, in this place. Back home there was no place for anyone with a heart. She would have had to become a killer to survive. But here … she belongs here. She has important things to do."

"What important things, Miranda?" He brushed her hair behind her ear, nuzzling the soft curls of her hair, breathing in her scent. Lemons, she smelled of lemons. "I've seen some funny things lying in that bed. I know she's important. But what is she meant for? Where is she heading?"

"I don't know. But getting here was worth the price."

He nodded. He knew it was true. There was no arguing. "She'll be safe?" he asked.

"There's no telling. We gave her the best chance she could have had." She raised her head and whispered softly in his ear. "We have to let her go."

He shivered, his eyelids drooping. The darkness was thickening still, and the pain was fading. He should have felt relieved, but instead he was only afraid. With his body the way it was, the pain going away could only mean that he was slipping away. He didn't know how he was still standing; each moment he swayed more and more, and the wind threatened to blow him hard to the ground. "I'm cold, Miranda."

Her sweet voice in his ear: "I know. Not long now."

"Will you stay?"

"Until the end."

"And then?"

She pulled away from his chest and looked into his eyes, radiant with the sun at her back. "Look at those eyes." She grinned. "Big bear eyes." She took his hand and took a step closer to the cliff edge, and he followed. She peered over the lip, turning her face into the wind and looking down the pristine coastline in all its chalky beauty, cast in hues of fading heliotrope as the sun's last light faded.

She let go of his head and turned to face him, her dress afloat in the wind, composed and perfect as a wax doll. "Come on home."

He nodded, and closed his eyes. He knew what he had to do.

But he needed a moment. It would take all the strength he had left to do it right. Then something had changed—there was an absence in front of him.

She's gone.

Miranda wasn't by his side any more. There was only the grass, the chalky precipice, and the rolling surf far below. He almost wept, but shook himself.

Stay focused. You're at the end. One last step. You can do it.

He crept forward until his toes were upon the cragged lip, and he took in the waves and the infinite sky one last time. He was looking at the world through a telescope now, a long dark tunnel that stretched on forever. The pain faded to a dull ache deep in his bones. He was tired, done. He had done what needed doing. Now he could rest.

He closed his eyes and held his arms out to the side.

Miranda's voice uttered from the wind, "*Come home.*"

Don leaned forward, and then he was falling. All the while his stomach fluttered and the rocks rushed up toward him, he was smiling.

CHAPTER 24

Sarah walked the cobbled streets of New Canterbury for a long while that night. Everyone else was too shut up tight in their homes to notice her making her way around the cobwebbed, dilapidated ruins at the edge of the city, away from the pools of precious light afforded by their power reserves. Her white dress glowed in the night, spotless and pure under the full moon. The dress plimsolls she was wearing were ungainly on the uneven cobbles, but with the rifle in her hands, she felt sure.

Nothing stirred but the trickling Stour, a blanket of twinkling reflected stars on black waters nearby. She breathed deep and walked sure, feeling Robert by her side. It was a silly thing, to think that being married could change anything; it was just a ring and a few words after all. She didn't believe in God.

But everything had changed. She felt more a woman than she had ever done before. People had always been kind, what with her divvying out the city's literature and schooling the children. But she had always been the nice girl, the gawky one bumbling around in her warehouse.

Never before had she felt maternal power in her bosom like this. She was the mother of the city, now. She knew it, and she saw it in others' eyes.

And her husband could never leave her. A part of Robert had nested inside her and gave her new strength, and a part of her now rested in him. She could almost feel his hands on her now, hear his voice uttering the minutiae of her surroundings, calling out things to notice and be wary of, muttering plans for mounting their defence come morning.

Which is exactly what she would do. At first light she would rally the city's guard—her guard. Pride was a thing to be cautious of, but she had been afraid to even touch a gun only days ago, and now she had taken a troop of those just like her, and made them a force worth reckoning.

Sarah smiled as she patrolled the city streets, a white wraith in the night.

Sometime after midnight, Allison and Heather appeared together on the roadside. By their stillness and the fixed hold of their gazes, she knew they had been watching her for some time. "What are you two doing here?" she said.

"Come inside, Sarah," Heather said, her hands clasped at her sides.

"Shouldn't you be in the clinic?"

"There is no more I can do for those people."

"Fine. Get some sleep, then. I'll need you come sunrise for militia duty. We're going to practice, and practice, and keep going until we tear those targets apart." She moved forward over the cobbles, stepping carefully, making her way past the both of them. "Nobody's getting past us," she muttered. "We'll kill them all."

She felt their eyes on her, and a well of anger rose up in her chest. She hated that feeling, the visceral sense that they were worried about her, as though she were unhinged or crazy.

And? How do you think you look? said a voice deep in her head. *Your books go up in flames and you turn into Xena the Warrior Princess?*

She almost laughed at herself, but caught the giggle in time. She couldn't afford to play silly games now.

"You haven't eaten," Allie said. "Your feet must be all blisters by now, in those shoes. Just come inside, you stupid mare. Let us fuss over you."

A swell of affection almost knocked Sarah off her course. Again, she almost succumbed to laughter. But she twisted her face into an expression she knew could melt ice, and glared at the two of them. "I'm not sure what you think is going on," she said, "but we don't have time to put our feet up. Look around, there's nobody else left. We're in charge. Us."

"That's why you need rest. People are looking to you, Sarah, and they need to be able to rely on you. There's no sense in you patrolling out here by yourself. Come on in with us, eat a hot meal and get some rest, and …"

"Take off that dress," Heather said.

Sarah looked down at herself, a white figurine amidst crumbling ruins of a bygone world. "I'm still wearing it," she said. And it was so. She had been wandering around for hours, and the veil still trailed from the back of her head.

"Come on inside," Allie said.

Together, Allie and Heather took Sarah's arms and guided her inside, crooning over her and muttering soothing words.

Sarah wanted to tell them to quit being so ridiculous, but she found that her mouth was glued together and her feet felt like they were made of lead. Maybe they were right. She was getting weak. "Fine, I'll eat."

"And you'll sleep."

"Fine." She stepped under the hall's roof and shivered as she was embraced by the warmth of the hearth fire in the far corner. She hadn't noticed how cold she was. Her stomach growled like a snarling dog. She sighed, sagging onto a bench and looked at her hands, feeling the tightness of the dress squeeze the air from her lungs. She propped the rifle beside her, and suddenly it seemed ten times heavier.

"What can I bring you?" Heather said.

"A change of clothes," she said. "And a blanket."

"You can't sleep here. We'll get you to bed."

"I'm not going home. I don't want to set foot in that place until Robert gets back." She glared at them until Allie nodded.

"A blanket," she whispered, patting Sarah's hand as she pushed a bowl of broth in front of her.

Sarah ate while Allie stripped off her white garments as though she were a child. She was lucky to have them, but she couldn't bring herself to thank them. Not yet, not now. A pall of determined vigour possessed her despite her exhaustion, pushing her on to the last.

She couldn't relax, couldn't show weakness. Not now. Because somewhere out there, Robert was fighting for them. And elsewhere, people were fixing to raze her city to the ground.

Sarah ate and slept, and dreamt of a honeymoon that never was.

CHAPTER 25

It was a crisp dewy morning, and Norman was in hell. Pain had festered in his chest since mounting up in New Canterbury. Even then he had known this trip might be the end of him, and he had come anyway.

This morning, cold woke him. He knew the Echoes were close. The farther north they rode, the stronger they seemed.

Before he could climb from his sleeping bag, the cold pulsed and thrummed in his chest, and he braced himself helplessly. This time he didn't slip; he was hurled from his body into a blackness so uniform it seemed rich and velvety, like treacle.

He had time for one thought to bullet through his head. *Dear god, what now?*

Then a terror to belittle all others shot from a mere pinprick to all-consuming enormity at impossible speed, and suddenly Norman hovered above millions of screaming, enslaved *things*, filthy and deformed.

So I've cracked after all. Well, at least now I'm sure.

Then he screamed. Screamed, the way children do when

confronted with an experience so alien and beyond their control that their only recourse is blind terror.

Something had thrust its way into his mind, deep into the gooey bits where he, the thinking, feeling Norman, lived.

"It's people," said a high, sweet little voice. A tiny figure now floated beside him, a young girl with fire-red hair, the same girl who had stood over him in his dream.

"You again!" he said. "What do you want?"

"Nothing. I didn't bring you here."

"Then what the hell is this?"

Talking to your own delusion. Great. Keep digging that hole, Norm.

But he couldn't shake the iron certainty that this *was* real. The horrors under them were too far beyond reckoning, but something told him the girl was a living, breathing person somewhere out there. He sensed power.

"I'm on a mission," the girl said simply.

"Aren't we all?"

She ignored him.

"You speak strangely," he said.

"I came across the sea. Enger Land is a strange place, like Wonderland gone topsy-turvy."

Wonderland gone topsy-turvy. I like that. Craziness gone crazy.

"Look, they hurt so much," she breathed.

Norman yelled as something yanked him closer to the writhing shadows, as though his face were being pressed up against stinking mud.

God, it's her.

She turned him over like a leaf in the wind. Maybe they were both here because of some higher power, but between them there was no contest. The ease with which she threw him around was frightening.

"You're special," he said.

Where had that come from?

"Lots of people say that." Her voice was tiny, and tired—too tired to come from that sweet, young mouth. "I just want to go home."

They hung there together and Norman shook his head. "When will all this end?"

Sick amusement trickled down those invading fingers stuck in his head, her amusement. "I gave up asking," she said.

"So I suppose we're on some kind of journey together? Some Abra Kadabra quest?"

"Maybe."

He nodded. What else could he do?

"One question," he said.

She looked at him, so alone and small it made his heart lurch in his chest.

"*Did* you bring me here?"

She blinked slowly, and those prying fingers yanked free from his head.

"See you soon," she said.

Then the screaming people were gone, and Norman span. In the blur he caught flashes of great silvery strands, titanic legs the breadth of entire galaxies, converging on eight blinking eyes—

The spider, the Great Weaver!

—and then he was shivering, encrusted in an icy skin. By the time the spinning stopped he was back in the stables, and Robert was calling his name.

It was time to mount up.

*

They had been moving for over a week, and by now Norman cursed himself every other moment. Constant, jolting impacts of the horse's hooves sent blinding pain coursing his body. As mile after mile passed by, they skirted the smouldering wreckage of towns and villages. More than a few members of the expedition erupted in frantic searches for their kin in the rubble.

In a way, Norman felt like a hypnotist, drawing his mesmerised flock towards a meat grinder. Because that was the truth of it: a lot of them were about to die, and it might be for nothing.

But he would do it, because that was what needed to be done. After all he had been through, he still spurned his Great Destiny. But he had learned that much, at least: some things just needed to be done.

The cities had all fallen behind them now and they were heading into the unknown. Nobody had ventured this far north for years. The Northlands had been respectfully left to their own devices as the South had scrabbled to form its alliances and rebuild something of what it had lost. Of what really went on here, they had little knowledge.

Apparently, not all had crumbled. If this coalition from Scotland really was real, it was possible another society like theirs was bent on re-creating the Old World, their two orders separated by a strip of no-man's land in between.

But it could also be that nobody waited out here but thieves, trading posts, rival gangs and any lone farmsteads strong enough to hold their own. The farther north they travelled, the more it seemed the latter was the case. Norman's hopes for finding the stranded emissaries dwindled fast.

But he couldn't let on. He was a leader now, and that meant holding the course for the sake of everyone else.

This is what Alexander had to deal with all those years … All those years I was whining at his side.

He wished he had paid a little more attention to how Alexander had dealt with it. He had always known he would have to lead, eventually.

They had passed bodies by the roadside for as long as they had travelled north. Most were thin, beaten and desiccated. Some were whipped into bloody horrors.

Every so often they would pass a farmstead or a town or campsite, raided of food and women and children, along with anyone strong enough to walk. The rest had been either shot or driven off. A few had been burned on pyres of straw and kindling—burned at the stake like medieval witches.

Norman's stomach turned at the sight of that calibre of barbarism. To think their countrymen had become that. He did his best to steer the group clear of those pyres, but still they all saw plenty. And there was no skirting the endless carpet of bodies that lay in the army's wake. Even the thieves and highwaymen who had ruled this land had fallen victim to the relentless tide of anger and retribution; their bodies peppered the same ground as those they would have called their prey.

The North belonged to the sigil of the pigeon, now.

After travelling along a motorway for some miles they crested a hill and saw yet more wilderness ahead, stretching away towards a jagged collection of mountains. The land was growing rougher, sparser, and a low-lying fog was becoming ever present. Also there was simply a sense of something different, a prescient thrumming deep in his bowels. He knew they all felt it, but couldn't describe it.

"This is the place. Radden," Robert said. It wasn't a question.

"Yes," Norman said. He didn't doubt it either.

The road ahead had something *other* about it, off-hue, as though it wasn't quite aligned with the rest of the world. After checking the map, they found that their target was the tallest of the mountain peaks: a flat-topped shear slab of rock over two thousand feet high called Dreymont's Peak.

By then the land was made up exclusively of heather, windswept fog-ridden moorland and dense forests older than any creation of man. Out there could be anyone, and anything, hidden amidst the ruins and the endless tracts of wilderness.

"They're up there," Robert said, looking toward the

peak. All of them had gathered along the edge of the A590, the carriageway they had been following, their mounts shuffling restlessly.

"Maybe," Norman said.

Faces all around them were uncertain and hesitant. Now that they were here, he sensed their apprehension. They would either find salvation or death here. Norman waited for Robert to take the lead, but for once he seemed caught up in his own thoughts, staring up at the distant slopes.

"Alright," Norman said, clearing his throat. The closer they came to this place, the more the pain in his chest gave way to that ugly, creeping cold. It tingled in his lungs, prickled his skin. He tried to ignore the Echoes wandering from horizon to horizon.

Whatever power was playing with him like a rag doll, it lived here.

He forced himself to turn to the others and saw that even they were ready and waiting, big burly men and ruddy-faced women who looked far wiser than he could ever hope to be. He nodded and took a breath. "We best get on with it."

They were well into Radden County's barren foothills when they saw the smoke of the first campfires on the horizon.

NINTH INTERLUDE

"We're here."

James and Alex had crested a hill that gave them a panoramic view of the landscape, sloping down towards Victorian ruins and, beyond, endless miles of moorland and mountains. In the far distance, he caught the paleness of the ocean.

Close by, pigeons cooed. At first it had only been a few from the coop back home following them. But along the way they had picked up more and more, until eventually it seemed the horizon was alive with their fluttering wings in all directions.

Something had changed in the birds just as it had in him, as though they sensed the force awakening inside him.

Alex was quiet, his face taut and twitching.

"What is it?" James said.

Alex nodded. "I know this hill," he said. "This is where I first saw it, saw the fires and the empty cars and falling planes. I came here the day of the End." He nodded down at the huddle of cottages and townhouses ahead, dark with vines and saplings and moss. "Welcome home, James."

The two of them remained on the hilltop for some time, taking in the sheer scale of their surroundings, dwarfed by the primal enormity of it all—the mountains and the lakes, the ancient woodlands and tortured heath clothing the moorland. James shivered despite his exhaustion and the tired slumping of his steed under him.

Yet still he itched. His calves and feet were numb, his crotch pummelled to jelly, yet all along their length, they itched to be moving forward, desperate to get wherever they were going. Still, he was being led like a goat being lured by a carrot on a stick.

Alex seemed to be waiting for him to make the first move. But now that he was here, he had no idea what to do. All he could think of was to keep moving and hope inspiration struck. But what was there to go on bar the itch itself—and what good was a feeling you had to be somewhere if you had no idea what your business was when you got there?

It was a wonder to be back at his birthplace, to know that he and Alex had come from here, right here, when the world had been bustling and alive. But now it was only another abandoned husk, rotting out in the wastes, without a single sign of life. This place was dead.

So why am I here? Why, for the love of God?

Because if he had come all this way for nothing, he would never forgive himself. He had put all they had worked for in jeopardy, and left Beth to those snivelling rats. All this had to be worth it, *had* to be.

He slapped his reins and urged his faltering mount onward, descending toward the ruins of Radden. It wasn't until they reached the foot of the hill and they had entered the blanket of thick fog that wreathed the entire county that he got his first sign.

Standing there amidst the land cloud with his hands clasped demurely before him, as though awaiting an appointment, was Him—the man he'd seen in his vision, dark streaks throbbing like bubbling tar under his eyes. He grinned a predatory grin, holding out his arms in welcome. "Finally!" he cried.

James blinked in shock and yanked on his reins. His mount bucked and he had to grasp the saddle horn grimly until he could wrestle it back to exhausted standstill. The grinning man was gone.

By then Alex was beside him, his eyebrows raised. "What did you see?"

"He was there, right in front of us! Where did he go?"

Alex looked into the mist. "Who?"

"It was Him. The one with the dark marks."

Alex looked again at the blanket of whiteness all around them and turned back to him quizzically. "You're sure?"

"He was there!"

Alex didn't break his gaze for a long time. Eventually he sighed and nodded. "Where next?"

James didn't bother asking whether he believed him. He nodded ahead, and the two of them rode on into the mist, moving closer to the gnarled ruins. Somewhere, James heard an echoing cackle, one that seemed to emanate from the ground and the very air itself. The hair on the back of his neck stood on end.

*

Alex let James ride on a while before unravelling the scrap of paper in his pocket. One of the pigeons had appeared with the scroll tied to its leg a few miles back. He wasn't sure why, but he had plucked up the scroll and hidden it from sight before James had seen. He had a bad feeling about it—he had given express instructions for the others to wait for them, no contact.

Now he read the message in a single quick glance and cursed. "Malverston," he fumed.

James's little crush might cost them the entire deal he had built up with Newquay's Moon. Whatever she had done, it had gone and gotten her in trouble.

Best not to tell James. He was distracted enough already. Better to get this silliness dealt with first, or he'd have to clean up the mess back home by himself. And he needed James back in fighting form.

Failing to quell his disquiet and guilt, he followed on and threw the note into the mud.

CHAPTER 26

Billy woke amidst leaf litter, staring up at a sky wreathed in fog. Dirt cliffs lay on either side of her, leading up to the forest floor above. She was in a long furrow where thick mud and dead leaves had collected until knee deep. Her back ached, and her skin was tight around her eyes. She had been crying in her sleep.

For a moment, her head was empty and she just lay there surrounded by the wilderness, the twig-strewn soil and the pigeons in the trees. The pigeons were everywhere, just as they had been before she had stepped through the archway. This was their home, their real home.

It would have been easy to stay like that forever. Her body was a bag of hurt, she was thirsty and tired, and she didn't much want to go anywhere. Just to stare at the sky and trace her fingertips through the crinkled leaves would be enough.

But then it all came back, with a rush and a roar that brought a scream to her lips.

"Daddy!"

Then she remembered: the darkness, seeing Daddy so

weak and lonely so far away, then cutting at the monster and running through the trees while they chased her. They had chased her a long time and she had laughed all the while—laughing but crying, half blinded by tears as big as raindrops, because Daddy was gone now, gone away forever just like Ma and Grandpa. They had been so far behind that they would never have caught her because her legs were like magic with the itch, moving over the ground and finding the places with the best grip so that it felt like she was flying.

For a while she had kept running and she had been angry; the Panda Man had promised she would know what to do once she got here. But now that she was free and running, she had no idea why she was here. As she had run for the trees, she had seen the whole landscape spread out flat and enormous around her; there was nothing but trees and grass and mountains. Nothing to do, and nobody to help.

And he was nowhere to be seen. He hadn't come to her when the monster had taken her, hadn't done anything to save Daddy like he had promised. He had just let him die and there had been nothing she could do to stop it, because he had taken her so far away she could never get home.

Where was he now? Where was he? He was a liar, a big fat liar!

How long had she been hiding here, reaching out with her mind? It felt like forever. The day she had touched the dark-haired man and showed him the darkness could have been yesterday or a week ago.

She couldn't hear the cries of the monster's friends

anymore nor the shuffling crash of their feet moving through the underbrush. The forest was silent and old and musty, dead save for the pigeons' cooing. But they were still out there, looking for her.

It was so old, this place. Older than even Stonehenge.

How do you know, silly? You've never been here before.

She knew. She knew just like she had known where to go all this time, just like she knew Daddy was gone now—she felt it inside her, a black empty space where he used to be that now rang hollow and throbbed with pain so deep it made her want to retch.

She cried a little while as that pain rose up and swept over her for the first time. It was all real. New Land, the Panda Man, the Archway, the teashop, the pigeons, the Medicine Ladies—all that madness and magic and silliness was what dreams were made of, fuzzy and unreal and make believe. It had been so easy to go this far believing that she would just wake up curled in Daddy's arms by the fire, and she would be back at the farm before everything had gone wrong. It had been so easy to believe it was all just some silly dream.

But it wasn't. There was no denying the pain in her belly now, that emptiness where all her family had lived before. It was all black and hollow now, and she was alone.

I'm alone, she thought. *Alone.*

She shivered and gripped the ground as though she would fall off, digging gouges in the mud and crying out, not caring if they found her and took her away. Fresh tears burst onto her cheeks and she choked on her own spittle, curling into a ball.

A lone voice stopped her, croaking and ancient and decrepit: "Stop that whining, young lady."

She opened her eyes and saw above her a crooked figure contrasted sharply with the morning fog. It was a woman of incredible age, her weathered skin like leather, pockmarked with dark spots and gnarled lengths of wiry hair upon her cheeks and neck. She was wearing odd clothes that were so clean Billy thought she was looking at one of the picture frames from Before, her jeans bright blue and whole, a soft-looking white blouse fluttering upon her shoulders. Billy gasped when she saw the glittering jewels on the many rings she wore on both hands, and the pendant loops hanging from her earlobes.

"Who are you?" she whispered, frozen by fright.

She didn't need an answer to know the woman wasn't from this place, nor any place she could get to. She wasn't even from the place between spaces from when the Panda Man appeared. She was from much farther away than that. Billy shuddered under her watchful eye.

"Name's Martha," she croaked. She teetered a little on the lip of the ditch and took a deep breath. "Phew, I hate passing between places these days. It's a young person's game." She looked at Billy's confused face and nodded. "Confused, I bet?"

"Yes."

"Fol sends his regards. The lazy bastard can't be here right now. I never understood the rules—magic is magic right? But everyone's got to play by rules, and he's no different. Don't worry, you'll see him again. For now, you got me."

Billy looked at her a moment, then rested her head on the ground. She didn't care about the Panda Man or his secrets anymore. "Go away," she muttered.

A beat passed, then the woman spoke in a scolding rattle. "I've come a long way to slap your little behind, so you listen good."

Billy sighed, but turned to her to meet her gaze.

The woman nodded. "Things are just getting started. We may not be from the same level, but I know Radden when I see it, and this place is special no matter what world you're hopping around in."

"I don't …"

"Hush. You can't go giving up now. Things have been awry too long already. We were supposed to have our candidate all those years ago. But the Chadwick boy turned his back, and things have slipped just that little bit more because of it. You must have noticed things are a little off around here? I got no phone signal, for one. And I saw all those wrecks on the motorway. Something did a real number on this world." She shook her head. "It might be too late to put everything right already." Her eyes bulged in their sockets. "But we got another chance with you. All you have to do is stay alive long enough to do your job." She gestured down at Billy, her crooked finger shaking. "What you got yourself down in the dumps, for? You're so close."

"My daddy," Billy said. She didn't know who this lady was or what she was talking about, but it didn't matter.

"He's gone and I'm all alone."

"Awwh, is she awl alooone?" Martha teased, affecting a soft bubbly lilt. Then her face hardened. "We all got problems, Billy."

Billy froze, a single tear trickling from her jaw. "How do you know my name?"

"We all know you, Billy. We've been waiting a long time for another one with the Gift to come along. And now you're here, and there's plenty to do."

"What?"

Martha made to speak, but then a crash rang out nearby, and a host of grumbling voices filtered through the trees. The monster's friends.

Martha looked unsettled and took a step back. "Looks like my time here is done already. I can't be seen, you understand. It'd confuse folks." She took a strange thin metal brick from her pocket and clicked a button on its side. Billy gasped when its dark face lit up with fantastic colours and figures, but Martha's face didn't change a mote. "Just checking the time," she said, rolling her eyes. "God, it must suck, living in this place. I wouldn't last a day without the net."

"What net?"

Martha laughed a harsh old lady's laugh, and pointed her finger down at Billy once more. It wasn't shaking this time. "You got stuff to do, and you're gonna do it. I'll kick your arse if I have to come back here again."

"What?" Billy cried. "I don't know what to do!"

"Sure you do. You just have to stop feeling sorry for

yourself. Do what feels natural. It'll come to you."

"And then?"

"Then … you fight. You're going to have to fight to stay alive, I'm betting. The Chadwick boy won't stop until the very end." Her eyes fluttered with a glimmer of emotion. "Shame. He was such a bright spark." Then her eyes hardened. "But the dice just didn't roll that way. We got you, now. So you keep breathing, you hear?"

Yet more crashes came from the underbrush, closer this time. Martha backed away. "Time's up, little one. I've got a roast in the oven, and my soap starts in ten minutes." She shrugged. "Not that that means anything to you people."

Billy shook her head. More silliness.

Just keep going. I've come too far to stop now.

But how was she supposed to do anything now, if all the Panda Man could send was this strange lady?

"I don't know where to begin," she said, hugging her knees.

The old lady smiled, revealing a mouth full of rotten brown teeth. "For starters, you get out of the ditch. You've got work to be doing, young lady."

Billy struggled to her feet. By the time she looked again, Martha was gone. It was as though she had never been there at all; a glimmer of a world far, far away. But when Billy clambered out onto the forest floor, footprints inset with the word *Timberlands* were outlined clearly on the ground.

The crashing was closer.

Billy started running once again, and this time she put all thought out of her head. Soon enough, her legs were flying once again, and she realised she was heading for the cliffs ahead. She had no idea why, but she trusted that her feet would carry her to the right place.

What else was there to do?

*

Evelyn leapt back with a start, holding her hand to her chest despite herself. It had been a long time since anything had given her a genuine fright. To have one now because of this fool!

"Aha, my dear, I didn't see you there!" Lincoln cried, high above her on the catwalk.

She bent down and picked up the blowtorch he had dropped not two inches from her head. She would have verbally skinned him if he'd been anyone else, but looking at the jovial old fool hanging up there like a white-haired monkey, grinning while the world was about to end around him, she couldn't bring herself to do it. He looked more alive than he had done in years.

Can't say my own heart isn't hammering to a young person's rhythm, she thought. Sensing its last few beats. Death has that way about it.

"Progress?" she said.

"Slow. We don't have enough hands. Even if we did, we don't have a whole lot to work with. Nobody's risking going out for supplies after the siege, whether they're still out there or not." He was grinning even now.

They both stood by the main gate, which was a hive of

activity. Volunteers and guards clung to it like limpets with welding equipment, attaching strengthening beams that criss-crossed the iron gate doors. Farther away, others were threading the tops of the walls with razor wire and hammering in lengths of sharpened pipe.

Don't forget the drawbridge and the moat. We're turning this place into a medieval fort.

Lincoln clambered down with great vigour despite his frail, shaking limbs, waving away Latif's attempts to help with blustering dismissal. He popped onto the ground beside her and took a bow.

Evelyn allowed herself a weakness. She hugged him close and tight. There was no sense keeping up her veil any longer. They were all the same now; there would be no special dignity for the elders when that army arrived.

He seemed surprised, his busy eyebrows disappearing into the thick steel-coloured mane atop his head, but he held her until she let go.

"It won't make any difference, will it?" she said.

"Not a damn bit." He smiled, and there was none of the pretence of the eccentric about him now. He turned with her to stare at the milling droves, each of whom bore intense expressions of concentration. "But it doesn't matter. We can't just sit and wait for those bastards to come get us. We have to do something. Busy hands make a clean conscience."

She was quiet. Real, childish fear stirred deep inside her at the thought of what was coming. She saw a flash of what this place would look like soon enough: pockmarked by bullet holes, blackened by fire, strewn with bodies. Even if they survived, things were going to get real ugly before they got better. "Maybe the messengers will bring others. Maybe there are a few still out there who'll come to help."

He nodded and looped his arm around her shoulders as though the two of them were newlyweds overlooking their new homestead. "Maybe." He sighed. "Maybe."

He squeezed her hand tight, and they stood that way for some time.

TENTH INTERLUDE

The ground opened up without warning, vanishing into a rabbit hole aperture at least ten feet wide. James yanked on his mount's reins to keep from falling in, and called for Alex to hold. The itch in his legs pulsed, crawling as though he had a sack full of worms in his trousers. His heart was racing.

"This is it," he muttered.

He sensed Alex's eyes on him from behind, burning into the back of his head. He said something but he sounded so far away, so very far—obscured by a rushing noise that seemed to rise up from the ground and wrap James in a pall of sonorous whining. He blinked, feeling drunk but unable to stop himself, climbing down from his mount and moving toward the hole. By the time he reached its lip he was almost scrabbling like a man dying of thirst diving for water. But then Alex gripped him roughly around the shoulders. "What the hell's gotten into you? I said not to go near it."

"I have to! Let me go, Alex. Let me go, I have to go inside!"

That doesn't sound like me, he thought. But he couldn't

help himself.

He needed to get down there. He *needed* to. There was no choice in the matter. If he waited any longer, then the itch would drive him mad. Already it was bubbling up out of his legs and into his abdomen, leaping ever higher toward his chest. It was a kind of fever, a madness, it was …

"Destiny," he cried, struggling free of Alex's grip. "It's my destiny. You have to let me go down there. All this time you've filled my head with all those stories about how I can change things and help people and really make a difference—well here it is, *this* is what I'm meant for." His mouth kept running like a spooked horse, and there was a desperate, dreamy note to it he didn't recognise. "This is where I belong, not running around playing castles with all those fools and farmers!"

"James." Alex stepped around the side of him and James was sobered by the blankness in his face. "James, what's wrong with you? This isn't you."

"It is me, and I have to go down there." It was obvious. Couldn't he see? Why was he standing in the way like that? Alex was hurting him, being in the way, ensuring that the itch plagued him, like a splinter in the brain. Anger spiked sudden and unstoppable, and he flung his arms into the air with a bellow of frustration. "I have to!"

"Why?"

"I … don't … know!" he screamed.

Alex blinked and looked around at the fog-strewn moorland. "This is nuts. You can't know what's down there."

James fumed. "I knew this place was here. Explain that."

"I can't. I just know that something's wrong."

"You don't know. I know. It's me who's got the fork in the road in front of him: either I'm about to have a complete meltdown, or I'm about to do something really fucking important."

"I can't risk losing you."

"You have the others," James spat.

"The others can't complete the mission like you can."

James barked a harsh laugh. "For a moment I thought you were saying you loved me."

"Of course I love you." Alex's lips tightened and his brow furrowed in anger. He was blushing. "I'm here, aren't I? Did I not just ride day and night through the bloody wilds on this wild goose chase just to make sure you didn't get your stupid self killed?"

"You came because you couldn't let your prize monkey slip through your fingers, Alex. That's the way it's always been. You've given me and the others everything we could ever want, and I wouldn't trade my life for anything, but let's not forget that you love the fairy tale in your imagination more than you could ever love any of us."

Suddenly, the air between them was different. The closeness had shifted. It wasn't the two of them standing in the foreign land, but James alone standing in a place that tormented him by its very being, and Alex standing in his way, keeping the answers over the horizon.

Stop while you're ahead, James. You don't mean this. It's just this crazy place.

But he couldn't stop. And there was something in Alex's face that looked broken, fractured so deep that all the fight had been knocked out of him. Without a word, he stepped aside. "It's your life, James," he muttered. He couldn't meet his eye. He sighed, and squared his shoulders, looking off toward the horizon. "I don't believe in all this crap about visions and special powers. I believe in people, the dirt and the sky, science and the real world. But I don't have a choice, sometimes. We live in a world we can't explain, and I've seen enough strange things to know that there's more going on.

"My life is about changing what I know I can change. If I don't, there's a chance nobody else will, and I can't let that happen. And I know you have the same way about you— it's a rare thing, so rare that I don't assume there are others like us out there. We can save what we're so close to losing. It's in our grasp.

"But like I said, it's your life. I never wanted to make a slave of you."

James wanted to reach out and grasp him, to tell him that he *knew*, to thank him for being the one to drag so many up out of the dirt. But the itch was still ablaze, and there was so much anger welling up in him that he took a step back instead. "You make slaves of everyone, Alex. We both do. That's who we are. We see things through, and we don't care who gets caught in our wake." He swallowed. "I don't know if that's what I want to be."

Alex was quiet for a long while. The fog of Radden Moor curled around their ankles and the whistling wind blew the crisp scent of wildflowers through the chasm that had erupted between them.

Alex nodded slowly, as though seeing him anew. "Go down. You have to go. But I'm not going with you. All this mystic puff might play a part in all this, but I don't have time to scratch around clues and chase mysteries. Maybe this is something, and maybe it's just crazy—for all I know you really do remember this place. You were just a baby, but it's possible. So go."

"Why do I get the feeling you're talking about something else here?"

"Don't play games, James. That girl and you ..."

James's heart hammered. "Beth. Her name is Beth."

Alex shook his head. "You can't afford these distractions. We have things to do, big things, and you need to keep your focus. You're so close to greatness. You can't give in now."

"I love her, Alex. And loving somebody isn't giving in; it's part of being alive. I don't want to live like that—"

He managed to bite back the last bit with extreme effort, but still it echoed in his head.

I don't want to end up like you.

"Like you said, you have a destiny. If you keep along this path, you'll be turning your back on it, and on me." For the first time that James could remember since he had ousted Paul, the zealot who had tried to kill James so many years ago, Alex was angry. Fury radiated from his eyes, and his jaw squared with leaping muscles.

He shook his head. "You come all this way and you want to do this now?"

"Go, James. Get it over with. Get it out of your system. We have business to do back home."

James cursed and stepped into the hole. It sloped down precipitously. He had expected it to really be like a rabbit hole, all soft earth and hanging roots and wriggling worms. But instead it widened out into a tunnel of mixed grey and obsidian stone, tall enough to walk at a stoop.

He stopped on the verge of where the grass gave way to bare rock, and turned back to Alex.

Alex wasn't looking at him. He had retreated a short distance away and was staring at the distant ruins of Radden with his hands in his pockets, shirt tails caught in the breeze. James felt a sinking sensation, and couldn't shake the feeling that things had changed for the worse between them.

He ducked down into darkness and, steeling himself, descended into the Earth. It was pitch dark here and he had to feel his way along walls slimy with moss, slipping on the sharp gradient every few steps and cursing, but ahead he could see an amber glow. He didn't have to look closer to know that it was the light of burning flames; these were the tunnels he had seen in his vision back at the farmstead, alight with bracketed torches.

He stumbled down, feeling more alone by the moment. He hadn't bet on going this far without Alex.

All his life he had been by Alex's side, preparing and learning all he could, training for the day when he would have to carry the banner of their cause. Had he just thrown it all away to tumble down a rabbit hole?

He shivered as he remembered the green book Alex had

given him when he had been a boy. The gold-leaf title was emblazoned on his memory: *Alice in Wonderland*. They had read that book cover to cover more times than he cared to imagine. That was the night Alex had first told him about his destiny, when they had begun their journey together.

Now it ends with another idiot tumbling down a hole in the ground. How bloody poetic.

The darkness didn't last long. The slope evened out and he passed the first of the torches, its light blinding even though he had been on the surface only a short while ago; he realised how thin and empty the blue-grey light that spilled over Radden County was. Now that the gradient had vanished, he could see all along the tunnel's length, and in the distance he could make out a brighter space, an opening that sent his already racing heart into overdrive.

All thoughts of Alex melted away as he pulled himself along. He wasn't walking anymore—the itch in his legs had taken over completely. He was being hauled along like a puppet on strings.

This must be what the pigeons feel like. It feels like flying.

The air was growing colder with each moment. Despite the flaming torches lining the walls in such an enclosed space, he was shivering in moments, not from the macabre surroundings, but from the chill. His breath puffed in vapour before his eyes, and he heard the crackle of ice crystals forming on his clothes.

By now he was almost sure he *was* flying. He couldn't feel his legs moving at all.

The cavern was only feet away, and beyond, he sensed

movement. Something was in there waiting for him. He was moving so fast and there was no stopping it, and he endured momentary panic, windmilling his arms. But there was no forestalling it now. He had arrived.

The tunnel ended and he passed into a cave the size of a small cottage. The light here came from old wax candles which burned with an acrid odour, and the walls were smooth and pure black. Delphic inscriptions had been carved into them in undulating messy lines; not the beauteous work of some ancient scribe, but more like the last scratchings of a thousand trapped madmen.

The cavern was cold and bright, empty bar a single hardwood desk at its centre, inset with a brass crest the size of a bicycle wheel, depicting a swinging pendulum. And sat there, upon a leather stool with his feet perched casually up on the desk top, was Him.

The man from his vision. The man with the dark marks under his eyes. He was staring at James with the expression of a wolf that has cornered its prey. He almost expected him to lick his lips with relish. As James emerged from the tunnel, He spread his arms wide and gestured to a free stool in front of the desk. "Mr Chadwick, at last," he said.

His voice was smooth and seductive, and James felt sick at the sound of it. How easy it would be to fall under its sweet spell.

He blinked. The itch had gone, suddenly and totally. His knees almost buckled, and he stumbled forward toward the desk.

Is this it, then? Have I really gone mad?

"No, not mad," the man said, grinning such that a mouthful of shining sharp teeth glowed in the light. "You've woken up, is all. Now you're seeing, really seeing."

Did he just read my mind?

"Don't let it fool you. It's just a parlour trick," the man said. His eyes glimmered with amusement.

James stepped closer, drawn forward by his mesmerising gaze. "Who are you?"

"I'm so glad you asked that, because I love this part." He kicked his feet off the desk and stood up, tracing its edge and running his fingertips over the brass crest. His hands took flight over his head and he began gesticulating grandly, his voice lyrical and otherworldly. "I am no one thing. I've walked alien forests in a cloak of tar, bringing darkness to purple skies, and those between the trees called me Nightfall. Elsewhere I've walked the coast of an endless ocean in the guise of a wolf. Over mountaintops made islands by the thickest clouds, I've flown as the Raven. The eons have given me many names. I am Shadow, I am the Eventide, I am the Shroud and the Veil, Jet and Sable, Obsidian and Sloe. Of all things touched by darkness, take your pick, for all have known my hand."

He came to stand in front of James and took a low bow. "You may call me Fol, and I need your help," he finished.

James stared dumbly. "My help?"

"I'm on a mission." He placed a long-nailed alabaster hand on James's shoulder. "I've been waiting years for you to finally wake up."

James grimaced. The hand on his shoulder was cold,

colder even than the arctic air of the cavern. "I have no idea what you're talking about," he said. James's breath puffed up between them. When the man replied, his breath did not.

"Quite." He gestured to the desk and the stool before it. "Step into my office, take a seat." He seemed perpetually amused, but James didn't get the joke. He sat without resistance, resigned to the absurdity of it all.

The man sighed as he propped his feet back up on the desk and relaxed back in his chair, lacing his fingers behind his head. "It's not often I get to put my feet up," he said. Then the amused twinkle in his eyes flashed out like a candle extinguished. "I've been watching you and yours since things around here hit the fan. I've seen what your blond-haired friend has done with a bad lot. You only see a few like that in a long stretch. I knew I could trust him to keep you breathing until you were ready."

"You're talking about Alex?"

"Don't worry yourself. He doesn't know any more about me than you. In fact, you're the world expert on all things Fol as of now."

"Lucky me."

Fol barked. "And he has a sense of humour! Things aren't all bad, after all."

James couldn't help twitching. His laughter wasn't comforting at all, but unsettling. He wasn't sure whether Fol was about to clap him on the back or stab him to death. He had that way about him, endearing yet dangerous. And what of all this, anyway? How could any of it be real? The torches in the tunnel seemed to burn without fail, and the air in here was colder than he would have thought possible.

"I'm either crazy, or ..."

"Or there's something else been going on all this time that nobody told you about," Fol said, his lip thrust mockingly.

James shook his head. "Or something else nobody else knew about," he muttered.

Fol seemed pleased. "You're sharper than you look, Wonderboy. No wonder you're the one I need."

"Stop stalling," James snapped. "I'm here. I'm not raving about how stupid and crazy all this is because I'm keeping it bottled. But if I'm here for some reason then tell me now, or I'm out of here." The anger came thick and fast, stemming from newfound desperation to get back to Beth. The itch had been smothering those feelings, and now the itch was gone he couldn't believe he had really left her. He had left her.

Fol held up his hands. "Fair's fair." He dropped his feet from the table once more and leaned forward over the desk. Again, his fingers traced the crest of the pendulum, and James's heart skipped a beat when he focused on it. Then Fol took a breath and nodded as though having made a decision. "Things are broken," he said.

James waited for more, but Fol was staring at him hard. "Broken?"

"That's right. Big things. We're talking cosmic-scale shitstorm, here." He jerked his head to the tunnel. "You might have noticed things aren't quite as they should be. Six billion missing people tends to give most people an inkling of that."

James sat up straighter. "You know what happened at the End?"

Fol shook his head, his sharp teeth glinting as he grinned in derision. "Can't believe you people call it the End. This is just the beginning, boy. Things are set to get a hell of a lot worse. And not just for this place. Things are setting to go to hell just about everywhere."

"So far as we know, it already has. We haven't heard from the rest of the world since I've been alive."

Fol shook his head in irritation. Suddenly, the sardonic humour was gone. "I'm not talking about this puny world. All that sea and land and sky you see in front of your eyes is nothing—*nothing*—compared to what I'm talking about. I'm talking about *everywhere*, James. All where, all times, all worlds. Something's knocked it all wobbly, and it's all going to come crashing down if we don't do something to stop it."

"You're crazy."

"Look who's talking. Who'd believe you if you told them about what you've seen already?"

"Alex would believe me."

Fol sat back in his chair. "I need you, James. You're special."

James grunted. "I've had people tell me that since I could walk. What's so special about a bookworm who keeps pigeons for friends?"

"Don't play dumb. You're different, and I know you

know it. Something that's been asleep inside you has woken up, something that you can't explain and can't control. You know things you shouldn't." It must have showed on James's face because Fol looked pleased. "It's destiny."

"Alex told me all about destiny. And I've spent my whole life trying to live up to it."

"I'm not talking about whatever you idiots have been doing, your little *mission*. I'm talking about real destiny, a real mission. I'm talking about saving the bloody universe, kid."

James drew a long sigh.

Just another man with an agenda, looking for a pawn. I'm sick of being somebody else's tool.

"I can't. I have responsibilities." He was thinking of Lucian, Agatha, Lincoln and the Creeks back home, all scrabbling to deal with those slimy Malverston wannabes because of him. And Beth, always Beth, drowning in their perverted stares. "I have people who need me." He would kill every one of them as soon as he got back if they had so much as smelled her hair. He could feel their hot blood on his hands already. "I have business that needs doing."

Fol was looked at him in a way that made James feel as though he was being read, front to back, every bit of him probed and catalogued. "You're exactly what I need," he said quietly. His eyes weren't glittering anymore. They were as dark and matte as the obsidian rock above their heads. "You've already made the first step. Sacrificing the girl … I didn't think you had it in you. But you did it. Taking the next step will be easier."

James was on his feet before he had fully computed Fol's words. Then he was gripping the pallid figure by the collar, at the same time furious and terrified—terrified because he sensed Fol could eviscerate him with a single twitch, but not caring. "What did you say?" he said, his voice shaking.

For the first time, Fol looked unsettled. "The girl. Your little Beth Tarbuck. You gave her up, James, and I have to say I doubted you had it in you—"

"WHAT ARE YOU TALKING ABOUT?" James roared, flinging the stool back so hard that it exploded into splinters against the far wall.

Fol's face fell. "He didn't tell you," he muttered. Then he shook his head. "Son of a bitch is cold."

"Didn't tell me what?"

Fol's smile slid slowly from his face. "Destiny catches up with everyone in the end, James. And hers just caught up with her." He grunted. "The fat mayor's coming for her head. And it looks like your fearless leader's been keeping it to himself."

James dropped Fol's collar and bounded across the cavern in a few enormous strides. His legs were no longer possessed by the itch, but something altogether more powerful: a primal, basic power deep inside every person that could only be awakened by a certain kind of fear—the fear of losing somebody they couldn't live without.

"James!" Fol was on his feet. He looked alarmed, the dark marks under his eyes suddenly grey instead of black. "You can't. I need you. We all need you. The End ... it really is just the first hiccough. If you don't come with me now, we might lose our only chance to put things right. They're all still out there, James. All those people, all those lives. We can save them, and everyone else."

James shivered even through all his terror and fury. "They're still alive?" he uttered, frozen mid-stride. "All of them?"

Fol's eyes glimmered. James could see he wasn't a predator at all, not really. He was only a messenger of a much higher power. "Help me," he said.

For a moment James mouthed, his mind a hive of deafening buzzing. But then Beth's face emerged from the sludge, and he shook his head. "I can't," he gasped, and then he was running back along the tunnel, his breath coming in mindless seething gasps, his fingers clasped into fists.

"James!" Fol cried.

James didn't stop, couldn't stop. His hands were bunched into claws, and he was going to use them to tear the heart right out of Alexander Cain's chest.

CHAPTER 27

The temperature dropped fast as they ascended. At first Norman thought it was the sight of the snowy peak thousands of feet above, but he soon realised it was the icy bite of the coastal winds. The mountain chain that formed the backbone of the county shielded most of it from the elements, creating the permanent blanket of fog that rolled down their slopes off the Atlantic. But Dreymont's Peak stood in the path of a valley that cut right through to the ocean side.

The mountainside was steep and harsh, carpeted with shining boulders that looked like scorched glass, thrusting up from the deep heather and boggy moorland and puncturing the clouds.

It had taken Norman this long to notice because of the storm of Echoes and muddy thoughts prying into his mind from all directions. Macabre sensations plagued him along with myriad Echoes, each of them stronger and more vivid than the last. Men, women and children from bygone eras passed in their droves, reliving countless snippets of lost happenings. He couldn't ignore them like before; they were everywhere.

He had thought for a while that he had finally snapped, that he might in fact be lying on the roadside kicking in delirium and foaming at the mouth. But that just didn't seem right. The sights and sounds were real and visceral, so much so that he couldn't bring himself to doubt he was in the here and now. And there was also the pain: it was gone.

He hadn't felt a single twinge since they had crossed into Radden County. Instead he was left with the cold—but he didn't dare imagine it was the same cold the others felt from the mountainside gale. The surreal bone chill was now so strong it burned his insides.

He couldn't help but be reminded of the raging cold the elders described when they spoke about the End. All the survivors had felt it.

Am I feeling what they felt all that time ago? Is this place really different, somehow?

Whatever was going on, it wasn't normal, and the others were blind to it. He was just as alone here as he had been back in Canary Wharf.

I hate this place. I've been here five minutes and I hate it, he thought bitterly. Even being free of pain wasn't worth the crawling feeling in his gut, like he'd eaten a vat of earthworms.

Let's just get this done and get out of here.

"Wind like this could freeze piss before it hit the ground," John DeGray shouted above the high whistle, holding his coat tight about him and leaning low on his mount.

Richard was consulting the map Lincoln and Latif had drawn for them, and pointed ahead, farther up the steep slopes.

Norman nodded and waved them on, hiding his face behind the collar of his coat to screen his face from the wind. He hoped their destination wasn't too far up because the gradient looked as though it only increased closer to the peak, and the horses were already having trouble. He didn't like the sound of approaching potentially hostile land on foot, especially if the enemy held the high ground. In terms of military tactics, what they were doing was already outrageous enough. They were ragged and worn, each of them travel weary and weak and hungry, uncertain of the terrain. If they were attacked, they wouldn't have a clue where to run. And if the route downhill was cut off with an ambush, then that would be that.

No amount of reconnaissance would make up for their ignorance of this place, even if they had time for that. Their enemy knew this place, and they didn't. It was go in blind or turn back for home. And they had come too far to stop now.

Robert was still beside him, somehow sitting up straight and alert despite the chill and the fact that they had been riding over twenty straight hours. It had been days since they had stopped properly, a restless and tense night shacked up in a barn on the outskirts of Leeds. Remnant gangs had prowled the night, thrown into turmoil after being decimated by the passing army, looking for blood and self-destruction. They had come close to opening fire several times, and few of them had slept at all.

Robert looked as indefatigable as ever, scanning the moorland below them with his hawk eyes, his jaw working.

Norman waited until the others had passed before leaning over in the saddle. "You see something?"

"No." His working jaw clicked. "That's the problem."

Norman frowned. "Why?"

"They called for help. They'd have made it easy to find them."

"They said they were pinned down on the mountain. That's why they're up here in the first place instead of back by the radio tower."

"If they were pinned down, we'd see the people pinning them down."

He turned and continued after the others, leaving Norman to look again with a touch more dread. He followed after, suppressing a shiver.

Just get it done. Get it done and go home.

*

"Wait!"

Lucian threw himself against the side of the cliff and cursed under his breath. His arms trembled, clinging to the dewy crumbling rock, and the bones of his fingers gave way little by little. It was early morning, and they had finally managed to slink away from the camp.

A gust of wind buffeted him and the others as they each pressed themselves flat against the flat rock and, under the cover of moonlight, looked down in search of the voice beneath them.

"What?" he hissed.

A strangled cry, then a grunt. A shadow writhed somewhere below in the darkness, amongst the glint of campfires spread across the moor. Lucian squinted, gritting his teeth as the racket of tumbling pebbles rang out in the night. He picked out one of the men clinging on to a ledge by the fingertips of one hand, the rest of him hanging out into space.

"I'm slipping!" the man hissed.

Lucian spat a mouthful of curses and swung his head up to Max, ten feet above him. Max's eyes twinkled in the penumbra, inky pits that confirmed Lucian's own thoughts.

They couldn't stop. By now they had surely been missed back at the camp, and the cover of darkness wouldn't last. They had to be on the ridge by morning, when they were betting on the guards being changed.

He locked eyes with each of the others in turn and nodded firmly, so that they would all see it. A blackness slithered in him, something that was a part of him but which he had tempered all the long years he had been part of the mission and lived under Alexander's rule. He had played house, organised celebrations and sat on committees, and he had been what his friends and family had needed him to be. But that wasn't what he was, not really.

Inside there was a wildness that not even Alexander and all his books and talk of destiny could temper. Deep down he was all grit and blood and the smell of the earth. And here, right now, hanging hundreds of feet above Radden Moor with a barbaric horde below him and his insane brother high above, he felt something give way—the last mental barrier that had bottled up the real him all this time.

"Climb," he said.

The others began scrabbling upward once again, and he was left looking down at the lone man flailing in mid-air. For a moment, he picked out a pair of shocked white eyes below him, capped underneath by the blackness of a gaping mouth. But then he had turned and he too was climbing.

Together they hauled themselves higher, armed with scant knives and the one unreliable pistol, a thread of burly, bloodied muscle clinging to the rock face. Only another hundred feet and they would reach the lip of the cliff and they would be a mere dozen yards from the lone tent atop it.

And then? Lucian thought. *Just what is it you plan to do when you get up there? You really think you can put a gun to James's chest and pull the trigger?*

He grunted at his own thoughts and kept on climbing, blinking soil from his eyes and ignoring the deep ache in the bones of his fingers and toes. They had to get there first. The night was wearing on, cooling toward a wet glistening morning, and it would be all too easy for the rest of them to slip too.

And don't go getting ahead of yourself. James's dog won't be far away. That tent is going to be guarded.

Despite the slab of granite-hard determination resting on his chest, he felt a quiver of anxiety. Somehow he couldn't quite shake the feeling that all this was too easy.

They all froze as a single cry rang out from below, accompanied by a shower of falling scree. They remained still in the night air until an almost inaudible thump rose up from far below, then they began climbing once more. None of them spoke.

All the while, the fires of the camp burned on the moorland floor, and the slaves continued forging weapons. Now that they were higher, they could see the campfires in detail. They carpeted the land for as far as the eye could see. Lucian's heart skipped a beat every time he laid eyes on the vast tracts of conflagrations, like bobbing fireflies. He had no idea that there were so many people out there.

There must have been at least ten thousand people, and they were all fixing to march south. Time was running out.

*

The riders from New Canterbury crested a rise and came to a plateau cut into the mountainside, still some thousand feet from the summit. Norman half expected fanfare. The other half expected a hail of gunfire.

But there was nothing over that ridge but more black sparkling rock, petrified tree stumps, and rivulets of melt water from the higher snowdrifts.

Robert had corralled them into a rigid tactical formation with the marksmen at the front and the fastest riders at the rear. Rifles had been raised, shoulders tensed, foreheads greased with sweat.

Norman had been ready to find the emissaries of their saviours, or death. But to find nothing threw him completely. It felt as though somebody had planted a fist squarely in the seat of his stomach.

"Tell me we haven't been had," Richard whined.

"The distress call was broadcast. Somebody sent it," John said, though hurriedly. He plucked at his sleeve while his bushy eyebrows twitched in spasm. "Are we sure these are the coordinates?"

"Yes, I'm bloody sure!"

"Calm down," Norman said. "They could still be here."

"Like arsing hell they could. Those campfires down there can only be one thing. The army is here, Norman. We've walked right into the hornets' nest."

"We don't know that."

"Stop playing, Norman. I haven't seen a friendly light since we left Leeds—and that place was the terminus of the train to fucking nowhere." Richard spat at the ground under him and snarled. Norman had never seen him like this. He'd put Richard down as a petal of a man.

It seemed he wasn't quite like his master. While John looked terrified of all that moved, every windswept leaf, and every shadow thrown down by the passing clouds, Richard looked fit to tear the world a new one.

"We didn't ride out here into the middle of nowhere just so that we could turn around and go back home empty handed." Richard was breathing deep, almost hyperventilating. "We didn't leave everyone back home wide open when those bastards could be coming to kill—"

He caught himself, his lip trembling, and looked away.

The others shifted uncomfortably as Norman urged his mount and cantered forward, milling to and fro as he scanned the mountain. But Richard was right. There was only the black rocks and mossy scree. No sign of an encampment, nor any sign that anybody had come this way. Not even a message scrawled in the dust.

It was as though nobody had been up here for centuries.

For all we know, that could be the truth of it. No, it can't be. It can't!

He bit his tongue to keep the very same lamentations as Richard's from spilling out, but he could do nothing to stem the fitful, raging thoughts from shooting through his mind.

We have to find them—find them or die. I can't go back to those faces, all those staring faces, and tell them we found nothing.

Suddenly, he realised he had been relying on this so much that he had no idea what to do. He had assumed that they would either succeed or die. He hadn't anticipated that they might have to lope all the way home and stand beside their brothers and sisters and await the coming droves after all.

The thought of that was enough to drive bile into his throat.

I can't go back to Allie with nothing.

He couldn't watch the hope fade from her eyes.

"I hate this place," he muttered.

The others were muttering audibly now, their formation

breaking. Cries of frustration and disgust were carried on the wind—the deep, gurgling murmur of unrest from a crowd about to abandon good sense.

John was attempting to talk Richard down, pulling the map toward him and consulting their notes. But his apprentice was inconsolable, and in a sudden surge of rage, Richard tore the map to shreds, throwing it to the wind before John could utter a wail of dismay.

The muttering quietened and turned to sighs that were so much worse than anger, for they were sighs of resignation.

Norman's heart leaped.

No. I can't let them go. I have to keep them with me. If they go now, I'll never get them back.

And that would be so much worse than returning home empty handed—returning unscathed but with half their number scattered and the other half ready to give up.

Time to play the Chosen One.

"Listen to me. Listen, all of you."

They turned to him grudgingly.

"We're going to check this place out. As soon as we're sure there's nothing here, we ride for home. We can still make a difference back there."

Grumbling.

He spoke over them. "They need us. We can't afford to feel sorry for ourselves."

"We just rode hundreds of miles to look at a pile of rocks!" Richard roared.

"Yes, we did. And now we know that we did everything

we could. We know where we stand."

"In fucking quicksand."

Norman surged forward and gripped Richard by the lapels. "You're a good kid, but don't think I won't beat you blue," he growled.

Where did that come from?

But he knew. It came from the place Alexander had been moulding inside him all these years, the piece of him that they all needed.

Richard's eyes were wet and wide. "I'm sorry," he said.

Norman let go of him and turned to the others. "Look around. Make sure there's nothing that can help us. Be ready to move. Our people are counting on us."

The muttering stopped. Norman didn't break his act until he had reached Robert's side and the formation had broken to scout the area.

"How did I do?" Norman tried a smile.

Maybe there's hope for me after all.

But Robert had barely blinked. His gaze was fixed on the ridge. "Don't let them ride," he muttered. His tone was low and fierce.

Norman felt his thin smile slide from his face. "What?"

"Don't move. Keep your eyes down."

Norman tensed, but couldn't help glancing into the corners of his field of vision. "Why?"

"They're here."

"The Scots? You're sure? Why didn't you say anything—?"

"No. Not them. *Them.*"

Fire-hot liquid dread coagulated in Norman's mouth. "You're sure?"

"We're beaten."

Norman turned to all two hundred and fifty pounds of his rippling tower of a body, and gaped. To hear those words come from that mouth stung like a slap to the face. "If you're so sure then why haven't the rest of us noticed anything?"

But before he could finish his sentence he caught a whiff of something in the wind: a rotten note that denuded the crispness of the breeze. He had smelled that before, in the woods around Canterbury. He would have known it anywhere—the smell of sweat and dirt and old blood.

"We have to put our guns down," Robert said. His voice didn't waver a note, but there was a sheen to his eyes that took all the fight out of Norman. It was like looking at the button eyes of a china doll.

"We can fight, Robert." Norman was thinking fast, desperate to claw back some good fortune from this mess. "We could capture one of them and make them tell us what they're planning, their strategy—"

"Tell them to put their hands up."

"So what if they're close? We could still get to cover. We can make a stand."

"Norman." Robert blinked once. Those doll eyes were blank. "Time's up."

And in that moment he knew it was true. As though rising up from the ground itself, myriad figures crested the ridge. And right in front of him, billowing in the wind atop a rusted flagpole, was the sigil of the pigeon.

The breath whistled out of him. He slumped, and for the first time since arriving in Radden, a bolt of pain ran through his fractured ribs.

Doesn't matter how special this place is. I'm betting bullets still kill here.

"Put your hands up," Norman said, turning slowly to the others.

Their faces were all drawn, eyes bulging. They had each frozen in place at the sight of the creeping ragged figures. For a moment, they sat stupefied on their saddles, but then Norman saw just how many figures surrounded them— they were outnumbered threefold, at least—and suddenly he was barking with a voice that didn't belong to him. "I said put your hands up, now! Weapons on the ground. Do it or die."

I hope that puts a stupid smile on Alexander's face, wherever he is.

A great clatter kicked up as the others shrugged their rifles to the ground and laced their fingers over their heads just as Norman had. Norman was ready to follow Robert's lead, but the great tree of a man hadn't moved, not even to drop his own weapon. Norman waited as the sigil came closer and the figures became men and women with sunken, starved faces and skeletal bodies, bearing all manner of firepower—the kind of heavy-duty military gear that could tear them all to shreds. They didn't stand a chance.

And the others knew it. Panic was creeping into their eyes.

Norman waited a moment longer, but Robert was blank—Norman realised the blankness in him was a depth of fury he'd never seen. Robert had stalled; Norman could see the battle to keep still in the micro-expressions on his face.

It was taking all he had to fight his own demons.

Norman was on his own. He wheeled around with his hands still on his head and that voice that wasn't his burst forth yet again. "Look at me. All of you, look at me! Don't look at them. They're nothing. You all keep watching me. We're going to be fine."

"Like hell," Richard squeaked. "We're dead—we're so dead."

"No. We're going to be fine."

John DeGray was looking at him as though from a great distance. "There's a time for pep talks." His voice was shaking with adrenaline. "I don't think this is it."

"Shut up. I said keep your eyes on me." He was tense, leaning over and ignoring the blinding pain in his chest and the bite of the bone-chill of this crazy place, breathing fire and pulling their gazes toward his through sheer force of will. "We are all going to be fine. We're going to go along with them because we're smart, and we're going to watch and learn. And when the time is right, we're going to get out of here."

By the time he stopped, the ragged men and women had formed a silent solid circle around them, watching. But the riders from the South ignored them, each of them watching for Norman's word.

Norman nodded to them, and then turned to a dark-skinned man holding the flagpole. "Alexander Cain and the people of the South send their regards," he said.

The man, with skin like stretched moleskin, didn't say a word. He turned to his companions and made a claw-like symbol with his free hand, and then turned back to Norman and strode towards him.

The circle closed in on the riders. The stench of dried blood grew stronger. All those blank faces came closer, hungry and tortured faces turned ugly by anger and pain.

Amongst all this, Norman had forgotten just who these people were: farmers and traders, everymen, people whom they had once called friends. All of them had been starved out by the coalition in their pursuit of keeping the Old World alive.

They had brought this on themselves.

They were led away in silence.

Norman found himself watching Robert. Their ragged captors had ripped his weapons from him, hissing like wildcats, leaping back out of range of his enormous arms and Obsidian's nipping teeth. But Robert had shut down.

In the end, Norman saw why. He followed Robert's gaze as they crested the ridge and began the long descent back towards the moorland floor, and saw what Robert must have seen when they first arrived—what had locked up his gears.

He knew why he hadn't seen it before, well hidden as it was. It was easy to forget how much more Robert saw than the rest of them, how unprepared they were for any of this.

Below the ridge was a pit thirty feet long and four feet wide, freshly dug out of the earth. A thin layer of soil had been kicked over its length, but it wasn't enough to hide the horrors therein. A myriad of blank, staring faces, and naked bodies tangled and white as porcelain. Arcs of blood as black as treacle. At least a hundred people lay partially exposed in the ground, piled on top of one another, their bodies ripped and torn. They stared at the sky, unseeing, their radio message never answered.

The emissaries from Scotland. They really had been here. But they had been no more of a match for the army than anybody else. And there was no telling where in the vastness of the North the rest of their people called home—if any of them remained.

Well, Norman thought. Now we know.

Nearby lay a spoil heap of pebbles and scree. It must have taken an army to dig that pit out of the thin, rocky topsoil. An army of slaves.

Their captors led them down the mountain and over miles of moorland, toward the distant campfires they had seen during their ascent. Soon they were being led on a hidden switchback path, ascending yet again. They were heading toward a cliff top. A single tent billowed in the wind on the peak above it.

CHAPTER 28

Allie and Heather kept a close watch over Sarah, but she didn't need it. Allie scarcely recognised her.

The days had passed so slowly that at times it seemed that the leaves falling from the trees would freeze in mid-air and the clocks would wind back on themselves. New Canterbury's militia took turns on sentry duty, scouring the hills and forests for any sign of change. But things seemed frozen, shut up and waiting.

Allie couldn't take it, sitting up on the rooftops, jumping at every shadow.

What are we waiting for? For our families to come home? Or for the fire-starters?

It was getting harder to tell by the minute.

They had quickly run out of things to say. The hollow ring of the silence between them was more frightening than the night watch. They were friends, good friends, she and Sarah and Heather.

They were best friends and they had nothing left to say to one another.

All they could do was sit and watch and wait.

This isn't me. I don't worry. I never worry. Even when Dad died. I always knew I would be okay.

But this was different. She had fought long and hard in London to be somebody, and scratch out the label of Town Gossip hanging over her head. Before she had been assigned to Norman and Lucian's scavenging party to Margate, she had been content to wallow on the sidelines, taking what she needed and doing the bare minimum on the duty rota. Going into the wilds had been sobering.

She would never forget the sight of the skeletal refugees crawling toward them, desperate for help. She would never forget riding away from them as though they had the plague.

The game's changed. New rules, and nowhere near as many players.

So here she was, sitting in the hot seat. People looked at her as though she had a clue as to what she was doing—and that was the most terrifying thing in the world.

Looking back, she could barely recall the old her. Only in the blur of distant memory could she make out a shadow of the stupid, little ignorant snot she must have been.

Who would have guessed?

Presently she sat up on the rooftop of an old Edwardian three-storey house beside Higgins and his young companion, whittling away the hours playing a card game she didn't understand, nor cared to learn the rules for. She could feel a thin smile stretching her lips, though she did her best to hide it. Smiling at a time like this felt inappropriate, but she couldn't help herself.

"What's so amusing?" the kid kept saying.

"Nothing." She would play her hand, lose, and the deck was reshuffled.

It took her a long time to work out why she was smiling. She didn't pursue it, just let it simmer away in her subconscious and bubble to the surface. When it finally popped up, she had to stifle a laugh by masking it with a cough.

Norman. It was him.

She realised with sudden piercing clarity that she was holding it all together for him. That scrawny, clueless idiot who everyone thought was a saint—but she knew was just as clueless as she was—was why she had gone all the way to London, had patched up that girl, had dragged her sorry behind all the way back here to stand guard and babysit the city folk. He brought out something in her, the part of her that made her what she wanted to be.

Bloody hell, I love him, a voice whined in her head. *I can't believe I'm in love with that fool.*

But there it was, bared in front of her. You didn't get to pick who you loved.

The more she thought about it, however, the more inevitable it seemed. They were in the same boat, she and him. Not long ago he had been just as lost, just as useless. Sure, he had a public face, and he hadn't been able to get away with slacking off, but they had shared that same unignited spark.

Despite the pain and suffering of all this mess, it had brought out the good in both of them.

What if he doesn't come home?

He will. He has to. If he doesn't, I'll kill him.

She shook away mental images of the horrors he and the other riders might be facing up north. There was no use thinking about it.

"Hold the fort," she muttered. "Keep them safe, keep them breathing. They'll be back." She pulled her knees tighter to her chest and flicked another card down onto the slate roof tiles. "He'll be back."

Higgins grunted. "You must have a touch of the Sight, lady."

She frowned. "What?"

"You're right. He's back." He was standing and facing down into the streets. His face was tight and disbelieving.

Allie struggled to her feet. "Who?"

"Him."

She stood up, gripping him by the sleeve. Though she was a head shorter, she tore him down to her height through sheer vehemence. "Who, damn you?"

Higgins's face bore the toothy smile of a child waking on Christmas morning. "Him. He's back."

"Norman?" Allie breathed. Her heart skipped a beat.

Higgins shook his head. "Mr Cain. Alexander Cain has returned to us!"

She blinked and nodded. A flood of relief, tainted slightly by disappointment, suddenly swept the cobwebs from the day. "You're sure?"

"See for yourself, lady." He gestured to the cobbled streets below, where she could now see a lone, robed figure striding from the abandoned outer edges of the city.

He had grey-blond thatched hair, tall and wiry, with a ruddy, wise face akin to the Greeks of old. Even from this distance, there was no mistaking the Messiah of the South. Allie let loose an enormous sigh, deflating like a knackered old balloon, and watched him stride toward the city. As though sensing his arrival, people who had been locked up for days in their own homes thrust out their heads through boarded windows and barred doorways, squealing with wordless delight. The droves who had clamped themselves to Agatha and her sermons in the cathedral came running, most of them far too old for more than a careful shuffle, but hurrying still.

He was swamped in moments. The crowds of New Canterbury were upon him before he could reach the building where Allie still stood. Higgins and the kid had scampered away to join the crowd, but she couldn't move. A wave of exhaustion that she had been denying until now crashed over her.

People were jabbering. Many were crying. Some just screamed, down on their knees.

How does one man do that? How can people believe that much in flesh and blood?

But it was a pointless question, because she knew she believed just as much as they did.

Alexander Cain had been unheedful and selfish. He had given his and all of their futures to his mission. She knew he must have played a least some part in the debacle they now faced. And in that way, he would never stop.

But he was here. He had played his hand when nobody else had in a game nobody understood, just as she had been doing up here with Higgins and the kid. In the end he had lost big, but there he was, standing down there in the street.

He had come back to them.

Allie was about to head for the window and climb down when she saw the crowd fragment and face down the street. The crying and wailing was stemmed. And amongst them, Allie saw that Alexander looked shocked.

She turned to follow their gaze, and there at the end of the street was the militia. Regimented in strict rows, rifles and pistols at the ready, two hundred of the people of New Canterbury stood puff-chested and erect upon the cobbles. Among them were Heather and the wife of Ray Hubble, and countless others whom Allie would never have believed would take a stand.

But here they were, a formidable line amidst the ruin and chaos.

At their head, Sarah Strong stood front and centre, her red hair and angular face aglow with dogged temerity.

I wouldn't have it any other way, Allie thought. By the time she reached the streets, Alexander and the crowd had joined the militia, and the two groups became one. Heather and Agatha were amongst those armed, a doctor and a senile old lady, standing arm in arm with the young and brave.

Allie took a pistol for herself.

The two crowds of militia and civilians chattered and mingled for a long time, nuzzling like a separated bitch and her pups. Coldness had grown between those prepared to fight and those who would never be ready, but those divisions now dissolved, spurred by a strength that even Alexander would never have been capable of on his own.

Alexander appeared before Allie and Sarah and the others. He stared right down at them as though seeing them for the first time. He wasn't smiling, nor was he serene like she had expected. He had found a humbleness somewhere out there in the wastes. He seemed more a mortal man than she remembered.

But that did nothing to lessen the shock when he, Alexander Cain, saviour of mankind, bowed to them. Then he threw his arms over Agatha, who evidently scarcely recognised him, and rested his head on her shoulder. Agatha patted his cheek and crooned.

Alex held her tighter.

It took Allie some time to realise she had been crying.

Sarah appeared beside her at some point. They took one look at one another, and knew exactly what the other was thinking about: Robert and Norman.

"They'll be back," Allie said. "They will."

Sarah's eyes swam. Seeing her smile was like watching the end of a long winter. "Men always come crawling back."

CHAPTER 29

Lucian crouched amidst ferns, his breath caught in his throat. The stunted pistol in his hands felt flimsy, liable to snap if he manhandled it too much, but it was better than nothing. The others would have to make do with the knives.

It felt wrong, holding back like this while the others crept forward from the cliff edge toward the tent. The canvas structure was much larger than it had looked from below; more of a tepee, at least twenty feet across and ten feet high.

His fingers burned with inaction, and the muscles in his legs felt wound up tight like springs. He had always been in the thick of things, been the first to jump. Sticking out back and waiting for somebody else to do all the hard work ate at him by the second.

But that was the way it had to be. If they were lucky they would have one shot from the pistol. They had to make it count.

He didn't trust the others to sink the round into its target. He didn't care how tough they were or what hellholes they were from. There were too many lives hanging on whether the little metal ball in the pistol's chamber found its mark. He didn't trust anybody to do it but himself.

The sun had risen some time ago, but there was still plenty of cover thrown down by the gnarled trees lining the cliff. Zigzagging between slate and mottled heather and twisted shadows, the dozen hulking men crept toward the canvas tent like leopards slinking closer to a grazing gazelle. They were ten metres away, then eight, then seven …

Max's last words to him reverberated in his head. "You wait until we're in and I give the signal, you hear? And don't give me that look. Stubborn as bloody anything, you are. Don't make me come back out here and kick your arse."

Lucian grunted—what passed for a peel of laughter in his book. His jaw ached from the tension. He made a conscious effort to keep breathing; every scrap of concentration was going to count. As soon as they were inside and the guards were down, he would have to move fast. He picked out his route to the tent's entrance over and over, tracing every inch, imagining the precise movement of each step. There was no room for failure.

Four metres, three …

Max turned, low to the ground, and gave Lucian a last nod.

Lucian nodded back, though he knew there was something wrong. But they all knew something was wrong. They had felt it since they had first slunk away from the forge. It had all been too easy.

But there was nothing they could do about that. A case

of the willies was no excuse for losing your bottle.

He could see the acceptance in the glint of Max's eyes. Whatever was about to happen was beyond their control.

One metre …

Lucian's finger touched the trigger, and he braced to spring forward.

The rest happened in the space of three seconds. Max pulled back the canvas flap, revealing the orange glow of a crackling fire inside, and the others spilled inside silently, blades glinting. Max followed after, and the flap fell back behind him. Flickering shadows were thrown against the tent walls, caricature silhouettes of odd proportions and exaggerated gestures: men with sickle-like machetes raised over their heads, bearing down on their victim; tussling brutes tearing at one another's faces; torsos impaled and limbs disfigured in real time.

The rumble in Lucian's ears was deafening. He listened for the tiniest sign, the one that would release him, the slightest let-up in the shuffling of feet and sloughing of clothing that would mean the tables had turned. He waited as long as he dared, then launched himself from the thicket. Every footfall made its mark, every inch of him coordinated for balance. His last reserves of strength all went into that last dash.

It went by in a flash and he tucked up into a ball in mid-air, rolling through the canvas flap and into the midst of a silent bloody brawl. A blurred vision of torn flesh, faces twisted into snarls of fury and pain, and undulating flames flashed before his eyes. Then he was standing again with the pistol raised, at the ready.

He's here! The thought rang like a gong through Lucian's mind.

Sitting right in front of him was a figure draped in a long cloak with a balaclava around his face. Lucian had seen the very same man back at New Canterbury the night Rayford Hubble had been killed, when he and Norman had chased the culprits into the woods to exact revenge. He had seen the man by the firelight then, but it had been Norman who had gotten close, trying like a fool to make peace.

Lucian had been covering him from the treeline. He had been the one to put a bullet in one of the slimy bastards. He had never stared the masked man in the face.

If he had, he would have known him immediately. He would have recognised him just as he recognised him now. James Chadwick's emerald eyes glowered behind the layers of cloth. Sat on a stool with one leg crossed over the other and a book in hand, as though the riot erupting around him were distant and immaterial, he had been staring at Lucian even as he had first entered the tent, as though he had been waiting for him.

It's true. God, it's really true. He's here.

In the split second he had to react, while aiming the pistol between myriad struggling shadows, Lucian realised that while he had been scheming and plotting all this time—while he had assumed ever since Max had first walked by his side that the one behind all this really had been his brother—he had never truly accepted that James could still be alive.

You're dead, he thought. *I saw you die.*

Max's voice bellowed from the other side of the world, made sonorous and inhuman by the slowness of time's passing. "LUCIAN, NOW!"

Those emerald eyes flickered to the pistol, then up at him. James didn't speak a word, but the meaning was clear. *Well?*

Lucian gritted his teeth and steeled himself. But those eyes had a hold on him; it was as though they gripped his fingers and bent them back away from the trigger. Lucian's hand shook violently and he willed his finger to squeeze—

Damn it, damn it!

"LUCIAN, KILL HIM!"

Do it or they'll die. Alex, Norman, Agatha, all of them.

But he's your brother, another voice whispered insidiously.

I have to!

Alex lied once. He could have lied again. It could all have been a lie.

"LUCIAAAN!"

Lucian bellowed with the fury of a stabbed bull. He felt all the hurt and pain from all his days would pour out through his mouth. Something in his throat tore. All the while the pistol trembled.

Then, with a gasp and a screech of rage, he dropped it. The pistol clattered to the ground, and all the fight drained out of him. He collapsed on his haunches in front of James's stool and looked up at him.

He closed his eyes, sighed, and hung his head. "Damn

it," he muttered.

The battle inside the tent came to an abrupt end. The hulking brutes he had dragged up here, though they still had the sudden and dangerous strength of kicking mules, couldn't defy physics; none of them had eaten anything more than thin gruel for days, and after the long walk north and forging by the fires, their energy levels were depleted. Under the prolonged struggle in the tent, their captors had gained the upper hand fast.

They hadn't realised how weak they were, how tired and uncoordinated. The element of surprise hadn't been enough. The floor of the tent was painted with blood. They had fought to the last breath and taken at least four men screaming with them to the floor, but those who remained flagged even in the few scant moments Lucian sat crouched on the ground.

Then it was all over: the tent flap was cast wide and at least a dozen more men piled in. The light filtering through the tent walls was cut off by yet more shadows surrounding them on all sides. Only the weak embers of the dying fire illuminated the last-ditch struggle. All the while Lucian squatted immobile on the ground in front of James, and James in turn kept his eyes fixed on him, unmoving, unspeaking.

The men were screaming now, roaring in wordless protest at their fate, even as they were eviscerated and dismembered with brutal, hacking blows, tackled and strangled and wrestled to the ground, covered in streams of hot vital blood. Only Max and two others stood. The beast of a man had three dirt-ridden men hanging from his neck and shoulders like parasites, beating and pulling at him—yet still he swung to and fro, knocking back yet more ragged figures, staggering and weak, but vicious to the last. He fought with such vehemence that his attackers couldn't land a blow. He was flagging fast, but for now he was holding them off.

Lucian might have been able to help him if he had the strength to stand. But all will, all control, had abandoned him.

He finally roused when Jason appeared at the tent's entrance. He stood there for a mere moment, an apparition that moved between places without traversing the distance between—he was that fast. Lucian only had time to register the joyful malice in his glittering eyes, then he vanished from the flap. He reached Max before Lucian could yell a warning.

Max stopped turning and yelling at once. He blinked rapidly and his face paled. Frank, childish surprise crossed his face as he looked down at the foot-long, curved knife embedded in his thorax. Crimson spurted down his shirt front as he looked up into Jason's eyes.

The other two men had fallen, and in the monster's presence, everyone had frozen and grown silent. For a moment the only sound was a gurgle deep in Max's throat.

"I remember you," Jason whispered to his victim. He smiled, a hyena's bloodthirsty grin. A bandage plastered over his cheek stretched taut—

So the fucker is mortal, Lucian thought distantly.

—and he leaned in close to Max's ear. "I remember sticking your mate just like this." He twisted the knife with a brutal jerk, and blood spurted from Max's lips. "Say hi to him for me."

Max grunted a final time, the tendons on his neck standing out as he lost his battle with gravity. Then his knees buckled and he slammed to the ground. His eyes were glassy and dead before he hit the floor, completing a carpet of gristle and torn flesh surrounding Lucian and James.

Jason sighed and flexed, his face vested with gratification that looked all too sexual. He wiped a trickle of blood running from his bandaged cheek and sucked it off his fingers, looking Lucian square in the eye. He winked.

He was alone.

Far away, an agonised cry rang out from the forging fires as some poor wretch was whipped. All around him the ragged men and women who had vanquished his motley crew stood staring down at him, their eyes flitting between him and James.

At first he thought they were silently begging permission to finish him. But then his peripheral vision began to gather the full meaning of those stares: they seemed awed.

"This is him?" Jason said finally. He snorted. "This one?"

James nodded. The balaclava over his face remained firmly in place, but any doubt that it was really him had long since faded. His eyes, though, they were different.

The very sight of them made Lucian's heart skip a beat. When they had been kids, those eyes had been soft as pudding. Now they could have belonged to a psychopath.

Jesus. Jesus.

Jason sauntered around behind James, wiping Max's blood from his curved knife on the seat of his trousers. The last spitting embers of the fire threw his matted hair and blackish-brown skin into harsh relief. He looked Lucian up and down as though appraising a disappointing mare at an auction. "Short-arse McGee, here?"

Lucian bared his gritted teeth at him. "Let's say we go outside and see if you can stick me with that thing before I cut you in half. We'll see who ends up shorter."

A muscle jumped in Jason's jaw as he smiled. He looked energised rather than insulted. Lucian couldn't help but frown; how did you browbeat a man who treated death threats like a dog playing fetch?

James flicked his head to the side, and Jason in turn waved his hand lazily at the others. The pathetic creatures all around them grunted and muttered, but none of them spoke up as Jason's eyes widened the slightest degree. They filed out hurriedly, tramping over the corpses of those who had been slaughtered, rolling the bodies like sacks of meat and kicking them out into the forest.

Then it was the three of them: Lucian, Jason, and James.

It took Lucian several attempts to say, "How? How are you here?"

James leaned forward. He was still holding the book in his hand. Now he closed it with great care, and Lucian groaned aloud. The book was green, inset with golf leaf. *Alice in Wonderland.*

Alexander had given that to James when they had just been kids. He would have known it anywhere.

"He lied," James said.

Lucian flinched at the sound of his voice. It was too real, a glimmer of a past he'd rather have forgotten—hell, he had tried to forget, stamped it down into the dark corners of his mind.

Lucian opened his mouth, and his dry tongue rasped against his mouth like sandpaper. "Alex?"

"He lied to all of you."

Lucian said nothing.

James looked into the fire's ashes and stood, pacing around on the bloodied floor. Jason stood aside for him to pass, watching, waiting—Lucian imagined he could see his snout twitching like a bloodhound's. An eruption of fluttering made him turn to the entrance, where a ruffled pigeon had just pushed through the flap, which proceeded to fly up and alight upon James's outstretched finger. The bird cooed in seeming contentment.

He wanted to deny it was really Him, the Pigeon Keeper. His brother. He *needed* to deny it.

But every passing moment was mounting up evidence that made it impossible. It was almost too much: after all this time, James was suddenly and undeniably *there*.

"I knew he lied," he said eventually. "I knew from the second that first feather was left on Alex's doorstep that it was you." He shook his head. "But he knew long before that, didn't he?"

James didn't move, his back to him, facing the fire-pit.

Alice in Wonderland drew Lucian's gaze, lying on the ground right before him, taunting him with its reality.

"Where have you been all this time?" Lucian breathed.

"Here. North. Around."

"Why didn't you ever come back?"

"To what?"

Me. You could have come back for me. I could have done with having my brother around, the one who saw the world in front of his face instead of some stupid vision. I might not have turned out such a tetchy prick.

Lucian swallowed.

The entrance rustled yet again, and this time when Lucian looked up he saw Charlie standing there, gaunt faced. Lucian could have sworn the boy was burning a hole clean through his skull. "I was hoping you'd made a break for the cliff," he said. His voice was flat, bearing no resemblance to the juvenile squeak it had been when Lucian had first hauled him blubbering and squealing like a pig from the sewers of New Canterbury. "There's so many people keeling over down there. I thought maybe one of those bodies was yours." He stepped into the tent and leaned over to whisper in Lucian's ear. "I hoped I'd get the satisfaction of watching you suffer a little longer."

Then he stood up and shifted with noticeable apprehension. "So, I did it …"

"You did," James said. His eyes were unreadable.

"You said I'd get revenge."

"You will."

"So I can take him?"

"No. You'll leave him be. We have things to discuss."

Charlie's body twitched as though struck. Lucian heard the echo of the unverbalised protest.

"You heard, boy. Go on, get." Jason waved his hand dismissively. "You did your part, now get back to those fires. Lazy bastards are slacking off while you stand there yammering."

Charlie's voice was low, quivering. "You promised." He was blushing, but he was holding his own. Lucian had to give it to the kid, he had balls. The feral monkeys who had cut down Max and the others had scampered away from James and Jason as though chased by demons. And here he was squaring off against them on his own.

If he wasn't lobbying to cut out my heart, we might get along just fine.

"You'll have what you're owed. I keep my promises, Charlie. But we judge only on what choices people make; we punish only the sins we know."

"I know a damn good one. He killed my father!"

"Did he?"

"*Yes!*"

"How do you know?"

"Because I told him," Lucian said. "It's true."

Charlie's lip was shaking, his eyes red and wide. "See? He admits it."

James returned to his stool and whispered sweet nothings to the pigeon for a while. "It was Jason and I who killed your father, Charlie. You know that. He's a casualty of our cause just like so many who've sacrificed. Lucian was defending himself."

"My father would never have hurt anyone. He was forced to break into that city."

"Exactly. We made him go. And he got killed. End of story."

Charlie gesticulated wildly. "So what? That's it? How do I get what's owed to me if he gets a clean slate?"

"You will get what's owed to you—what's *really* owed to you. And what's owed to you depends on the choices Lucian makes, here and now. But killing your father wasn't a choice, it was a necessity."

"I … You can't … You son of a bitch. You tricked me."

"I never lied."

Charlie was blinking, blank-faced. His face was dripping with silent tears. "What was all this for? Why the tricks, having me bring him here, having me babysit him down there?"

"I needed him to come to me. I needed to know he was still my brother deep down, even if he's sitting on the wrong side of the fence." James sighed and rubbed at his face under the balaclava, his eyes shining with pain.

Somebody cleared their throat at the tent's entrance and one of the ragged women poked her head in, face pinched and scarred by eczema. Even her cruel face was fawning and watchful as she addressed them. "You were right. They sprung the trap."

"How many alive?"

"All of them."

"Where are you keeping them?"

"Here. Outside."

James straightened. "Bring them in." He turned to Charlie. "As I said, I have business with my guests. Go, now. Make sure they're ready. It's time."

Charlie's lip curled. "What makes you think I'm doing anything for you?"

Jason squared his shoulders but James held up a hand to quell him. "Don't forget why we picked you and your father up in the first place. They starved you out, stole your home, and they'd do it again if it meant holding onto what we've all already lost."

"So what? It won't bring my father back."

"No, it won't. But it will stop them making more orphans while they chase the Old World's shadow."

Lucian felt Charlie's eyes burning him again, but couldn't look at him anymore. A few seconds later, he heard Charlie tramp outside with a curse.

A moment later, a great many more footfalls became audible. Lucian tried to peer through the crack in the entrance, but it was quickly thrown aside again, and a group of people were shunted inside. His guts, turned to slurry, slithered up under his tongue when Norman, Robert, Richard, DeGray and a whole troop of others from back home were marched in with their hands bound. They each in turn registered shock at the sight of him, but Lucian gained control of himself with colossal effort and hardened his brow, shaking his head minutely. They got the message; their faces had grown blank by the time they had been wrestled into kneeling positions beside Lucian.

If this was how bad things were, they needed to be solid, make it look like they'd planned this.

In moments the tent was busy with over a dozen captives. A good number, if they could get the upper hand.

"I hope this isn't my bloody rescue mission," he muttered.

"Don't flatter yourself," Robert said, kneeling beside him.

"We thought you were dead," Richard whispered on his other side.

"Shut up," Lucian said.

"Screw you. I came here for Scots, not your sorry arse."

Lucian blinked at Richard's stony expression and leaned across to look at DeGray. "What happened to your star pupil?"

John DeGray, rotund and sweaty as always, shrugged. "Turns out one of us has a spine."

Lucian smiled when he saw Norman beyond Robert, but Norman was staring up at Jason with a snarl.

Jason sauntered up to him, this time not even looking to James for permission. "How's the chest?"

Norman spat up into his face. Lucian could have laughed if he hadn't felt so hollowed out. The kid had been saving up a good hock that basted Jason's face and bandaged cheek with a stringy lather of spittle and snot.

"Nice," Lucian said.

"Glad you're alive," Norman said without taking his eyes off Jason. Then he addressed the bespittled wolf standing over him. "Feeling better all the time."

Jason wiped away the spittle with a disturbing lack of disgust. "You sure you want to waste your time?" he said to James. "I could finish this now." He waggled his knife.

"Yes. Leave them."

Jason shrugged. "Little cat-and-mouse never hurt anyone, I guess."

"Go help Charlie. He'll need it."

Jason snorted. He was grinning right up until it became obvious to everyone that James was being serious. Then the smile slowly faded from Jason's mouth, and he grunted. "Fine," he said, licking his lower lip. Lucian sensed his bottled rage even from six feet away. "Fine."

He stalked past them all and exploded from the tent, waving for the last guards to leave with him. James waited until it was just him and the people of the mission. Casually, he placed the pigeon on his shoulder and crouched to pick up the pistol Lucian had dropped, glancing at Robert and nodding as though words of significance had passed between them.

"I was just starting to like him," Lucian said. "Where'd you get your dog, James?"

"The same place I found all these people: where you left them."

"Don't tell me you found that one curled up in a hole begging and pleading like some charity case. I know born killers as well as you. He's been looking to hurt anything that breathes since the cradle. I suppose that's why you can keep him on a leash: all this is the perfect excuse for people like him. Carte blanche for genocide. Congratulations."

"He has his uses."

"I bet."

Robert, at James's head-height even though he crouched on his knees instead of being sat on a stool, seemed to expand, somehow taking up more space as he said, "So it's you. You're the one."

"It's a pleasure."

"What have you done with the rest of our people?"

"We have fires that need stoking, and blades that need sharpening."

Norman leaned forward to catch Lucian's eye. "You two know each other?"

Lucian's gut twisted. "Used to."

James caught his eye, but said nothing.

"You bastard," Richard said. His acne-scarred face was quivering, his thin frame looking even more brittle than Lucian remembered—he had always given him a hard time, but it was only now that he realised just how young Richard was.

Shit, he's just a kid.

Richard glowered despite his cracking voice. "Everything we sacrificed, all the progress we've made—"

"Richard, shut up!" John hissed, eyeing the gun with sweat rolling into his eyes. "Just shut your mouth. You'll get us killed."

"No!" Richard cried. "No. I don't care." He rounded on James. "You've undone everything, set us back decades. You'll send everyone back to the stone age."

"Yes. I will."

"How could you? How could you cause so much pain?"

"I could ask you the same question. How many times did you stop to think about the mouths that went unfed so that you could keep rooting through libraries, fat and plump?"

"We're fighting to make everyone's lives better."

"In the long run. Eventually. When the world turns for the better. That's the mantra, isn't it? But in the meantime, it's fine to trample over anyone in your way?"

"At least we're doing something."

"So am I. I'm putting an end to the plague Cain started. What I helped him start."

Richard said nothing.

Robert made as though to stand, dropping back only when James waggled the pistol once more. "Fine, you're a saint. Tell someone who gives a toss. Stop playing and end it."

James ignored him, strolling along past each of them in turn, inspecting them, until he came to stand in front of Norman. He paused and the two of them shared a look; though Norman looked confused, Lucian was impressed by the temerity of his gaze.

"I have to hand it to you, Norman. I didn't think you could live up to all those stories Alex wrapped you up in. But here you are. You surprised me."

"Turns out I'm full of surprises," Norman said. "Why don't you come a bit closer and I'll show you." Lucian almost jerked at how different he sounded, how powerful. He sounded like a different man altogether.

He even talks different, like a leader, like …

James is right. Just like how Alex always painted him in the stories. Give him a few days and he'll be ten feet tall and throwing lightning bolts.

Lucian took a moment to peek at the knots binding the others.

Damn, tight.

They'd never get out of them on their own. But still his spirits were buoyed. The idiots had got themselves caught, but it hadn't broken them. They were all raring to take some scalps.

"What are you doing, really? What's this all about?" Lucian said.

James laughed, a harsh rasping noise. Lucian wondered what was under that balaclava. "This is about justice. And don't bother with playing innocent. We both know nobody's innocent here."

"We hurt you. You're angry; I get it. God knows, if it had been me … I'd have burned every damn thing Alex ever touched to the ground a long time ago. But I know you. You always saw what he saw. You knew the Old World held the answer. You believed in the mission—you knew it was the way forward!"

"Take a look outside this tent. You'll see every able body in the land setting to tear apart all that's left of what Alexander Cain has done."

"No, what I'll see is madmen and criminals looking for blood, holding hostage whoever else you've left alive."

"The suffering is temporary, a pinprick compared to

what's to come if the mission goes on. Because that's what it'll take to save the Old World—that's what it's always taken. A few have to be raised above the masses and treated like Gods, and all the while those under them get pounded into the mud."

"That's not true."

"Tell me something, Lucian. Did Alex ever do something that wasn't in aid of his great destiny? Did he ever do something that didn't make you think he was willing to throw somebody—anybody—away to get the job done?" He turned to Norman. "Tell me … Did he ever ask you even once whether you wanted to have the life he made for you?"

Norman didn't answer.

"That's what I thought."

"How do you know all this?" Norman grunted. "Just who the hell are you?"

"I was the Chosen One," he said simply. "Before you, before any of your friends here, it was me with the great destiny, standing by his side."

Lucian sighed, watching the wave of pain glaze Norman's eyes. "You don't remember, Norman. You got hurt. You forgot. But it's true."

Norman mouthed openly for a time, but eventually he shook his head. "I don't care. It doesn't matter. Just tell us what you want. If you're going to kill us, then do it."

"I want to give you the choice I never had. I want to offer you the chance to stand on the right side of the line."

Robert barked. "Sign up with you?"

"You can't be serious," Norman said.

Lucian squared his shoulders. "James, don't do this. Just stop. You can still stop."

James whirled to face him and for the first time Lucian truly saw his little brother behind those emerald eyes. "I can never stop, Lucian. Not ever," he whispered.

"And we'll never stand with you."

James nodded slowly. "Then you'll watch. You'll watch while I put right all the wrongs."

"I don't believe it. You and I grew up with the people back home. You were angry enough to do some bad things, but I don't think you could ever hurt your own family. I know you, James."

Their eyes met for a long, burning moment, then the pistol was rising into the air, and for the first time in memory, Lucian McKay felt a chill roll along his spine.

James raised his free hand and loosened the balaclava around his face. He let it fall, and for a moment the tent was alive with a dozen gasps of terror.

It was a face cleaved of flesh. Half a face. A monstrosity.

Where cheeks should have been, there were fleshy holes, windows to a mass of lolling, uncontained tongue, teeth, and exposed jawbone. The eye sockets were sunken underneath, the structure of the skull simply gone. The remaining skin below the eye line, trailing down his neck and into his collar, was a single mass of shining scar tissue.

The jaw parted, and the reaper-like face contorted as James said, "You know me?"

Lucian had time for a single thought to run through his

mind. *God ... God. What did we do to you?*

Then he was looking into those mad green eyes once more, and he saw James's finger depress the pistol's trigger.

The pistol let forth thunder and blinding light. A wet crunch followed close behind his head, and he yelled in protest. "James, don't!"

But the gun fired again, and again, and again, moving to each of the crouched figures behind him, all long the back row. Each round sent Lucian's head spinning faster, his vision blurred. Somewhere amidst the gunfire were myriad pleas and screams. He couldn't tell how many were of those being slaughtered, and how many were his own.

James finished his arc along the back row, then with deliberation trained the pistol at the farther end of the first row—at DeGray.

"NO!" Richard roared, throwing himself in front of John. Master and apprentice cowered against one another.

In James's momentary pause, Lucian bellowed, "STOP, STOP, WHAT DO YOU WANT? I'LL DO ANYTHING! JUST STOP!"

James looked at him and nodded. "You're right. He shouldn't have to pay for his elders' mistakes."

Then before any of them could utter another sound, he raised the pistol an inch and fired.

John DeGray's eyes bulged. He let out a simple, "Oh," and crumpled into the spreading pool of the others' blood.

"No," Richard moaned. "No!" He crawled over to him and crouched over the rounded form of his master. "No, no, you're fine, you're fine."

But Lucian could already see the professor's empty stare, the glazed eyes, the same look he'd seen countless times in his life and haunted his dreams.

"Finish it," Lucian said to James.

James shook his head. The hollowed horror of his exposed cheekbones tightened. "The rest of you are staying here. I want you to watch us march away and know they're all dying, and there's nothing you can do to stop it. Once you feel something like that, you see things more clearly. You see the truth." He was backing away, and his ruined face twisted with a shadow of old pain. "You'll see."

Then he disappeared from sight, and they were left with the bodies and the blood and the lingering vortices of black smoke.

*

James signalled for his guard to follow and walked amongst them along the cliff edge when Jason appeared from the forest. Afar, he could hear a great clatter of stumbling feet and clanging metal.

"The boy's doing his job," Jason said.

"Good."

Jason looked to the tent. "You left some of them alive?"

James didn't answer.

"All this time you've been hollering about the great evil of their ways, and how we got to stop it. We burned half the sods from coast to coast to beat them down. We got their ringleaders right here in front of us. We could end this now."

He didn't seem perturbed, more intrigued, as though seeing James in a new light. "Or maybe you just said what had to be said for a shot at getting back at your shit-crazy big brother."

"Are they ready?"

Jason picked at the dirt under his fingernails with his foot-long knife. "Every one of them. Just say the word. You're sure you don't want to finish them?"

"Leave them."

"Fine." Jason swaggered forth and descended the cliffside path, heading for the campfires. "More fun for me." His voice dripped with sick delight.

James nursed the pigeon upon his shoulder, and watched as the dark hordes slowly crested the distant hills. It was time to end this.

ELEVENTH INTERLUDE

James burst out into the lacklustre daylight that lay lank and drooping on the rocks and trees, and picked out Alex's shadow not far from where he'd left him. He didn't stop running. His fingers curled into fists so tight that his nails cut into his palms.

Alex registered momentary surprise at the sight of him rushing forward, but then James collided with him and they both went crashing into the damp moss and heather, James bellowing all the while. He landed on top of Alex and his arms were pumping before he knew it, beating his face again and again. Stars of pain exploded along the skin of his knuckles as he made contact with nose, brow, chin and cheek, striking again and again.

He was yelling without end, hitting as though he would never stop.

And Alex just lay there and took the beating. While his skin split and his face crumpled into bloodied pulp, he didn't raise a hand to defend himself.

"How could you?" James was yelling, wailing. His vision blurred with tears. "What have they done to her? Tell me!"

"James," Alex said, then spluttered as James landed another blow, tearing his bottom lip. "James!"

James raised his arm yet again, but this time he cried out and his fist just hovered there beside him. He choked a few times as the world span in front of him, then he said, "Tell me, now."

Alex groaned in pain and coughed. "Malverston. The Tarbuck sister, she tried to kill him. The town rose up. He came for Beth, took her. He's going to … make an example."

"How long have you known?"

"James …"

"*How long?*"

Alex swallowed. "Since Northampton."

James's jaw fell ajar. By now they could have her all the way back to Newquay's Moon. "No," he said. "You can't do this to me."

"What did you find down there?" Alex said. "What happened?"

Fol and the tunnels seemed so far away now that James could barely understand the question. "Why would you do this? You didn't even want to come here."

"You needed to come here. We're so close to signing the treaty. We're so close. I needed you to have a clear head."

"You were going to let her die."

"The mission demands sacrifices." Alex swallowed. "I make no apologies. I did what I've always done, what I had to."

"I can't put people I love into danger for some idea,"

James said, fighting nausea.

"We have to. We have no choice." He wheezed, spluttering blood. "It's our destiny."

James felt his lip curl, and backed up, rolling off him. "Not mine."

"James!"

"Nothing's worth her life."

Through the pain, Alexander fixed him with a new look; James finally realised as he stumbled to his feet that it was confusion. He didn't understand.

Alex would never understand. That was the way he had always been. It was only now that he was seeing it with clear eyes.

But he wouldn't be that.

He ran towards their horses, and the cloud of pigeons at the distant treeline exploded into the sky.

To hell with destiny. Both of them. I'm done with madness.

CHAPTER 30

Alexander approached the log atop the hill slowly, with ceremonial timidity. It seemed like a hundred years ago that he had come up here to talk with Lucian, but it could only have been—what, weeks? Maybe a month or two.

No time at all. Yet everything had changed.

He sat on the log and grimaced at the pain in his hips from his long, solitary trek.

Where had the time gone? He was an old man.

He'd failed them all. From the very beginning, he had failed them. It was woven into the fabric of this place and their whole order—the obsession, the sickness that had been born in his heart on End Day.

A fluttering beside him made him turn. A lone pigeon was walking the length of the log toward him. Its leg was tied with a tiny scroll that made his heart flutter. He untied it, numb with resignation, and unrolled the scrap of paper. It was yellow and mottled, torn from the pages of a book.

He read it aloud to himself and realised he knew exactly what book it had come from: his father's copy of *Alice in*

Wonderland. Once upon a time, he had given that book to a little boy with emerald eyes. '*My dear, here we must run as fast as we can, just to stay in place. And if you wish to go anywhere you must run twice as fast as that.*'

So that was it. They were coming.

He knew it was so, just like he knew this was the last of the gifts the pigeons would bring him.

As he sat and looked over the city that was preparing its last stand, another line from that same old green book popped into his mind. '*Off with their heads!*'

He sighed, long and hard. Nothing to do now but wait, and pray.

Somewhere out there, they were on the move.

*

The light was dying fast. In the last few minutes the afternoon had given way to evening, and heavy dark clouds had rolled in off the mountains. They lingered on the bloody tent floor for a few minutes, dazed and listless, but already the starless black of night was upon them.

"No …" Richard was sobbing, rocking to and fro upon the hulk of John DeGray's lifeless body. "Come back, please. I'm not ready."

Norman fought his way back to sense. His head pounded with the echo of gunshots, and flashes of his old dream were rising up into the forefront of his mind's eye, fluid and unstoppable, just like the bile rising in his throat.

The storm, the city, the dripping faces. He had been

hurt. He had forgotten.

His dream must have been from the night terrible things had happened, whatever they were. Still his memory was foggy. Though he sensed a break in the amnesia ahead, it was still only distant blinding specks of garbage. And there would be time for that later.

For now, they had to get back home.

Slowly the ringing cleared and he became aware of Robert and Lucian grunting in an awkward kneeling dance beside one another, back to back, tackling the bindings on their hands. Lucian had grabbed hold of a knife from one of the dead and was sawing back and forth dangerously close to Robert's wrists.

The tent looked like an abattoir, its flapping sides slicked with gore, its floor carpeted with staring mangled corpses, all centred around the black ashes of a toppled fire. The smell was somewhere between burning charcoal and a butcher's board.

Richard still wept, shuddering upon John's body, which looked like a beached whale upon the ground.

He was gone. They were all gone, broken beside one another. Just another bunch left dead on the road Alexander Cain had sent them all along. They had called DeGray the professor. Looking at him he realised that they would never get back the knowledge he had had. Another part of the Old World had just winked out forever.

He struggled against his own bindings as Lucian's cutting allowed Robert to give a brutal tug and break free. They both moved fast after that, turning over the bodies of the fallen and patting them down for supplies. While he wrenched and pried at the fibres cutting into his wrists, he scrambled over to Richard and knelt over him. "Richard, we have to go."

Richard ignored him, weeping still, caressing his master's groomed locks of grey hair.

"Richard. There isn't time."

"I don't care," he whispered. "It doesn't matter now. Nothing matters. We can't stop it."

"We can still make a difference."

Richard choked back a sob. "Why? So we can starve in some hole and forget about the Old World?" He looked at the professor's body afresh and his horror seemed redoubled. "He knew so much. He could have done so much more. And now he's just ... gone."

"Yes, he's gone. But he wouldn't want you to stay here."

Richard laughed weakly. "He never wanted me to be here. *He* didn't want to be here." His face crumpled. "I made him come. I killed him."

"You took a stand, and so did he. He knew the risks."

"I can't go on without him. I don't know what to do. I can't do his job. I'm not ... I'm not strong enough. I'm not him."

Norman looked at him a long while and saw an echo of himself. "No," he said finally, "you're not him. Men like him are different, and we'll have to walk in their shadows for the rest of our lives—but only if that's how we choose to see it. Or, we can remember them, and do what we can in the best way we can, instead of trying to be what we aren't."

Richard swallowed.

Norman reached into John's pocket and took out the black king chess piece he had been holding hostage these long years. Never had Richard claimed it from him. Now Norman held it up in the fading darkness. "He believed in you. God knows I know what it feels like to have all that weight dumped on your shoulders. But all we need is something to keep us going. You're right. You're not ready. Neither am I. And nobody ever really is.

"But we can't let that stop us. Because they didn't let it stop them. So here's your prize, Richard." He slipped the king into his pocket. "I'll hold onto this. One day, you will be ready. And when that time comes, it'll be yours. But you have to work for it. You have to keep fighting."

Richard staunched his cries and wiped the spittle from his mouth, leaning back on his haunches. He pulled off his coat and laid it over DeGray's face. He was silent while Robert and Lucian freed them both from their bindings and went back to gathering supplies, letting Norman do what needed doing.

At last, he nodded. "Alright," he said.

Norman squeezed his shoulder. "The road will be long. Are you ready?"

Richard glanced at Norman's pocket and his eyes sharpened. "I'm ready."

Norman swept up and joined Robert and Lucian. They laid out what they found and were disappointed. None of the bodies had anything but knives or machetes. A few had only sharpened scrap metal or farming tools. It wouldn't be much use to them against an army.

Of those who had ridden north from New Canterbury, only four remained. They might never find the others taken down to the camps.

But they would have to go back and do what they could. If they moved fast enough they might be able to warn somebody. It was all they had left.

"So what now?" Richard said.

Lucian scowled. "We get back."

"How?"

"We'll figure it out," Norman said. He said it without thinking, though his mind seemed bogged down in a sudden quagmire. A strange light filtered in from outside, akin to that of the Echoes. A strange undulation coursed his bowels, and he was suddenly sure that something was coming. He kept still and waited as the others argued.

"We get back to the mountain and look for our horses. That's the only way to be sure we'll find mounts," Robert said. "I know the path."

"That'll take too long," Lucian said.

"It's the only choice we have."

"We can search the camps," Richard said. "They must have horses."

"They'll have taken them."

"Maybe there will be some left."

"Don't be stupid."

"Screw you!"

"Be quiet, both of you!" Robert said. "Let me think."

Norman wasn't listening. The little girl who had

appeared in the tent's doorway took up all his attention, sucked him in, and suddenly seemed to span all of space. As soon as he looked upon her, he knew—she was different. Special. It was written in the air over her head.

She was very young, no more than ten years old. Fire headed and freckle faced, she held a stubby little knife out in front of her and took a hesitant step toward them. Norman blinked, surprised that any child could approach four bellowing men, covered in blood with a stack of knives at their feet.

But there was strength in her eyes that made him feel weak.

Robert, Lucian, and Richard stopped arguing as soon as she crossed the threshold. A silence longer than any Norman had ever endured stretched out between them, so total that he thought the world's clock itself had wound down.

Then she raised her little knife still higher and said, "You." She pointed at Norman. "You're the one." Her voice was soft, lilting. Irish. Just like the old man they had found outside New Canterbury.

She was close now, close enough for him to see her in full even in the gloom. It was her. The girl from his visions. Even as he realised it his mouth was forming her name—a name he couldn't have known, yet he knew it. "Billy?"

She nodded. "I'm here."

"I see that," he said lamely.

"You know this girl?" Lucian said.

Just like you knew about James. We all have our secrets,

Norman thought.

"I know her."

"Where did you come from? Did you escape from the camps?" Richard said.

She shook her head. She didn't even seem to notice the bodies lying on the ground behind them. "I came from home. Far away."

Robert kneaded his forehead. "We don't have time for this."

Norman fought away flickering film snippets of the dark-eyed man sneering at him in those very same visions. This was his doing. "He sent you?" he said.

I sound like a bloody lunatic. Like those travelling gypsy fortune-tellers Lucian used to chase away every summer.

Billy nodded. "I'm here to help."

"With what?"

She shrugged.

Lucian grumbled. "Will the madness ever stop?"

"Daddy says all the best people are mad," Billy said without a hint of humour. Her eyes were steely. Norman wondered what she'd seen. She was so filthy, so ragged, that she looked feral. Yet she spoke softly, and there was nothing of the wild about her. She was like a forest nymph.

"She's probably in shock," Lucian muttered. "Don't worry, kid. We'll get you to a safe place." He rounded on Norman. "Stay focused. We need to get home."

Norman spent a moment wondering how he could explain himself to the others without them labelling him insane, but there was no way around it. They lived in a mad world, where people vanished and pigeons heralded coming death. "We'll get there," he said.

"How?" Richard cried, throwing his hands into the air. "We can't. They took our horses. We'll never get back in time."

"Don't worry," said Billy. She smiled, an impish look in her eye. "I have a friend who knows a shortcut."

Norman smiled. "A friend?" He had barely spoken to this girl, and even then it had been in a dream, yet he felt like he knew her, knew her well.

She shrugged. "I hope he is." She took a step back and jerked her head in the direction of the cliff. "Come on. Hurry."

Robert looked bemused, Richard forlorn, Lucian angry.

"You're here to help us?" Robert said slowly. "Who sent you?"

"I'll explain along the way," Norman said. "There's a lot to tell."

Lucian gripped him by the shirt. "Hang on. This is nuts, Norman. I know we're going through a lot here, but I need you to keep it together. You're tougher than this now. Don't crack on me."

Norman yanked himself free. "Listen to me. If I'm right, we're about to see some weird crap. But it's the only way. So why don't we get on with it?"

"Norman, she's a shell-shocked little girl."

"No, she isn't. Now we've all seen some weird things, but we keep going; we live with it. So let's take a leaf out of that book. Let's go."

Robert looked him hard in the eye. "Are you sure about this?"

"I've never been more sure of anything."

Robert nodded slowly. "Good enough."

Lucian scowled for a long moment, then shrugged. "Fine, whatever. Next stop, crazy town."

Norman nodded to Billy. "Lead the way."

Billy had been waiting without expression. The girl took flight from the tent, dashing with nimble strides along the cliff.

They followed at a run, clumsy by comparison but keeping pace.

"Are you ready?" Lucian said.

Norman nodded. The pain in his chest had never seemed so distant. The road had been long and tough, but he was finally who he had always been meant to be. "I'm ready."

They paused together on the cliff edge and watched as the first of James's army came into sight. Dark figures carrying long burning torches cast the pale ragged mass into harsh relief.

Thousands. Endless thousands, all moving south, all marching under the banner of the pigeon. In time they filled the horizon, and the torches they carried lit up the colossal emptiness of a world rotten, fallen, and on the brink of tumbling one last time into true darkness.

END OF VOLUME II

Coming Soon

(Can't wait? Put your name down at
http://eepurl.com/bnmr35 to get
email notifications when I release a new book.)

FROST

A Ruin Novella…
Autumn 2015

What caused the End? Where did the mysterious tech-stash under London come from? Who knew about the coming apocalypse?

Secrets are revealed in **Frost** (Ruin #2.5), the prequel that tears the world of Ruin wide open, peeking behind the curtain of All Where.

FRAY

Part 3 of the epic Ruin Saga…
Early 2016

The epic final instalment in the *Ruin Saga*.

Thanks for reading, folks.

Thanks for reading, folks. I hope you enjoyed the ride. If you have a spare moment, I'd greatly appreciate it if you could drop by your retailer's website and leave an honest review. Every nugget of feedback helps me provide a better reading experience.

Join My Mailing List

Join my mailing list at http://eepurl.com/V4niL to keep up with new releases and great deals.

No spam, nothing fancy, just some treats for being great fans, and the heads up on anything I'm working on.

Anybody looking to be an advance reader, get in touch at contact@harrymanners.net!

A Pendulum Universe Book

Something has gone wrong. A pendulum's swing is dying. If it stops, everything stops. The fabric of all existence is in danger. Shadows are moving, long-sealed doors have fallen ajar, and the balance of an infinitude of worlds has shifted. On one world, something has gone very wrong, indeed: the End. Six billion people have vanished, leaving a barren Earth populated with scattered survivors. While man struggles with mere survival and the eternal plagues of betrayal and retribution lay waste to already crumbling cities, a much greater mission begins. So opens a universe that stretches far beyond Earth, across deserts and tundra, kingdoms of past and future, and ancient forgotten worlds between the cracks. If there is any hope, it lies in a precious handful, creatures of destiny scattered across all of reality. The success or failure of their gathering will decide the fate of countless lives. Bringing them together will cause destruction, pain and death. Some will run, some will fight, and some will turn to darkness. Only one thing is certain: the End was just the beginning.

Acknowledgements

Once again, my thanks go to family and friends for all their understanding and encouragement. I could never get a single word out there without them.

My cover designer, Levente Szabo, has outdone himself once again. His artwork is a pleasure to slap on the front of my books.

My editors Amy Eye and Alex Roddie provided some fantastic information that showed up the gaps in my research, and patiently sifted the endless tide of typos. Full credit to them for being such patient and accommodating people.

Special thanks to fellow indie author Sandra Fairbrother for her wonderful contributions.

About the Author

Harry Manners lives in Bedfordshire, England with his family. When he's not writing, he studies Physics at the University of Warwick, reads a ton-load of books, and generally nerds out—for which he is staunchly unapologetic.

Website:

www.harrymanners.net

Facebook page:

www.facebook.com/OfficialHarryManners

Twitter:

@harry_a_manners

Blog:

www.harrymanners.wordpress.com.